Dear Reader,

Welcome to the second of three books about the rowdy McKettrick cousins, the Creeds.

Dylan Creed, seasoned hell-raiser and erstwhile rodeo cowboy, suddenly finds himself the full-time father of a two-year-old daughter. Like his brother, he's come back to Stillwater Springs, Montana, to face down his demons, but his high school sweetheart, librarian Kristy Madison, shakes him up more than any bull he's ever ridden in the rodeo! Will he stick around long enough to help Logan make the Creed name mean something again?

I also wanted to write today to tell you about a special group of people with whom I've recently become involved. It is The Humane Society of the United States (HSUS), specifically their Pets for Life program.

The Pets for Life program is one of the best ways to help your local shelter: that is to help keep animals out of shelters in the first place. Something as basic as keeping a collar and tag on your pet all the time, so if he gets out and gets lost, he can be returned home. Being a responsible pet owner. Spaying or neutering your pet. And not giving up when things don't go perfectly. If your dog digs in the yard, or your cat scratches the furniture, know that these are problems that can be addressed. You can find all the information about these problems—and many other common ones—at www.petsforlife.org. This campaign is focused on keeping pets and their people together for a lifetime.

As many of you know, my own household includes two dogs, two cats and four horses, so this is a cause that is near and dear to my heart. I hope you'll get involved along with me.

With love,

LINDA LAEL MILLER

MONTANA CREEDS: DYLAN

HQN™

ISBN-13: 978-1-60751-760-3

MONTANA CREEDS: DYLAN

For Sam and Janet Smith, my dear, funny friends.
Thanks for some of the best advice I've ever received:
Go to Harlequin!

Also available from

LINDA LAEL
MILLER

and HQN Books

The Stone Creek series
The Man from Stone Creek
A Wanted Man
The Rustler

The McKettricks series
McKettrick's Choice
McKettrick's Luck
McKettrick's Pride
McKettrick's Heart
A McKettrick Christmas

The Mojo Sheepshanks series
Deadly Gamble
Deadly Deceptions

**Don't miss all the adventures of the
Montana Creeds**

Logan Now available
Dylan Now available
Tyler April 2009

And in August 2009, return to Stone Creek in

The Bridegroom

MONTANA CREEDS: DYLAN

CHAPTER ONE

Las Vegas, Nevada

HE'D KNOWN ALL DAY that something was about to go down, something life-changing and entirely new. The knowledge had prickled in his gut and shivered in the fine hairs on the nape of his neck throughout the marathon poker games played in his favorite seedy, back-street gambling joint. He'd ignored the subtle mind-buzz as a minor distraction—it didn't have the usual elements of actual danger. But now, with a wad of folded bills—his winnings—shoved into the shaft of his left boot, Dylan Creed knew he'd better watch it, just the same.

Down in Glitter Gulch, there were crowds of people, security goons hired by the megacasinos to make sure their walking ATMs didn't get roughed up or rolled, or both, cops and cameras everywhere. Here, behind the Black Rose Cowboy Bar and Card Room, home of the hard-core poker players who scorned glitz, there was one failing streetlight, an overflowing Dumpster, a handful of rusty old cars and, at the periphery of his vision, a rat the size of a raccoon.

While he loved a good fight, being a Creed, born and bred, Dylan was nobody's fool. A tire iron to the back of the head and being relieved of the day's take—fifty-odd thousand dollars in cash—was not on his to-do list.

He walked toward his gleaming red extended-cab Ford pickup with his customary confidence, and probably looked like a hapless rube to anybody who might be lurking behind that Dumpster, or one of the other cars or just in the shadows.

Someone was definitely watching him; he could feel it now, a for-sure kind of thing—but it was more annoying than alarming. He'd learned early in his life, though, just by being Jake Creed's middle son, that the presence of another person, or persons, charged the atmosphere with a crackle of energy.

Just in case, he reached inside his ancient denim jacket, closed his fingers loosely around the handle of the snub-nosed .45 he carried on his frequent gambling junkets. Garth Brooks might have friends in low places like the Black Rose, but *he* didn't. Only sore losers, crooks and card sharps hung out in this neighborhood, and Dylan Creed fell into the latter category.

He was within six feet of the truck before he realized there was someone sitting in the passenger seat. He debated whether to draw the .45 or his cell phone in the split second it took to recognize Bonnie.

Bonnie. His two-year-old daughter stood on the seat, grinning at him through the glass.

Dylan sprinted to the driver's side, scrambled in and lost his hat when the little girl flung herself on him, her arms tight around his neck.

With his elbow, Dylan tapped the lock-button on his armrest.

"Daddy," Bonnie said. At least, in *his* mind the kid's

name was Bonnie—Sharlene, her mother, had changed it several times, according to the latest whim.

"Hey, babe," Dylan said, loosening his grip a little because he was afraid of crushing the munchkin. "Where's your mom?"

Bonnie drew back to look at him with enormous blue eyes, thick-lashed. Her short blond hair curled in wisps around her ears, and she was wearing beat-up bib overalls, a striped T-shirt and flip-flops for shoes.

I'm only two, her expression seemed to say. *How should I know where my mom is?*

Dylan turned, keeping one arm around Bonnie, and buzzed down the window. "Sharlene!" he yelled into the dark parking lot.

There was no answer, of course, and he knew by the shift in the vibes he'd been picking up since he stepped through the back door of the Rose that his onetime girlfriend had bailed. Again.

Only this time, she'd left Bonnie behind.

He wanted to swear, even pound the steering wheel once with his fist, but you didn't do things like that with a kid around. Not if you'd grown up in an alcoholic cement mixer of a home, like he and his brothers, Logan and Tyler, had, jumping at every thump and bump. And there was more to it than that: besides the fact that he didn't want to scare Bonnie, he felt a strange undercurrent of exhilaration.

He seldom saw his daughter, thanks to Sharlene's gypsy ways—though she always managed to cash his child-support checks—and being separated from Bonnie, never knowing what was happening to her, ached inside him like a bruise to the soul.

Bonnie settled into his lap, laid her head against his chest, gave a shuddery little sigh. Maybe it was relief, maybe it was resignation.

She'd probably had one hell of a day, given how the night was shaping up.

Dylan propped his chin on top of her head for a moment, his eyes burning and his throat as hot as if he'd tried to swallow a red-ended branding iron. He leaned forward, turned the key in the ignition, shifted gears.

Logan. That was his next thought. He had to get to Logan. His brother was a lawyer, after all. And while Dylan had the money to pay any shyster in the country, and he and Logan were sort of on the outs, he knew there was no one else he could trust with something this important.

Bonnie was *his* child, as well as Sharlene's, and by God, she deserved a stable home, decent clothes—the getup she was wearing looked as if it had doubled as a dog bed for a year or two—and at least one responsible parent.

Not that he was all that responsible. He'd been a rodeo bum for years, and now he was a *poker* bum. He had all the money he'd ever need, thanks to a certain shrewd investment and a spooky tendency to draw a royal flush once in practically every game, and he'd done some high-paying stunt work for the movies, too.

Compared to Sharlene, for all his rambling, he was a contender for Parent of the Year.

He didn't find the note and the shabby duffel bag on the backseat until he got out to South Point, his favorite hotel. Holding a sleepy Bonnie in the curve of one arm while he stood waiting for a valet to take the truck, he read the note.

I'm having some problems, Sharlene had scrawled in her childlike handwriting, slanting so far to the left that it almost lay flat against the lines on the cheap notebook paper, *and I can't take care of Aurora anymore.* Aurora, now? Jesus, what next—Oprah? *I thought giving her to you would be better than putting her in foster care. I went that route, and it sucked. Don't try to find me. I've got a boyfriend and we're hitting the road. Sharlene.*

Dylan unclamped his back molars, shifted Bonnie's weight so he could take the ticket from the parking guy and then grab the duffel bag. He'd have his own gear sent over from Madeline's place, where he usually crashed when he was passing through Vegas. Madeline wouldn't like it, but he wasn't about to take his two-year-old daughter there.

South Point was a sprawling, brightly lit hotel. Dylan stayed there whenever he came to the National Finals Rodeo—if Madeline, a flight attendant, was on one of her overseas runs or seeing somebody else at the time—and the establishment was family-friendly.

He and Bonnie were family.

There you had it.

After he'd booked a room with two massive beds, he ordered room-service hamburgers, French fries and milk shakes. While they waited, Bonnie, only half-awake, lay curled on her side on the bed farthest from the door, her right thumb jammed into her mouth, her eyes following every move he made.

"You're gonna be okay, kiddo," he told her.

She looked so small, and so vulnerable, lying there in her ragbag clothes. "Daddy," she said, and yawned broadly before pulling on her thumb again, this time with vigor.

"That's right," Dylan answered, turning from the phone to the duffel bag. Inside were more clothes like the ones she was wearing, a kid-size toothbrush with the bristles worn flat and a naked plastic baby doll with Ubangi hair and blue ink marks on its face. "I'm your daddy. And it looks like we'll be doing some shoppin' in the morning, you and me."

There were no pajamas. No socks. No real shoes, for that matter. Just two more pairs of overalls, two more sad-looking T-shirts, the doll and the toothbrush.

Rage simmered midway down Dylan's gullet. *Damn it*, what was Sharlene *doing* with the money he sent to that post office box in Topeka every month? He knew by the way the substantial check always cleared his bank before the ink was dry that her grandmother picked it up for her, the day it came in, and overnighted it to wherever "Sharlie" happened to be.

He had his suspicions, naturally, regarding Sharlene's spending habits—cocaine, animal-print spandex, tattoos for the fathead boyfriend du jour, if not herself. Bonnie, most likely, had subsisted on fast food and frozen pizza.

Dylan's jaw tightened to the point of pain; he consciously relaxed it. None of this was Bonnie's doing. Unlike him, unlike Sharlene, she was innocent, forced to live with the consequences of other people's mistakes.

Not anymore, he vowed silently.

Much as he would have liked to put all the blame on Sharlene, he knew it wouldn't be fair. He'd known who—and what—she was when he'd slept with her, nearly three years ago, after a rodeo, in a town he couldn't even remember the name of now. They'd holed up in a cheap room and had sex for a week, then gone their separate ways. A few clueless months later, Sharlene had tracked him down and told him she was expecting his baby.

And he'd known it was true, long before he'd even laid eyes on Bonnie and seen her resemblance to him, the same way he'd known he wasn't alone in the parking lot behind the Black Rose.

Listless with fatigue and probably confusion, Bonnie merely nibbled when the room-service food came, and then fell asleep in her overalls. Was she still on formula or something? Should he send a bellman into town for baby bottles and milk?

He sighed, shoved a hand through his tangled hair.

In the morning, he'd take Bonnie to a pediatrician—after buying her some decent clothes so the doc wouldn't put a call through to Child Protective Services the minute they walked in—for a routine exam and to find out what the hell two-year-olds actually *ate.*

When he was sure Bonnie was sound asleep, the bedspread tucked around her, he called Madeline. She'd be expecting him, though to her credit, not at an even remotely reasonable hour, since theirs was a sleep-over-when-you're-passing-through kind of arrangement.

He needed his clothes, and his shaving gear, and his laptop.

"It's Dylan," he said, to Madeline's hello.

"You winnin', sugar?" She'd cultivated a Southern drawl, but every once in a while, the Minnesota came through, with its faintly Scandinavian lilt.

"I always do," Dylan murmured, looking at his sleeping child.

"Then we ought to celebrate," Madeline crooned. "Find us a sexy movie on pay-per-view and—"

"Look, Madeline, I can't make it over there tonight. Something—er—came up—"

"Where are you?" There was a snap in Madeline's tone now. She wasn't possessive—he'd have driven fifty miles out of his way to avoid her if she had been—but she had turned down other offers for the duration of his stay in Vegas, she'd made that abundantly clear, and she clearly wasn't happy about being stood up.

"I'm at South Point," he began.

"Damn you," Madeline said, downright peevish now, "you picked up some—some *woman,* didn't you?"

"Not exactly."

"What do you *mean,* 'not exactly'?"

"I'm with my daughter, Madeline," Dylan said, patient only because he didn't want to disturb Bonnie. "She's two years old."

The croon was back. "Oh, bring her over here! I just love babies."

Dylan actually considered the offer, for a nanosecond. Then he remembered Madeline's penchant for impromptu sex, the smell of stale pot smoke that permeated her condo and the bowl of colorfully packaged condoms in the middle of her coffee table.

"Uh—no," he said. "She's pretty tired."

He sensed another huff building up beneath Madeline's drawl. "Then why did you bother to call at all?" she purred. In a moment, the claws would be out, poised to rip him to bloody shreds.

"I need my stuff," Dylan admitted, ducking his head a little, the way he had on the playground when he was a kid, in anticipation of a blow. "If you'd just put it all in a cab and send it this way, I'd be obliged."

"I wouldn't *think* of doing that," Madeline said. "I'll drop it all off on my way to the club." Her slight emphasis on the last two words was a clear message— if he was going to be a no-show, far be it from *her* to sit home alone watching pay-per-view.

"Madeline, you don't have to—"

"South Point? That's where you said you are, isn't it?"

"Yes, but—"

She hung up on him.

Dylan sat down on the edge of his bed, opposite Bonnie's, and propped his elbows on his thighs. Madeline would want to come straight up to the room, probably to see if he'd lied about the company he was keeping, and he didn't want her waking Bonnie. But unless he could talk Madeline into sending his things up with a bellman, which didn't seem likely, he'd have no other choice.

He'd have to leave Bonnie alone to go downstairs, and that wasn't an option.

Twenty minutes later, the phone rang, causing Bonnie to stir in the depths of some baby-dream, and he pounced on it, whispered, "Hello?"

"I'm downstairs," Madeline said. "What's your room number, sweetie?"

Dylan suppressed another sigh. God, he hated being called "sweetie." "Twelve-forty-two," he said.

Madeline, a leggy redhead, almost as tall as he was, at six feet, whisked her shapely self to his door with no measurable delay. Looking through the peephole, he saw that she was flanked by a bellman with a loaded cart. Her shiny mouth was tight, and her eyes narrowed slightly.

Reluctantly, Dylan admitted her.

She immediately scanned the room, her gaze landing on Bonnie, while the bellman waited politely to unload some of the stuff from the cart. Dylan handed him a tip and brought in the laptop, his shaving kit and his suitcase himself.

"She is *precious!*" Madeline enthused, looming over Bonnie's bed.

"Be quiet," Dylan said. "She's had a rough day." A rough *life* was more like it. As soon as he got rid of Madeline, he'd bite the bullet and call Logan. They'd made some progress lately, he and his older brother, but the ground could get rocky at any time, and asking big brother for help was going to be hard on his pride.

Madeline put a *shh* finger to her plump mouth and batted her false eyelashes. Put her in a big Vegas head-dress, with feathers and spangles, a skimpy costume, high heels and fishnet stockings, and Bonnie, if she chanced to wake up and see a stranger standing over her, would have nightmares about showgirls until she died of old age.

He took Madeline by the elbow and gave her the bum's rush toward the door. "Good night, thank you, and what do I owe you for the favor?"

She patted his cheek. "We'll settle up next time you come through Vegas," she said. She paused. "The hotel could probably provide a babysitter, then we could—"

"No," Dylan said flatly.

Blessedly, and none too soon, Madeline left.

Dylan showered, shaved, brushed his teeth and headed for bed in his boxer briefs; he hadn't owned a pair of pajamas since grade school.

But he had Bonnie to think about now. He couldn't go parading around in front of a two-year-old in his shorts—even if she *was* asleep.

Fatherhood, he thought, was getting more complicated by the minute. Especially since he didn't know jack-shit about it—his experience had been limited to a few brief visits with Bonnie whenever Sharlene deigned to light someplace for a month.

He pulled on a pair of jeans and a T-shirt, and then he crashed.

He'd call Logan the next day, he promised himself. Or the next day, or the one after that...

KRISTY MADISON BUSTLED around her big kitchen, opening a can of food for her white Persian cat, Winston, gathering her notes for that night's book-club meeting at the library, grabbing her cell phone off the counter where she'd been charging it during a quick trip home for supper.

She wished she could stay in tonight, soak in her big claw-foot bathtub and read a book, but the reading group had been *her* idea, after all. And it had turned out to be a popular one—twenty-six people had signed up.

Privately, Kristy wondered how many of them simply wanted a close-up look at Briana, Logan Creed's love interest. Before Briana had taken up with Logan, she'd been just another single mother, pulling down a paycheck at the casino on the outskirts of Stillwater Springs, homeschooling her two boys, Josh and Alec, and generally minding her own business.

Kristy bit her lower lip. Thinking of Logan inevitably led to thinking about *Dylan,* and that was still too

painful, even though it had been five years since she'd
seen him. He'd been in town recently—the busybodies
had made sure she knew—but he hadn't sought her out,
and she'd been half again too proud to chase *him* down.

Looking at her own reflection in the dark glass of the
kitchen window, Kristy saw a slender woman with fash-
ionably mussed, midlength blond hair, blue eyes and
good bone structure. But there were shadows under
those eyes, her hair needed a trim, and what the hell
good did *bone structure* do a person, anyway? She
looked okay in the picture on her driver's license—that
was the extent of the advantage, as far as she'd been able
to determine.

Winston, ignoring his food bowl, gave a loud and
plaintive meow and slithered across the cuffs of Kristy's
black jeans, leaving a dusting of snow-white hair.

Now, she'd have to lint-roll—again.

Other women carried mints and lipstick in their
purses—Kristy had a tape-covered stick.

"I know," she told Winston gently. "You want to cuddle
and watch *Animal Planet,* but I've got to work tonight."

Winston's reply was another meow—this time, he'd
turned the "pitiful" meter up a few notches.

"You can have an extra mackerel treat when I get
home," Kristy promised. "I won't be late—nine-thirty
at the outside."

Winston, unappeased, turned and made his way
between the various paint cans and wallpaper samples
littering the kitchen floor. With a disdainful flip of his
bushy white tail, he disappeared into the dining room.

Kristy had been renovating her big Victorian house
forever, or so it seemed. She was used to tripping over

stuff from Home Depot, and so was Winston, but all of a sudden, it seemed more like a never-ending hassle than the noble restoration effort she'd undertaken as soon as she'd signed the mortgage papers.

"I'm tired of my life," she told her reflection. "I want a new one."

"Too bad," her reflection replied. "You made your bed, and now you have to sleep in it. Alone."

No husband. No children.

A few more birthdays, a few more cats, and she'd qualify as a crazy old maid. Kids would start saying she was a witch, and avoid her house on Halloween.

Kristy turned away from her window-self, tugged her purse strap onto her shoulder, dropped her cell phone into the bag, along with her notes and a copy of that month's book-club selection, and headed for the back door.

No matter how blue she might be, the sight of the Stillwater Springs Public Library always lifted her spirits, and this evening was no exception. She loved the squat, redbrick building, with its green shutters and shingled roof. She loved being surrounded by books and readers.

She and a few other people who'd grown up in or around the small western Montana town had fought some hard battles to get the funding to build and stock the library after the old one burned down.

Parking her dark green Blazer in the spot reserved especially for her, Kristy hurried toward the side door, keys jingling. The main part of the library had closed early that night for plumbing repairs in one of the restrooms, but the two small meeting rooms would be open—the reading group in one, AA in the other.

She hung her purse on a peg, washed her hands at the sink in the little kitchenette between the meeting rooms and started wrestling with the big coffee urn.

Sheriff Floyd Book was the next to arrive—he carried in a box of books from his personal car and greeted Kristy with a smile and a nod. "I knew if I didn't get here too quick, you'd make the coffee," he teased.

Kristy laughed. "Everything in place for your retirement?" she asked, setting out columns of disposable cups, packets of sugar and powdered creamer and the like.

"Everything except *me*," Floyd replied, through the open doorway leading to the AA side, already setting out books and pamphlets for that night's meeting. In Stillwater Springs, nobody was anonymous, but for the sake of what was called The Program, everyone pretended not to notice who came and went from the side entrance to the library on a Tuesday night. "I can't hardly wait for that special election. Hand my badge over to Jim Huntinghorse or Mike Danvers, and kick the dust of this town off my feet—for a few weeks, anyhow. Dorothy and I are all packed for that cruise to Alaska."

"Soon," Kristy soothed good-naturedly. She'd been too busy, until the mention of the woman's name, to notice that Mrs. Book was nowhere around. "Dorothy isn't coming to the reading group meeting? She signed up."

Dorothy Book was confined to a wheelchair, following an automobile accident some years before, and there were people who said she wasn't right in the head. Kristy had always liked Dorothy—so what if she was a little different?—and she'd been looking forward to having her come to the group's first meeting.

Floyd shook his head. He'd looked weary lately,

worn down to a nubbin, as Kristy's late mother used to say. Maybe it was the buildup to his retirement, the stresses of his job, and the uncertainty of the special election, but it seemed to Kristy that he was more strained than usual.

"It's hard for her to get in and out of the car," the sheriff told Kristy. "And she hates fussing with that wheelchair. I'm hoping the cruise will put some color back in her cheeks and a twinkle in her eyes."

Kristy stopped fiddling with the coffee things. Floyd Book was the sheriff of a sprawling county—he'd been elected to the office when she was in the second grade and had held it ever since. Until her dad died, just six months after her mother's passing, Floyd had been a regular visitor out at Madison Ranch. He and Kristy's father had been best friends, sharing a love of fishing, horseback riding and herding the few cattle Tim Madison had been able to afford to run on that hardscrabble place.

A pang struck Kristy as she started to ask Floyd, straight out, if something was wrong and if so, what she could do to help. This was a night, it seemed, for painful memories to come up.

"You all right, Kristy?" Floyd asked, crossing the hallway to lay a brawny hand on her shoulder. "You went pale for a second there. I thought you were going to faint."

"I'm fine," Kristy lied. She'd been raised as a tough Montana ranch kid, expected to say she was fine whether she was or not.

But the ranch was abandoned now, the barn leaning to one side, the sturdy old house empty. The last time Kristy had forced herself to go out there and stand on the high rise where she used to ride Sugarfoot, her beloved palomino gelding, she'd actually *felt* her heart break into pieces.

Her parents were both dead, and she had no brothers or sisters, no aunts—now that Great-Aunt Millie had passed away—or uncles, no cousins.

Sugarfoot was gone, too, buried in a horse-size grave in the middle of a copse of trees bordering the Creed ranch. After sixteen years, more than half her life, Kristy still cried when she visited her best friend's final resting place. People urged her to get another horse—she'd loved riding, and she'd been uncommonly good at it, too—but somehow, she just didn't have the heart to love something—or someone—that much and risk another loss.

She'd lost so much already.

Her parents, Sugarfoot…

And Dylan Creed.

"Kristy?" the sheriff prompted, peering worriedly into her face now. "Maybe you ought to go home. You might be coming down with something. I could tell the reading-club ladies the meeting's been postponed."

Kristy summoned up a smile, straightened her shoulders, looked her father's old friend straight in the eye. "Nonsense," she said. "We've already postponed it once. I'm just a little tired, that's all."

Floyd didn't seem entirely convinced, but a few of the AA regulars were straggling in, so he finally turned to go and greet them, the way he had every Tuesday night for years—ever since Dorothy's car accident, and that scandal about him running around with Freida Turlow behind Dorothy's back. He'd wept, sitting at the kitchen table with Kristy's dad, out on the ranch, over the pain Dorothy had suffered, not only because of the wreck on an icy road, but because he'd betrayed her with another woman.

It was the first and only time Kristy, watching and listening unnoticed from the hallway, had ever seen a grown man cry.

Her kindly dad had put a hand to Floyd's shoulder and said, "It's the drinking, old buddy. That's what's messing up your life. You think I don't know you carry a flask everywhere you go? You've got to do something."

And Floyd *had* done something. He'd joined AA, gotten sober and, as far as Kristy knew, been a faithful husband to Dorothy from then on.

Kristy left the kitchenette for the reading group's meeting room, and by some cosmic irony, Freida Turlow was the first to arrive.

An athletic type, attractive in a hardened sort of way, Freida, like Kristy, was a lifelong resident of Stillwater Springs. Except for college, neither one of them had been away from home for any significant length of time.

Kristy was a hometown girl—she'd never wanted to live anywhere else, even after her parents both died during her junior year at the University of Montana. By contrast, Freida, who was at least a decade older, had indeed been Kristy's babysitter on the rare nights when her mom and dad went out dancing, or to play cards with friends, seemed out of place in Stillwater Springs. She was ambitious and well-educated, and virtually ran the local real estate office. Her brother, Brett, was a classic jerk, sleeping on her couch and famous for stealing money from her every chance he got.

Tonight, her dark chin-length hair pinned up at the back of her head, Freida wore a running suit and sneakers and carried that month's reading selection under one arm. Like Kristy, Freida had lost her family home—the gingerbread-laced minimansion Kristy now owned—and she was touchy about it. She'd offered to buy back the old house several times, at higher and higher prices, and had gotten progressively more annoyed at every polite refusal.

Kristy understood Freida's desire to reclaim the venerable Victorian, even sympathized. But that house, except for Winston and her job at the library, which she'd held ever since she got her degree, was all she had.

Where would she go, if she sold it back to Freida?

"News on the real estate front," Freida told her, with no little satisfaction. "I've got an offer on Madison Ranch—or at least, the promise of one."

Kristy froze. The old place was run-down, but it was big—totaling some thirty thousand acres. Prime pickings for the movie stars and Learjet executive crowd who'd been snatching up properties in Montana over the past couple of decades.

Only the probate tangle had kept it off the market this long.

Technically, the local bank owned Madison Ranch now, though the name had stuck, because there had been Madisons living on that land since that part of the state was settled. They'd foreclosed two months after Kristy's dad died.

Freida allowed herself a smug little smile.

Then Briana Grant came in. There were rumors that she and Logan Creed were secretly married or would be soon, and sleeping together either way. Briana, a pretty woman who always wore her strawberry-blond hair in a tidy French braid, certainly hadn't confided the nature of the relationship to Kristy, though the two of them were friendly.

Seeing Freida seated at one of the chairs surrounding the conference table, her book open before her, Briana stopped on the threshold, looked as though she might turn on one heel and bolt.

"Come in," Kristy urged her, smiling. Inside, though, she was still shaken by Freida's smug announcement that she had a promising prospect to buy Madison Ranch, and no amount of telling herself it didn't matter anyway seemed to help.

Briana hesitated, then met Freida's gaze, lifted her chin a little, and took a place at the table.

"You've got your nerve, showing up here, after all the trouble you've caused my poor brother," Freida told her flatly.

Briana flushed, but didn't give any ground. Sheriff Book had picked Brett Turlow up for questioning a couple of times, after a break-in at Briana's, but that was all Kristy knew. She wasn't much for gossip.

"Everybody's welcome here, Freida," Kristy said staunchly. While the Stillwater Springs Public Library wasn't exactly a hotbed of violent controversy, she'd had some experience keeping order. A lot of townspeople used the place as if it were a free day-care center, and once in a while, there was a little dust-up when two voracious readers wanted to check out the only copy of some recent bestseller.

Freida stood, her movements stiff and precise. She

grabbed her purse and her book and sniffed, "I don't know why I stay in this town, with all the riffraff coming in these days." With that, she swept grandly out.

Tears stood in Briana's eyes.

Kristy sat down beside her friend, took her hand. "*She's* the one with nerve, calling *anybody* riffraff, with that brother of hers," she said gently.

Briana sniffled, managed a smile and then a nod. She hugged her library book to her chest like some sort of treasure.

After that, the other members of the book club began trailing in, by chatty twos and threes. Those who wanted to helped themselves to the coffee in the kitchenette, and though they watched Briana with interest, surely speculating about her and Logan Creed, they included her in the discussion.

All in all, Kristy thought, as she locked up an hour later, when both meetings were over, it had been a worthwhile evening, though Winston probably wouldn't agree.

Back in the Blazer, and alone in the library parking lot, Kristy gripped the wheel with both hands and laid her forehead against her knuckles for a long moment.

She felt strangely on edge, hyperalert, as though something big were about to happen, but big things simply *didn't* happen in Stillwater Springs, Montana. Not often, anyway.

She rallied, made herself sit up straight, start the motor, head for home. Winston was waiting, and so was her claw-foot bathtub, along with the page-turner she'd been trying to finish for a week.

Maybe Sheriff Book had been right.

She might be coming down with something.

And maybe that monster-memory she'd been fighting to keep submerged was about to break the surface, finally, and ruin her carefully constructed life.

CHAPTER TWO

FIRST THING IN THE MORNING, after half an hour trying to spoon room-service oatmeal into Bonnie's tightly closed mouth and finally giving up, Dylan checked out of the hotel and went looking for a Wal-Mart.

Bonnie needed a car seat, and a whole slew of other things.

So he put her into a shopping cart, and the two of them wheeled around. He guessed at her clothes sizes, and she kicked up a fuss when he went to try some shoes on her, but after a brief struggle, he won. In the toy department, he snagged a doll almost as big as Bonnie herself, mounted on a plastic horse no less, but she didn't show much interest in that, either.

"Toys," an older woman told him sagely, leaning in to whisper the wisdom, "have to be age-appropriate."

"Age-appropriate?" Dylan pushed his hat to the back of his head.

The woman tapped the box containing the new doll, sitting tall and straight on her horse. "This is for children five and up. Your little girl can't be any older than two."

"She's small for her age," Dylan replied automatically, because he didn't like other people telling him what to do, even when they were right. But once the meddlesome shopper had rounded the bend, he put the doll back on the shelf and rustled up a soft pink unicorn with a gleaming horn and a fluffy mane. According to the tag, it would do.

And Bonnie took to it right away.

After making a few more selections, and paying at the checkout counter, they were good to go. Dylan made a couple of calls from the truck and located a pediatrician on the outskirts of the city.

Jessica Welch, M.D., operated out of an upscale strip mall. She was good-looking, too, with long, gleaming brown hair neatly confined by a silver barrette at her nape. Not that it mattered, but when Dylan met a woman—any woman—he noticed things about her.

"Who do we have here?" Jessica Welch, M.D., asked, chucking Bonnie, who had both arms clamped around Dylan's neck, under the chin.

Bonnie threw back her head and screamed out one of those ear-piercers that go through a man's brain like a spike. Ever since Dylan had hauled her into the waiting room, a full forty-five minutes before, she'd been clinging to him. He'd been the only father present, and the looks he'd gotten from the various mothers waiting with quieter, better-behaved kids weren't the kind he was used to getting from people of the female persuasion.

Dr. Welch was unmoved. Screaming children were not uncommon in her day-to-day life, of course. "This way," she said.

Dylan and Bonnie followed her down a short corridor and into a small examining room. Bonnie didn't let up on the shrieking, and she'd added kicking and squirming to the fit; hostilities were escalating.

"I guess she thinks she might get a shot or something," Dylan said, completely at a loss. By then, Bonnie had knocked his hat off, and she was pulling his hair with both hands.

Dr. Welch simply smiled. "Let's have a look at you, Miss—?"

"Bonnie," Dylan said. "Bonnie Creed."

Bonnie Creed. He liked the sound of that.

The doctor examined the papers on her clipboard. "And you're her father," she said. It was rhetorical, a conclusion not a question, but Dylan felt compelled to answer all the same.

"Yes."

"I would have known by the resemblance," Dr. Welch said. As it turned out, she had a few tricks up her sleeve. By letting Bonnie listen to Dylan's heart through a stethoscope, she got the kid to quiet down.

"Any significant health problems?" the doctor asked, finishing up with the routine stuff, like looking into Bonnie's ears with that little flashlight-type thing and peering down her throat.

"Not that I know of," Dylan said. "She's been—er—living with her mother."

"I see," Dr. Welch replied solemnly.

"I was hoping you could tell me what to feed her and stuff like that," Dylan went on. He felt his ears burning. By now, the doctor was probably wondering if she should notify the authorities or something.

"I take it you haven't been around Bonnie much," she said thoughtfully.

"It was kind of sudden. Sharlene decided she couldn't take care of her anymore, and left her with me." He probably looked and sounded calm, but if Dr. Welch drew her cell phone, he and Bonnie would be out of there in a flash and speeding for the open road. *Damn.* He should have called Logan. Then he'd have some kind of legal backup at least—

"I'll need a number where I can contact you, Mr. Creed."

Dylan gave her his cell number and hoisted a reaching Bonnie off the end of the examining table and back into his arms.

"Two-year-olds," Dr. Welch went on, with a sudden smile, "usually prefer a semisoft diet—some baby food, not the infant variety. Anything that's easy to chew."

"No bottles or anything?" Dylan asked.

"One of those sippy cups, with the lid," the doctor said. "Bonnie needs a lot of milk, and juice is okay, too, provided you watch the sugar content."

Dylan figured he ought to have been taking notes. What the devil was a sippy cup, anyhow? And didn't just about everything have sugar in it?

He kept his questions under his hat, having already made a fool of himself. If the doc didn't take him for a child abductor, it would be a miracle.

Dr. Welch gave Bonnie a couple of shots—the kid barely noticed—ferreted out a list of healthy foods for children and sent them on their way. Dylan paid the bill, and he and Bonnie left. Until they were fifty miles north of Vegas, he checked the rearview mirror for a squad car every few minutes.

As it happened, Dylan didn't have to call Logan, because Logan called him—at an inconvenient time, as usual.

Logan was getting married to Briana Grant, that was the gist of it, and there was no talking him out of it, Dylan learned, when he took his brother's call on his cell phone, seated in a truck-stop restaurant somewhere along the winding road homeward. Bonnie, in the provided high chair, kept flinging strands of spaghetti at him—she was covered in the stuff, and so was he.

And he was losing patience. "Look, Logan, I—" He paused when Bonnie stuck her whole head into her plate and came up looking like some pasta-Medusa. "*Stop that, damn it*—"

Bonnie merely giggled and preened a little, like all that goopy spaghetti was a wig she was modeling.

"Are you with a woman?" Logan asked.

"I wish," Dylan said. "I've got to hang up now—I said *stop it*—but I'll get there when I can. If I don't show up in time, go ahead without me."

After that, Dylan barely registered what his brother said.

Logan asked him to get word to Tyler, he remembered that much, and relay the message that he wanted to talk to their younger brother, in person.

As if. Tyler was in pissed-off mode. There would be no getting through to him, and Dylan said so, in so many words.

Then Bonnie started throwing spaghetti again.

This time, she hit the woman in the next booth square in the back of the head.

Dylan ended the phone call, no closer to asking Logan for help than he had been in the first place, scooped up the demon child, tossed the bills to pay for the meal onto the cashier's counter and fled.

Now, he'd have to find a place to hose the kid down.

He cleaned her up with baby wipes, purchased along with the unicorn, a plastic kid-toilet, the little tennis shoes and the new outfit she'd pretty much ruined.

"Potty," she said, as they pulled out of the truck stop and onto the highway. "Daddy, *potty*."

"There's no way we're going back in there," Dylan said. "We're probably banned from the place, thanks to you. Eighty-sixed, for all time and eternity."

"Potty," Bonnie insisted. Besides *Daddy,* that seemed to be the only word she knew. He'd sneaked her into at least four different men's rooms since they'd left South Point that morning. Held her on the seat so she wouldn't fall in and looked the other way as best he could.

Her lower lip started to wobble. "Potty," she said pitifully.

"Oh, hell," Dylan muttered. He pulled the truck over, located the miniature pink toilet, and set it down behind some bushes. Then he unfastened Bonnie from her car seat and carried her, spaghetti stains and all, to the john.

He turned his back.

She must have gotten her pants down on her own, because he heard a cheery little tinkle. When he finally turned around, she was grinning up at him, her hair crusted in spaghetti sauce, and grunting ominously.

Dylan had ridden the meanest bulls on the rodeo circuit, and until he and Cimarron, the bull to end all bulls, met up, he'd never been thrown. He'd held his own in bar brawls and backstreet fights where losing meant getting your head slammed against the curb.

Bluffed his way past the toughest poker players at the toughest tables in the toughest towns in America.

But a little girl *pooping*—now, that was a new one.

"Wipe!" she crowed, upping her known vocabulary to three words.

"Not a chance," Dylan said. But he got some more baby wipes out of the truck and handed them to her.

She must have used them, because when she came past him, her pants were up and she was pulling the potty-chair behind her. Gnarly as the whole experience had been, Dylan felt a rush of pride. The kid was independent, for a two-year-old. She'd even thought to dump the evidence.

"We need a woman," he told her, once they were back in the truck and he'd used yet another baby wipe to wash her hands and fastened her into the car seat, which was so complicated it might have been invented by NASA. "*Any* woman."

But it wasn't *any* woman who came to mind.

It was Kristy Madison.

No way, he told the image.

After that, they drove for hours, and a little past three in the morning, they hit the outskirts of Stillwater Springs, Montana.

Dylan owned a house on the family ranch—Briana and her kids had been living there up until recently, when they'd moved in with Logan, but there had been a break-in and some vandalism, and he didn't know if Logan had arranged for repairs yet.

So he headed for Cassie's place.

When they pulled into her driveway, light glowed through the buckskin walls of her famous teepee. Dylan had spent a lot of happy hours in that teepee, with Logan and/or Tyler, pretending to be Indians plotting a raid on a white settlement.

Now, with Bonnie asleep in her car seat and clinging to that naked, inked-up doll like it was her last friend, the pink unicorn spurned, he got out of the truck and headed toward the teepee.

Cassie, a bulky and singularly beautiful woman and the closest thing to a grandmother he'd ever had, sat watching low, flickering flames in the fire pit inside the teepee. It might have been a picturesque scene, if she'd been wearing tribal gear, but double-knit pants, bulging at the seams, neon-green high-top sneakers and a sweatshirt with a picture of Custer on the front, with an arrow through his head, lacked the punch of a fringed leather dress and moccasins.

Custer was a nice touch, though. From his benignly confident expression, the arrow didn't bother him much.

"Dylan," Cassie said, looking up. And she didn't sound surprised.

"I need help," he told her. No sense beating around the bush with Cassie; she could see right through a person.

She smiled. Nodded. Moved to rise.

He extended a hand to help her up.

Led her to the truck.

She drew in a breath at the sight of Bonnie, still sleeping the sleep of the just. "Yours?" she whispered.

"Mine," he confirmed and, once again, he felt that same swell of pride.

"Where is her mother?"

"God knows." Dylan got Bonnie out of the car seat, her head bobbing against his shoulder. "I'm going to petition for full custody, but I need Logan's help to do that."

"There are a lot of lawyers in this world," Cassie pointed out quietly. "Why Logan?"

"Because this could be—well—tricky."

"Dylan Creed, did you steal that child from her mother?" They'd reached the gate by then, and Cassie led the way up the walk, onto the porch. Jiggled the knob on the door.

Evidently, she *couldn't* see through him. Not always, anyway.

"No," Dylan said. It was late—or early—and he was too wrung out from the long drive and the stress of looking after a two-year-old to go into the story. "Give me a little credit, will you? I'm not a *criminal.*"

"But you're looking over your shoulder for some reason," Cassie whispered, switching on a lamp in the familiar living room of her small, shabby house. She took Bonnie from him, murmured soothingly when the little girl fussed in her sleep.

"I don't have legal custody," Dylan answered. "Until I do, I'm keeping a low profile, in case Sharlene changes her mind. I'll tell you the rest in the morning."

Cassie stared into his eyes for a long moment, then nodded again. "All right," she said, making for the spare bedroom. "I'm putting this child to bed. There's cold chicken in the refrigerator if you're hungry."

Grateful, Dylan let himself drop onto the couch, and before he knew it, the sun was up and Bonnie was standing beside him, tugging playfully at his hair.

He grinned, glad to see her. She was wearing one of

Cassie's massive T-shirts, tucked up here and there with safety pins, to make it fit, and she was clean.

God bless Cassie. Despite her obvious misgivings, she'd given Bonnie a much-needed bath, and probably fed her, too.

"Daddy," Bonnie said angelically, stroking his beard-stubbled cheek with one very small hand.

And if Dylan hadn't known before that he'd do anything to keep and raise this child—*his* child—he knew it then.

"DYLAN'S OUT AT CASSIE'S place," Kristy's hairdresser, Mavis Bradley, told her, when she came in for a lunch-hour trim. "I saw his truck parked in her driveway when I came in to work."

A thrill went through Kristy, part dread, part anticipation. She waited it out. If Dylan *was* in town, he'd soon be gone. That was his pattern. Come in, stomp somebody's heart to bits under his boot heel and leave again.

"And Cassie was at the store, not an hour later, buying training diapers and toddler's food in those plastic cartons that cost the earth," Mavis rattled on, before Kristy could come up with a response. "That's what Julie Danvers told me, when she came in to have her nails done."

Kristy took a moment to be glad she'd missed Julie. There was some bad blood between them, at least on Julie's side, because Kristy had been briefly engaged to her husband, Mike, and he hadn't taken the breakup well. Now they had two children, a big house and a thriving business, and Mike was a candidate for sheriff. It was a mystery to Kristy why that particular water hadn't gone under the proverbial bridge.

"Interesting," Kristy said, because she'd known Mavis since first grade, and she'd just keep prattling on until she got some kind of reaction. Everybody for miles around knew Kristy and Dylan had been passionately in love, once upon a time, and Mavis certainly wouldn't be the last person eager to tell her Dylan was back.

"Now what would Cassie need with stuff for a little kid unless—"

"Mavis," Kristy broke in. "I have no idea."

"Think you'll see him?"

Kristy actually shrugged. No use pretending she didn't know who Mavis was asking about. "Maybe around town," she said, with a nonchalance she certainly didn't feel. "We're old news, Dylan and I."

"So are you and Mike Danvers," Mavis parried coyly, "but Julie gets her panties in a wad every time he mentions your name. Which, apparently, is quite often."

Kristy had to be careful how she answered that one. Everything she said would go out over Mavis's extensive network within five minutes after she'd paid for the haircut and left. "That's silly. Mike and Julie have been married for a long time. They have two beautiful children and a great life. So Mike mentions my name once in a while? Stillwater Springs is a small town. He probably mentions a lot of people's names."

"Well," Mavis said doggedly, "I'd think you'd at least *wonder* about why Cassie might buy diapers, and there's Dylan Creed's truck parked in front of her house so early in the day that he must have rolled in during the night—"

"I don't wonder," Kristy lied, and very pointedly. If Dylan had a child, it would be the height of unfairness on the part of the universe. *She* was the one who longed for a houseful of kids. Dylan had never wanted to settle down—he'd just pretended he did, for obvious reasons. "What Dylan Creed does—or doesn't do—is simply none of my concern."

"Hogwash," Mavis said. "Your ears are red around the edges."

"That's because you've been poking me with the scissors at regular intervals. Are we nearly done here? I need to get back to the library."

Mavis blew out a breath. "The *library*," she scoffed. "You were a cheerleader in high school. You were a prom queen. *And* Miss Rodeo Montana, first runner-up for Miss Rodeo America. Who'd have thought Kristy Madison, of all people, would end up with a spinster-job? It reminds me of that scene in *It's a Wonderful Life,* when Donna Reed is this miserable old biddy because George Bailey was never born—"

"Oh, for heaven's sake, Mavis!" Kristy was ready to leap out of the chair by that point. Tear off the plastic cape and march right out into the street with her hair sectioned off in those stupid little metal clips. "Some of us have moved beyond high school, you know. And what's so terrible about being a librarian?"

Mavis softened. In the mirror facing the chair, her pointy little face looked sad. "Nothing," she said quietly.

"I'm sorry," Kristy said, immediately regretting her outburst. "I didn't mean to snap at you. It's just that—"

"It's just that," Mavis continued kindly, "when anybody mentions Dylan Creed, you get peevish."

"Then why mention him?" Kristy asked wearily.

Mavis squeezed her shoulder with one manicured hand. "I didn't mean any harm. I was just thinking you might be *glad* Dylan was back. I know you've had a hard time, Kristy—losing your folks the way you did, and the ranch and Sugarfoot, practically all at once. I'd like to see you happy again—and you were happy with Dylan, until that blowup the day of his dad's funeral. So would everybody else in Stillwater Springs—like to see you happy, I mean."

Kristy fought back tears, not because of the sad memories, but because she was touched. Mavis, in her own clumsy way, *did* care about her, and so did a lot of other people. "I *am* happy, Mavis," she said. "I have my job, my house, my cat—"

"Well, I've got a job and a house and *four* cats," Mavis argued cheerfully, "but it's my Bill that makes my heart go pitter-pat."

"You're lucky," Kristy said. And she meant it. Mavis had been married to the same man since the day after her high school graduation and though she and Bill had never had children, it was common knowledge that they were still as deeply in love as ever.

Mavis finished the haircut without mentioning Dylan again, which was a mercy, and Kristy rushed back to the library to grab a sandwich in her tiny office behind the information desk. It was Wednesday, and business was slow enough that her two volunteer helpers, Susan and Peggy, could handle the traffic.

Story hour was coming up at three, though, and it was Kristy's baby. She still hadn't chosen a book, and that stressed her a little. She was a detail person, and few details were more important to her than doing her job well.

So she finished her sandwich and went out into the main part of the library, headed for the children's section. It was always tricky, deciding what story to read, because the kids who gathered in a circle under the mock totem pole in the tiny play area ranged in age from as young as three to as old as twelve. The rowdy ones came, after swimming lessons over at the community pool, still smelling of chlorine and sunshine and always a little soggy around the edges, and the ones with working mothers invariably arrived early.

Harried, Kristy went from book to book, shelf to shelf.

Finally, she fell back on an old standby, one of the Nancy Drew mysteries she'd loved in her own youth. The boys would snicker, and the little ones wouldn't understand a word, but she knew just listening was part of the magic.

Yes, today, it would be *The Secret in the Old Clock.*

It would do the girls good to hear about smart, proactive Nancy and her lively sidekicks, George and Bess. And it wouldn't hurt the boys, either. Call it consciousness raising.

The time passed quickly, since Kristy stayed busy logging in a pile of returned books, and when she looked up from her work, she saw at least a dozen kids gathered in the play area, waiting.

"Showtime," Susan whispered, smiling. "I'll finish the returns. And I can stay right up till closing time tonight, too. Jim's off to Choteau with his bowling league."

Susan, in her midfifties, was supercompetent. Her staying meant Kristy could leave at five o'clock, instead of nine, like a normal person, and paint at least part of her kitchen before she nuked something for supper and tumbled into bed with Winston to read awhile and then sleep.

"Thanks," Kristy said, giving her friend a shoulder squeeze.

Carrying *The Secret in the Old Clock,* she made her way to the play area, took exaggerated bows when the kids clapped and cheered. They always did that, mainly because they liked to make noise in the library, where it was normally forbidden, but Kristy got a kick out of the whole routine anyway.

She settled down on the floor, cross-legged. "Today," she announced, "Nancy Drew."

True to form, the boys groaned.

The girls giggled.

The latch-key kids were just happy to see an adult.

Kristy made a production of opening the book. That, too, was part of the show. Always a flourish— kids liked that. Her own mother had made reading— and being read to—so much fun, using a different voice for each character and sometimes even acting out parts of the story.

And when she looked up, ready to begin, her heart jammed itself into the back of her throat and she couldn't say a single word.

Dylan Creed had appeared out of nowhere. He was sitting, cross-legged like Kristy, at the edge of the crowd, holding positively the cutest little girl Kristy had ever seen within the easy circle of his arms.

Kristy swallowed.

There was no doubt the child was his—the resemblance made Kristy's breath catch.

Dylan's blue eyes danced with mischief as he watched her.

She cleared her throat. "Chapter One," she began.

And then she froze up again.

One of the bigger boys started a chant. "Nan-cy! Nan-cy!"

All the other kids picked it up. Even the angelic being in Dylan's lap clapped her plump little hands together and tried to join in.

Dylan let out a sudden, piercing whistle.

Silence fell.

The little girl turned and looked up at him curiously.

"The lady," Dylan said, "is trying to read a story. So you yahoos better settle down and listen."

Somehow, Kristy managed to get through three chapters of the book, but it was a lackluster perfor-mance, for sure. Her gaze kept straying to Dylan and the little girl, and every time that happened, she felt her neck heat up.

At last, mothers started wandering in and collecting their charges. Kristy tried to look busy, but that was hard, given that she was still sitting on the floor with nothing but a book to fiddle with. Worse, her legs had gone to sleep, and she knew if she stood up too suddenly, she'd probably fall on her face.

In front of Dylan Creed.

Why didn't he just *leave,* like everybody else?

"Nice job," he said, and Kristy was startled to realize he was sitting right beside her. The little girl was playing with the large plastic blocks the Friends of the Library had provided for the play area.

Was he making fun of her?

Kristy swallowed again. Gulped, was more like it.

"She's beautiful," she croaked, inclining her head toward the child.

Dylan nodded. "Her name is Bonnie," he said.

What do you want? That was what Kristy would have asked if she hadn't been too chicken, but what tumbled out of her mouth was, "I heard you were passing through."

Great.

Now he'd think she'd been panting for any Dylan Creed news that might come her way.

"I'm not passing through," Dylan replied, watching Bonnie with a soft light in his wicked china-blue eyes. "I'm planning to stay on—tear down that old house of mine, now that Briana and her boys don't need it anymore, and build a new one. I'm going to have a barn, too, and some horses. Maybe even run some cattle with Logan's herd."

Why was he telling her all this? Did he think she cared?

Did she care?

No, no, a thousand times *no.*

Get a grip, she told herself.

Okay, so Bonnie could have been *her* little girl, as well as Dylan's, if things had turned out differently. But they hadn't, and that was that.

She had a house and a job and a perfectly good cat.

An excellent life, damn it.

"That's nice," she said, easing her legs out straight and giving them subtle shakes to get the circulation going again so she could stand up and walk away with some degree of dignity. Go about her business. Tell Susan she had a headache and wasn't staying until five.

But that would be a lie.

It was her heart that ached, not her head.

"How have you been, Kristy?" Dylan asked.

What was this, Be Kind to Former Lovers Week? "Fine," she said.

One corner of his mouth tilted upward in a sad little grin. "Up until the last time I talked to Logan, I thought you were married to Mike Danvers."

The name fell between them like a lead weight.

Kristy recovered quickly, but not quickly enough. Something moved in Dylan's eyes while she was coming up with her response, even though it only took a split second. "It wouldn't have worked out for Mike and me," she said.

"Like it didn't work out for us," Dylan said, and try though she might, Kristy couldn't get a bead on his tone.

"We were young," she heard herself say. "The world was falling apart. Your dad had just been killed in that logging accident, and both my folks—"

"Daddy!" Bonnie whooped suddenly, shrill with joy. "Daddy! Daddy! Daddy!"

She ran at Dylan and he scooped her up in his arms.

"Potty!" Bonnie yelled triumphantly.

Dylan sighed. "Would you mind taking her to the women's room?" he asked Kristy.

Glad of an excuse to break out of his orbit, if only for a few minutes, and hoping to God her legs had woken up, Kristy got to her feet, took Bonnie by the hand and escorted her to the bathroom.

Because so many of the children who came to the library were small, Kristy was used to that particular duty. But this was *Dylan's* little girl. He'd conceived this beautiful moppet with some nameless, faceless woman— not with her.

Damn it. When they'd made love all those times, before the rodeo and death and a lot of other things came between them, they'd always ended up choosing names afterward. They'd call a boy Timothy Jacob, for their fathers. A girl, Maggie Louise, for their mothers…

When she and Bonnie stepped out of the restroom, Dylan was waiting in the corridor, leaning against the wall with that indolent grace that seemed to emanate from his very DNA.

"Thanks," he said.

"You're welcome," she replied.

He hoisted Bonnie up into his arms. "Good to see you again, Kristy," he said, his voice a little hoarse.

"You, too," Kristy said. Fortunately, he left before the tears sprang to her eyes.

Thanks.

You're welcome.

Good to see you again…

You, too.

Kristy ducked back into the women's restroom, turned on the cold-water faucet and stood splashing her face until the burning stopped. But she still heard the voices, hers and Dylan's, though this time, they came from the long ago.

When the moon strays off into space, Dylan Creed, and the last star winks out forever, I will still love you.

He'd smiled, and stroked her hair, and kissed her, sending fire skittering along her veins all over again. *You read too much,* he'd teased. *I love that about you. Our kids will have a chance at being smart, with you for a mother.*

You're smart, too, Dylan, she'd protested, meaning it.

Not book-smart, he'd replied. *I can't talk in poetry the way you do.*

Does it matter? she'd asked, her heart brimming with tenderness.

Nothing matters but you and me, Kristy.

Nothing matters but you and me.

CHAPTER THREE

DROPPING BY THE LIBRARY had probably been a tactical error, Dylan admitted to himself; it had been a spur-of-the-moment thing, a sudden compulsion to see Kristy again, if only from a distance.

As it happened, though, she'd just rounded up a herd of kids for story-time when he and Bonnie came through the front door, and he'd been drawn into her circle immediately. There might as well have been beating drums and a fire pit, like the one in Cassie's teepee—the gathering had that same kind of elemental, visceral attraction.

Kristy was still beautiful—five years of living without him to complicate her life had only made her more so. She seemed more centered and serene than before, though it had pleased him to notice that his unexpected presence had thrown her a little.

The only bad part was the hurt he'd glimpsed in her eyes when she'd registered Bonnie's identity.

He glanced over at his daughter, buckled into her car seat and hugging her inky doll. By rights, the toy should probably be burned, since it had to be germ-central, but he couldn't bring himself to take it away. Maybe later, when Bonnie was asleep, he'd douse the thing in Lysol or something.

In the meantime, cruising through the shady streets of Stillwater Springs, he was careful to keep to the speed limit. All he needed was Floyd Book or one of his deputies pulling him over and asking for some kind of proof that he hadn't committed parental kidnapping. He had the note from Sharlene, found in his truck with Bonnie and the duffel bag, but who knew how much weight that would carry?

Logan would, of course. Logan could draw up papers, get everything on the up-and-up.

He headed for the ranch, partly in the vain hope that Logan would be there, and partly because it was home.

"This is where I grew up," he told Bonnie, as they drove under the newly repaired *Stillwater Springs Ranch* sign hanging over the main gate.

"No," Bonnie said cheerfully, chewing on the doll's punk-rocker hair.

Four words, now. The kid was developing an impressive vocabulary, all right.

The work on the barn was almost finished—new timbers supported it, and the roof had been replaced.

Dylan parked the truck, rolled down his window as one of the workmen came toward him, grinning.

He recognized Dan Phillips, a guy who'd graduated a few years ahead of him, at Stillwater Springs High.

"Logan around?" Dylan asked, though he knew the answer.

Dan shook his head. "Off to Las Vegas to get married."

"The barn's looking good," Dylan said.

Dan stooped for a glimpse at Bonnie. "Didn't know you were a family man, Dylan," he commented, with a twinkle.

"I'm full of surprises," Dylan replied. "You happen

to know if Logan arranged to have my house fixed up after that last break-in?"

"Took a crew over there and did it myself. Logan asked me to have Briana's and the boys' stuff picked up and moved here, and I did that, too."

That was something, anyhow, Dylan thought, still unaccountably disappointed that Logan wasn't home. He and Bonnie could get some groceries and move right in. Cassie had made them welcome, but her place was small and he didn't want to impose any longer than necessary.

"This must be old home week," Dan went on, just as Dylan was about to shift gears and drive overland to his place to figure out what he and Bonnie would need besides groceries. "I just saw Tyler. He's holed up in that old cabin of his, out there by the lake, and he asked me not to tell anybody he's around. Don't figure he'd mind your knowing, though."

Dan figured wrong, but Dylan saw no reason to say so. "I'll stop by and say howdy," he answered easily. *If I'm lucky, little brother won't run me off with a shotgun.*

"Starting on the house next," Dan said, with a nod toward the venerable old place. "Putting in some pretty fancy rigging—new master bathroom and a state-of-the-art kitchen to start."

Dylan grinned. Logan still expected to stay on, settle down, raise a pack of kids with Briana.

He'd believe it when the last of the bunch grew up and got married.

But, then, considering how he felt about his own child, it was possible Logan really *had* set his mind to "making the Creed name mean something," as he put it.

"Be seeing you," Dylan told Dan, because that was what you said, in the boonies, when you wanted to make a polite but speedy exit.

Dan nodded, executed a half salute and went back to work.

Dylan headed for his own place.

"Potty," Bonnie said solemnly, as they bumped and jostled across the field, going around the orchard and the cemetery.

Sooner or later, he'd have to visit Jake's grave, but that was way down on the list.

"Hold your horses," Dylan answered, his tone affable. "We're almost home."

"It's just plain silly to get all bent out of shape just because Dylan Creed showed up at story hour with absolutely the most gorgeous child in the universe," Kristy told Winston, long about sundown as, standing on the top rung of a folding ladder, she swabbed sunshine-yellow paint around the framework of the archway between the kitchen and dining room.

Winston, having just devoured his usual feast, groomed one of his forepaws meticulously and offered no comment.

"I mean, it isn't as if he's ever had any trouble attracting women," Kristy went on, wiping a splotch of paint from her nose with the sleeve of the oversize men's shirt she'd bought at Goodwill for messy jobs.

"Meow," Winston said, halfheartedly.

"It's just that it was sort of a shock, that's all."

Bored, Winston turned, fluffed out his bushy tail and hied himself to the living room. He liked to curl up on the antique bureau in front of the bay windows and watch the world go by. Slow going, in Stillwater Springs. Hours could pass before a car putted past.

"Typical," Kristy said to the empty kitchen. "Nobody listens to me."

In the next instant, somebody rapped at her back door, and Kristy nearly fell off the ladder, she was so startled. What was the *matter* with her, anyway?

"Come in!" she called, because that was what you did in Stillwater Springs.

When Sheriff Book opened the door and stepped across the threshold, she was surprised, though not enough to take a header to the linoleum.

"You shouldn't just call out 'come in' like that," Floyd said, taking off his sheriff hat and setting it aside on the counter. "I could have been some drifter, bent on murder and mayhem." A little grin twitched at the corner of his mouth, softening his otherwise stern expression. "This isn't the old days, Kristy."

Kristy set her wet paintbrush in the aluminum tray of sunshine-yellow and climbed down the ladder, smiling. "Coffee?" she asked.

Floyd shook his head, sighed. "Trying to cut down," he said. "Keeps me awake at night."

Kristy stood there, waiting for him to get to the reason for his visit.

"You mind sitting down?" the sheriff asked, sounding tired.

Uh-oh, Kristy thought. *Here comes the whammy.*

Once she was seated at the table, Floyd took a chair across from her. "I guess you know the bank finally untangled that probate mess over the ranch," he said quietly. "And Freida's got that movie-star fella all set to buy it."

Kristy's throat thickened. She nodded. "She told me it was going up for sale now that all the legal processes are complete." She was curious as to why Floyd had dropped in to tell her something like that.

"It's an old ranch," Floyd went on, his expression downright grim. "A lot happened out there, over the years."

Kristy felt an uneasy prickle in the pit of her stomach. "Floyd, what are you getting at?"

"I think there might be a body buried on the place," Floyd said.

Kristy's mouth dropped open, and her heart stopped, then raced. The monster-memory stirred in the depths of her brain. "A *body?*"

Floyd sighed. "I could be wrong," he said, but the expression on his face said he didn't think so.

"Good God," Kristy said, too stunned to say anything else and, at the same time, strangely *not* surprised.

The sheriff looked pained. "There was a man— worked for your daddy one summer when you were just a little thing. Some drifter—I never knew his name for certain. Men like him came and went all the time, stopping to earn a few dollars on some ranch. But one night, late, Tim woke me up with a phone call and said there was bad trouble, and I ought to get out there quick. He didn't sound like himself—for a moment or two, I thought I was talking to a prowler. Turned out he'd caught this drifter fella sneaking out of the house with some of your mother's jewelry and what cash they had on hand, which was plenty, because they'd sold some cattle at auction that day. There was a fight, that was all Tim would tell me. That there'd been a fight. I dressed and headed for the ranch, soon as I could. And when I got there, your dad changed his story. Said the drifter had moved on and good riddance to him."

Dread welled up inside Kristy, but she said, "That must have been the truth, then." She'd never known her father to lie about anything, however expedient it might be.

But Sheriff Book shook his head again. His eyes seemed to sink deeper into his head, and there were shadows under them. "I took his word for it, because he was my best friend, but there was more to the story, and I knew it. Tim looked worse than he'd sounded on the phone. It was a cold night, but he was sweating, and he had dirt under his nails, and on his clothes, too. You know he always cleaned up before supper, Kristy, and this was well after midnight."

Kristy couldn't speak, couldn't bring herself to ask the obvious question: Did Sheriff Book think her father had *killed* a man?

"Few days later," the sheriff went on, clearly forcing out the words, "on a Sunday morning, I came by the ranch for a look around, when I knew you and your folks were at church. And I found what I figured was a freshly dug grave in that copse of trees over near where Tim's property and the Creed place butt up."

Kristy felt a surge of relief—he'd seen *Sugarfoot's* grave that morning, not that of a human being—but it was gone in a moment. Back then, Sugarfoot had been alive and well.

Floyd reached across the table, squeezed her ice-cold hand. "I asked Tim what was there. He said an old dog had strayed into his barn and died there, and he'd buried the poor critter in the midst of those trees." He thrust out another sigh. "I was the sheriff. I should have done some digging, both literal and figurative, but I didn't. I *wanted* to believe your dad, so I did, but I've always wondered, and now that I'm about to retire, I've got to know for sure. It isn't just the coffee that keeps me up at night, it's certain loose ends."

Kristy thought she was going to be sick. "You're going to—to exhume—"

Floyd nodded. "I know Sugarfoot's buried there, Kristy," he said gruffly, hardly able to meet her gaze, "and I'll do my best not to disturb his remains too much. But I've got to see, once and for all, if there's a dog in that grave with him—or a man."

"You seriously think my father—*your best friend*—would *murder* someone and then go to such lengths to hide the body?" Now, Kristy was light-headed. Her heart pounded, and the smell of paint, unnoticed before, brought bile scalding up into the back of her throat.

Don't remember, whispered a voice in the shadowy recesses of her mind, where migraines and nightmares lurked. *Don't remember.*

"I think," Sheriff Book said quietly, "that there *was* a fight, and things got out of hand. If Tim did kill that drifter, it was an accident, and nobody will ever convince me otherwise. He'd have been real upset, Tim, I mean, with you and your mother in the house—that would have made the fight one he couldn't afford to lose. In Tim's place, I'd have been scared as hell of what that fella might do if I wasn't up to stopping him."

Kristy got up, meaning to bolt for the bathroom, then sat down again with a plunk. "But Dad called you," she muttered. "Would he have done that if he'd killed somebody?"

"He was in a panic, Kristy. He probably called first and thought later."

"Dad's gone, and so is Mom. You're about to retire. Can't we just let this whole thing…lie?"

"If we can live with knowing what we do. I don't think I can, not anymore—I've got an ulcer to show for it as it is. Can *you* just go on from here like nothing was ever said, Kristy?"

She bit down on her lower lip. "No," she said miserably.

If there *were* human remains buried with Sugarfoot—more likely beneath him—the scandal would rock the whole state of Montana. Tim Madison's memory, that of a decent, hardworking, honorable man, would be fodder for all sorts of speculation.

How would she handle that?

"Why now?" she asked, closing her eyes briefly in the hope that the room would stop tilting from side to side. "After all this time, Floyd, *why now?*"

"I told you," he replied gently. "My retirement. And with that land going up for sale, and some jerk from Hollywood bound on bringing in bulldozers to make room for tennis courts and whatnot—"

Kristy froze. She'd known, of course, that *someone* would buy Madison Ranch eventually. It was prime real estate. But not once had she considered the possibility that that someone might destroy poor Sugarfoot's grave.

Tears filled her eyes, and all the old wounds opened at once.

"I'm sorry," Sheriff Book said.

"When he died," Kristy murmured, "Sugarfoot, I

mean—I wanted to die, too. Crawl right into that grave with him and let them cover me with dirt."

"You'd just lost your mother then," Floyd reminded her. "And your dad was already sick. It was a lot for one young girl to bear up under. But you *did* bear up, Kristy. You kept going, kept living, like you were supposed to."

A long, difficult silence fell. Kristy broke it with, "You do realize what an uproar this is going to cause, if you find—find something."

Grimly, Floyd nodded. "Might be I'm wrong. There's no need to get the community all riled up if there's really a dog sharing that grave with Sugarfoot. I can keep the whole thing quiet, Kristy, at least for a while. But this is Stillwater Springs, and folks are always flapping their jaws. Word could get out, and that's why I came over here to talk to you first. So you'd know ahead of time, in case—well, you know."

Kristy nodded.

The sheriff stood to go. "You going to be all right?" he asked. "I could call somebody, if you want."

"Call somebody?" Kristy echoed stupidly. Who? Who in the whole wide, upside-down, messed-up world would drop everything and rush over to hold the librarian's hand?

Dylan, she thought.

"Maybe you oughtn't to be alone."

"I'm fine," Kristy said. Stock answer.

Major lie.

"Lock up behind me," Floyd said.

Kristy nodded.

But he'd been gone a long time before she even got out of her chair.

THE HOUSE WAS HABITABLE, as it turned out, if sparsely furnished. Dylan figured he and Bonnie could live there, in comfort if not style, but he'd need to rig up some kind of bed for her, get her a dresser.

More shopping, he thought unhappily.

And with a two-year-old.

"Whoopee," he muttered.

"Potty," Bonnie said.

"Learn another word," Dylan replied. The little pink toilet was still at Cassie's place, so he had to lift Bonnie onto the john again, bare-assed, and wait it out.

In the end, Cassie offered to babysit at her place while he laid in grub and the other necessities.

He bought Bonnie a miniature bed, one step up from a crib, with side rails that could be raised and lowered. It was white, with gold trim—French provincial, the saleswoman at the only furniture store in Stillwater Springs called it. The piece, she said, was designed to grow with the child.

Dylan paid cash and the woman promised an early-morning delivery. He still needed some other stuff, but since he meant to tear down the house anyway, he couldn't see torturing himself by buying a decent couch and a new dinette set right then. He could get all that later—or maybe the trailer he meant to lease and set up on the property as temporary digs would have some rigging in it.

But the kid would need milk in the morning, to put in her sippy-thing, and cereal, too.

So he braved the grocery store in town.

Once he'd carted everything back out to the ranch and put it away, he headed back to Cassie's to pick up Bonnie. She could sleep on the bed that night—it had been there when Briana moved in—and he'd take the lumpy old couch.

At least they'd be in their own place, he and Bonnie. It was a start.

As he drove past the casino, his truck wanted to pull in, but for the time being, he was out of the poker business. He was, after all, a father.

He had responsibilities now.

And strange as it seemed, he liked the feeling.

It was all good—except for the potty thing and the flying spaghetti.

He *definitely* needed a wife, if he was going to pull this thing off.

He immediately thought of Kristy.

"Oh, sure," he told himself out loud. "Just walk right into the library, one fine day, and suggest letting bygones be bygones because, lo and behold, you've got a two-year-old daughter and you could sure use a hand raising her."

Put like that, it sounded pretty damn lame.

And Kristy would probably bash him over the head with the nearest heavy book.

Still, Bonnie needed a mother, and he couldn't think of a better candidate than Kristy Madison, with her soft storyteller's voice and her calm practicality. If he'd had to get somebody pregnant, why couldn't it have been her, instead of Sharlene?

Now *there* was a useless question.

After what had gone down the day of Jake's funeral, Kristy had crossed him off her list, gotten herself engaged to Mike Danvers. Good old solid Mike, student body president, Boy Scout and future owner of his dad's Chevrolet dealership.

He wouldn't get arrested for fighting with his own brothers after a family funeral, not Mike. No sir, he was the original solid citizen, not a hell-raising Creed. One word from Kristy and he'd probably beat feet down to the jewelry store to make a down payment on that honking diamond he'd given her.

Since Dylan was thinking these thoughts, and some that were even worse, when he pulled into Cassie's yard, it took him an extra second or two to realize that the big white Cadillac SUV parked next to the teepee probably belonged to Tyler.

The rodeo insignia in the back window clenched it. Only champions had those silver-buckle decals, and Tyler had been a world-class bronc-buster, among other things.

He did TV commercials, too, and posed for cowboy calendars, half-naked. Taking a page from Dylan's book, he'd done some stunt work, too, though mercifully they'd never wound up on the same movie set.

Dylan was flat-out not ready to deal with his younger brother just then, but leaving wasn't an option, either. For one thing, he didn't run from confrontations, unless they were with women. He'd come for Bonnie, and he wasn't leaving without her.

So he got out of the truck and walked toward Cassie's front door.

Best get it over with. He'd pass the word to Tyler, if Cassie hadn't done it already, that Logan had been trying to get in touch with him, get Bonnie and all her assorted gear, and leave.

Tyler was on the floor when Dylan walked in, on his hands and knees, with Bonnie on his back, one hand gripping the back of his shirt collar, the other raised in the air, bronc-buster style.

And she was laughing as he bucked, careful not to throw her.

She was a Creed, all right. Thank God she was a girl, or she'd probably end up on the circuit, risking life and limb for a rush of adrenaline and some elusive prize money.

Of the three Creed brothers, Tyler was the youngest, and the tallest, and the one with the hottest temper. His hair was as dark as Cassie's, and he wore it long enough to brush his collar.

He turned his head, saw Dylan and stopped bucking. Eased Bonnie off his back and got to his feet.

His deep blue eyes were arctic as he straightened to his full height.

As a kid, he'd had music in him, so much that it flowed out through the strings of his cheap guitar and just about everything he did. Between Jake's drunken escapades and his mother's suicide when he was still young, though, something had shut down inside him and never started up again.

"Logan wants to talk to you," Dylan said, because with Tyler, even "hello" was shaky ground.

"So I hear," Tyler answered. "Of course, I don't give a rat's ass."

Cassie wooed Bonnie into the kitchen, promising her a cookie, after casting worried glances from one Creed brother to the other.

"If you're trying to get my back up, Ty, you're going to have to do better than that. What brings you back to Stillwater Springs?"

"I was about to ask you the same thing," Tyler answered, turning to look when Bonnie's giggle chimed from the kitchen. "Cute kid," he added, and for a fraction of a second, his eyes warmed. "Bonnie, isn't it?"

"That's right," Dylan said, still waiting for the explosion. He and Tyler had had several run-ins over the years; the brawl after Jake's funeral was only one of them. A couple of seasons back, they'd collided at the same rodeo, and Ty's girlfriend, probably wanting to make him jealous, had been all over Dylan.

He hadn't taken the bait, but the girlfriend—he couldn't recall her name—had ditched Tyler, stayed out all night and claimed she'd been with Dylan, in his hotel room. It wasn't true—for one thing, there'd been *another* woman sharing his bed, and he wasn't into threesomes—but Tyler, with that perennial chip on his shoulder, hadn't believed him.

There would have been a fight, right there behind the chutes that day at the rodeo, if ten other cowboys hadn't jumped in to pull them apart.

"I'll be leaving now," Tyler said. "I just came by to say hello to Cassie."

Dylan nodded. There had to be more to it, of course—Tyler hadn't set foot in Stillwater Springs, as far as he knew, since Sheriff Book turned them all loose the morning after Jake was laid to rest—but he knew better than to try to get an answer out of his brother.

"See you," he said.

"Not if I see you first," Tyler replied. As kids, that had been a running joke. Now, Tyler meant it.

A bleak feeling settled over Dylan. He and Logan were speaking, anyway, though they still had things to work through. But that wasn't going to happen with Tyler, he could tell.

Tyler was a loner, and he clearly intended to stay that way.

"What's he doing here?" Dylan asked Cassie, in the kitchen, after Tyler left. The SUV started up with a roar outside.

She sat at the table, Bonnie on her knee, deftly spooning toddler grub into the kid's mouth. "Why didn't you ask him?" she asked. She'd been trying for years to get the three of them to reconcile and act like brothers, and despite an almost complete lack of success, she still seemed to think it could happen.

"Might as well ask the totem pole down at the library," Dylan said, opening the fridge and helping himself to a can of soda. Pre-Bonnie, he'd have had a beer, but since you never knew when you might have to rush a kid to the emergency room with some sudden malady, he figured he'd better lay off the brew.

Cassie smiled to herself. "You've been to the *library?*"

Dylan popped the top on the soda can and took a swig. "I *can* read, you know. I was dyslexic as a kid, but I've learned to compensate."

"That isn't what I meant," Cassie said sweetly. How many nights had she sat with him, at that same table, going over the "special lessons" he'd been assigned after a battery of reading tests?

"Ah," Dylan said. "Yes. Did I see Kristy—that's what you're asking."

"And?"

"I saw her."

"Well, don't overwhelm me with information, here."

Dylan sighed. "I saw her. She's still a looker. She's still got a way with kids. End of story."

"Or the beginning," Cassie said, smiling at Bonnie.

"Don't get any ideas," Dylan warned, though when it came to Kristy, he'd been getting ideas himself. Cassie couldn't possibly know that, unless she used her X-ray vision.

"Poor Kristy," she said, looking solemn now, even sad. Frowning as she gazed over Bonnie's head, past Dylan, to some unseen world only she could navigate.

"What do you mean, 'poor Kristy'?" Dylan asked, knowing he shouldn't, but too worried to resist. When Cassie worried about people, they tended to meet with severe and immediate problems.

"She could use a friend, that's all," Cassie mused.

It *wasn't* all, of course.

Dylan set the soda can aside with a thump. He'd have tossed it, but Cassie recycled. "What's going on?" he demanded quietly. "You didn't have one of your dreams…?"

"No," Cassie said. "I just know these things." She brightened. "Call it an old Indian trick."

"Cassie," Dylan pressed. "Tell me."

"Go see her," Cassie replied, looking up into his face. "She's alone, at her place. I'll look after Bonnie, give her a bath and supper and put her to bed."

"I can't just show up on her doorstep, Cassie. What am I supposed to say? 'Hi, my foster grandmother sent me'?"

"You'll think of something."

"I was planning on taking Bonnie out to the ranch."

"That can wait, Dylan. I'm not sure Kristy can."

"She'll probably slam the door in my face."

"You're a big boy. Deal."

Dylan sighed. He'd never taken Cassie's so-called psychic abilities very seriously—she'd as much as admitted that she told her Tarot clients whatever she thought they wanted to hear—but there were times when her instincts struck too close to the bone for comfort.

He bent, kissed the top of Bonnie's head and left.

Ten minutes later, he was knocking at Kristy's door, still wondering what the hell he was going to say to explain being there in the first place.

She was wearing old pants, a man's shirt and a lot of yellow paint when she opened the door.

And she'd been crying. Her eyes were puffy and her nostrils were red around the edges. Seeing Kristy in tears was devastating, but at least he wasn't the *cause* of them this time—as far as he knew.

"Everything okay?" Dylan asked, stricken. Just call him the Wordmeister, he thought glumly. He'd always been able to talk his way into—or out of—any situation—unless that situation involved Kristy Madison.

"No," she said. Her voice shook a little. Then she launched herself at him, wrapped both arms around his neck. *"No!"*

CHAPTER FOUR

DEAR GOD.

It should have been against the law to smell the way Kristy did—a tantalizing combination of rich grass after a heavy spring rain, leaves burning in autumn, talcum powder of some kind and paint thinner. For a precious moment, Dylan simply held her against him, breathed her in, closing his eyes tightly against the rush of emotion he felt.

Like most precious moments, that one was brief.

Kristy quickly bristled in his arms, pulled back, raised her chin and sniffled. The vulnerability in her cornflower-blue eyes turned to defiance.

"I apologize," she said stiffly, as though he were a stranger she'd collided with in a crowded airport, not the first man who had ever made love to her. "I've just been under a little stress lately and—"

Dylan drew a long breath, let it out in a sigh as he closed Kristy's front door behind him and hooked his thumbs through his belt loops. "Kristy," he said. "This is me. Dylan. Something's up with you, or you wouldn't have practically tackled me on the threshold."

Kristy gave an answering sigh, and her usually straight shoulders sagged in a way that tugged at a tender place in Dylan's heart. "Come in," she said, with about the same level of enthusiasm she might have shown a visiting terrorist wearing a suit of dynamite.

Dylan saw no reason to point out that he was already in—he simply followed Kristy through the house, expecting to wind up in the kitchen. When folks around the Springs had something to discuss, or just wanted to jaw awhile, they tended to congregate at the table, with the coffeepot and the refrigerator close at hand.

He'd visited the huge Victorian once or twice, with his dad, when Jake stopped by to collect an overdue paycheck from old man Turlow. The place had seemed dark and oppressive to him then, but Kristy had brightened it up considerably, with lace curtains and lots of pale yellow walls. The floors were gleaming oak, probably sanded to bare wood and then refinished.

That, too, would be Kristy's doing.

She liked a lot of light and space—used to dream of living in the Turlow house one day.

It only went to show that *some* dreams came true, anyway.

A giant folding ladder stood just inside the kitchen doorway—Kristy ducked around it, Dylan walked between its runged legs.

"Coffee?" she asked. He saw the struggle in her face, but eventually, she couldn't keep herself from adding, "You shouldn't walk under ladders."

"That's a stupid superstition," Dylan countered, with a twinkle. "And, yes, please, ma'am, I *would* like some coffee."

"I wasn't referring to the superstition," Kristy insisted loftily, standing on her toes to fetch two mismatched mugs down from a cupboard. "Things could fall on your head, like a bucket of paint."

"Still waiting for the sky to come crashing down, I see." Dylan grinned, but tension twisted inside him like a screw turned too tight. He regretted those flippant words as soon as he saw them register in Kristy's face. Behind that flimsy facade of bravery, she was crumbling.

Perhaps the sky *was* falling.

"Are you going to tell me what's wrong," he persisted, "or do I have to look it up on the Internet?"

A flush rose in her face. She poured coffee, carried the two cups to the table, and pulled back a chair with a practiced motion of one foot. "For Pete's sake," she said irritably, "*sit down.*"

"Not until you do," Dylan replied. "I'm a gentleman."

Kristy snorted at that, dropped into her chair. Added insult to injury by rolling her eyes once, for good measure.

Dylan took the chair next to hers, idly stroked the big white cat that immediately jumped into his lap.

"Sheriff Book was here a while ago," Kristy said, elbow propped on the tabletop, her chin resting forlornly in her hand.

"Go on," Dylan said.

Her eyes filled with fresh tears. "He thinks my father may have—may have killed someone."

Stunned, Dylan set down the mug he'd just picked up and stared at Kristy, waiting for the punch line. Tim Madison, a murderer? Impossible. Kristy's dad had been a soft-spoken, kindly man, hardworking and generous with what little he had.

Jake Creed, on the other hand, had been possessed of a legendary temper, and if Sheriff Book thought *he'd* offed some poor bastard, Dylan could have believed it. Although he didn't tolerate criticism of Jake well, particularly when it came from his brothers, deep down he'd never had many illusions about the sort of man his father was.

"That's crazy," he said, finally.

Kristy sniffled again, tried a sip of her coffee, made a face and put it down again. "I know. But the county is going to dig up Sugarfoot's grave. He tried to soften the blow, but Floyd clearly believes my father killed a man, probably by accident, and buried him with—with—"

Dylan longed to displace the cat and pull Kristy onto his lap, to offer her what comfort he could, but he didn't move. She'd loved Sugarfoot, that old horse of hers, with a near-sacred constancy.

The way she *hadn't* loved him.

When he spoke at long last, the words scraped his throat like a swallow of rusty barbed wire. "Suppose they *did* find a body in that grave besides Sugarfoot's? Your folks are gone, Kristy, and so is Sugarfoot. This can't hurt any of them."

Stupid, stupid, Dylan thought, in the next instant, raking splayed fingers through his hair as the frustration hit him.

The Madisons couldn't be hurt, or the horse, either— but Kristy could.

She'd lived in or just outside of Stillwater Springs all her life. It was her home, the only place she'd ever wanted to be, which had been a big part of the problem between the two of them back in the day. She'd been Holly Homemaker, he'd been a hell-raiser and a rodeo cowboy with a penchant for the open road.

Welcome to Heartbreak Hotel.

Kristy bit her lower lip, reached out and closed her paint-splotched hand over Dylan's. Tried gamely to smile. "I know you didn't mean that the way it sounded," she said, with a gentleness that bruised him. He was used to rough-and-tumble, growing up with Jake and his brothers and then riding the professional circuit. He could *be* gentle, especially with Bonnie, or a lost or injured animal, but finding himself on the receiving end was different, and downright unsettling.

Dylan cleared his throat. Gearing up to make another attempt, because he was a Creed, and therefore nothing if not persistent. Even when it meant digging himself in deeper, he had to keep shoveling.

"Why didn't you ever get another horse after Sugarfoot?" he heard himself ask. Damn, but he hadn't intended to say that, either. It just rolled right off his tongue before he could rope and hogtie it.

A faraway, wistful look deepened the bluer-than-blue of Kristy's eyes. "It costs money to keep a horse," she said, after a very long time. "A *lot* of money. Librarians don't exactly pull down the big bucks, Dylan."

"You bought this house," Dylan reasoned.

"I received a small inheritance when my great-aunt passed away a year and a half ago," Kristy said, in a why-am-I-telling-you-this-when-it's-personal tone of voice. "I made the down payment on the house and moved in."

The cat had already gotten bored; having shed white hair all over Dylan's T-shirt, he probably figured his work there was done. Now, he was batting a toy mouse around the kitchen floor.

"You and your great-aunt's cat," Dylan mused, recalling how Kristy had always wanted a large family and lots of pets. Being an only child, she'd said, was too lonely.

"Oh, Winston didn't belong to Aunt Millie," Kristy replied. "He was Freida Turlow's, and when she moved out after I'd closed on the house, he started turning up on my doorstep at all hours of the day and night. Freida's been annoyed with me ever since—it's as if she thinks I wooed him away from her or something."

Dylan remembered Freida Turlow clearly. She'd tried to seduce him, the night of his sixteenth birthday, and he might have taken her up on the offer, too, if he hadn't already been in love with Kristy.

"Freida's always annoyed with somebody," he observed, barely stopping himself from saying right out loud that, faced with a choice between living with the imposing Ms. Turlow or with Kristy, he'd have thrown in with the cat.

Kristy's eyes turned bleak. For a few minutes, she'd forgotten about the possibility of impending scandal, but now Dylan could see that the respite was over. "Freida will be the worst," she said, with soft despair, "if it turns out that Floyd's suspicions are right."

"What will you do," Dylan ventured to ask, "if he is?" He was surprised by the suspense he felt, awaiting her answer. It would be one hell of an irony if, just when he'd decided he'd be able to settle down on the ranch and make a home for his daughter, Kristy chose to leave town for good.

"I don't know," she said. "I think—I think it might sour things—the house, my job at the library—" She paused, took another run at getting her point across. "You know how small towns are, Dylan. It was bad enough when my parents died within a year of each other, and the ranch went for debts and taxes. Everybody felt sorry for me. People would *never* let a story like this rest, and I'm not sure I could face all that pity and gossip again."

All that pity and gossip.

Kristy looked as though she'd like to take those words back, choke on each one whole before giving voice to them. Dylan supposed there had been plenty of gossip, when he came back to Stillwater Springs to ask her to wait for him, a few months after the breakup following Jake's funeral, and she'd waved Mike Danvers's huge engagement ring under his nose and basically told him to get lost. He'd always supposed, though, that any *pity* making the rounds had been reserved for him.

That was one of the reasons he'd stayed away so long—as a ragged kid, with the notorious Jake Creed for a father, he'd had all the sympathy he could take. Charity baskets left on the front porch, at Christmas, Thanksgiving and Easter. Well-meaning church ladies offering him their sons' cast-off clothes. And all the rest of it.

The biggest reason, though, had been Kristy herself.

He'd ridden the meanest bulls in rodeo. Scraped his knuckles and bloodied his nose in a score of bar brawls—and those were the ones he'd *won*—but he'd known that seeing Kristy going about her wifely business around town, picking up mail down at the post office, pushing a shopping cart through the supermarket aisles, intermittently blossoming with another man's child, would bring him to his knees.

So, except for brief forays, when he'd brought his bull, Cimarron, back to the ranch, not knowing what else to do with him, and hired Briana Grant—now Creed—

to look after his empty house, he'd stayed as far away as possible.

Bonnie—and Logan's telling him, during his last visit, that Kristy was still single—had changed everything.

Coming to terms with all that was going to take a while.

And now there might be a body moldering on the old Madison place.

His coffee had gone cold, but since the conversation had come to a halt and he didn't know how to start it up again, he sipped some java.

That was another thing that hadn't changed.

Kristy's coffee was still bad.

He smiled at the thought.

"Tell me about your little girl," Kristy said, and he knew by the way she framed the request that she'd been working up her nerve during the silence.

"You probably already know as much about her as I do," Dylan admitted. "She's two. Her name is Bonnie. She likes listening to you read aloud."

Kristy seemed to relax a little, though there was still a tense undercurrent. "I take it her mother is out of the picture?"

"God knows where Sharlene is," Dylan said, sighing. Then he met Kristy's gaze, and held steady. "Sharlene was a mistake, no denying that. But Bonnie— well—she's the proof that something good comes out of everything."

Everything but a horse's grave, in a peaceful copse of trees, added the voice in his mind. Now that the possibility had had a chance to sink in, he knew instinctively that the sheriff and his crew *would* find something besides Sugarfoot's bones when they dug that hole.

Kristy's smile was misty. "I envy you," she said.

Again, Dylan was taken aback. He'd forgotten Kristy's capacity to surprise him—one of the things he'd loved best about her. "Why?" he asked, honestly puzzled.

"Because you have a child," she said slowly, and with amused patience.

"I just hope I can keep her," he answered. The worry that Sharlene would change her mind and take Bonnie back circled in the darkest depths of his mind, liable to drag him under when he least expected it.

Kristy raised one eyebrow. Waited.

"I plan to file for permanent custody when Logan gets home from Vegas," he explained. "Until then, I'm pretty much hanging out there in the wind." He studied Kristy, remembering—no, remembering wasn't the right word, because he hadn't actually forgotten in the first place—how good it had felt to hold her tightly again.

"You didn't—*steal her,* did you?"

"You're the second person who's asked me that," Dylan said. "No, I didn't kidnap my daughter. Sharlene left her in my truck while I was inside some dive in Las Vegas, playing poker, along with a note saying she couldn't take care of her anymore."

Kristy's mouth dropped open. "She *left a child alone in a truck?*"

"She was around someplace, keeping an eye out."

Like *that* made a difference. He'd probably never know what Sharlene would have done if he hadn't found Bonnie. Even if they happened to have a reasonable conversation at some point, Sharlene wasn't likely to be honest and straightforward.

"Oh, *well*," Kristy said skeptically, "that changes everything."

"Sharlene isn't the brightest bulb in the marquee," Dylan allowed. "But in her own crazy way, I think she was doing what she thought was best."

Kristy pulled in her horns a little. Sighed again. "Why not simply call you, if she felt overwhelmed by the responsibility of caring for Bonnie, and ask for help?"

Dylan didn't like the answer that came to him, liked saying it out loud even less. "She probably thought I'd say no, so she didn't give me the chance."

A short silence fell, during which Kristy regarded Dylan long and hard. "*Would* you have said no?" she finally asked.

"Of course not," he said, mildly affronted. "Bonnie is my *daughter.*"

"Excuse me," Kristy countered, "but *some* guys would have *married* the mother of their child."

Just like that, she'd gotten his hackles up. That was another thing he'd forgotten about Kristy—her gift for pissing him off royally. "I didn't love Sharlene," he said tautly, "and she sure as hell didn't love me."

"Did either one of you love Bonnie?" Kristy asked.

Dylan had to unclamp his back molars before he could reply. "I never missed a child-support check," he said.

"Aren't you noble?" Kristy challenged, bending one knee and sitting on her leg, which was still another thing he recalled about her. Her forehead was furrowed, her eyes slightly narrowed. "Did you ever *see* Bonnie, before you found her in your truck? Did you ever take care of her when she was teething, or had the flu? Did you even carry her picture in your wallet?"

"Yes," Dylan growled, leaning in a little. "I saw Bonnie whenever I could catch up with Sharlene. *No,* I wasn't there when she was teething, or if she had the flu." He raised his haunches, pried his wallet out of his back pocket and flipped it open to the discount-store photo of the one person in the entire world he was absolutely, positively sure he loved. "Sharlene's grandmother sent me this," he finished, confounded by his own fury. After all, none of this was Kristy's fault—not directly, anyway. "Along with a bill for Sharlene's boob job. It seemed they both thought she'd have a better chance of landing a husband with a big set of knockers."

Kristy blushed.

Dylan didn't care. If she wanted to play hardball, so be it.

"Did you pay it?"

For a moment, Dylan wasn't sure he'd heard the question correctly. *"What?"*

A smile teased at the corner of Kristy's lush and highly kissable mouth. "Did you pay the bill for the boob job?"

"No," he said.

She laughed.

And then, remarkably, he laughed, too. "Your coffee is still awful," he said.

"And you still get your back up too easily."

"Do I?"

"Yes."

He needed to leave, pick Bonnie up at Cassie's and get her settled out at the ranch. But first he had to know for sure that Kristy was going to be all right.

Spotting a small blackboard on the wall next to the back door—Kristy's grocery list was on it, in her precise librarian's handwriting, all loopy and firm—he crossed to it, picked up a stubby piece of blue chalk and scrawled his cell number below *broccoli*.

"Call me," he told Kristy, turning to see her clearing their cups from the table with brisk, efficient motions, "if you need anything."

"I won't," she said. "Need anything, I mean."

Her stubbornness. Her pride. It was all coming back to him now.

"Why didn't you marry Mike?" he asked. He felt entitled to ask that question; turnabout was fair play, after all.

She sighed, turned to face him. He could tell that holding his gaze was an effort, but she managed it. "I came to my senses," she said.

Now, what the hell did *that* mean?

"Mike is a nice man," she went on, when Dylan didn't speak. Although he'd come in through the front door, he was at the back now, with one hand on the knob. "He deserved to be happy."

"He looked pretty happy to me, that night I ran into the two of you in Skivvie's Tavern." The vision filled his mind's eye; he might as well have been in that darkened bar again, watching Mike and Kristy dancing to a slow song playing on the jukebox, Kristy making sure Dylan got a good look at the diamond glittering on her left hand. He could feel the sawdust and peanut shells under the soles of his boots, smell cigarette smoke and draft beer.

"I was using him," Kristy said forthrightly. "When I realized that, I broke our engagement. A few months later, he married Julie. End of story."

End of story? After that night at Skivvie's, Dylan had left Stillwater Springs, his tires flinging up gravel, swearing he'd never set foot in his hometown again. He'd spent the better part of a year drowning his sorrows in cheap whiskey, dodging bill collectors and backing down from the one thing he was really good at—bull-riding.

He'd probably have drunk himself to death, in fact, if an old friend, a retired rodeo clown named Wiley Spence, hadn't gotten him by the shirt collar one night in Cheyenne, after bailing him out of jail, and threatened to call Logan if he didn't get his act together pronto.

Kristy wasn't the only one with pride. Although he and Logan had been estranged back then, he'd known his big brother would track him down and probably throw him into the nearest treatment center. He hadn't wanted Logan to see him down and out. So he'd laid off the booze, except for an occasional beer, cleaned up and gotten back into the rodeo as soon as he'd scraped together an entry fee.

None of which was Kristy's concern.

"Thanks for the coffee," he said. And then he left.

DYLAN WAS GOOD AT LEAVING. *Very* good at leaving.

Kristy banged the mugs around in the sink for a few moments, then decided to wash them later, when she wasn't apt to break off the handles.

What had she expected?

Well, she certainly *hadn't* expected him to show up at her front door that evening, that was for sure. And if anyone had told her she'd—well, *throw herself* at him the way she had, she'd have called them crazy.

The hardest thing to face was the knowledge that if

he'd kissed her, she'd have let him make love to her right there in the front hallway.

The thought made her cringe.

And yearn.

It was a wonder she hadn't gotten pregnant, back when they were still together, as often as they'd made love.

Things would have been so different if *she'd* been the one to conceive Dylan Creed's child, not this Sharlene person with the breast implants.

Her gaze swung to the blackboard, and Dylan's number, written hard and fast and slanting to the right. Like she would call *him,* even if there were ten muggers in the house and the place was on fire to boot.

She marched over and resolutely wiped away the blue chalk with the palm of her hand, leaving a streaky smudge.

But erasing the number hadn't helped.

It was already burned into her memory, like the letters on the old sign over the gate out at Stillwater Springs Ranch.

She let her forehead rest against the blackboard.

And tears came. Again.

She'd lost so much—her parents, Sugarfoot, Madison Ranch, the home and family she and Dylan might have shared, if they hadn't been such hotheads.

Winston curled around her ankles, meowing uncertainly, and a tear plopped onto the top of his head. He looked up, in a curious way, as though wondering if it was raining.

His expression made Kristy laugh.

And laughing made her square her shoulders, dry her cheeks with the back of one hand and pull herself together.

Maybe all hell would break loose when Sheriff Book and his crew opened Sugarfoot's grave.

Maybe Dylan Creed was back in town for good, with his child and his wicked smile and his death-to-women body.

She was no gutless wonder, and no stranger to trouble. Whatever came her way, she'd handle it.

Somehow.

THE FIRST NIGHT IN THE ranch house was a sleepless one for Dylan, and not just because he spent half of it trying to comfort Bonnie, who'd taken to calling for her mother during their fast-food supper and hadn't quit until she'd fallen asleep against his chest, after one last, hiccoughy sigh.

Sitting on the beat-up old couch that, like the bed and the kitchen table, had been in the place since the last Creed had lived and died there—his great-uncle, Mick—his chin propped on top of Bonnie's sweat-dampened head, Dylan felt real despair.

He hadn't expected raising a child to be easy; it wasn't that. Now that the novelty of being with him was wearing off, Bonnie was missing Sharlene, and it was likely to get worse.

You're a real tough guy, Creed, he told himself silently. When Bonnie had cried, and then wailed, he'd felt like crying right along with her. Almost called Cassie in a panic, ready to beg her for help.

Cassie? Who was he kidding?

It was Kristy he'd wanted to call.

When the *hell* were Logan and Briana coming back from their damned honeymoon, anyhow? Briana was a mother—a good one, from what he'd seen—and she'd surely know what you were supposed to do when a kid started crying and wouldn't stop.

The knock at the back door startled him.

Careful not to wake Bonnie, he stood, carried her with him through the kitchen, crossing the dark place worn into the linoleum by decades of passing feet.

Tyler peered in at him through the glass.

Dylan scowled a little, then nodded.

Tyler came in. "Is that old bull in the pasture yours?" he asked, as though nary a harsh word, let alone a fist, had ever flown back and forth between them.

"Yes," Dylan answered, whispering. "Do you know anything about kids?"

Tyler grinned. "Only that that's about the cutest one I've ever seen."

Bonnie stirred against Dylan's chest, whimpered a little. Her face felt hot against his shoulder, even through the cloth of his shirt. He carried her into the bedroom, laid her down carefully on the bed, made sure the inked-up rubber doll with the wild hair was within reach, and sneaked back out into the kitchen.

By that time, Tyler was going through the cupboards.

"No whiskey?" he asked.

"I'm a beer man these days," Dylan answered quietly, wondering what the unexpected visit was all about. Five would get you ten it wasn't a social call. "In the fridge."

Tyler opened the refrigerator door, recoiled as if he'd found a live rattler coiled inside. "The cheap brand?"

"Beer is beer. Keep it down, will you? The kid's been screaming for three hours straight and she'll probably start up again if you wake her."

Tyler extracted a can from the six-pack and popped the top. His expression was unreadable. "Is she sick or something?"

"I don't know. Her forehead felt kind of warm when I was holding her a minute ago."

So much for the inscrutable singing cowboy. Tyler looked alarmed. He set aside his beer—hell, it was the *cheap brand,* anyway—headed for the bedroom and bent over Bonnie, touching the backs of his fingers to her cheek.

He frowned, gazing at Dylan, who stood in the doorway.

Back in the kitchen, Tyler said, "I think she has a fever. You got any baby aspirin?"

"No," Dylan said, more scared than he was about to let Tyler see. "She was upset earlier—like I said, she cried a lot—it's probably just that."

"Why was she crying?" Tyler demanded, as though he thought Dylan had been pinching the kid or something.

"She wanted her mother," Dylan answered. Tyler wasn't much comfort, but he was better than nothing.

"Oh," Tyler said, picking up his beer again, taking a swallow.

"Yeah, oh," Dylan said, annoyed.

"I still think we should take her to a doctor."

"Gee, all this concern. It's almost like having a brother."

Tyler frowned angrily. "I'm going to town to get some baby aspirin," he said. "While I'm there, I'll ask the pharmacist if he thinks Bonnie needs medical attention."

In spite of himself, in spite of all that had gone down between him and Tyler over the years, Dylan felt a sudden rush of relief, and something a lot like affection.

He was swallowing the lump that had risen in his throat when Tyler went on, already headed for the door.

"I'll be back," he said.

A few moments later, Dylan heard his brother's rig start up outside.

He checked on Bonnie again—he'd have sworn she *did* have a fever—but decided to do his pacing in the kitchen so he wouldn't disturb her sleep.

When Tyler blew in again, forty-five minutes later, he had baby aspirin, cough medicine, a stuffed animal of indeterminate species and a digital thermometer.

"If this thing reads above a one-oh-one, according to the pharmacist, Bonnie should be taken to the emergency room."

Dylan frowned, examining the unfamiliar plastic stick in its bright green box. "Where does this thing—go?"

Tyler chuckled. He made quite a picture, standing there in Dylan's kitchen, full of avuncular concern. The bad-ass cowboy, spilling a toy dog, if that was what it was, along with a bottle of aspirin and a carton of children's cough syrup onto the table.

"In her *ear,* shit-for-brains," he said.

"Oh," Dylan said, squinting at the instructions on the back of the box.

Tyler grabbed the whole works right out of his hand. "Give me that," he said, after the fact. "Bill—that's the pharmacist—told me how to use it."

"Great," Dylan said.

"I ran into a friend of yours while I was at the drugstore," Tyler added, as an aside. "You might get company any minute now."

"What?" Dylan asked, irritated all over again.

Tyler grinned, rummaging in the drugstore bag again and pulling out a packet with a sterile wipe inside. Damned if he hadn't thought of everything, old Uncle Ty. "The thing's got to be sanitized," he said.

"Who—?"

Tyler wiped down the thermometer, dispensing with all those offensive Dylan germs, and headed for Bonnie.

"Ninety-eight point seven," he announced, in a low but triumphant voice, after gently easing the end of the thermometer into Bonnie's right ear. "She's probably fine."

Suddenly, Dylan felt unaccountably territorial.

Bonnie was *his* daughter. He should have been the one taking her temperature.

As if in direct response to his thought, she woke up at precisely that moment, looked around, and let out one long, piercing shriek, followed by a plaintive, "Mommmmmmmeeeee!"

"I see what you mean," Tyler said.

Vaguely, Dylan heard a knock at the back door. He tried to pick Bonnie up, but she flailed both arms and kicked like she'd been raised by wolves.

And then Kristy swept in, like an avenging goddess, and scooped Bonnie up into her arms.

"There, now," she murmured, stroking Bonnie's back. Gradually—*very* gradually—blessed silence filled the room. "I'm here, sweetie. I'm here. Everything will be all right."

Over Bonnie's head, Kristy gave Dylan a what-were-you-*doing*-to-her kind of glare.

"She was out of cat litter," Tyler explained.

"Huh?" Dylan asked, stung by Kristy's look and, at the same time, glad as hell that she was there.

"That's why I happened to run into Kristy at the store. She stopped by for a bag of cat litter."

"You could have warned me," Dylan growled, after Kristy had carried Bonnie out of the bedroom.

"Ah, hell," Tyler answered smugly. "That wouldn't have been any fun at all."

CHAPTER FIVE

SOMETHING HAPPENED to Kristy, as she held Dylan's child, there in that old, run-down ranch house that warm summer night. Something sacred and inexplicable and eternal, the kind of shift that comes along once or twice in a lifetime, if that often. It was like the meeting and melding of two colliding universes, at a quantum level.

Bonnie seemed to feel it, too. She looked up at Kristy with wide, startled eyes, then flung both her small arms around Kristy's neck and held on for dear life.

"Mommy," she said.

Kristy didn't have the heart to correct the child. Over Bonnie's head, her gaze connected with Dylan's. She saw his jaw tighten, and a blue storm flared in his eyes.

"You have chalk on your forehead," he said.

Still dealing with her own internal cataclysm, Kristy merely stared at him, uncomprehending.

"Guess I'll be getting back to the cabin," Tyler said.

Kristy barely heard him, had only the vaguest sense of his leaving the ranch house kitchen for the dark, yawning world beyond the door, while she and Dylan and Bonnie remained where they were, like the stunned survivors of a meteoric impact. About as mobile as Stonehenge, Kristy couldn't even swallow, let alone speak.

Dylan broke the spell, stepped forward, put his arms out for Bonnie.

Visceral, mother-wolf resistance flared through Kristy, almost painful in its intensity, but Bonnie was *Dylan's* daughter, not hers. She was still rational enough to know that, anyway.

So she surrendered the little girl. It felt as though some vital part of her was being torn away.

Dylan murmured to the child, now nodding against his shoulder, and carried her back to the bedroom. As if pulled along behind by an invisible tether, Kristy followed.

Miraculously, Bonnie fell into an immediate sleep, most likely exhausted from all that shrieking.

Kristy, slowly returning to a state that *resembled* normalcy, found the bathroom, stared at her reflection in the mirror over the sink. A great splotch of blue chalk stained her forehead, from when she'd rested it against the blackboard in her own kitchen, earlier that evening, like the mark of some primitive initiation rite.

She cranked on the water tap, lathered her hands and then her face with soap, and washed the chalk away.

When she returned to the kitchen, Dylan was there, pouring coffee.

He looked exhausted—and grim.

"I was only trying to help," Kristy said, without apology, remembering the strain she'd seen in his face when he reached for Bonnie a few minutes before.

He smiled wanly, raised a coffee mug in a half-hearted toast. "I know," he said, husky-voiced. "And I appreciate it."

Kristy longed to ask if he'd felt what she had, when she

was holding Bonnie in her arms, but she didn't quite dare. Why *would* he have felt it, standing several feet away?

"You seemed pretty angry," she ventured, after working up her courage for several moments. "When Bonnie called me 'Mommy.'"

"Not angry," Dylan said, extending a cup to Kristy. "Frustrated. Scared as hell. I'm not very good at this parental thing, it seems."

Kristy saw his vulnerability in his eyes, and in his countenance, and she was touched by it. She'd never known Dylan Creed to be afraid of anything, or to doubt himself in any way. But one very little girl had changed all that.

"Give yourself a chance," she said, accepting the offered coffee. "You're new at this."

"When she screams for Sharlene like that—" Dylan began, turning away from her then, to gaze out the night-darkened window above the sink. "It tears me apart."

Kristy wanted to cross that room and lay a hand on Dylan's taut, muscular back, but she refrained. Things were too crazy; she felt too dazed and wrung out. She was standing on the brink of something huge and dangerous, and one wrong move would send her tumbling over the precipice.

He turned then, and faced her, and she felt another shift, almost as staggering as the first. *What was happening here?*

If she stepped outside, would she find the world changed, the stars in different places, the moon filling most of the horizon instead of riding like a small round balloon above the starkly etched rim of mountains?

It seemed alarmingly possible.

"What do I do, Kristy, the next time Bonnie calls for

her mother? And the time after that? What's worse, what do I do if Sharlene wants her back?"

She set the coffee aside on the table then, and went to Dylan, regardless of that incendiary *something* pulsing in the atmosphere, ready to explode at the slightest spark. Laid her hands to his upper arms, tilted her head back to look into his troubled face.

"You can do this, Dylan," she said quietly. "You're just tired and a little overwhelmed, that's all."

He kissed her forehead, lightly, briefly.

Spark #1.

Despite the danger, Kristy laid her head against his shoulder, slipped her arms around his lean cowboy waist, but loosely. Sighed, because it felt so good, being close to Dylan again. He was solid and warm, hard and strong, and when he embraced her, it was a homecoming for Kristy. The healing of broken things inside her, the righting of ancient, forgotten wrongs, a sweet, soft benediction.

She finally got it then.

She still loved Dylan Creed, had probably never stopped.

The realization seized her throat closed and brought stinging tears of despair to her eyes. And she simply leaned into him, all her strength gone. All her willpower, evaporated.

He felt her shudder, hooked a finger under her chin and lifted, so she had to look at him.

"I think we're in big trouble here," he murmured.

"Me, too," she replied. "Me, too."

She watched a variety of emotions move in his face, like reflections on water. Then his embrace slackened, and he set her a little way apart from him, his hands resting on her shoulders.

"Go home, Kristy," Dylan said. "If you stay much longer, we'll wind up in bed. I don't think you're ready for that, and maybe I'm not, either."

As hard as it was, Kristy knew he was right on all counts. Her own emotions were at a fever pitch, and any decisions she made in that state of mind might have extreme consequences.

So she bit her lower lip, nodded slowly.

She wanted to look in on Bonnie, just once before she left, but she might not be able to leave if she did. So she headed for the back door, Dylan walking behind her, and descended the porch steps. Half sprinted toward her Blazer, waiting in the dark, her purse still in the backseat, along with the cat litter she'd gone out to buy earlier, the keys still dangling in the ignition.

She'd probably left the engine running when she arrived—Tyler must have shut it off when he left.

Just as she moved to open the driver's-side door, Dylan caught hold of her arm and turned her around.

And he kissed her, deeply, suddenly, and so thoroughly that she nearly melted. When it was over, she looked up and aside, too stricken to meet his gaze. Overhead, stars seemed to collide in blurry rushes of silver.

Dylan cupped his hands on either side of Kristy's face, made her look at him.

"Wh-what was that?" she asked shakily, once she caught her breath.

"I asked you to leave," he answered, his voice rough as dry gravel on a sun-baked country road. "And it was one of the hardest things I've ever done. I still think it's right, but that doesn't mean it's what I want. I need you to know that, Kristy."

Convoluted as the explanation was, Kristy understood it, because she felt the same way. She longed to stay, give herself up to Dylan completely, and devil take the morning after.

"You'll—you'll call, if Bonnie needs—"

The voice in Kristy's mind interrupted. *If Bonnie needs you? Get a grip, Madison. You're not her mother, and nothing is going to change that.*

"I'll call," Dylan promised gruffly. "Go now, Kristy. I want you real bad, and I can't hold out much longer."

At once exhilarated by his words and profoundly aware that she was on very dangerous ground, Kristy climbed behind the wheel of her Blazer. Oddly, she was struck by the pristine new-car *emptiness* of the vehicle— no baby seat strapped in the back, no toys scattered on the floorboards, no sippy cup in the console. No grocery lists or unopened mail—nothing but her purse.

It was definitely the conveyance of a spinster librarian.

Oh, for a glorious mess, the detritus of a busy, happy life.

Dylan slowly closed the door, stepped back, waved as she glanced his way once more before starting up the Blazer to go home.

It wasn't that she didn't love her job, or the broad painter's canvas that was her house. Until Dylan—until Bonnie—Kristy had been able to convince herself that it was enough.

Now, she knew for sure that it wasn't.

She wanted to be a wife and a mother *as well as* a librarian. She wanted a sex life, damn it.

Driving through the sultry night, Kristy rolled down her window.

She wasn't ready to go back to town, even though she knew Winston would be watching for her. So she took the familiar turn when she came to the tilting red mailbox with the name Madison faded to near-invisibility on its side. She bumped over the rutted driveway, drew in a breath when her headlights swept across the old, long-abandoned house she'd grown up in.

The barn had finally fallen in on itself, and the yard and flower beds—once her mother's pride—were hopelessly overgrown.

The loss swept over Kristy, undiluted, as fresh as if it had just happened.

She drove on past the house, jostling overland toward the copse of trees where Sugarfoot, and perhaps a murder victim, were buried.

The faintest, most disturbing memory niggled at the back of her mind, locked away, but struggling to break free.

Had she seen something, heard something, that long-ago night?

The thought made her stomach churn, and a migraine threatened. She took deep breaths until the ominous feeling subsided a little.

Shutting off the Blazer, she sat for a few moments with her eyes closed, trying to remember. Trying not to.

The old house was small. If there had been a ruckus between her father and that hired hand, how could she have missed it? How could her mother not have known?

Still, nothing came to her.

She got out of the SUV, walked toward Sugarfoot's grave.

It was a pilgrimage she'd made often, during the last several years, at all hours of the day and night. The fact was not lost on her that she seldom visited her *parents'* graves, except on their separate birthdays, on Memorial Day and sometime during Christmas week.

She'd come to terms with their passing, at least consciously—knew the essence of Tim and Louise Madison could not be confined to a coffin. But with Sugarfoot, it was different—as if not only her horse, but her *life* were buried here. All her dreams, all her hopes, all her faith that things could change for the better.

Sheriff Book, she soon discovered, had already been here. The grave itself seemed undisturbed, but the sunken mound was surrounded by yellow tape, supported by stakes driven into the ground.

It was actually going to happen, she realized, dazed.

They were going to dig up Sugarfoot's grave.

And they were going to find a human body.

Kristy put a hand to her mouth, fearing she was about to be sick. She didn't know *how* she knew Sheriff Book's suspicions were correct, but she knew.

She took deep breaths until the nausea subsided.

Her eyes were dry—tears couldn't reach the gouge of bleak certainty piercing her very soul.

"I'm sorry, Sugarfoot," she whispered, before turning to go. "I'm sorry."

She got back into the Blazer, drove toward Stillwater Springs, not looking at the old house as she passed it. At home, she soothed a disgruntled Winston and poured fresh litter into his box.

She took a long, hot shower, put on one of her oft-washed, oversize T-shirts, as she did every night.

She crawled into her huge and profoundly empty bed, intending to read for a while, in hopes of quieting her racing brain. But the words wouldn't stay put on the pages.

Leaning, Kristy switched off the bedside lamp.

Winston leaped onto the bed, snuggled close to her. Cat-comfort.

She smiled at his devotion, stroked his silken back with one hand.

Sleep was probably out of the question, but she had to try. She had to open the library promptly at nine the next morning, no matter what else was going on in her life.

But sleep came, and when it did, the dream pounced on her, smothering and heavy.

It was dark, and quiet, in the way only a country night can be, except for the rapid thump of her heart and the strange, shallow breathing of the man standing beside her bed. Although her eyes were tightly closed, a child's only real defense against monsters creeping out of the closet, she was aware of his gaze on her.

Daddy! she cried silently. *Daddy, help me!*

And then the door of her room crashed open.

There was a violent scuffle, swearwords exchanged in raspy voices.

Kristy didn't open her eyes until she heard her mother's voice, felt herself gathered tightly against her soft chest.

"Did he hurt you, Kristy? Are you all right?"

Horrendous noises, farther away now, coming from the dark kitchen.

The back door opening with a loud creak and a slam against the porch wall.

More swearing, sharp-edged and ugly.

Kristy clung to her mother, terrified.

They were fighting, her father and the man.

When would it stop?

What if her daddy got hurt?

It came then, the deafening blast.

The shotgun her father kept on the highest shelf in the pantry. A country kid, Kristy recognized the sound.

Kristy's mother screamed, a high, quivering wail of fear.

The sound sent Kristy surging to the surface of consciousness, shaking. She ran for the bathroom and retched into the toilet until there was nothing left to throw up.

SHE WAITED UNTIL DAWN to call Sheriff Book.

"I know what happened," she said woodenly, when he answered his home phone with a sleepy hello.

"Kristy?" Floyd asked. "Is that you?"

"I know what happened," she repeated.

"Are you all right?"

She shook her head, realized he couldn't see her. "No," she said.

Floyd was knocking at her back door within fifteen minutes, wearing civilian clothes and looking rumpled. She hadn't changed out of her T-shirt, but she had put on a bra and sweatpants, for the sake of decency.

Kristy had a strange, disembodied feeling as she described her dream to the sheriff, standing there in her cheery kitchen, with its fresh yellow walls and the first rays of sunlight streaming through the windows. *This must be what it's like,* she thought distractedly, *to be beside yourself.*

"I figured it had to be something like that," Floyd

said, when she'd finished. At some point, he must have ushered her to a chair—Kristy was surprised to find herself sitting down instead of standing up, and she had no memory whatsoever of the transition.

"What now?" she asked, barely recognizing her own voice. "What happens now?"

Floyd sighed. Drew back a chair and sat down across the table from her. "We'll dig today," he said quietly. "Then the M.E. will have the body—if there *is* a body—picked up and examined for evidence. There'll be some newspeople in town, most likely, asking questions and taking pictures. It'll be rough for a while, Kristy, I won't lie to you." He paused, blushed, looked away for a moment, before facing her squarely again. "But things will die down in time—get back to normal."

"And my father will be remembered as a murderer," she said.

"Tim Madison," the sheriff argued firmly, "will be *remembered* as a man protecting his daughter and his wife. He wouldn't have been convicted, Kristy, even if he'd confessed to the whole thing."

"This is what gave them cancer, you know," Kristy heard herself say, her voice drifting right over the top of Floyd's words like some slow-moving river. "Mom and Dad, I mean. Knowing what really happened that night. Keeping it in. They must have been so afraid—"

Sheriff Book reached out, squeezed her hand. "There's no way to be sure of that," he said gently. Then, after a long pause, "Did he hurt you, honey? That drifter?"

She shook her head. There were so many things she wasn't sure of, but she knew that much. She must have called out to her dad aloud that night, not just in the panicked silence of her mind. He'd gotten there in time.

"No," she said, but she gave a cold shudder as the full extent of the danger she'd been in crashed over her.

"You want me to call Dylan?" Floyd asked.

Kristy started slightly. She'd erased Dylan's cell number from the blackboard. Why had *his* name been the one to leap to Floyd's mind?

Floyd smiled, evidently reading her thoughts from the expression on her face. "I saw his truck parked out front last night," he said. "While I was out making my rounds."

"Don't call Dylan," she said. "I'm fine."

"You're sure? You don't look too good, if you don't mind my saying so."

"I've got to open the library at nine," she told him.

"Hang the library," Floyd answered. "History won't stop if it's closed for a day or two."

He didn't understand. She couldn't just pull the shades and wait for the sky to come down on her head in big blue chunks, for reporters to knock on her door and the phone to ring off the hook with crank calls and requests for interviews. She had to keep going, keep busy—or go completely insane.

"I'll be all right," she insisted, but without enough conviction, apparently, to suit Sheriff Floyd Book.

He leaned forward a little in his chair, studied her with worried eyes. "This could get rough before it's done, Kristy. Why don't you leave town for a week or two—or even a month? Lie low till the worst is over, anyhow?"

Running away wasn't in her. Tim and Louise Madison hadn't raised her that way. And Stillwater Springs was *home,* the eye of the coming storm, yes, but also the place she most needed to be to weather it.

And weather it she would, or die trying.

BONNIE'S BEDROOM FURNITURE was delivered first thing that morning, and, having passed a sleepless night, Dylan found himself grumbling a lot as he set things up.

Bonnie, on the other hand, had slept like the Angel of Purest Innocence, and she was full of the dickens as a result. While he turned the last screw in the bed frame, she managed to knock over the new mattress leaning against the wall and immediately started jumping up and down on it.

"Bonnie," he said.

She ignored him. Healthy child suddenly turns deaf.

"*Bonnie.*"

She met his gaze, her eyes impish and wide. "Story," she said.

"Story?" Where had *that* come from?

A little mulling solved the mystery. Bonnie had taken to Kristy in a big way, and she associated her with their visit to the library.

Hence: story.

"We don't have any books," he said.

"*Story!*" Bonnie insisted, jumping harder and higher.

Of course it was Kristy she wanted, not a chapter of Nancy Drew.

"Unless you want to hear an article from *Western Horseman,*" Dylan said, "you're out of luck." He'd found a moldering stack of his uncle's favorite magazine on a shelf in the cellar, and that was the extent of the reading material on hand. "And stop jumping—*now.*"

Bonnie indulged in one more spring, then landed in a gleeful, giggling heap of wild-child in the middle of the mattress. If she was like this at two, what would she be like at sixteen?

It didn't bear thinking about.

Dylan's cell phone rang in his pocket, and he flipped it open without looking at caller ID. "Hello?"

"D-Dylan?"

Sharlene. And she was crying.

He handed Bonnie the pink unicorn, hoping that would keep her occupied, and strolled casually into the kitchen. His stomach was wedged into the back of his throat.

"What do you want?" he rasped, bracing one hand against the counter for support. He could hear Bonnie jumping on the mattress again.

"I made a mistake," Sharlene blathered. "I want Aurora back."

Dylan closed his eyes. He'd feared this moment, known it was coming, but it still caught him unprepared. "I call her Bonnie," he said evenly. "And she's staying with me."

"Clint said he'd bring me to fetch her—all the way from Texas. You've got to give her back to me, Dylan. I can't live without—Bonnie."

Clint, of course, was the boyfriend. He'd certainly outlasted most of his predecessors—though for all Dylan knew, there had been a changing of the guard in the short interim since Sharlene had ditched Bonnie back in Vegas.

"Maybe you should have thought of that before you abandoned her in my truck, Sharlene," Dylan said. The jumping had stopped; out of the corner of his eye, he saw

Bonnie in the doorway, watching him curiously, with her lower lip plumped out in a pout. In went the thumb.

"You don't know how it was," Sharlene argued pitifully. "I lost all my money in a slot machine, and Clint was mad at me, and I knew you'd take care of—"

"Bonnie," Dylan supplied tautly. "Look, we're not going to talk about this right now. Little pitchers, and all that."

"At least tell me she's okay."

Dylan seethed. All this concern—from a woman who'd left a two-year-old child to fend for herself in a parking lot behind one of the sleaziest bars in Vegas. At night.

"She's fine," he said.

Bonnie unplugged her thumb just long enough to say fretfully, "Story."

Translation: Kristy. *I want Kristy.*

"If we can't talk now, we'll talk in a few days," Sharlene went on, confident as hell, for somebody who would probably have trouble scraping up enough cash to cover the states between Texas and Montana, even by bus. "I know you're in Stillwater Springs, Dylan. And we're on our way, Clint and me."

Figuring out where he was had been no great intellectual leap—he'd talked about his home town, his brothers and the ranch a lot when they were together. But maybe Sharlene was smarter than he'd given her credit for; she'd guessed, somehow, that he'd fight to keep Bonnie, do anything he had to do to protect her.

She wanted something.

Specifically money.

He hated being conned, but he'd hate losing his daughter more.

"Spill it, Sharlene," he said.

"If we just had a few thousand to tide us over until Clint gets on with one of the oil companies—"

"You'd do what?" Dylan rasped.

"We could rent a little house. Get settled and every-thing. Then, in a couple of months, we'd bring Bonnie home—"

Bonnie is *home,* Dylan thought. And he'd be damned if he'd let Sharlene cart his baby girl off to Texas, to live under the same roof with this Clint yahoo, whoever he was. What would happen to the kid the *next* time Sharlene blew her child support and decided she couldn't take care of Bonnie?

"How much, Sharlene?"

If Bonnie realized who he was talking to, she gave no sign of it. She just watched him, pulling hard on the thumb.

He listened while Sharlene consulted the boyfriend, her voice muffled. She probably had a hand over the receiver.

"Three thousand," she said at last. "I'll give you a number and you can wire it. Before the end of the day, Dylan."

"And in return for this, I get—?"

"A few more months with Bonnie."

The depraved bitch. She was willing to *sell* two or three months of her daughter's life. He shouldn't have been surprised, given Sharlene's history, but he was.

"All right," he said, after a long moment spent fighting for control. He found a pencil and an old envelope in one of the kitchen drawers. "Give me the information."

She did, her voice sweet and lilting, now that she'd gotten what she wanted.

"Before the end of the day," she repeated, in parting. And hung up in his ear.

He scooped Bonnie up and the two of them headed for town.

He wired the money to Sharlene first thing.

It wasn't that he'd miss a few thousand dollars; it was the proverbial drop in the bucket, compared to the shares he owned in Logan's company, and it would buy him time to sue for permanent custody. Despite all of that, giving in to what amounted to gross extortion went against his grain, big-time.

He gravitated toward the library, once he'd sent the wire.

He needed to be near Kristy, if only for a little while, and besides, Bonnie wouldn't let up on the "Story" thing.

Kristy was behind the front desk when they walked in, and she looked up immediately, as if an alarm had gone off or something.

Kristy looked like five miles of bad road, though she was clearly trying to put on a front for the library patrons. Dylan saw right through the act, and with unsettling clarity.

"I guess we need a few books," he said lamely, when he got to the desk. "Bonnie keeps wanting a story."

There were deep shadows under Kristy's eyes, and she looked gaunt, as though she'd lost ten pounds overnight. With chagrin, Dylan remembered that the authorities were about to dig up her horse's grave, and that they expected to find the body of a man her father had murdered in the process.

He'd been so wrapped up in his own worries— Sharlene's call being at the top of the list—that he'd nearly forgotten what Kristy was going through.

"I think I can help you with that," she said, with brisk good cheer. The words sounded hollow, though, and forced.

She rounded the desk, winked at Bonnie, who was clinging to Dylan's neck like a kudzu vine, and led the way to the children's section. She selected *Curious George, Goodnight Moon* and *Everyone Poops.*

Dylan did a double take at that last one.

Kristy gave a slight, slanted grin. "Well," she said, "they do, you know."

"I'm not reading that out loud," Dylan said, feeling his neck heat up. "Anyhow, Bonnie knows how to do that, trust me."

"Chicken," Kristy responded. "It's not about knowing how. It's about being comfortable with normal bodily functions."

Why hadn't he just stayed in the truck? Driven to Missoula or someplace, where they had actual bookstores, and bought the kid a stack of cheerful tales he wouldn't be too embarrassed to read?

Resolutely, she carried the three selections to the desk and set them down to be checked out.

"Now, what can I get for *you?*"

So *that* was it. She remembered his dyslexia, and probably thought he was illiterate and needed all the reading practice he could get.

Dylan was both touched and insulted.

He leaned in close, whispered in her ear *exactly* what she could get for him and enjoyed the flood of pink spilling across her cheekbones. At least it gave her some color. Before, she'd been pale as milk.

"Dylan Creed," she sputtered, casting anxious glances

around, as though worried that one of the library patrons might have overheard. "I was talking about a *book*."

He merely grinned. Gestured with his free arm for her to have at the shelves and find him a tome. Bonnie was straining in the curve of his other arm, wanting to go play by the totem pole with a bunch of other little kids.

"Is it story hour?" he asked, letting Bonnie down so she could join in.

"No," Kristy said. "Their mothers are all getting their hair done, or at the dentist, or buying groceries."

She walked purposefully into the stacks, and Dylan followed.

Reaching the M section, she extracted Larry McMurtry's *Lonesome Dove.*

"Already read it," Dylan said. "Five times. Didn't even have to move my lips. Want to quiz me on the story line?"

Irritation flared in her eyes, quickly followed by pain. "You could have watched the miniseries," she said.

"Did that, too," Dylan admitted, nodding toward the book in her hands. "It opens with two pigs trying to kill a snake. I don't remember if the TV version did or not."

Kristy looked both ways. "I need to talk to you. In private."

He'd been waiting for that, he realized, since he'd walked into the library and caught sight of her face. "What time do you get off work?" he asked, watching Bonnie at the periphery of his vision, wondering if he'd be afraid, his whole life, of someone stealing her when he wasn't looking.

"Five," she said. "Susan is going to cover for me."

"I'll pick up some steaks, and we'll have supper at

my place, then," he replied. "Once Bonnie is asleep, we'll talk."

She looked hesitant, then nodded. "Can I bring anything?"

He shook his head. It was just a steak dinner, not a night of wild abandon between the sheets, but he was exhilarated at the prospect.

"I have to bring *something*," she said.

Dylan didn't bother to protest again. It was what country folks did, when they were invited to somebody's place for supper. They showed up with a cake pan covered in foil, or a cold salad in a sealed plastic bowl.

He'd been away far too long. "Knock yourself out, then," he said.

After that, they were all business. He signed up for a library card—the first he'd ever had—and checked out the books for Bonnie, including the one about poop.

Bonnie didn't want to leave, but she lightened up when she saw the books. "Story," she said.

"Story," Dylan confirmed.

The next stop was the grocery section at Wal-Mart. The mom-and-pop place had long since closed down, and Dylan missed it, even though he'd been caught shoplifting a package of gum there when he was seven, and Jake had whipped his butt all the way back to the truck.

He picked out steaks, potatoes for baking, salad makings and assorted trimmings. Got more milk for Bonnie's sippy cup, and a roasted chicken for lunch.

Once they'd settled up at one of the checkout counters, he loaded Bonnie and the groceries into the truck and started for home, taking a different route just because they had the time.

Which was how he ended up with the horse.

CHAPTER SIX

IT WAS THE SORRIEST-LOOKING critter Dylan had ever seen, that horse, standing in the middle of the road, lead-rope dangling from its old rope halter. Its ribs showed, and it was so coated in mud that he couldn't tell what color it was.

"Horsie," Bonnie said, pleased.

"Sit tight," Dylan told his daughter, though there was no danger of her breaking out of the car seat rigging—not yet, at least. Give her a few weeks, and she'd figure out how to spring herself, for sure.

After pulling to the side of the road and shutting off the truck, he got out and walked slowly toward the horse, careful not to look the animal directly in the eye. That would have been nonverbal predator-speak. "Hey, buddy," he said soothingly. "Bad place to stand. I almost hit you."

Up close, he saw scars in the animal's dirty hide, but it was the hopeless resignation in its eyes that made his gut grind. A thatch of cream-colored mane indicated that the gelding might be a palomino, but there was no telling for sure.

Dylan took a light hold on the halter with his left hand, stroked the horse's quivering, slatted side with his right. "Easy now," he said, leading the animal out of the road. "Easy."

They'd no more than reached the shoulder when a blue pickup came tearing around the corner, horn blasting. The pricey new vehicle screeched to a dusty stop, and a teenage boy leaped out, a short lunge-whip in one hand, and started for the gelding, apparently unconcerned by Dylan's presence.

The gelding shivered and backed up a few feet.

Dylan kept a loose hold on the lead-rope. "Hold it," he told the kid.

The boy stopped, blinked, stared at Dylan as though he'd sprung up out of the ground. Contempt curled the young man's lips—he was good-looking, and faintly familiar. "That's *my* horse," he said. "Step aside."

"You're not going to take that whip to him," Dylan said, standing his ground. "Whether he's yours or not."

"Do you know who my *father* is?" the kid demanded, after a few moments of high dudgeon, during which he was apparently too indignant to speak.

"I don't give a rat's ass who your father is," Dylan replied evenly.

The kid reeled off the name of an ultrafamous movie star.

"I'm still not impressed," Dylan said. "Do you want to try again?"

"We're here to buy a ranch for *major* bucks," said the kid. "You cross me, and you'll be sorry, cowboy. I promise you that." He raised the lunge-whip.

Dylan caught hold of the boy's wrist and squeezed until the whip dropped to the dirt. "You're the one who's going to be sorry," he said, "if you so much as *touch* this horse."

"I'm only trying to train him," the boy whined, rubbing his wrist and flushing a little around the ears as he tried to get the circulation flowing back into his fingers.

"That's no way to teach an animal anything but fear," Dylan said. Even without the famous last name, he would have figured the kid for a city slicker, not a local. His clothes were too well-cut for rural Montana, his haircut too casually perfect. He'd had the best of everything—and too much of it—all his life, and it showed. "How'd you come by this fella, anyway?"

"I was test-driving him," the boy said. "He belongs to some drunken old man. I agreed to pay five hundred dollars if I like the horse."

It made sense to *ride* a horse before buying it—but whipping it was another thing entirely. "What's your first name?"

The boy thrust his chin out. "What's yours?"

Dylan simply waited, still holding the lead-rope.

"Caleb," the kid finally admitted, flustered. "Caleb Spencer."

"Dylan Creed," Dylan said, but he didn't put out a hand the way he normally did when he made somebody's acquaintance. "Around these here parts, *Caleb*—" okay, so he was troweling on the rube act a little heavy, but the kid clearly thought he was a hick, so why disappoint him? "—we don't mistreat animals." He paused, let the words sink in for a few moments. "So you just head on back to wherever it is you're staying and I'll look after the horse."

"You can't just take him," Caleb complained. "He's almost mine!"

"Watch me," Dylan said. He took out his cell phone,

glanced back toward the truck to make sure Bonnie was where he'd left her and speed-dialed Dan Phillips, the foreman of the construction crew at the main ranch house, with a quick jab of his thumb. "Dan? Dylan. Listen, I'm on old highway 14, near the Wilkenson place. Yeah, right by that big bend in the road. Could you send somebody over here, pronto, with Logan's horse trailer?"

"Sure," Dan said.

Caleb kicked the ground with the toe of one very expensive loafer. "I'm going to call the sheriff," he threatened.

Dylan clicked off with Dan, poised to call Floyd next. "I'll take care of that one for you," he said affably.

At that, Caleb, finally getting it, turned on his heel and stormed back to his truck, a new, fancy rig too powerful for a kid his age to handle. Although the vehicle *could* have belonged to Caleb's illustrious father, it was probably the brat's very own.

"You'll hear from my dad's lawyers!" Caleb yelled in parting.

"I'm looking forward to it," Dylan replied cheerfully.

"Stupid hillbilly!" Caleb climbed behind the wheel, slammed the door shut, gunned the engine to life.

Dylan grinned and waggled his fingers in a mocking farewell.

"Hell," he told the horse, when the boy and the bad-ass truck were gone.

Dan showed up within twenty minutes, Logan's trailer hooked up behind his work truck. Getting out of his rig, Dan approached, examined the horse with a thoughtful frown.

"He's in bad shape," he said.

Dylan forgave his friend for stating the painfully obvious. "From what I can figure, he belongs to old Gunnar Wilkenson," he explained. "I thought the humane society had fixed it so Gunnar couldn't keep horses anymore, gotten a court order or something, but I guess he just overlooked that little detail."

"You know Gunnar," Dan said. "He 'don't much cotton' to outside interference, especially of the organizational variety."

Dylan had a dozen memories of Gunnar Wilkenson, all of them unpleasant. He was a wizened gnome of a man, perennially dirty, more often drunk than sober. The old fart had been batching it in a tumbledown house a mile or two up in the hills since God started kindergarten.

He'd have to pay Gunnar a social call, but first he meant to settle the gelding in Logan's barn and drop Bonnie off at Cassie's. Since the old man was as likely to shoot as offer a welcome, taking Bonnie along on the visit wasn't something he meant to do.

"Where to?" Dan asked, after they'd loaded the gelding.

"Logan's barn," Dylan answered. "I'll get Doc Ryder to come out and look him over as soon as I've been to Gunnar's place."

Dan grinned. "If I hear shots," he said, being as familiar with the old coot's temper as Dylan was, since as teenagers both of them had been peppered with rock salt from his shotgun for stealing pears out of his orchard, "I'll send the sheriff. You're not taking the munchkin with you, I hope."

Dylan shook his head. "Thanks, Dan," he said.

Cassie was home watching her after-lunch soap

operas, fortunately, and she was ready, willing and able to tend to Bonnie for an hour or two.

Dylan headed straight for Gunnar's shack, alone.

The place looked even worse than it had the last time he'd been there—the yard was overgrown, and crowded with rusted-out wrecks in various stages of disintegration. Bald tires, broken bottles and a lot of other trash practically obscured the house from view.

Gunnar, short, stout and red-faced from years of swilling cheap booze and nursing grudges, hobbled out to greet Dylan, the familiar shotgun in one hand. Over the years, it had become a fifth limb, as grimy as its owner.

Everybody has a dream. Dylan would have bet his latest poker winnings that Gunnar's was to shoot some poor bastard and get away with it.

"You come to steal my pears?" Gunnar demanded. His voice squeaked like a hinge in need of oil, high-pitched and petulant.

"No," Dylan said easily. "I came to buy a horse."

"Ain't got no horse," Gunnar said. "Not anymore, nohow. I had ole Bingo, but I'm sellin' him to that movie star's kid."

"He's out of the horse market," Dylan said. "And quit waving that damn goose-blaster around before somebody gets hurt."

"He said he'd give me five hundred cash for that horse if he could ride it!" Gunnar protested, still clutching the shotgun in both hands, hands streaked and crusted with filth. The man reeked pungently enough to make Dylan's eyes water. "I was countin' on that five hundred dollars!"

Dylan took out his wallet, pulled out a thousand in hundred-dollar bills.

Gunnar's shriveled, toothless mouth revealed his interest. He was practically drooling.

"I'll need a bill of sale," Dylan said, keeping the crisp bills just out of snatching distance. Once, as a kid, he'd bought a dog from Gunnar, for the same reason he was buying Bingo, and since the animal was off someplace when the transaction took place, he'd given the devious old son of a bitch the requested twenty dollars and promised to come back for the dog. When Logan, with his brand-new driver's license burning a hole in his jeans pocket, brought him out to Gunnar's a couple of hours later, they found the reprobate digging a grave— he'd shot the "stupid mutt," he claimed, because it "turned on" him.

The recollection scalded the pit of Dylan's stomach and roiled up into the back of his throat, even after all this time. Gunnar hadn't given back the twenty dollars, of course, and when Dylan had complained to his dad later, Jake had laughed and said it served him right for making a fool's bargain. *Let that be a lesson to you, boy. And we don't need a damn dog around here, anyway.*

"Let me get somethin' to write on, then," Gunnar fussed, turning to head for the house at a peculiar little trot, "if you're going to be an asshole about it."

Dylan smiled to himself. Folded his arms and stood in Gunnar's junked-up yard, waiting. When it came to being an asshole, old man Wilkenson had met his match.

Gunnar returned pretty quickly, considering the hitch in his get-along, and thrust a receipt at Dylan, hastily scrawled on the back of a piece of cheap lined notebook paper. "Roundin' up the horse is your problem," Gunnar warned.

Dylan withheld the money until he'd examined the receipt. "You got any other four-legged critters on the place, Gunnar?" he asked, with what was calculated to sound like mild curiosity.

"Just a worthless dog," Gunnar said. "Tried to run him off, but he still hangs around. Tipped over my garbage, too."

Dylan wondered how Gunnar differentiated the garbage from the rest of his yard. And as if on cue, said worthless dog belly-crawled out from under one of the rusted-out junkers. He didn't look a hell of a lot better off than the horse, being scrawny to the point of emaciation. His brown coat was full of nettles, and his eyes seemed to plead with Dylan.

Oh, what the hell, Dylan thought. He peeled off another two hundred dollars of his poker winnings and bought the dog, too. Made Gunnar go through the whole exercise of writing a receipt all over again.

When the process was complete, Dylan hoisted the dog gently into the backseat of his truck, noting that it whimpered a little. Most likely, it had been kicked a time or two, when it got too close to Gunnar.

Using his trusty cell, he called the veterinarian, Doc Ryder, to arrange a visit to the horse and make an appointment for the dog, too. Doc, who answered his own phone as often as not, said to bring "the little guy" right in— he'd see to the gelding on his rounds the next morning.

Hal Ryder was a kindly old duffer with white hair and calm, quiet blue eyes. "What's this fella's name?" he asked, once Dylan had reached his office and set the dog on the battered examining table.

"Damned if I know," Dylan said. "I just got him."

"Half-starved and probably wormy to boot," Doc said, checking the mutt over with the kind of intuitive skill only years of experience could develop. "Where'd you get him?"

"From Gunnar Wilkenson," Dylan answered. "The horse, too."

Doc flushed. "That old son of a bitch," he said. "I've got half a mind to call Floyd and tell him Gunnar's broken his probation again. He has a rap sheet for cruelty and neglect that goes back to Noah's Ark."

"I have no objection to that," Dylan remarked, "but Floyd's got a lot to reckon with right now." He wasn't about to go into detail; if there was a body buried on the old Madison place, he wouldn't be the one to pass the word.

In a flash, he knew Doc had already heard the story. It showed in his wrinkled road map of a face.

"Hell of a thing for Kristy to have to deal with," Doc said. Keeping one hand on the dog, he dug a sealed packet containing several syringes out of a drawer in the examining table. "Folks will be flapping their jaws about this for years."

Dylan watched mutely as Doc brought the dog up to date on his shots. So far that day, he'd acquired a horse and a boot-shy mutt, unable to turn his back on their plights. The urge to rescue *Kristy* was half again as strong.

"I'd never have figured Tim Madison for the type to kill a man," Doc said.

"Maybe he didn't," Dylan suggested, but he was doubtful, and he knew Doc heard that in his voice.

"I guess if you catch somebody robbing your house, there's no way of telling what you'd do," Doc went on.

He called in his assistant, and the dog was led off for X-rays and blood tests. It cried pitifully at being separated from Dylan.

"Guess not," Dylan said. *I'll be here waiting for you when they're finished, boy,* he promised the dog silently.

"Reckon you're back in Stillwater Springs to stay, if you're acquiring a menagerie," Doc prattled on. He was good to the bone, Doc was, but he gossiped like an old lady.

"Reckon so," Dylan said, getting out his wallet. There were prescriptions, on top of the other charges, and he bought the special food the doc recommended, too.

"Kristy could use a friend," Doc said.

The assistant reappeared with the dog, who seemed both surprised and reassured to see Dylan waiting for him. He licked Dylan's hand in pathetic gratitude.

Dylan let Doc's latest comment slide. He wanted to be a lot more than a friend to Kristy, but instinct told him to move slowly. She was, after all, the only woman who'd ever broken his heart, and if he cared too much, and things blew up, he wasn't sure he could handle it.

"Pretty woman like her," Doc went on, shaking his head. "I can't believe she isn't married, with a batch of kids."

When Dylan didn't take the bait and offer a response, Doc followed him and the dog right through the front door of the office and out into the parking lot.

"Guess maybe she's been waiting for you all this time," Doc said.

"Thanks for taking care of—" Dylan looked down at the dog. "Sam," he decided. Yes. It suited the mutt.

Doc chuckled and shook his head. "Still a Creed,

through and through," he said. "Might as well try to get the facts out of a stone wall as you."

"It's a proud family tradition," Dylan replied. He *did* like Doc, though, so he smiled.

Doc nodded, lugging the bag of special chow and heaving it into the back of the truck. He was strong, from years of pulling calves and colts and hefting big dogs on and off his examining table. "I'll have another gander at Sam tomorrow, once I've seen to the horse."

Dylan nodded. Sam was in the passenger seat by then, ready to roll.

"Once his medicine has kicked in and he's had a few good meals," Doc said in parting, "Sam will rally pretty quickly."

Cheered, Dylan nodded again, got into the truck and drove off.

"I've got a little girl," Dylan told the dog, once they were under way, "and you'll have to be nice to her. No biting."

Sam perked up his ears and tilted his head to one side, panting. His eyes, formerly dim, were already brightening with cautious hope.

They went back to Cassie's to pick Bonnie up—she was immediately taken with Sam, and when she gave one of his ears a happy tug, he licked her face and made her laugh. Finally, they were on the way home, stopping briefly at Logan's place to make sure the horse had settled in.

It was standing in the breezeway, the stall door open behind it.

"So you're a Houdini type, are you?" Dylan grinned. "An escape artist?"

He led the gelding back into the stall, made sure it had adequate feed and water and worked the latch again.

Before he got to the barn door, the horse was out a second time, plodding along after him.

They repeated the lockup.

The horse worked the latch.

"Damn," Dylan said, more in admiration than frustration. He'd encountered lock-pickers before, but this cayuse seemed to have a special talent for it. Use a padlock, and he'd figure out the combination.

Just to see what the horse would do, he got into the truck and drove it a few yards down the driveway while Bonnie crowed, "Horsie! Horsie!"

The animal followed.

Resigned, Dylan headed slowly for his own place, Bingo ambling doggedly behind the truck.

AT SIX THAT EVENING, Kristy pulled into Dylan's yard, gussied to the gills in makeup, a white ruffled top and her best black jeans. The sight of the palomino gelding grazing near the clothesline practically stopped her heart.

It *wasn't* Sugarfoot, of course. But it might have been—the conformation was the same, like the coloring.

"He followed me home," Dylan explained, when he appeared on his back porch. His gaze moved over her outfit with a blue glint of frank appreciation.

Slowly, Kristy approached the horse, drawn to him in the same powerful way she was drawn to Bonnie. "Except for the scars, he looks like—"

"Sugarfoot," Dylan finished for her.

The palomino's golden coat was still moist from a recent washing. Kristy breathed in the scent of horse, and memories she'd held at bay for a very long time welled up inside her, caught in her throat.

"I meant to put him up in Logan's barn until I get my own built," Dylan went on, appearing at her side now. Bonnie toddled after him, along with a very skinny dog. "But he wouldn't stay put."

"Where did you get him?"

"He belonged to Gunnar Wilkenson," Dylan said.

Kristy's temper flared. "Gunnar's not supposed to have—"

"Bingo's safe now," Dylan assured her quietly. "Think we ought to give him a different handle? New life, new name?"

Kristy didn't miss the word *we*. She took a step back from the horse, afraid of caring too much, fearing it was already too late.

She cared about Dylan.

She cared about Bonnie.

And now, here was this horse, a sad, mistreated version of her beautiful, healthy Sugarfoot, a living ghost, come back to haunt her.

"It's okay, Kristy," Dylan said huskily.

"Poop story!" Bonnie yelled.

Both Dylan and Kristy laughed, and the tension slackened a little.

"Did you read that book to her already?" Kristy asked.

"No," Dylan answered. "I'm philosophically opposed to the subject matter."

"Wimp," Kristy teased.

Dylan grinned. "Come on inside," he said. "I'll put the steaks on. I've already whacked up a halfway decent salad."

Leaving the horse, like leaving Bonnie and Dylan the night before, was a tearing-away, the swift removal of a bandage from a raw wound. It left Kristy almost breathless.

"I think you're right—he ought to have a different name," Kristy said, breezily decisive. Now that she was in Dylan's actual presence again, telling him about the night her father had killed a drifter didn't seem so urgent as before. "The horse, I mean."

"Like what?" Dylan asked.

Kristy looked back at the gleaming, golden horse. His hide, scarred as it was, glistening with fresh salve, seemed to soak up the fading light of a summer day. "How about Sundance?"

"I like it," Dylan said.

Warmth settled over Kristy's heart, lingered like some magical mist. "He's yours?"

"Yep," Dylan answered. "I could use some help training him, though. For all I know, he's never even had a saddle on his back."

They entered the kitchen, Bonnie and the dog leading the way. The smell of freshly washed and chopped vegetables offered a singular welcome, and Kristy spotted three giant steaks on the cutting board, seasoned and ready to broil.

Her stomach growled in anticipation.

Dylan poured some red wine into a jelly jar and handed it to her.

"Here's to stray dogs, old horses and little girls," he said, picking a beer can up off the counter and raising it slightly.

"To dogs, horses and little girls," Kristy replied, wondering why she suddenly felt like crying. She blinked, looked away, gulped down some of the wine. "Are we expecting someone else to join us?" she asked, when her voice returned, referring to the trio of steaks.

"The third one's for Sam," Dylan said, with a nod to the dog. "As you can see, he could stand a little beefing up. Pardon the unintended pun."

"Is there anything I can do to help?" Kristy asked, remembering the potato salad she'd left in the Blazer. She'd been so taken with the horse that she'd forgotten all about her deli-bought contribution to the meal.

"Nothing that ought to happen in front of a two-year-old," Dylan joked, but his eyes smoldered, a pair of blue blazes in his tanned face. His beard was growing in, a golden stubble, and Kristy refused to remember how that stubble used to feel against the bare skin of her breasts and her belly and her thighs.

Supper was a deliberately low-key affair, but Kristy felt overheated and pleasantly anxious throughout, even though the back door was open to the cool of the evening and the swamp-cooler was roaring away on a windowsill on the far side of the room.

Once they'd finished eating, Kristy put Bonnie into pajamas and brushed the child's teeth, then read her the poop story. Bonnie went directly to sleep.

Dylan was just finishing up the dishes when Kristy returned to the kitchen, one finger pressed to her lips.

Dylan dried his hands with a wad of paper towels and offered to pour more wine. Kristy demurred, since she had to drive home later.

"You wanted to talk to me?" Dylan prodded.

Kristy sighed, sat down at the table. Nodded.

He joined her. "What's up?"

She watched his face tighten as she described the dream she'd had the night before, the drifter in her room, the scuffle and the shouting—and finally the shot.

"Did he hurt you?" Dylan asked, just as Sheriff Book had, when she'd related the story to him.

"No," Kristy said. "Thanks to my dad."

Dylan's face was ghastly; he looked as though he'd like to dig that drifter up himself and kill him all over again. "Nobody's going to blame Tim for what he did," he said gruffly, after shoving a hand through his hair.

"That won't stop the talk," Kristy said.

"Probably not," Dylan agreed.

If Dylan asked her why she'd thought it was so important to relate the resurfacing of that terrible memory to him, Kristy wouldn't have known how to answer. Fortunately, he didn't.

"Will you help me with the horse, Kristy?" he said instead, after another lengthy silence.

"You don't need my help," Kristy replied. "You're better with horses than I ever was. I'm onto your plan, Dylan. You want me to work with Sundance so I'll forget about Sugarfoot, and that's never going to happen."

"I've got Bonnie, and a custody suit to file and win. A house and barn to build. And that horse—"

"Don't you *dare* say it needs me, Dylan Creed." Even then, Kristy could feel the animal tugging at her, heart to heart, calling to her in the silent way horses always did.

"What are you afraid of?" Dylan pressed.

Kristy bit her lower lip, averted her eyes, but in the same inexplicable way Sundance grasped at the tattered edges of her soul, Dylan drew her gaze back to his face.

"Caring," she said, finally, in a very small voice.

"I saw how you looked at that gelding," Dylan replied, "how you touched him and came up with a name in two seconds flat. Don't look now, but I think you're past that point where *caring* what happens to Sundance is a choice."

Yes, Kristy thought miserably. *Just as I'm past the point of no return with you, and with Bonnie. I'm in so far over my head, I can't even see the surface.*

"He'll have to go back to Logan's," she said, "until your barn is up. It's not safe, otherwise, because of the bears."

A grin tilted one side of Dylan's mouth upward. "They're still hanging out in the orchard and the old cemetery, are they?"

Kristy nodded. "Briana ran into one not long ago— it almost got her *and* her dog. If Logan hadn't come racing into the orchard in his truck, honking the horn—" She closed her eyes. In the old days, when her dad was still running cattle, she'd seen what was left of spring calves, when the bears got them, and a shudder went through her at the recollection.

"My brother didn't tell me about that," Dylan said. "No surprise there. There's a shitload of stuff Logan hasn't told me. And *damn* it, when is that yahoo going to quit honeymooning and come home?"

"You could call him, you know," Kristy said.

Dylan's sigh was heavy. He was not, and never had been, the patient sort. "I'll wait," he told her.

Just then, Kristy's cell phone rang. She picked up her purse, rummaged for the annoying thing and answered. "Hello?"

"Kristy? This is Floyd Book."

Kristy's heart caught, slid like slick-soled shoes on a floor waxed for dancing. "Floyd," she said, to let Dylan know who was calling.

He raised his eyebrows, leaned forward slightly in his chair.

"Hold on a second," Kristy told the sheriff. She scanned the unfamiliar buttons on her phone—she rarely used the thing—and found the one marked Speaker. Pressed it.

"Dylan's listening, just so you know," she told Floyd.

"Probably a good thing," Floyd said, sounding weary. "I'm glad you're not alone."

Kristy's stomach jumped. "Bad news?"

"Worse than I expected," Floyd said. "You're sitting down, I hope."

"Spit it out, Floyd," Dylan put in.

"We found *two* bodies in that grave," Floyd told them grimly. "Besides the horse."

Kristy was struck speechless. She simply stared down at the phone, lying there all shiny and sinister on Dylan's kitchen table.

Dylan picked up the slack. "The drifter and—?" he prompted irritably.

"We *think* one of them's the drifter," Floyd answered. "The second body has been tentatively identified, by what's left of her clothes and the color of her hair, as Ellie Clarkston."

Kristy put a hand over her mouth, sure her supper was about to surge up into her throat. Ellie Clarkston, the cute redheaded teenager who had disappeared during a family camping trip a few years before, at nearby Flathead Lake. A frantic, lengthy and entirely fruitless

search had been conducted, once she was reported missing, and the girl's grieving parents had finally given up and returned to their home in another state.

Kristy had run across one of the posters that had been taped and tacked up all over western Montana in a desk drawer at work, just the other day. Studied Ellie's photograph for a long time before crumpling the paper into a tight ball and tossing it away.

"Kristy?" Floyd asked. "Are you still there?"

Dylan reached across the table, closed his hand over hers.

"I'm here," she managed. "What happens now?"

"There'll be an investigation. The bodies have already been transported to the M.E.'s office in Missoula." Floyd paused, cleared his throat. "Dylan, I've already told Kristy I think she ought to leave town for a while, since the press is bound to be all over this thing. She won't listen to me. Maybe you can convince her."

Dylan said nothing, but his hand tightened comfortingly around Kristy's.

"I'm staying," Kristy said, still dazed, but sure of that much. "Ellie Clarkston disappeared *after* Dad died. That means—"

"I know what it means, Kristy," Floyd said patiently. "Whoever murdered this girl is still out there someplace. And it probably isn't a coincidence that they buried her where Tim buried the drifter. The second killer must have known what Tim did."

The room spun around Kristy. Both her parents had worked hard all their lives, and they'd been prudent with their money. Were they being blackmailed, all

those years? Had someone seen her dad burying the
man he'd been forced to shoot, defending his wife and
daughter and himself, and demanded money in return
for silence?

Was that the *real* reason why her parents had lost
everything—the ranch, their savings, their health and
their most cherished hopes?

She could think of only one living person who had
even suspected what happened that long-ago night,
besides herself, and that was Sheriff Book.

Oh my God, Kristy thought. *Oh my God.*

"We'll get to the bottom of this, Kristy," the sheriff
promised. Surely he knew what she was thinking. He
wasn't a stupid man.

Kristy nodded. "Yes," she said, her voice too bright,
too shrill. "Yes. I know."

"I'm trying to keep this quiet," Book went on, "but
I'm afraid it's been leaked, and now that the M.E. is
involved, it's out of my hands."

Dylan nodded thoughtfully at that, but didn't say
anything.

Kristy and the sheriff—the man who might have
killed poor Ellie Clarkston *and* blackmailed her father
into his grave—said their farewells. Kristy closed her
phone and stared at Dylan.

"He knew," she whispered. "Sheriff Book knew all
along—or at least suspected—that my dad had shot that
man and buried him in Sugarfoot's grave. What if *he*
was blackmailing my folks all that time? What if *he*
killed that Clarkston girl?"

"Whoa back," Dylan said. "That's some major
conclusion-jumping."

"*Floyd Book was the sheriff,* Dylan. Why else would he have kept silent, never followed up on his suspicions, dug up that grave long before now?"

"Your dad was his *best friend,* Kristy."

Kristy bit her lower lip. "So he claims," she answered. "But most people wouldn't turn a blind eye to something like that, no matter who was involved." She swallowed. "Would you? If you wore a badge and you'd taken an oath, would you just look the other way?"

Dylan was a long time answering.

"No," he finally said, his tone bleak. "No, I wouldn't."

CHAPTER SEVEN

FOR KRISTY, the very air buzzed with portent, but nothing happened for three full days after that fateful call from Sheriff Book, confirming that two bodies had been found sharing Sugarfoot's tree-shaded grave. She was a woman going through the motions, braced to withstand a personal apocalypse, and yet she managed to function.

She fed Winston, night and morning.

She went to the library every day.

She kept everything at a careful distance—her frightening attraction to Dylan Creed, her growing attachment to little Bonnie, the deep desire to work with Sundance until he was restored to wholeness. Until he had, in turn, restored *her,* by means of that magical alchemy peculiar to horses.

It was only during the oppressively hot, quiet and long nights that she allowed the evening her life had changed forever to surface and play out on the screen of her mind, like scenes from some macabre theater production, full of shadows and slashes of crimson.

But when Zachary Spencer came rushing into the library on the third morning, his handsome face full of avaricious interest, Kristy knew the shit, to put it crudely, had finally hit the fan.

"We *have* to talk!" the actor said, leaning across the counter at the main desk, his elegant nose an inch from Kristy's.

Kristy gripped the edge of the counter, felt herself go pale. She'd met Spencer once or twice, he'd asked her out and she'd refused, not because she disliked him, but because there was no zip between them.

Her friends thought she was crazy. Didn't she *know* he was a star?

"Mr. Spencer," Kristy said, stiffly polite, "I'm busy."

"This is important," Zachary insisted. "It's a *movie!*"

"A what?"

He strode around back of the counter, took her by the arm and shuffled her toward the back office. He'd spotted it because her name was stenciled on the door in big letters.

Library patrons, young and old, stared as they passed.

"It's got everything!" the actor emoted, as soon as they were alone. "Murder! Mystery! Human pathos!"

Kristy gaped at him. He'd heard about the bodies found in Sugarfoot's grave, obviously. The eye of the storm had passed, and now she would be swept up in the whirlwind.

"It's *your* story, Kristy!" Zachary ranted on, flinging his arms out from his sides, his enthusiasm bordering on the manic. "I can offer you major money for an exclusive—"

"Wait," Kristy breathed, shaken. Feeling her way around behind her desk and falling into her chair. "You're talking about making a *movie* about what happened?"

"*Yes,*" Spencer said, pacing now, shoving a hand through his artfully trimmed but undeniably thinning brown locks. She'd have bet he was already shopping for a hair transplant. "All you have to do is sign an agreement, giving me permission to write and direct the project, and cash the check!" He stopped pacing, braced himself against the edge of her desk, looming over her in a way that made her push back her chair a few inches, setting the small, swiveling wheels to creaking. "What do you say, Kristy? Do we have a deal?"

"I don't—"

"Surely you can use the money! You're a small-town *librarian*—"

Kristy's spine stiffened. "Yes. I'm a librarian. But so far I've managed to keep a roof over my head and I—"

Zachary huffed out a sigh. "All right, I guess I came on a little strong—"

"Ya think?"

"The press is already zeroing in on Stillwater Springs," Zachary reasoned. "This is a *big* story. Once it gets out, a lot more people will be after you to sign over the rights—books, movies, all of it. Kristy, I *want* this."

In Zachary Spencer's world, Kristy supposed, wanting something was reason enough to get it. On Planet Kristy, there were variables.

"How *much* money?" she asked. She was only human, after all, and while she certainly didn't live from hand to mouth, she did worry, at odd times, that she'd end up sick and broke, the way her parents had. They hadn't made it as far as old.

The figure Zachary Spencer threw out then made Kristy blink.

She could buy back the ranch, with a fortune of that magnitude, and have plenty left over. Make sure Sugarfoot's final resting place was never bulldozed and replaced with a tennis court.

"I'd have to think about this," she said evenly. "Consult a few people."

"All right," Spencer agreed, albeit with theatrical reluctance. It was no wonder he was famous, with a row of Oscars and other prestigious awards to his credit. His face, though aging, reflected his every emotion. He fumbled a little, pulled out a checkbook. "At least let me *option* the project."

"Option—?"

"That means I pay you, and you agree not to sell the rights to anyone but me within a specified period of time."

"I know what it means," Kristy said. She'd begun to feel dizzy by then, and a mild headache pounded behind her right temple, intensifying with every beat of her heart. "Suppose, at the end of this 'specified period of time,' I decide I don't want any books written or movies made?"

"Someone will do it anyway," Spencer admitted, after a lengthy silence. "You can profit by this, have some admittedly limited influence over the projects, or you can stand by, penniless, and watch writers and directors and actors and producers make of it what they will."

Not, Kristy had to confess, at least to herself, a very appealing choice. "I could sue," she said, grasping at the proverbial straws.

Zachary laughed rawly at that, a hard sound, devoid of humor. "And they'd settle. But you couldn't stop the books, Kristy, *or* the movies. Even now, there are films of the gravesite and your parents' house up on the Internet—check for yourself if you don't believe me."

"And selling the rights to you would prevent all the

unauthorized stuff?" Kristy asked. She was actually just thinking aloud—she knew there would be no keeping a lid on such a juicy drama, and if she allowed speculation to run rampant—

"It would forestall it. I could have the papers drawn up today. My legal people would make sure we had a claim by applying for copyrights and the like."

Kristy bit her lower lip, thinking hard. In essence, she was trapped—damned if she did make a deal with the devil, damned if she didn't.

"I'd want something else," she ventured. "Besides the money."

Spencer waited, exuding intensity.

"I know you've been talking to Freida Turlow about buying Madison Ranch. You'd have to promise to back out of the agreement, if you've made one. Let me buy it instead."

The still-perfect face fell slightly. "There's a problem," Zachary ground out, not quite meeting Kristy's eyes.

"What sort of problem?" she asked quietly.

"It seems there's another buyer, somebody who's willing to top every bid I make on the place."

"Who?" Kristy's voice, barely more than a whisper, shook. Why hadn't Freida mentioned that? The woman delighted in getting under Kristy's skin, and the sale of Madison Ranch to a stranger was a good way to achieve that end.

Zachary's broad shoulders rose and fell in a combination shrug and sigh, slightly too artless to *be* artless. "I don't know. Some cattle company—that's all Ms. Turlow would tell me."

Kristy tilted her head back, shut her eyes.

No one, but *no one,* in or around Stillwater Springs had the kind of money Zachary Spencer could offer. So this mystery buyer had to be an outsider, another movie star, perhaps. Or a CEO soaring back to earth with a golden parachute strapped to his back.

If she couldn't buy back the ranch, what was the point in splashing her dead parents' secrets across the silver screen, or in some tell-all "true crime" book?

Hopelessness washed over her.

"I'll think about it," she said, finally opening her eyes.

When she did, she saw a freshly written check lying on the desk in front of her. The amount would have paid off her mortgage, even after taxes.

She gasped.

"And that's just the option," Zachary said, pressing his advantage. "Yours to keep, just for agreeing not to sell the story to anyone else during the next ninety days."

Kristy stared at the check for a long, long time. Then, with a sigh, she asked, "Where do I sign?"

LOGAN WAS BACK, at long last, and he had a shiner the size of a manhole cover on his right eye. But he looked stupidly happy, standing there on the back porch at Dylan's place, dressed like any Montana rancher in scuffed boots, jeans, a T-shirt and an old flannel shirt, worn thin by hard use.

"Must have been one hell of a honeymoon," Dylan drawled, unwilling to let his brother see how relieved he was by his return. He'd taken his sweet, shit-ass time coming home, Logan had.

Logan laughed. "Tyler gave me the black eye," he

said cheerfully. "Said he came to town and waited around till I got back just for the pleasure of punching me in the face."

"Sounds like Tyler," Dylan agreed, stepping back so Logan could cross the threshold.

"Nice horse," Logan commented, indicating Sundance with a nod of his head. "Looks pretty beat-up, though."

Bonnie, who had been playing quietly—for once—looked up from where she sat on the hooked rug in front of the refrigerator, Sam stationed patiently at her side.

Logan's dark eyes widened slightly as they fell, for the first time, on his niece.

"Well," he said huskily, going to Bonnie and crouching to stroke Sam's head. "Hello, there."

"Poop," Bonnie said.

Dylan laughed, though his throat felt sick and his eyes burned slightly.

"I'm your uncle," Logan told her. There was a note of shy wonder in his voice—he was actually *choked up,* Dylan concluded, surprised. The Logan he knew was a lot of things—shrewd, tenacious, the strong, silent type. But sentimental? No. Not Logan.

"Poop," Bonnie repeated.

A distinctive smell filled the air.

"I don't think she was commenting on my character," Logan observed, grinning.

Dylan sighed, scooped his daughter up and carried her to the bathroom. The cleanup job, closely supervised by a concerned and ever-vigilant Sam, took fifteen minutes, and when he got back to the kitchen, Bonnie riding his right hip, he found that Doc Ryder had arrived.

He sat at the table with Logan, the pair of them drinking coffee.

"You actually changed a diaper," Logan remarked, his eyes dancing as he watched Dylan. "Never thought I'd see the day."

"Your time's coming," Doc told Logan, with a chuckle. "At least, from what I've heard, anyhow."

Logan knew as well as Dylan did that Doc had heard plenty, and passed most of it on, bucket-brigade style, to seven hundred and twenty-eight of his closest friends.

"I hope so," Logan said quietly, watching Bonnie again. "I really hope so. And so does Briana."

Doc finished his coffee, slapped his thighs with his gnarled hands and stood. "I'll have a look at Sam here and be on my way. Checked out the gelding on my way in. Seems sound to me, if a little skittish, but I wormed him and gave him his shots. If Gunnar had seen to that, I'd know about it."

Dylan nodded. "Thanks, Doc," he said. "What do I owe you?"

"You'll get a bill," Doc replied, squatting in front of Sam to examine him. "You look a whole lot better, fella," he told the dog, "now that you've had a bath and a good meal or two."

Sam tried to lick his face.

Doc dodged the dog tongue with affectionate grace and another chuckle. Ruffled Sam's ears before straightening to his full height, knee bones popping like muffled gunshots in the room.

"I'm getting too old for this stuff," he lamented good-naturedly. "Too bad I don't have a son to take over the practice, so I could retire like Floyd is about to do."

Dylan and Logan exchanged amused glances; Doc had been threatening to retire since they'd lost their baby teeth.

"Guess I'll die with my boots on," Doc said, sounding resigned.

"How's Lily?" Logan asked. Lily was Doc's daughter, his only child. She'd visited every summer after her parents' less-than-amicable divorce, a wistful little girl, always on her dad's heels.

"Made me a grandfather six years ago," Doc said, somewhat sadly, "not that I ever see her *or* little Tess. Lily was always more her mother's girl than mine."

Dylan, the father of a daughter himself, felt a pang at this. Only denial had kept him from missing Bonnie every moment he'd been away from her. Denial and poker and stunt work.

Gossip though he did, Doc didn't commonly open up about his personal life. That day, he looked smaller than usual, and more stooped. He really *was* getting old, and the thought saddened Dylan, blew over him like a chilly wind on a lonely winter night.

"Tyler was crazy about Lily," Logan reflected thoughtfully. Dylan recalled their youngest brother's crush on Lily Ryder well. Around the time they both hit high school, though, Lily's mother had remarried, and the happy couple had moved back east somewhere, taking Lily with them. After that, she hadn't made many more long summer visits, as far as Dylan recalled.

Doc nodded, hand resting on the doorknob, eyes far away. "Wild as Tyler was, I've often wondered if Lily wouldn't have been better off with him than that flyboy she married. *He* was a piece of work—had himself a pretty little flight attendant stashed in every city on his route."

"Was?" Dylan asked.

"Flying for a major airline wasn't enough for him," Doc answered, coming back into himself with a visible start, giving a little shudder. "Burke Kenyon had to barnstorm on the weekends, in some jerry-rigged little plane he built himself. Crashed it right into a viaduct one day."

Neither Dylan nor Logan spoke. If Doc needed to vent, they'd listen.

"I don't know why I'm telling you all this," Doc said, with a haunted expression and a smile that didn't quite make it to his eyes. "I guess it just wears on me, knowing Lily blames herself for Burke dying the way he did."

Dylan swallowed hard.

Logan cleared his throat, cast a nervous glance in Dylan's direction. "Why would she do that?" Logan asked gruffly.

"She'd served Burke with divorce papers when it happened," Doc answered. "Lily doesn't confide in me much, but I think she believes he might have crashed that plane deliberately because she was leaving him."

By that point, Logan was looking at Dylan, not Doc, and the expression in his eyes, one of painful reluctance, set off some alarms in Dylan's head.

Doc said his goodbyes and left.

Bonnie toddled off into the living room, followed by Sam, and when Dylan checked on her, he found her curled up on the couch, sound asleep. Sam rested dutifully on the floor, as close to her as he could get.

Dylan went back to the kitchen. He'd been chomping at the bit to talk to Logan about filing for custody of Bonnie, but he knew now that something else was up. Something big.

"What's going on, Logan?" he asked his brother.

Logan stood in the middle of the kitchen, hands on his hips, elbows sticking out. "It's about Dad," he said.

Dylan's back molars clamped together; he consciously relaxed his jaw. Jake Creed was a sore spot between them, for all their separate efforts at being real brothers again, and if Logan was going to start up on the old man, the way he had after the funeral, they'd be back at square one.

"Save it," he said.

"I can't," Logan replied grimly. "It's too important."

"What?" Dylan snapped. Whatever was coming, he knew he didn't want to hear it. He also knew he didn't have a choice.

"Sit down," Logan urged, drawing back the chair he'd occupied when he and Doc were jawing earlier.

Dylan scraped back a chair of his own, sank into it. Glared at Logan as he sat down, too.

"Brett Turlow didn't kill him, Dylan," Logan said. Their dad had been a logger, tough as the trees he'd felled for a living. Brett Turlow was the boss's son, jealous of Jake, and everyone—including Sheriff Book—had always suspected Brett of cutting the chain that released the truckload of logs that had fallen on Jake, though Turlow had always sworn it was an accident.

Dylan didn't say a word. The memory of that loss scoured and scalded inside him, painful enough to take his breath away. He'd seen Jake lying in the intensive-care unit of a Missoula hospital, shortly after his death, hopelessly crushed, lying amid a tangle of recently disconnected tubes and wires. In his weaker moments, he pictured the so-called accident that had taken his father's life, heard the thunder of those rolling logs, the sound of splintering bones. He saw the blood and imagined the pain Jake must have experienced.

Logan moved as if to lay a hand on his shoulder, then plucked an old piece of paper out of his shirt pocket instead. Handed it over.

Dylan shook his head. Knew his eyes wouldn't focus on the words written there.

So Logan read them aloud.

Blood pounded in Dylan's ears; he heard the letter in bits and pieces.

"'If you've looked this far—'" Logan paused to explain that he'd found the note in a box of family pictures "'—you're ready to read this pitiful missive from your soon-to-be dearly departed father—'"

Dylan closed his eyes, endured while Logan read on.

"'I tried, but I could never get the hang of living.'" Logan stopped, cleared his throat, then went mercilessly on. "'It was just too damn hard. So today, I mean to go up on the mountain, just like always, and rig a logging chain—'"

The rest was apology.

Excuses.

As if the old man had ever given a shit how his actions affected anybody else in the universe.

"He killed himself," Dylan ground out, when Logan finally fell silent, refolded the paper, and tucked it back into his pocket. "The rotten, selfish son of a bitch *killed himself.*"

Logan didn't answer. He didn't have to.

"Does Tyler know?" Dylan asked presently.

Logan nodded. "I told him," he said, hoarse with the memory.

"Where is he now?" Protecting their little brother was an old habit with Dylan. Even when they were pissed off at each other—the three of them had been known to stand back to back, in the middle of a brawl with each other, and take on all comers.

"I don't know," Logan replied wearily. "I'd gone to Dad's grave. I heard somebody behind me, turned around, and there was Tyler. He sucker punched me, and I went down."

"And then you told him Dad committed suicide. Why, Logan? Out of spite, because he hit you?"

"Give me some credit, Dylan," Logan rasped. "I told him because I knew he'd take off and I might not get a chance to talk to him for *another* five years."

"If you hadn't broken his guitar after Dad's funeral—"

Logan shut his eyes. Opened them again. "Do you think I don't regret that, Dylan? I was drunk. You were drunk. Hell, we *all* were, and Tyler kept playing that damned song, making Dad out to be some kind of fallen hero—"

"Maybe he needed to believe that, Logan. Did that ever occur to you?"

Logan sighed. "Not then," he admitted.

Dylan was still seething, but Jake was at the root of his anger, not Logan. "And you just dropped it on him, at Dad's grave, of all places? He had to be told, I know that—but shouldn't we have done that together, you and me?"

"I wasn't sure we'd have that option," Logan answered. "Like I said, he's gone."

Dylan glanced back over one shoulder, and through the living room doorway, he saw Bonnie still napping away on the couch. Pre-Bonnie, he would have been in his truck by then, bent on finding Tyler before he did anything stupid, but now he was a father. Bonnie depended on him. He couldn't just take off and leave her, no matter how urgent the mission seemed.

"You do recall," he said fiercely, "that Tyler's mother killed herself and he didn't talk for a year after that?"

"I haven't forgotten," Logan said, looking as dismal as he sounded.

"Shit," Dylan said.

Neither of them spoke for at least five minutes.

During that time, Dylan thought about Tyler, and about Jake, about the whole dysfunctional mess they called a childhood. But he also thought of Bonnie. If things were going to be different for her than they'd been for him and Logan and Tyler—and *by God* they were—he'd have to set aside his anger with Logan and ask for his help.

So he told Logan, quietly and calmly, about Sharlene, and Bonnie's birth, and how he'd found her in his truck that night in Vegas. The story poured out of him and, pride or no pride, he couldn't hide his desperation to keep and raise his daughter from the brother who knew him so well.

"Do I have a chance in hell?" he asked, when he'd finally finished.

"A fairly good one," Logan said. "If you've still got the note Sharlene left, saying she couldn't take care of Bonnie any longer."

Dylan let out a sigh of relief so deep that it left him a little light-headed. "I'm pretty sure I could buy Shar-lene off," he said, keeping his voice down, though

Bonnie probably wouldn't have understood what he was saying, even if she hadn't been asleep. "But once the money ran out, she'd be back. And if I didn't give her what she wanted, she might snatch Bonnie. Then there's the boyfriend—Logan, I've got no idea what kind of man he is—"

"We'll file in the morning," Logan said. "Where's the note?"

Dylan had stashed Sharlene's scrawled excuse in a jelly glass at the back of one of the cupboards. He got it out, handed it to Logan.

Logan read it, gave it back. "Put this in a safety-deposit box at the bank," he said. "There was a break-in when Briana lived here, if you'll remember, and we can't lose this. It's the best proof we have that Sharlene is unfit to raise a child."

"Leaving Bonnie in the truck isn't enough?" Dylan asked.

"From the judge's perspective, that will be hearsay. Your word against Sharlene's. If she decides to fight for Bonnie, you can bet your ass she'll show up in court dressed like a Sunday-school teacher and ready to make you out to be a rodeo bum. A lot of touching tears will flow. The judge might see through it. *Or* he or she might fall for the whole thing and grant Sharlene sole custody."

"I can't let that happen, Logan."

"I'll do what I can. Except for the note, Sharlene's holding the high cards, Dylan. She's Bonnie's mother, and she's bound to say she just got overwhelmed trying to raise a child by herself, without any help from you. If anything happens to the note, she could even claim you *stole* Bonnie from her."

"Damn it, I'm Bonnie's *father,* and I've paid child support ever since she was born!"

"A lot of family-court judges are still pretty old-fashioned," Logan reminded him. "Especially in rural Montana. They usually sympathize with the mother. I'm not saying things will shake out that way, but you've got to face facts here. Sharlene might roll over, especially if there's a settlement involved. She might also decide to play the wronged single mother, struggling to raise a child on her own, or even demand that you marry her."

Dylan opened his mouth, closed it again. He could protest all he wanted, but Logan was right. A clever attorney, should Sharlene be smart enough to hire one, paying the retainer out of the money he'd just sent her, could make him look pretty bad. And while no one could legally force him to marry the woman, he knew he'd do even that to keep Bonnie.

He was a former rodeo cowboy, with no visible means of support.

He was single.

He'd been a chronic womanizer since he and Kristy broke up—bimbos would come out of the woodwork, prepared to testify that he was a party animal, a boozer and a brawler, just like his old man.

And plenty of people around Stillwater Springs would agree with that assessment.

He braced his elbows on his thighs, splayed his fingers and shoved them into his hair, his head hanging.

Logan's hand landed on his right shoulder, squeezed. "There's one thing working in your favor," he said.

Dylan didn't look up. Or shake off his brother's hand, as he might have done any other time. "What?"

"I'm the best damn lawyer since Clarence Darrow," Logan replied, with a grin in his voice. "And I play to win."

Dylan lifted his head, met Logan's gaze. "You'd damn well *better* win," he said.

KRISTY MET ZACHARY SPENCER at the Marigold Café, as agreed, as soon as she left the library that night. He'd brought the papers along, outlining their option agreement. The check he'd given her earlier, in her office, was tucked carefully in her wallet, between two twenty-dollar bills, where it seemed to give off some kind of vibratory energy.

Thus far, she hadn't seen any reporters or newspeople in town, but that didn't mean they weren't lurking behind telephone poles or speeding in her direction.

Zachary stood when she entered the café.

Everybody in the place watched as she walked to his table, waited while he pulled back her chair, and sat down.

"They're staring," she whispered.

"They're jealous," Zachary answered. "Of *me*. You are one good-looking woman, Kristy Madison."

The compliment didn't register; Kristy was too nervous for that. At the edge of her vision, Kristy spotted Mike and Julie Danvers, dining with their two perfect children, both of whom were sporting huge Mike Danvers for Sheriff buttons.

Mike pushed back his chair, straightened his tie and approached Kristy's table, while Julie seethed visibly behind a rigid campaign smile.

"Kristy," Mike said. He was a chubby man, not overly tall, with a broad, guileless face. While Kristy had no doubt of his integrity, she didn't think he had the toughness it would take to be a good sheriff. Except for their breakup, things had gone his way all his life. It was different with his opponent, Jim Huntinghorse, who'd grown up poor on a local reservation.

"Hello, Mike," she said, smiling. She nodded toward Zachary. "Mike Danvers, this is Mr.—"

Mike flashed a smile and stuck his hand out to the movie star, who rose from his chair as gracefully as if they'd met in a swanky L.A. restaurant instead of a diner in Stillwater Springs, Montana. "I know Zachary," Mike boomed, as the two men shook hands. "I wanted to thank you personally for that contribution you made to my campaign."

Zachary cleared his throat diplomatically. "Well, you're welcome, Mike," he said. "But I'd be less than honest if I didn't tell you that I wrote a check to Jim Huntinghorse for the same amount."

Mike's confidence seemed to wane a little, but he recovered quickly enough. "I appreciate it just the same," he said.

Zachary nodded affably. Sat back down at a nod from Mike. "If I can ever manage to buy a chunk of land around here," Zachary said, "I mean to become a local, at least part-time. I've got kids, and good law enforcement matters to me."

Mike nodded, at something of a loss. He looked at Kristy, who was pretending to study the menu. As if she didn't know it by heart, since the Marigold was the only non-drive-through in town, and she ate there often.

"You coming to hear Jim and me discuss the issues tomorrow night, Kristy?" Mike asked hopefully.

Kristy looked up at him. With all that had been going

on, she'd forgotten about the Great Debate, to be held at the high school gymnasium. Until Floyd Book had found two bodies in her horse's grave, the campaign for the sheriff's job, along with Dylan's return to Stillwater Springs and Logan's recent marriage, had been the biggest topic of conversation going.

"I'll be there," she said mildly. In truth, she planned to vote for Jim Huntinghorse, but she prided herself on keeping an open mind. And she didn't want anyone saying she was hiding out, trying to escape the fallout brought on by Sheriff Book's discovery.

If indeed it *had* been a discovery, and not something he'd known about all along, and decided to reveal only because the possible sale of the land, and subsequent moving of Sugarfoot's poor remains, left him with no other choice.

She'd found it easy enough to avoid her dad's old friend over the last few days, but she knew it couldn't last. Stillwater Springs was too small a town for that.

"Julie and I just wanted you to know," Mike told Kristy lamely, after glancing back once at his clearly unhappy but still smiling wife, "that we don't think for one minute your dad would murder somebody."

Mike might think that. Julie would not be so generous.

Kristy put her smile on high beam. "Thank you, Mike," she said. "That's good to know."

At last, Mike said goodbye and went back to his family.

"He's nuts about you," Zachary observed, with dry amusement.

"He's married," Kristy said, in a tone calculated to put paid to the subject of Mike Danvers.

The waitress came.

Zachary ordered a steak, rare, grilled asparagus and a baked potato with the works.

Kristy asked for the same thing she always did—a chef's salad with Thousand Island on the side.

While they ate, Kristy was conscious of the intermittent stares slithering their way. Even after the Danvers tribe trooped out, Mike stopping to shake hands with someone at every table, she and Zachary were the center of none-too-subtle attention.

"They're saying I finally managed to get you to go out with me," Zachary said, apparently amused.

"This," Kristy said, "is *not* a date."

Zachary pulled a woebegone face, though his eyes sparkled with his trademark mischief. "Is there someone else?" he asked, with so much drama that Kristy wouldn't have been surprised to hear somber organ music.

There *was* someone else, of course, though Kristy wasn't about to share that with Zachary Spencer.

And, as luck would have it, that *someone else* was the very next person to walk through the front door of the Marigold Café.

As if he had radar, Dylan Creed stepped over the threshold and immediately swung his blue gaze straight to Kristy.

CHAPTER EIGHT

DYLAN HAD AGREED to have dinner out with Logan and Briana while Cassie looked after Bonnie and Briana's boys, Alec and Josh, at the main ranch house. He'd wanted a distraction from all that was weighing on his mind—the truth about Jake's death, filing for permanent custody of his daughter, and all the rest.

Instead, he got Kristy sitting with a movie star. *People's* Sexiest Man Alive a year or so ago, if he remembered correctly.

Dylan had no claim on her, of course, no right to say who she had dinner with and who she didn't, but he bristled just the same. And Logan knew it, prodded him from behind, murmuring, "Move it, lover boy. I'm hungry."

With more effort than he liked, Dylan tore his attention from Kristy. Waited while the hostess found a table for him and Logan and Briana.

"Cool it with the 'lover boy' stuff, all right?" he snapped to Logan. "I don't give a damn who Kristy goes out with."

Logan chuckled, and his dark eyes danced as he pulled back a chair for Briana, his beautiful, glowing bride. "Is Kristy here?" he asked, pretending surprise.

"I wouldn't have known that by the way you stopped cold in the doorway when you caught sight of her."

"Logan," Briana said sweetly, used to governing two rambunctious young sons and therefore highly diplomatic, "leave your brother alone."

Before sitting down, Dylan leaned to kiss his sister-in-law resoundingly on top of the head. "Thanks, beautiful," he said, glaring at Logan.

Logan simply grinned. Sat himself down beside Briana and took her hand.

They looked good together, Logan and Briana, Dylan thought grudgingly. Better than good. Obviously, the sex was beyond excellent, the energy of it crackled around the two of them like a live wire sparking blue on a rain-wet road, but there was more to the marriage than that.

Damned if his brother hadn't fallen in love for real this time, and Briana loved him, too.

Lucky bastard, Dylan reflected, still glaring at Logan.

Logan ignored him, reached for a menu. He and Briana sat with their heads close together, reading it.

"What looks good to you?" Briana asked her husband.

Logan, a *husband.* Incomprehensible.

Logan kissed her lightly. "What looks good to me isn't on the menu," he said.

"Please," Dylan said.

Logan grinned across the table at him. "Eat your heart out, little brother," he said.

Briana elbowed him playfully. "Stop it."

"Don't call me 'little brother.'" In Dylan's mind, that salutation belonged to Tyler.

"Touchy," Logan replied.

"I can still whip your ass," Dylan asserted.

"You're welcome to try," Logan said happily. Even the big shiner on his right eye didn't seem to dampen his spirits. It was disgusting, that was what it was. The man was almost high.

"Enough," Briana interjected, smiling. "We came here to have a nice meal and for Dylan to sign the custody petition you spent the whole afternoon writing up, Logan Creed. And if either of you think I'm going to referee a brawl just because the two of you are on testosterone overload, you'd better think again."

"You've already drawn up the papers?" Dylan asked, watching Logan.

"I told you I was the best," Logan said, as Briana pulled a legal-size manila folder out of her big purse. "I'll file them in the courthouse tomorrow, if you approve them."

Dylan all but snatched the documents out of Briana's hand. Read them quickly, then read them again, this time slowly, to make sure he hadn't missed anything. It was a habit he'd acquired because of his early struggle with dyslexia—when he'd told Kristy, the other day at the library, that he'd read *Lonesome Dove* five times, he'd been telling the truth. It had taken that many passes for the whole story to sink in.

He tapped the blank spot on the third page, where Logan had left room for a settlement amount. "You think I should pay Sharlene off?" he asked.

"I'm giving you the option," Logan said. "The amount—if there is one—is up to you."

Logan probably thought he was poor. A rodeo bum, a gambler and sometime stunt man. Dylan had never seen any reason to disabuse either of his brothers of the notion.

Now, it gave him a kick to say, "A million ought to do it."

Logan arched one eyebrow. "You have a million dollars?"

"A lot more than that," Dylan answered. "Thanks to the stock I bought in your company way back when I was winning buckles at the big rodeo. It split four times before you sold the outfit last year, and twice since."

Amusement—and respect—flickered in Logan's brown eyes. "I went over the stockholders' list a hundred times. I never saw your name on it."

"You wouldn't have," Dylan allowed. "I didn't use it."

"Clever," Logan said.

The waitress came, flirted a little, took their orders and left again. Five seconds after she'd gone, Dylan couldn't remember what he'd chosen to eat. He was too conscious of Kristy, over yonder charming that movie star.

"Why keep it a secret?" Logan asked.

For a moment, Dylan didn't know what Logan was talking about. Then he realized what his brother was referring to—the stock purchases he'd made while the boy wonder, Logan Creed, was wowing the financial community with his user-friendly legal-services Web site.

It came back to him, too, that he'd ordered the meatloaf special. Maybe he wasn't losing his mind after all.

"Should I have let you find out I was impressed by your success?" Dylan grinned. "That would never have done."

Briana shook her head. "Testosterone," she said.

"I'm not sure," Logan said, musing, "but I think I'm flattered."

"Don't let it go to your head," Dylan advised. "I still think you're an asshole ninety percent of the time." He turned to Briana. "Sorry, sis."

"I like the sound of that," Briana said, moving the custody papers out of gravy-range. "'Sis,' I mean. Not 'asshole.'"

The food came. They ate.

The meat loaf was probably good, but Dylan couldn't have sworn to it. What were Kristy and that actor talking about over there at that table on the far side of the café, anyway? Their heads were too close together to suit Dylan.

"Go over and say hello to her," Logan said, midway through the meal. "Do you realize you've salted those mashed potatoes four times? Your arteries are probably hardening as we speak."

Briana giggled. "Go," she urged Dylan. She was a looker, Briana was, with her red-blond hair pulled back into a French braid, her emerald-green eyes, and that knockout figure of hers. Why hadn't he noticed that, that long-ago night in front of the Stillwater Springs Wal-Mart, when her jerk of a first husband had ditched her in the parking lot with two boys and an old dog and nowhere to go?

He'd given her the keys to his house, since he wasn't using it anyhow, and the use of the old beater he'd driven in high school. He might have been able to win her over, if he'd stuck around and tried. Instead, he'd gone back to the rodeo circuit.

But even then his mind had been full of Kristy. He'd come back to settle his bull, Cimarron, at the ranch, and once he'd made all the arrangements for the animal's care by a neighbor, he'd shot out of that town like a greased bullet.

Briana excused herself and left the table, probably headed for the ladies' room.

"If I didn't know better," Logan remarked mildly, "I'd think you were lusting after my wife."

"She's primo," Dylan admitted.

"But you're still hung up on Kristy Madison."

Dylan felt a hot flush climb his neck. He pushed his plate away, his appetite gone. "Are you trying to pick a fight, Logan? Because I'm game, even if you *are* my lawyer."

"I've already got one black eye," Logan said. "I don't need another."

"Did you hit Tyler back?" Dylan asked. This was ground he knew how to navigate. The things he might have told Logan, if it hadn't been for their rocky history, were too raw to uncover.

"No," Logan said. That desolate look was back in his eyes.

Dylan was surprised. What Jake Creed hadn't taught him and Tyler about fighting, Logan had. "You just let him knock you down and get away with it? Who are you, and what have you done with my brother?"

"There's been enough brawling, don't you think?"

"I don't believe I'm hearing this."

"Believe it. I came back to Stillwater Springs to make the Creed name mean something good again, and punching Tyler's lights out, however badly I wanted to do just that, isn't on my to-do list."

"You *have* changed."

Logan watched with something like adoration radiating from his face as Briana approached the table, Venus in blue jeans. "Oh, yeah," he replied huskily, "I've changed, all right."

"Are you going to be insulted if I tell you I think that's a good thing?"

Logan chuckled, stood to pull back Briana's chair. "No," he answered. "You're going to find it a lot harder to insult me these days, little brother."

Dylan felt a muscle bunch in his jaw, but he didn't protest the moniker.

"I stopped to say hello to Kristy on my way back from the restroom," Briana announced brightly, as she sat down. "She introduced me to Zachary Spencer, and it seemed like a business dinner to me."

So, Dylan thought, Logan had told Briana the starcrossed-teenage-lovers story. He caught his brother's gaze and narrowed his eyes.

Logan grinned, unfazed. "I'd stroll right over there and say howdy, if I were you," he told Dylan. "That guy looks way too much like George Clooney to be safe around women."

"Well," Dylan answered, "you're *not* me."

Logan shrugged one shoulder. "If you want Kristy to think you're chickenshit, that's your business," he said.

Briana jabbed him with her elbow again, harder this time. "Logan!"

Dylan shoved back his chair and stood. Nobody knew which of his buttons to push better than Logan did, and he'd just pushed the one that opened half a dozen psychological missile silos. The thing none of the Creeds could abide—Dylan included—was being seen as a coward.

A gutless wonder, as Jake used to put it.

Logan's smile was self-satisfied to the max.

Briana looked worried. Like most women—with the standout exception of Sharlene—she probably hated public scenes.

"Remember," Logan said quietly, with a lawyer's moderation, "everything you do and say will find its way straight to the judge if Sharlene decides to counter your custody petition."

Inwardly, Dylan sighed. Nodded.

As he made his way toward Kristy's table, he drummed up his laid-back-cowboy smile. By the time he got there, he must have looked downright amiable, though his guts were churning. Was it possible to sweat on the *inside* of your skin?

"Hello, Kristy," he said, in a hat-in-hand voice. Actually, he'd left his hat in his truck, but he wished he had it then, so he could turn it idly in his hands.

"D-Dylan," she said. "Hello."

The movie star stood up, put out a hand. "Zachary Spencer," he said.

Dylan shook his hand. "Dylan Creed," he replied. "Good to meet you."

Spencer looked thoughtful. "That name sounds familiar," he said.

"I had a run-in with your boy, Caleb, over a horse," Dylan said.

Kristy's gaze flickered from him to Spencer and back again.

"I heard about that," the movie star said, without apparent ill will. "Caleb's too used to getting what he wants. Do him good to get a taste of the real world."

Recalling the kid, and the way he'd been set on taking a lunge-whip to Sundance, Dylan's jawline tightened.

Kristy, being privy to what had happened on the road the day before between Dylan and Caleb, made the connection, the realization plain in her face. After all, there weren't that many movie stars, or movie star's *sons,* knocking around Stillwater Springs, even with the run on real estate.

"He was about to *hit* that poor horse," she said to Spencer. "Your son, I mean."

"I talked to him about it," Spencer said. To his credit, he looked sincere about that, at least. "Join us?" he asked Dylan.

"I'm here with my brother and sister-in-law," Dylan said, unable to keep his gaze off Kristy. She was looking down at the remains of a big salad, which she'd hardly dented, and the color was high in her cheeks. "I just wanted to say hello to an old friend."

The movie star nodded, smiled affably and sat down.

Before he could give in to a primal and completely unreasonable urge to grab Mr. Hollywood by the front of his fancy shirt and pitch him head-first into the pie counter, Dylan turned and walked away.

"THAT WENT WELL." Kristy sighed ruefully, as soon as Dylan was out of earshot. She knew what he was thinking—that she was starstruck over Zachary Spencer, dazzled by his money and fame and all the rest, like practically every other woman in town.

"I know when I'm beaten," Zachary said quietly.

Kristy's eyes shot to his face. "Beaten?"

"Let's just say," Zachary went on, his tone gentle and

full of resignation, "that if we'd been standing on dry grass when all those sparks were flying between you and the cowboy, we couldn't have outrun the wildfire."

Kristy opened her mouth, closed it again.

Zachary reached across the table and patted her hand. "It's okay," he said. "You're probably too young for me, anyway."

Kristy heard herself laugh, and the sound caught her off guard. "Your last wife," she said, "was in her twenties."

"So you *have* been reading up on me." Zachary grinned.

"I've seen most of your movies," Kristy admitted lightly. Now that Dylan was out of her personal space, she could breathe again, and the heat was subsiding. "And I might have read an article or two."

"But you're not one bit taken with me, are you?"

"Not one bit," Kristy said, smiling.

"The cowboy?"

"I knew him when," Kristy answered, her smile fading.

"He's jealous as hell, you know. Because you're here with me."

Kristy sighed, annoyed with herself. She wanted to go to Dylan, tell him straight out that this wasn't a repeat of the Mike Danvers situation. At the same time, she was too stubborn to do something so openly codependent. Yes, there was something powerful happening between her and Dylan, but they hadn't made any commitments. They weren't even at the dating stage—and might never get there, the way things were going.

"He'll leave town," she said, and then could have bitten off her tongue. "It's only a matter of time."

"He's a rover, our Dylan Creed?"

"He's a rodeo cowboy," Kristy answered. "Same thing."

Zachary snapped his fingers. "Now I know where I've seen him before," he said. "He's done stunt work in a couple of my movies. He's one of the best in the business—absolutely fearless."

Absolutely fearless.

That was Dylan, all right.

And the only thing worse than loving a rodeo cowboy was loving a stuntman. Dylan might *claim* he wanted to settle down, make a real home in Stillwater Springs, but when he got bored, or ran low on money, he'd park sweet little Bonnie somewhere safe and be off again.

Remember that, she told herself.

Not that she'd ever taken her own good advice, at least where Dylan was concerned.

An hour later, the option agreement signed, Kristy let herself in through the kitchen door at home, and the instant she stepped into the darkened house, Winston shot past her in a white blur.

She paused, alarm prickling the pit of her stomach.

Was someone in the house?

It wasn't like Winston to dart out like that. His usual M.O. was to scrabble at the legs of her jeans with his forepaws until she picked him up for a nuzzle and some cuddling.

"Hello?" Kristy called.

Nothing.

She was being silly, that's all. She was on edge because of the extra bodies in Sugarfoot's grave, and the story that was about to break over her life like a tsunami. And Dylan.

She turned, after setting her purse aside on the counter, and called to Winston.

He ignored her, though she heard a snarly *meow* out there in the gloom.

What was the *matter* with that cat?

She closed the door, flipped on the lights, filled the coffeemaker and set the timer for morning. The house still felt strange, as though it had drawn in a breath and held it.

She was *really* stressed out.

As a matter of principle, Kristy forced herself to venture into the dining room, then the living room beyond. She switched on the lamps at either end of her chintz couch, listened.

Her imagination took off, despite her determination to behave like a rational person.

Suppose Sheriff Book was hiding somewhere, behind a door, or in the pool of dark at the top of the stairs, planning to finish her off before she told anybody what she suspected?

*Ultra*silly, she thought. She'd already told someone—Dylan—and Sheriff Book knew that, because she'd put her cell phone on speaker at Dylan's house that day, and the two men had talked to each other.

Besides, Floyd had been her father's best friend.

He'd come to her college graduation, stuffed into a suit he probably hadn't worn since his own college days.

He was kind to animals.

He fetched books to and from the library on a regular basis, because his invalid wife loved to read.

He was *not* a monster.

Kristy had just come to all these perfectly sensible conclusions when she heard a footstep directly overhead, in one of the guest rooms.

Get out now, her practical side warned.

But Kristy had another side—the stubborn one. This was *her* house, damn it, and she was more angry than she was afraid.

"Who's there?" she called, moving to the foot of the main stairway.

Still nothing.

"Hello?"

More footsteps, running ones, clattering down the hall, headed for the back stairs, leading to the kitchen.

She bounded in that direction.

There was a shout, followed by a crash, and then a figure in a black running suit landed in a heap at Kristy's feet.

Freida Turlow.

Stunned, Kristy nonetheless bent over Freida's huddled form. "Are you all right?"

Freida sat up. "I'm—I'm okay, I think," she said sheepishly.

Kristy put her hands to her hips. "Next question— what the hell are you doing, prowling around in my house?"

Tears streaked Freida's dusty cheeks.

Kristy bent to help her up.

"You never changed the locks," Freida said.

"Don't try to make this about me," Kristy replied, taking the woman by the arm and leading her to a chair at the kitchen table.

Freida hobbled a little. "I think I sprained my ankle," she said.

"Sit down," Kristy ordered.

The other woman sank into a chair. "I know this seems weird—"

"*Seems* weird?" Kristy countered, though now that the fine hairs on the back of her neck had lain down again, she was a little calmer. "Freida, you scared me half to death!"

"I'm sorry." Freida sniffled. "I was just—"

"Just what?"

"Homesick, I guess. I wanted to see my old room."

"You could have knocked on the door and said that, instead of creeping around like some—some burglar."

Freida's smile was dreamy, and singularly odd. "You've changed it," she said. "My room, I mean. Taken out the window seat, pulled up the carpet—"

To keep herself busy, since she wasn't, it turned out, as calm as she'd thought a moment earlier, Kristy filled the electric teakettle and plugged it in, got tea bags and cups down from a cupboard. "You knew I was remodeling, Freida," she said. "I would have given you the tour if you'd just asked."

Freida sniffled again. Her strong shoulders stooped a little, under her sweat jacket. She'd always been athletic, running in marathons, lifting weights. "I'm sorry," she repeated. "Oh, Kristy, I don't know what possessed me to—to trespass—"

Kristy softened a little. Her heart had stopped pounding, and she was breathing at a normal rate again. "I guess you've been under a lot of stress," she said kindly. "What with Brett getting into trouble and everything."

Freida's face tightened. "Oh, yes," she said. "Brett. My baby brother. He's in treatment in Billings, you know."

"I knew he was in treatment," Kristy said. "It must be a relief, knowing he's getting the help he needs."

"I shouldn't have treated Briana Creed the way I

did," Freida muttered, though her expression belied her words. "At the reading-group meeting, I mean."

Kristy didn't speak. She plopped tea bags into the cups and waited for the kettle to whistle out steam.

"You like her, don't you?" Freida prodded.

"Yes," Kristy said, peering out the window over the sink, hoping to catch a glimpse of Winston. She prayed he hadn't run away, or gotten hit by a car.

"Do you like me?"

It was such a strange question that Kristy turned to look at Freida, frowning. *Did* she like Freida Turlow? The answer was no, but she didn't *dislike* her, either. They had little in common, and there was a big difference in their ages.

"I've known you all my life, Freida," she hedged.

Freida seemed mollified. "Everything's changing," she remarked. "Mama and Daddy are gone. I don't live in this house anymore—and Brett—"

The kettle shrilled. Relieved, Kristy poured water into the two cups she'd set out and brought one to Freida. Sat down across the table from her.

"I hear there's someone else interested in the ranch," Kristy ventured. "Besides Zachary Spencer, that is."

For a moment, Freida's expression hardened, and Kristy didn't think she'd answer.

But she did, in her own good time. "It's a money game, real estate," Freida said, with a verbal shrug. "Some outfit called the Tri-Star Cattle Company put in a bid."

"Tri-Star Cattle Company," Kristy echoed. "I've never heard of them."

"I hadn't, either, before some lawyer called from Las Vegas and doubled Zack's last offer."

Zack?

Of course. Zachary Spencer.

Evidently, Freida and the movie star were chums, as well as business associates. Probably neither here nor there, Kristy concluded, but she filed the tidbit away in the back of her brain anyway.

"Why didn't you tell me?"

Freida sighed. "Because I regretted being so mean about it before," she said. "Okay, I lost my parents, and my home. But so did you, Kristy. I shouldn't have taken my own emotional problems out on you."

This was either the new Freida or a clone from outer space. "Did the bank accept Tri-Star's offer?" Kristy asked.

"They will if Zack doesn't top it within twenty-four hours," she said. "And I don't think he's going to. He said something about a place on the other side of Missoula, one that wouldn't need so much work."

"How much are these Tri-Star people willing to pay?"

Freida finally bristled. "Why should I tell you that?"

"Because I caught you sneaking around in my house, and I could have called the sheriff, but I didn't. You owe me a favor, Freida."

"Fair enough," Freida agreed, but only after mulling it over for a few moments. "Madison Ranch is a big chunk of land, with a lot of water and good grass for grazing. Tri-Star offered eight figures."

Eight figures. Even if she sold her family's story to Zachary Spencer, she wouldn't have enough to top an offer like that, and if she had, Tri-Star would probably just keep bidding.

The ranch was lost for good, and she might as well face it.

Freida stood, her tea untouched. "I'd better be going," she said. The strange tone was back.

A little shiver ran down Kristy's spine. "You're not yourself, Freida. Should I call someone?"

Freida gave a bitter little laugh. "Like whom? I'm all alone in the world, Kristy. Just like you."

Just like you.

Kristy took the high road, though it was hard. "Let me drive you home," she said, starting to rise.

"I'd rather walk," Freida said.

Kristy wasn't going to argue. She saw Freida to the back door, watched the other woman head for the gate in the garden fence, step onto the sidewalk beyond.

"Winston?" Kristy called, when she was sure Freida was gone.

He came then, rushing at her, winding himself around her ankles, purring apologetically. Kristy scooped the neutered tom up in her arms, nuzzled his neck.

"It's okay," she told him. "You're safe."

He answered with a doubtful and rather plaintive meow, and wriggled out of her grasp, landing on the floor with a graceful thump. Then he stood looking back at her, with his blue Persian eyes, oddly reminiscent, for a fraction of a second, of Dylan's.

The cat walked a little way, then stopped, looked back at her.

Kristy fumbled to fasten the dead bolt. Since Freida obviously still had a key, she'd get the locks changed first thing in the morning.

"Meow," Winston said, waiting.

Kristy approached him.

He led the way up the rear steps, skirting the crumpled painting tarp Kristy had forgotten there. She gathered it up, grateful Freida hadn't broken her neck when she tripped over the thing.

At the top of the stairs, she folded the tarp, set it aside.

Winston stood in the shadow-draped hallway, as if waiting for her again.

Was he trying to lead her somewhere?

"Way too Disney," Kristy told herself, primarily because she needed to hear another human voice, even if it was her own.

"Meoooow," Winston repeated insistently.

"All right," Kristy said. "I'm coming."

He proceeded straight into the room that must have been Freida's once—it was the only one where she'd torn out the window seat, and her visitor had definitely mentioned that.

An eerie feeling came over Kristy as she switched on the light in that empty room, its fine hardwood floor bare of the ugly lavender shag carpet she'd torn up even before tackling the master bedroom.

Winston sat, tail switching, in the center of the room.

"What?" Kristy asked, irritable now, and still on edge.

Winston got to all fours again and strolled toward the closet.

Kristy followed, frowning. Turned on the single bulb dangling inside the walk-in.

And gasped.

The drywall at the back had been torn out, to reveal the framework and insulation behind it. The crowbar

Freida had used to do the damage was still lying on the floor, covered in a layer of fine gray dust.

A picture came into Kristy's mind—Freida, manstrong, wielding that crowbar. Her stomach pitched; she imagined waking up in the night, seeing the woman standing over her bed, ready to bash her to a pulp with the heavy iron tool.

"Oh my God," Kristy whispered, dropping to her knees, suddenly unable to stand. *"Oh my God."*

Winston brushed against her again, meowing softly now, as though to comfort her.

Call the sheriff, she thought.

Clearly, Freida had been looking for something. Why else would she rip out a wall?

But what could it have been? Kristy would have gladly turned over any forgotten possession.

Gripping the closet doorjamb, Kristy pulled herself to her feet. Swayed slightly.

She *couldn't* call Sheriff Book, she decided belatedly—she was afraid to be alone with the man.

She waited, leaning against the woodwork, until she could trust her legs to support her. Then, every motion deliberate, she made her way into her own room, sat down on the edge of the bed, reached for the phone and dialed a number she'd tried to forget.

And when he answered, all she could get out was, "D-Dylan?"

CHAPTER NINE

THE INSTANT Dylan's name came out of Kristy's mouth, she wished she hadn't called him in the first place, and seriously debated whether to go on with the conversation or hang up.

It was too late, of course, to do that.

"Kristy? Is that you?"

She heard honky-tonk music in the background, laughter and the ring of bottles and glasses and the click of colliding pool balls. All of it coalesced, in Kristy's mind, transporting her to a smoky, neon-lit Skivvie's Tavern.

"Yes—I—" Kristy stopped, shoved a hand through her hair, groping for an excuse. "I'm sorry—I must have gotten your number mixed up with—"

The lame attempt was met with a frostbite silence on Dylan's end.

"I'll just say goodbye now and—" What was wrong with her? Why couldn't she complete a simple sentence?

Because she'd found a prowler in her house, that was why. And that prowler, a person she'd known all her life, had torn out the back of one of her closets with a crowbar. *And* because she didn't dare call Sheriff Book while she was home alone.

"Did that guy do something to you?" Dylan asked. He sounded sober, but he was Jake Creed's son. *That* man could have drunk half the county under the table, and never slurred his words.

"What guy?" Kristy asked, a split second before she realized that, of course, he meant Zachary Spencer. "Oh. No—no, it's nothing like that." She paused, struggling with herself, and finally lost the battle. "Are you at Skivvie's?"

The place was a dive—it should have been condemned long ago, in Kristy's admittedly librarianesque opinion. She'd seen more marriages break up because of that joint than she could count.

"Yes," he answered flatly, and there was a dare in his tone. He might as well have said, *What of it?*

"Okay," she said, sounding half again too perky.

"Jim Huntinghorse is here—campaigning," Dylan told her. "Logan and I decided to stop by and talk politics for a while. Briana's taking care of the kids."

Why was she still on the phone? Calling Dylan had been a mistake—he was going to think she was hysterical or hormonal or…something.

"Well, like I said, I called you by accident so I'll just say—"

"Cut the crap, Kristy," Dylan broke in. "I know when you're upset—and when you're lying. What's going on?"

She closed her eyes. "You're going to think I'm an idiot."

"Try me."

"When I got home from the café tonight, I found Freida Turlow in my house. She said she just wanted to see her old room again, but I—well— It scared me, Dylan."

"Did you call Floyd?" Dylan's voice was taut.

"Of course I didn't," Kristy whispered, as though Floyd Book might be hovering just outside her bedroom door, ready to pounce. Another shiver trickled ice-cold down her back. "Do you think I want to be murdered?"

Dylan laughed. "Yo, Kristy. Get a grip. You've been checking out too many thrillers from the library. Floyd is the *sheriff,* and he's a good man."

Kristy flushed. "I have not been reading thrillers," she lied. The truth was, she couldn't get enough of them, and the gorier they were, the better she liked them. "And you yourself said you wouldn't turn your back, the way Floyd did, if you thought your best friend had killed someone—"

"I'm coming over there."

"Dylan, no, I really—"

He hung up.

Kristy replaced her bedside phone in its cradle. Sat forlornly on the side of her bed, staring at the wall. "Are you *deliberately* trying to get yourself seduced?" she asked aloud. "Dylan, plus you, minus everybody else on the planet, equals *sex.*"

Skivvie's wasn't very far away—nothing was, in a town of less than ten thousand people—and hardly five minutes had passed when she heard Dylan's truck pull up outside. Before she could hike down the front stairs, he was pounding on the front door.

She let him in. "I suppose you think I want sex," she said.

Dylan stared at her.

She was pretty surprised herself. The heat of embarrassment suffused every part of her. "I didn't mean—"

"What's going on between you and the movie star?" Dylan demanded, shutting the front door behind him.

"Nothing!" Kristy retorted, then wished she hadn't taken the bait so easily.

Dylan folded his arms. His hair was a little rumpled, but he didn't look or smell drunk, so maybe he really *had* been talking politics with Logan and Jim over at Skivvie's, not trying to live up to his father's reputation. "You went out to dinner with him," he said slowly, but she saw uncertainty in his eyes. "He's famous and—"

"He's not my type, Dylan."

Dylan thrust out a sigh. "I'm sorry, Kristy," he said. "I shouldn't have asked. It was none of my business."

Inside, where she hoped it wouldn't show, Kristy was delighted. *Dylan was jealous?* "You can go now," she said quickly, because various parts of her anatomy were on the verge of meltdown. "Finding Freida here kind of freaked me out, that's all. I shouldn't have bothered you with it."

He took a step toward her.

"Don't you have to go home and look after Bonnie?"

"She's spending the night with Briana and Logan," Dylan said. And moved closer.

"Oh," Kristy said. "Logan and Jim must be expecting you back at Skivvie's pretty soon, then."

"The party broke up when you called," Dylan answered. His eyes were serious, hungry—and such a perfect blue that Kristy thought she could get lost in them, like a bird surrounded on all sides by nothing but sky, not knowing up from down or left from right. "There's nothing between you and the movie star?"

Kristy couldn't speak. She was afraid she'd ask Dylan to make love to her, then and there, if she did. She

seemed to have no control over her vocal cords at all—
everything that entered her mind immediately popped
off her tongue.

He reached out, hooked a finger in the waistband of
her jeans and tugged. The snap gave way, and then she
was pressed against him. He was hot and hard. He
was—Dylan.

All man. Uncompromisingly so.

Kristy gave a soft groan.

Dylan plunged the fingers of his left hand into her
hair, tilted her head back and kissed her so thoroughly
that her knees almost buckled. "Yes or no, Kristy," he
rasped, when their tongues untangled and their mouths
broke apart. "Yes or no."

If she'd had her wits about her, Kristy would have
pretended she didn't know what he was talking about.
But she couldn't pretend, and she couldn't say no.

Not to Dylan Creed.

That, of course, left only one alternative. "Yes,"
she whispered.

He lifted her into his arms, carried her up the stairs,
Rhett Butler style.

"Where?" he asked gruffly, when they reached the
second-floor hallway.

She pointed in the direction of her room.

His strides were swift, his arms strong. Although she
knew better, knew she would live to regret this night,
Kristy let herself be swept away. She had simply needed
Dylan too much, for too long.

The bedside lamp was still burning in her room.

Dylan laid her gently onto the bed, stared down at her
for a long, incendiary moment.

The whole encounter felt predestined to Kristy. Profoundly inevitable.

"Do you have—something?" she asked, turning her head aside on the pillow, mortified. She wasn't on any kind of birth control, and she didn't keep condoms around; she hadn't had any reason to, after Dylan left town. Her engagement to Mike had never gotten beyond the handholding-kissing stage.

Poor Mike. She'd told him she wanted to save herself for marriage.

As if.

"I have something," Dylan assured her, with a hoarse chuckle.

Kristy's gaze swung to him—she should have been relieved; instead, she was stung. "Always ready?" she asked, with just the merest touch of sarcasm.

"I just bought them, Kristy," he told her, popping the snaps on his shirt. "This has been coming on ever since I stepped into the library the other day, and you know it as well as I do."

She *had* known, she realized. Her body, dormant for so long, had begun to awaken again, not just when Dylan first walked into the library, but probably when he passed the city limits. She'd always had a special sense where Dylan was concerned, a kind of global positioning system.

He took a packet out of his jeans pocket, set it on the bedside table.

"You're sure, right?" he asked.

She bit her lower lip, nodded. Until Dylan made love to her, she wasn't going to be able to think straight.

"Fast, Dylan," she whispered, blushing with embarrassment and need. "Fast and hard, this first time."

He undressed her very, very slowly, shoes and jeans first. Then he stretched out on the bed beside her, kissed her again, nibbled along the length of her neck, flicked at her earlobe with the tip of his tongue. When he bared her breasts, he paused to weigh them in his hands, chafing the nipples until they tightened.

Kristy whimpered again, arched her back.

He suckled at her right breast, lightly at first, and then harder. At the same time, he slid a hand down under the lacy waistband of her panties, parted her, stroked her with an easy, languid circling of his fingers.

"Oh God, Dylan," she cried, "fast and hard— *please*— It's been so long— I *need*—"

He kissed away her words, kissed away her breath and her sanity.

But he knew how to make love to Kristy, knew what she wanted. What she'd *always* wanted, since the very first time, long ago, in the high summer grass of the orchard where the bears came to feed.

He drew down her panties, reached for the packet, and all the while she writhed and undulated beneath him, seeking the only thing that would satisfy her.

He was inside her in one deep, breathtaking thrust, and Kristy's starved body immediately seized upon him. He raised himself onto his knees, pulling her with him, and held her cheeks in his hands, watching her face while she rode astraddle of him. And then she came, in one sweet, violent spasm after another, her head flung back, and she shouted his name, shameless and wild in the throes of an ever-rising satisfaction.

Dylan never let up on the friction, but when she finally sagged against him, spent, her body still quivering from its very core, he laid her down on the pillows again, hiked her legs up over his shoulders and went after his own release.

Instinctively, Kristy grasped the brass rails in the headboard of her bed, knowing that even though she'd already given him everything, he would still want more. When the next orgasm began, it was more intense, more desperate, more shattering than any that had gone before.

When Dylan's powerful body plunged deep and stiffened, Kristy wrapped her legs around his hips and bucked beneath him, no longer sure whether she was giving or taking, whether they were two creatures or one, set ablaze, fused, and sure to be consumed.

At long last, Dylan fell to the mattress beside her, his breathing ragged and swift. She buried her fingers in his hair, felt his skin, moist along the length of her own perspiring body.

"Was that 'hard and fast' enough for you?" he asked, much later.

Kristy giggled, snuggled close to him. "You may have noticed that I enjoyed it," she answered.

"Are we going to regret this in the morning?" He kissed her eyelids, her temples, the corners of her mouth.

"Maybe," Kristy purred, her senses already stirring again. She found a lock of his hair around one index finger. "Probably. *Definitely.* But all I care about is right now."

He chuckled. Kissed her neck. And got out of bed, headed for the bathroom adjoining her room. When he came back, he had moonlight caught in his hair, silver glancing off gold.

And he was frowning.

She sat up, alarmed by his expression. "What?"

"How do I put this?"

Her heart beat a little faster, and not because there would be more lovemaking before the night was over, and still more. "Dylan, *what's wrong?* You're scaring me."

"Let's just say," he answered grimly, "that they don't make condoms like they used to."

Kristy's mouth fell open.

"It broke," Dylan said.

"Oh my God," Kristy whispered, flipping through a mental calendar and gasping as she made the mind-blowing leap. "What if I'm pregnant?"

He had been standing in the middle of the room, gloriously naked. Now, he came back to bed, stretched out, gathered Kristy in his arms. Kissed the top of her head. "Then I guess we'll have to deal with it," he said quietly, sounding almost wistful.

"Dylan!"

He propped himself up on one elbow, gazing down at her with an expression she couldn't read, because at some point, one of them had switched off the lamp.

When had that happened?

Dylan traced the outline of her cheek with a lazy index finger. He seemed to exude tension, for all the distracted ease of his touch, and Kristy knew his mind was miles away.

"Dylan?" she asked, very softly.

"If there *was* a baby, you wouldn't—well—get rid of it or anything, would you?"

The question stunned Kristy, electrified her, all but shorted out her circuits. *"No,"* she said, furiously. "Of *course* I wouldn't. Dylan Creed, why on earth would you think—" She stopped. Stroked his hair—his wonderful, spun-gold hair—when he buried his face deeper in her neck. "Bonnie's mother?"

Dylan lifted his head, and the moonlight shifted to his eyes, turned them silvery. "Sharlene," he said hoarsely, "probably wouldn't even have told me what she planned to do—or that she was expecting my baby at all—if she hadn't needed money. I paid her to go through with the pregnancy—it was the only way she'd agree to carry Bonnie to term. I was supposed to raise our child—that was the deal. But when Bonnie actually arrived, Sharlene cried and wailed and claimed she'd die of grief if I separated the two of them. My guess is, she'd already gone through most of the money I gave her and decided a monthly child-support check would be just the ticket. At the time, though, I believed she'd actually bonded with our daughter, sucker that I was." He sighed. "I'm sure Sharlene loves Bonnie, in her own crazy way. But she's toxic. I never should have left Bonnie with her."

"Why did you?" Kristy asked, very quietly. Her heart ached.

Dylan thought, shook his head. "If I had it to do over again, I'd probably marry Sharlene. That was what she wanted. But my dad had three wives, and he never loved any of them, any more than I loved Sharlene, and it was hell for Logan and Tyler and me, at least when we were younger. Tyler's mother was so unhappy that she—" He paused, swallowed once, then again. Couldn't seem to go on.

Kristy laid a hand on his chest, felt muscle and bone and a beating heart under his skin, strong and steady. "I know," she said softly.

He swallowed visibly, and his eyes glistened in the

darkness as he stared up at the ceiling. "I didn't want to wind up treating Bonnie the way my dad treated us," he said.

"You could never have been like Jake," Kristy told him. She was as sure of that as she was of anything in the world.

"He probably thought he wouldn't turn out like *his* old man, either," Dylan said. "Not when he was my age."

Kristy understood then. She finally recognized the demon that had driven Dylan away from her the first time and might well drive him away again, child or no child. Although he probably wasn't consciously aware of it, he clearly believed that Jake's hell-raising and sorry luck and hard drinking were no one-generation fluke, but imprinted in his own DNA, as well as Logan's and Tyler's. *That* was the real reason he'd let Sharlene keep Bonnie, whether he knew it or not. He'd thought, at the time, even with all Sharlene's shortcomings, that his little girl had a better chance for a happy life with her mother than with him.

Because he was a Creed and, therefore, tainted. Perhaps even cursed.

"Oh, Dylan," she whispered. "You're *not* your father."

He sat up suddenly, pulling free of her, turning his back to sit on the side of the bed and reach for his jeans. He didn't answer or face her, but went on getting dressed instead.

He was leaving.

Again.

"Look at Logan," Kristy urged, hoping he wouldn't hear the desperation in her voice. "He's married. He's *happy.* And he's Jake Creed's son, too."

Dylan turned at last, buttoning his jeans. The same

moonlight that had gilded his hair and turned his blue eyes silver etched hard shadows into his face now. "How long do you think *that* will last?" he snapped.

"From what I've seen," Kristy said gently, trying hard not to cry, "I'd bet on forever."

"Forever is a fairy tale," Dylan said brusquely, picking up his shirt, jamming his arms into the sleeves. "Logan had two wives before Briana. Both times, he was climbing the walls, trying to claw his way out, before the first anniversary rolled around."

Kristy wondered how he knew what Logan's first two marriages were like when he'd been estranged from his brother for so long. Since Jake's funeral, in fact. Since Dylan got so drunk after the services that he and both his brothers were arrested for disorderly conduct and destruction of private property.

They'd torn Skivvie's to pieces, along with each other.

She'd seen Dylan the next morning, after Sheriff Book let him go, and that was when they'd had the argument that eventually ended everything. He'd told her, standing on the sidewalk in front of Stillwater Springs' tiny courthouse and jail, that he was going back to the rodeo, and she could either wait for him or get on with her life, whichever she preferred.

She'd been stunned, and then angry. And ashamed, too, because everyone in Montana knew Jake Creed's *funeral,* for God's sake, had ended in a boozy brawl at Skivvie's.

"I don't know you anymore, Dylan," she'd said.

And he'd grinned, not in his usual engaging way, but cruelly. "Maybe you don't," he'd replied. He'd walked away from her without looking back, gotten into the secondhand truck he'd owned at the time and driven away.

Oh Lord. If only she'd known then what she knew now.

She sat up in bed, wrapped her arms around her sheet-covered shins, rested her forehead on her bony knees.

She knew by Dylan's voice that he was in the doorway—farther away, almost gone.

"If there's a baby—" he began.

Strength flooded Kristy; she could not have said where it came from. It was just *there,* all of a sudden, filling her. "If there's a baby," she said, propping her chin on her knees now, "I will raise him or her, and love them more than any baby has ever been loved before, in the history of this or any other world, and you can go straight to hell, Dylan Creed."

He hadn't moved, but his back was to her, and ramrod straight. He gripped either side of the door-jamb, like someone about to be blown away in a high wind, and gave a ragged laugh. "Oh, I'll probably get there one way or another," he said bitterly. "To hell, that is."

"You might be surprised," Kristy said, "to find out you're not the devil after all. That job's been taken."

"Are you just going to let me walk out of here?" he asked. "Without even checking to see if there are monsters hiding in closets or under beds?"

Kristy arched an eyebrow. Pursed her lips thoughtfully. Dylan didn't *want* to leave? That wasn't like him at all. He was great at exits, the king of the see-you-around-sweetheart saunter.

Without saying anything—what was there to say, after all?—she sighed, got out of bed, pulled on a robe. Pushed past Dylan into the corridor, flipped on a light.

The glare made her blink.

She marched to the room Freida had vandalized, showed Dylan the destruction in the closet.

He gave a low whistle, bending to touch the splintered drywall. "Remind me not to cross that woman," he said. It was as if the lovemaking—along with the heavy emotions it had brought to the surface—had never happened.

Except, of course, for the low hum throbbing in the nuclei of her cells.

"Crowbar," Kristy explained unnecessarily, pushing back her bangs.

"God, Kristy, did she threaten you?"

"No," Kristy said, after the briefest hesitation, which Dylan picked up on immediately. He turned, standing there in the closet, and looked straight into her face.

"But?" he prompted, the familiar muscle bunching in his jaw.

She lifted both shoulders, let them down again, thrust bunched fists into the pockets of her robe. It was yellow chenille, that robe, with a duck on the back, and she'd had it since her sophomore year in high school. Trust her not to have anything black and lacy and low-cut.

"I was a little scared," she confessed.

"Which is why you called my cell and then tried to convince me it was an accident?"

She drew in a breath to protest, but she could see by the quirk at the corner of Dylan's mouth that he wouldn't believe her if she lied. "I felt silly, Dylan. I called you in a panic, and then—"

He curved a finger under her chin. "And then you tried to backpedal," he said. "Why, Kristy?"

Because I love you.

She couldn't tell him that. She'd cry if she tried.

"I'm an adult," she said. "I've been taking care of myself for a long time now. No reason to stop managing my own life just because you're back in town." *For now.*

She didn't say that last part aloud, but it didn't matter. She could see that Dylan knew what she'd been thinking.

"No reason at all," he said slowly.

Kristy stepped back, swallowed. Averted her eyes so she wouldn't have to watch Dylan walk away.

Would he be back? Probably—and that only made matters worse, because with Dylan, it was a cycle. Get close, disappear. Come home, go back on the rodeo circuit.

Poor Bonnie.

Kristy was an adult. She could cope.

Bonnie could easily end up a victim, though.

The idea hurt so badly that Kristy grasped the door frame with one hand, following Dylan out of the guest room, so she wouldn't double over.

Dylan stopped, looked back at her. "Are you all right?" he asked.

Oh, just dandy, Kristy thought furiously. *You came here and you made love to me and now the force-field is back in place again and—surprise—you gotta be goin'.*

Things to do.

Hearts to break.

"See you," he said.

Kristy nearly *did* double over that time. *See you?*

The Dylan equivalent of slam-bam-thank-you-ma'am.

Well, what had she expected?

She trailed him down the corridor and the front stairs, saw him to the main door, shut it hard behind him, turning the dead bolt and putting the chain in place. Leaned against it when he was gone.

Winston appeared out of nowhere. "Meow," he said, looking almost ghostly in the relative gloom of the entry hall, where only the barest frayed edges of the corner streetlight reached.

"Oh, be quiet," Kristy replied, tightening the belt on her duck robe.

DYLAN CLIMBED INTO HIS TRUCK, slammed the door and started the engine with a roar. He leaned to glare at his reflection in the rearview mirror and snarled, "You dumb bastard."

Going home was out of the question, since Bonnie wasn't there.

Since Kristy wasn't there.

Hell, even his dog and horse were at Logan's place.

Skivvie's, once a favorite hangout, held no attraction at all.

He didn't feel like playing cards—he was in a mood, and that meant his game would be off. Poker required a kind of Zen attitude he couldn't muster under the circumstances, so going to the casino wouldn't help, either.

He'd head up to the swimming hole and skinny-dip, but at this time of night the mosquitoes would eat him alive.

Maybe Tyler was still around, though Logan seemed convinced their little brother had lit out after blacking his eye.

So he jostled his way overland, to the far side of Hidden Lake, where Tyler's log house stood on a high bank. It was the smallest of the three places on Stillwater Springs Ranch, but in some ways the best, since it was so secluded.

Dylan felt his hopes plummet as he rounded the last bend, saw the darkened windows and the empty driveway. Even the lake looked lonely, flickering under moving shards of moonlight.

"Hell," Dylan said.

He backed the truck up, turned around, still not ready to go home and face that old house. In a way, he felt guilty whenever he was there, intending as he did to bulldoze the whole shooting match to the ground and start over.

Starting over.

That was what Logan wanted to do: live down the Creed reputation, make the ranch—and the name—hum again. He'd even had some fantasies like that himself.

He'd marry Kristy, and the two of them would raise Bonnie, and a couple more kids, if they were lucky, and it would all be as perfect as a black-and-white sitcom from the 1950s.

Yeah, right. Kristy's father had killed a man, and hidden the body in a horse's grave. Let the secret eat him up from the inside.

And Jake? Well, he'd been a card-carrying son of a bitch, no two ways about it. Before he kicked the bucket himself, he'd put three good women in their graves—Logan's mother, Dylan's, and then Tyler's.

Still had a hammer in his hand and a coffin nail between his lips at two out of three weddings.

"Not bad, old man," Dylan said.

He pictured Briana's face, so full of love and hope. Those freckle-faced boys of hers, they clearly loved

Logan, too, though they still had a relationship with their birth father, who worked at an auto shop in town.

He thought of Bonnie, and then, inevitably, Kristy.

And was half-surprised to find himself driving along the cemetery road. He got out of the truck, in the glare of his headlights, to open the old gate—really just some weathered poles, wired together—lay it aside.

He drove on through, letting the gate lie.

Since there was nothing but footpaths once he got inside the cemetery, he parked the truck and walked to Jake's grave. Stood there, with just the moon, intermittently disappearing behind ragged clouds, to see by.

There were pockmarks in the ground, and the headstone was chipped. Dylan frowned, squatted to run his hand over the raw places on the marker.

"Bullet holes," Logan observed, stepping out of the darkness.

"Jesus," Dylan said. "You damn near gave me a heart attack."

Logan flipped on the flashlight he was carrying—had he been *trying* to sneak up on him?

"Sorry," Logan replied lightly.

"How did you know I was out here?" Dylan asked, a little annoyed at being caught visiting a grave in the middle of the night, like some—well—*grieving* person.

"Saw your headlights," Logan said. "I figured it had to be you."

"Could have been Tyler," Dylan answered, still crouched on the ground next to Jake's splintered headstone.

"He's long gone. Won't be back until he takes a notion to punch one of us out again."

The subject of Tyler was a sore one with Dylan. He'd been counting on tossing back a beer or two with his little brother, talking about everything but old times.

"He tries that with me," Dylan snapped, "I'll kick his ass."

Logan merely smiled at that. He looked weird in the glow of his flashlight, like a character in *The Blair Witch Project,* or Jake, when they were kids and he'd crept up on their "campsite" in the backyard, pretending to be a raving maniac, out for blood.

Not that he'd had to pretend all that hard. Being a maniac came easy to him.

"You said these were bullet holes?" Dylan asked.

Logan, dropping to his haunches, nodded. "Seems there are folks out there who still want to kill the old bastard, regardless of the fact that he's been dead for five years."

Having said this, Logan drew in a breath. It wasn't quite a gasp, but Dylan heard it as one.

"It's okay," he said. "You're entitled to your opinion. I didn't make up any songs about Dad being a hero, either."

They were both silent for a moment. Dylan was thinking of Tyler, and the way he'd fought so hard to believe Jake was a good man, the kind of father he'd needed and never had.

Something sour gathered in Dylan's mouth, and he spat.

"Bonnie all right?" he asked.

"Sleeping like a baby," Logan reported. "Briana's an old hand at taking care of kids, Dylan. Nothing's going to happen to Bonnie."

"Isn't it?" Dylan asked. The sour taste had been

replaced by a coating of rust, evidently. His voice scraped against his throat.

Logan stood. Dylan did, too.

"Mind telling me what that's supposed to mean?" Logan asked quietly, folding his arms.

Whatever his own misgivings might be, Dylan didn't want to throw cold water all over Logan's hopes for a future with Briana and the boys and the kids they expected to have together.

"Nothing," Dylan said.

Logan made a sound in his throat, a sort of contemptuous burst of breath. "Spare me the bullshit, Dylan," he rasped. "You're out here in the dark, wondering whether to cry or spit on the grave. I've been there. What's gotten under your hide?"

Dylan let out a long sigh. "Maybe I didn't do Bonnie any big favor, being her father," he said. "Now she's going to grow up as a Creed."

CHAPTER TEN

SLEEP, KRISTY SOON DISCOVERED, was out of the question.

She couldn't stop thinking about Dylan—reliving every kiss, every caress, every throaty man-sound he'd made in their most intimate moments. She actually considered taking a cold shower, but just imagining icy water pounding against her love-warmed skin, still pulsing with the echo of earlier responses, gave her goose bumps.

"I might as well do something constructive," she told Winston, who had curled up at the foot of the bed, perchance to dream. She got up, rummaged through a drawer, found sweatpants and a T-shirt reserved for painting and pulled them on.

Winston rose to all fours, stretched luxuriously and meowed.

There was still wallpaper to scrape in the little room in back of the kitchen, and door frames to paint—but somehow, the prospect was about as appealing as watching the wood dry, and television sounded even worse.

When no better ideas came to mind, Kristy padded down the back stairs to brew tea, Winston following, and double-checked that the lock was turned and the chain was on.

The phone rang, startling her, and Kristy reached for the receiver automatically. Who could be calling her at this time of night, besides Dylan? Speculation ran wild: maybe Bonnie was sick. Maybe he wanted to come back.

But the voice on the other end of the line belonged to Floyd Book. "I was driving by on patrol," he said, "and I saw your lights go on. Everything okay?"

Kristy's stomach curdled. "F-Fine," she lied. "Everything is fine." She forced a cheerful, I-don't-*really*-think-you're-a-murderer note into her voice. "Since when do you, the big honcho, have to work the night shift? Don't your deputies take turns keeping the mean streets of Stillwater Springs safe for democracy between sunset and dawn?"

Floyd chuckled, but it wasn't a happy sound. "Right now, one of them is on vacation. The other is on sick leave—he says it's flu, but I think he doesn't have the stomach for exhuming bodies. Passed out cold when he saw the girl."

A shudder went through Kristy, and she closed her eyes against images of crumbling flesh, disintegrating hair and old bones. It didn't help.

She thought of reporting Freida's break-in, but since she didn't plan to press charges and didn't want to give Floyd an excuse to stop by, she stuck with her original decision. "Has the girl's family been notified?"

"Yes," Floyd said, and there was a ring of sorrow in his voice. "There was no point in their viewing the body, but they identified the ring she was wearing. As soon as the forensics report is in, the remains will be released for a proper burial. I guess that'll bring the Clarkstons some closure, but the bottom line is, they've still lost

their daughter for good, and nothing is going to change that." He sighed heavily. "That damn election can't come too soon to suit me—but there was a time when I sweated out the vote-counting myself. Thought I'd die of disappointment, back when I ran against old Warren Holter fresh out of the army, if I didn't win."

Kristy wanted, suddenly and fiercely, to blurt out the question pounding in the back of her mind.

Did you kill that girl?

She bit down hard on her lower lip to forestall the urge. Since there was still a chance that Floyd Book hadn't figured out what she suspected, it was safer to keep her mouth shut.

"I won't keep you," he said, when she was silent. "Just wanted to make sure there wasn't any trouble at your place."

"Thanks," Kristy said. Her palm was moist, where she gripped the telephone receiver, and her fingers ached because she was holding it so tightly. "But I'm okay, really."

"If the reporters get after you too much, you call me," Floyd told her.

They said their goodbyes, and rang off.

Dylan had been right earlier, Kristy thought, once she'd replaced the receiver. She was letting her thriller-stoked imagination run away from her. Sheriff Floyd Book hadn't killed Ellie Clarkston. It was crazy to think he was capable of a heinous crime like that—he'd devoted his entire career to upholding the law.

Except, of course, when it came to the secret of Madison Ranch.

Even less likely to sleep than before, if that was

possible, Kristy went into her small study, off the living room, and logged onto her PC.

First, she ran a search on Ellie Clarkston and her disappearance.

Along with newspaper articles, there were a surprising number of private references to the case online, even after all this time. Everything from video clips of the parents, John and Barbara, pleading with the public for any scrap of information that would help them find their daughter, to weird amateur sites offering theories as far-fetched as alien abduction, governmental conspiracies and human sacrifice. There were blogs, too, devoted to probing the psyche of your average, run-of-the-mill serial killer, many with a tone a little too admiring for Kristy's taste, message boards for "fans" of poor Ellie and other young women like her. And worse, for their killers.

Kristy's blood ran cold, looking at all that stuff. It creeped her out to think there were people out there with nothing better to do than post the gleefully macabre dredges of their sick minds on the Web.

She clicked her way out of the cyber-landfill.

Surfing the Net was clearly no cure for insomnia, but she was still too antsy to read or watch TV, and except for a midnight run to Wal-Mart or bellying up to the bar for a tall one over at Skivvie's, which would certainly delight the gossips, there weren't a lot of choices.

She could shower, dress and go to the library to catch up on work, except that there *wasn't* any work to catch up on, because she was ultragood at her job, and besides, the dark of night seemed threatening, even oppressive.

If Sheriff Book hadn't killed the Clarkston girl, then

someone else had. Perhaps it had been a stranger, passing through—but what if the killer was a local? What if it was a person she spoke to all the time, in the grocery store, the post office, the library?

That idea was even scarier than the evil-stranger scenario.

She blinked when an instant message showed up in the lower right-hand corner of her monitor, as startling, in its own way, as Sheriff Book's unexpected phone call had been.

Hi, began the message. Why'd you rush off? The screen name, charmingly, was Gravesitter.

Who the hell was *Gravesitter?*

Common sense and curiosity squared off on the field of Kristy's mind, and curiosity won, as it usually did in any matter not related to her job. Who's asking? Kristy typed in response.

Saw your name when you stopped by our message board a few minutes ago, came the immediate and blithe answer, written e.e. cummings–style and full of misspellings. *And* neatly skirting her question. You should have stuck around. We're not a bad bunch.

No, Kristy thought grimly, *you just sit hunched over a computer in some gloomy basement room, knee-deep in dirty laundry and fast-food wrappers and greasy pizza boxes, chatting about the redeeming qualities of serial killers.*

Stopped in by accident, Kristy typed. Not my kind of thing.

Too good for us?

She bristled. *Well, yes, as a matter of fact,* she thought. *Not being a monster and a ghoul, I guess I am.* How had this guy—or woman—been able to send her an instant message, or any other kind? She certainly hadn't registered for any of the message boards she'd visited.

But, then, there were computer geeks everywhere—even in small Montana towns three miles from nowhere. A few patrons, mostly junior high kids, used the donated PCs at the library, and while she'd never tried to pick up their cyber-trail after they logged off and skulked away, she would now, and at the first opportunity, too.

The instant-message window came up again, with a chiming sound. Kristy? Are you still there?

Kristy? Are you still there?

How had this person known her name? It wasn't in her e-mail address.

WHO ARE YOU? Kristy demanded, punching the keys hard as she typed the demand.

Just a friend, came the response. By the way, it's good to know you're sleeping with Dylan Creed again. Some of us thought you were frigid.

Furious—and scared—Kristy logged off immediately—and then wished she hadn't. Now, there would be no way to trace the messages back to their source—or would there? How many Gravesitters could there be, out there crawling around the Web like spiders stalking flies?

Kristy logged back on. Ran a search.

Thousands. That's how many Gravesitters there were. Thousands upon thousands.

Kristy pushed back from the desk, got to her feet and paced, Winston matching her step for step.

Just a friend—by the way, it's good to know you're sleeping with Dylan Creed again—some of us thought you were frigid.

A local, obviously.

Freida? Sheriff Book? Julie Danvers?

Or just some high school kid, messing with her head?

It was time to stop playing Nancy Drew, she decided. Make herself a second cup of herbal tea—the first had grown cold—soak in a hot bath, relax.

Relax. Yeah, right.

After the Freida incident.

After Dylan's lovemaking had turned her soul inside out.

After Gravesitter's chummy little instant messages.

And with the looming prospect of a media circus, centered around the drifter her dad had killed, in her defense and maybe his own and her mother's, as well, and the finding of Ellie Clarkston's body. Not to mention her doubts about Sheriff Book, a man who'd been like an uncle to her, if not a second father.

She tried the herbal tea anyway, and the hot bath, too.

And when the sun rose the next morning, Kristy was on hand to greet it.

As IT TURNED OUT, filing the custody papers was sort of anticlimactic, as far as Dylan was concerned. Once it was done, bright and early the morning after he and Kristy had made love, there was nothing to do but wait for the slow wheels of justice to grind into motion.

Dylan had met Logan in front of the tiny courthouse in Stillwater Springs at 9:00 a.m. sharp, when the place opened, wearing his best jeans, polished boots and a freshly purchased white shirt with the folds still in it, only to find his big brother sporting a snazzy lawyer suit, dress shoes buffed to an intimidating shine and a tie.

Logan had read his expression, grinned and slapped his shoulder. "Relax, cowboy," he'd said. "There's no need to dress up."

This is *dressed up,* Dylan had thought, panicked. What if the judge thought he was a slob, and couldn't provide an orderly environment for Bonnie?

Except, they didn't see the judge. They didn't see anybody but Fred Brill, the bored and balding clerk who'd worked the front desk at the courthouse since Reagan's first term in office, if not longer. Logan saw that the documents were stamped and shuttled into the system, such as it was, and that was it.

"Now what?" Dylan demanded, as they walked outside again, onto the tree-shaded sidewalk.

"Now, we wait," Logan answered.

"Why'd you put on a suit, if you knew we didn't have to go before a judge?" Dylan asked, resettling his hat.

"Sometimes," Logan said, "I just like to look like a lawyer." He indicated the Marigold Café, just down the street, with a nod of his head. "Let's get some breakfast."

Since practically every parking space on Main Street was filled, an unusual phenomenon in Stillwater Springs at any time of day, they left their separate trucks in the courthouse parking lot and walked to the Marigold. There were vans bearing the logos of several national networks, and the closer Dylan got to the front door of the restaurant, the less of an appetite he had.

"They're here to get the story on Kristy's dad," he mused, worried.

"Yeah." Logan nodded. "And the Clarkston girl. Damn. Who'd do a thing like that?" It was a rhetorical question, with no answer expected, so Dylan didn't offer one.

He took hold of the door handle and pulled. He'd woken up on the wrong side of the bed that morning, because things had ended badly with Kristy the night before, after all that brain-bending sex, and because he kept imagining Sharlene and the current boyfriend zeroing in to grab Bonnie. The thought of a pack of newshounds baying at Kristy's heels did nothing to improve his mood.

The café buzzed with chatter. Dylan and Logan got the last two seats in the place and ordered coffee. When it came, Dylan took a sip and almost spat it out—the stuff tasted like battery acid.

Logan didn't seem to notice. He sipped away, scanning the crowd, taking people's measure, in that way he had. "I imagine Kristy's expecting a blitz, but it wouldn't hurt to warn her, just the same."

Dylan was up for an excuse to talk to Kristy. He felt bad about the way he'd acted last night, but the truth was, it scared the hell out of him, the things she made him feel. As teenagers, they'd had cosmic sex and thought they loved each other. Now, Dylan realized neither one of them had had a clue.

Love was a desperate thing, fierce and ferocious, capable of consuming a man like invisible fire.

Logan watched him intently. "Are you all right?" he asked, and he sounded as if Dylan's answer would really matter to him.

"No." Dylan sighed, rubbing his unshaven chin with one hand. The roughness matched his state of mind—sandpaper against bare and tender hide. "I don't think I am."

"Bonnie?"

"Partly," Dylan admitted. "I'm scared shitless, Logan. I can't let Sharlene raise her, but I don't know jack about bringing up a kid—especially a *girl* kid." He paused, at once holding back the question and forcing it past his throat. "What if I'm like Dad?"

"Make the same choices he did," Logan said quietly, "and you will be."

"Is that enough?" Dylan asked doubtfully. "Just making different choices, I mean? This hell-raising thing runs deep with the Creeds—all the way back to old Josiah's day. Even further, for all I know. Suppose it's genetic?"

One side of Logan's mouth quirked up in what looked like rueful amusement. "It's about time somebody tried to find out, don't you think? Dug in their heels and said, 'By God, this is it, it stops *here,* in this generation'?"

"You're really serious about this."

"You sound surprised," Logan said mildly.

The food came. The conversational din surrounding them had long since faded to a buzz, like distant bees droning in the orchard out home.

Logan, clearly hungry, tucked into a short stack with a side of ham. Dylan stared down at his own plateful of bacon and eggs and couldn't recall ordering it. He left his knife and fork where they were—wrapped up in a paper napkin.

"I don't mind admitting," Dylan said, at some length, "that I have my doubts. After all, you've been married twice already, and I've never known you to stay in one place long."

Logan chortled at that, chewed and swallowed. Took a sip of his coffee. "I guess I can't blame you."

"What happened, Logan? What made you even want to change?"

Logan mulled his answer over for a while before giving it, which was like him. "I got curious about our distant cousins, the McKettricks, after one of them—Meg—sent an e-mail via a half-assed Web site Cassie set up one time, when she was on a 'save the Creed heritage' kick. There are McKettricks all over the place, but the main bunch lives outside a little town in Arizona, called Indian Rock, on the Triple M Ranch. They're a rowdy crew—a lot like us in some ways—but they're a *family.* With all their differences, and their disagreements, they'll stand back-to-back to defend each other, when trouble comes. It struck a chord in me—I wanted that for the Creeds."

"We're related to the McKettricks?" Dylan marveled. "I knew a Jesse McKettrick on the rodeo circuit."

Logan grinned. Nodded. "Yup," he said.

Dylan shoved a hand through his hair, dared to dream, if only for a moment, that Logan's vision—a thriving ranch, a solid family, a new course for future generations of Creeds to follow—could be fulfilled.

Bonnie, growing up proud of her name, secure on a piece of ground she could always call home, no matter where she wound up living as an adult. Folks there, ready to take her part if she needed help.

The thought made Dylan's eyes burn. Suddenly, he wanted to print out that disk full of pictures Logan had given him a couple of weeks back. He wanted to *see* the people he came from—misguided, yes, but tough as hell. What were their stories? What had they hoped for, dreamed of? Who had they loved—and hated? Was there nothing left of them, save the dusty skeletons moldering in the old cemetery on the other side of the orchard, out there on the once-famous Stillwater Springs Ranch?

Logan seemed to read Dylan's mind, though most likely everything he was feeling in that moment showed plainly in his face. "There are letters, Dylan. Pictures. Even a few diaries. And because Josiah published a newspaper, there's microfilm, too, at the library. Kristy can help you access it."

All his life, Dylan had felt like a lone link from a rusty, broken chain. Now, he knew he was connected, not only to Logan and Tyler, and to the land itself, but to all those Creeds who had gone before and, more important, to those who would come *after*—starting with Bonnie.

And for Bonnie alone, whatever his misgivings, he knew he had to try.

"I'm in," he said quietly.

Logan smiled, nodded. "Good."

That was all. Just "good."

But it was enough.

THE REPORTERS WERE WAITING on the library lawn when Kristy, wan with dread and lack of sleep, showed up for work that morning. They were crushing the grass, trampling the flower beds, blocking the sidewalk.

Kristy thought about turning her Blazer around and simply driving off, but sooner or later, she'd have to face the music, and the longer she waited, the harder it would be.

A man with a slick hairstyle and capped teeth immediately shoved a microphone into her face. "Did you know all along that your father had murdered a man, Ms. Madison? Were you a witness?"

Kristy squared her shoulders, shifted her handbag from right to left, flipping through her key ring for the one that would open the library's front doors.

Business as usual, Madison, she told herself.

"There is no proof that my father murdered anyone," she said, with freezing dignity, pushing past him.

A woman she recognized from a morning show out of Missoula stepped directly into her path. "Can you confirm that there was a *second* body found on your family's property? That of Ellie Clarkston, the missing teenager?"

"I think that's a question you should ask the sheriff, not me," Kristy said. She and the newswoman engaged in a brief glaring match, and Lois Lane finally stepped aside.

Kristy got as far as the steps in front of the entry doors before another question hit her, striking from behind, with the impact of a stone.

"Is it true that you've sold the rights to the story to a major movie studio?"

Kristy didn't turn around. Her keys felt slippery in her numb fingers. "Nothing definite has been decided," she said. If she could just get inside, among the books— she always felt safe, surrounded by books.

The reporters would follow, of course. The library was a public building; she couldn't keep them out.

Her stomach rolled. She managed to open the door, cross the threshold. White-teeth and Lois Lane were right behind her.

She turned to face them. "I have a library to open," she said. "If you wouldn't mind—"

"Just give us a statement," Lois pleaded. "Anything."

White-teeth watched her eagerly, ready to thrust the microphone at her again.

"I'm not at liberty to comment," Kristy answered, because that was what people always said on the TV news. "Sheriff Book is conducting the investigation. Why don't you ask *him* about the case?"

A figure appeared in the doorway behind them, rimmed in sunlight, too bright to identify.

Another reporter, no doubt.

Kristy's heart skittered. She felt trapped, cornered—in this, her sanctuary, of all places.

"But you *did* sell movie rights to Zachary Spencer," White-teeth persisted.

And then, blessedly, the figure in the doorway solidified into Dylan. Wearing a deceptively easygoing grin, he came to Kristy's side, slipped an arm around her. She blinked at the whiteness of his shirt, fresh out of the package if the creases were anything to go by.

"The library's closed today, folks," Dylan said.

Before Kristy could protest, he'd shuffled her back through the library and onto the porch. Left with the choice of following or being locked in—since Dylan had taken the keys from Kristy's hand and given them an eloquent jingle—Lois Lane and White-teeth trailed after them, blended in with their colleagues waiting on the lawn.

Dylan locked the doors, nodded affably to the startled throng and squired Kristy to his truck.

"Dylan Creed," she sputtered, "*what* do you think you're doing?"

"We're going to a cattle auction," he said.

"To a *what?*" Kristy gasped when he opened the passenger-side door, gripped her around the waist with both hands and hoisted her into the seat. "I'm supposed to be working—"

"You really think you can *work* with that rat pack hanging around?"

Kristy sighed, settled back in the seat, closed her eyes. "Running away never solved anything," she said.

"Sometimes," Dylan replied, snapping her seat belt into place, "it's the better part of valor."

"That's discretion," Kristy said. "*Discretion* is the better part of valor."

"Gosh," Dylan teased. "Thanks for clearing that up." With another grin, he shut the truck door, rounded the front end and got behind the wheel.

"They'll only come back, and back again, until they get whatever it is they want."

"No sense in making it easy for them," Dylan replied, gunning the engine and giving the horn a merry farewell toot as they sped away.

"I can't just go to a—a cattle auction."

"Sure you can." Dylan grinned. He didn't speak again, until they were past the city limits, headed toward Missoula. Then, his expression changed. "I'm sorry about last night, Kristy."

Great. The best sex of my life, and he's sorry.

"Still worried I might be pregnant?" Kristy asked, with a little tartness to her tone. "Forget it. I checked the calendar. Not ovulating."

She *had* checked the calendar, so that part, at least, was the truth. Whether she was ovulating or not was anybody's guess.

"Too bad," Dylan said. "I think we'd make a great baby together."

Kristy stared straight ahead, because if she looked at Dylan, he might see what she was feeling in her face. "Do me a favor," she said. "Don't mess with my head. I'm on overload as it is."

"Which is why you need a distraction. And a cattle auction is nothing if not distracting."

"A cattle auction," Kristy said, a little *less* tartly, because deep down, she was glad Dylan had decided to play white knight back there at the library, "is dusty, loud and boring." She paused. "And where is Bonnie?"

"With Briana," Dylan answered easily. "Logan and I had breakfast together this morning, after we filed the custody papers, and we got to talking about bringing the ranch back to its former glory. The next logical step is to buy more cattle. He's meeting us at the auction, after he changes out of the monkey suit."

"The monkey suit?"

Dylan grinned. "The one he wore to the courthouse. Said it made him feel more like a lawyer."

"Oh," Kristy said. One of her exchanges with Freida Turlow came to mind. "Have you ever heard of a company called Tri-Star? They made an offer on my folks' place, and Freida's sure the bank will accept it."

Dylan shook his head. "Doesn't ring a bell," he said.

She studied him, out of the corner of her eye, still too proud to look directly at him. "Something's different about you," she remarked, at some length.

"Is that so?"

"*Yes,* it's so. What are you up to?"

"Besides kidnapping the town librarian?"

"Stop it."

Dylan laughed, and buzzed down his window, and the wind danced in his golden hair. He *had* changed, and just since the night before, too. He seemed more substantial somehow, less transient, more of a reality and less of a dream. "I'm still me, Kristy. The guy who'd like to get you naked, right now, if we weren't on a public road, and unwind some of that tension coiled up inside you with a good old-fashioned—"

"Dylan, *stop.*"

"Orgasm," he finished. "Damn, if I hadn't promised Logan I'd meet him at the stockyards in Missoula—"

Kristy squirmed. She felt hot and achy—and wet. Now, she'd be on the ragged edge, all day, anticipating another round of lovemaking with Dylan. Exactly as he'd intended.

She sighed again. Rolled down her own window. *"Don't."*

"Don't," Dylan repeated.

"Stop."

"Don't stop," he said. "Where have I heard that phrase before?" He cocked his head to one side, pretending to think hard. "Oh, yeah. It was last night. I went down on you, and you said, 'Don't stop—oh, please, Dylan, *don't stop.*'"

The reminder made Kristy blush—and want him to go down on her again, right there in the truck, in the broad light of day.

She groaned.

Dylan laughed.

By the time they reached the stockyards, where the cattle sale was to be held, he had her so riled up that if he'd pulled into a motel parking lot instead, or even into the bushes alongside the road, she'd have been begging before he got her jeans unsnapped.

Dylan signed up for a bidding number and examined the livestock as calmly as if he hadn't been seducing her with words all the way from Stillwater Springs. When Logan arrived, wearing jeans, boots and a T-shirt, he didn't seem at all surprised to see Kristy there on a day when the library should have been open for business. After studying her face for a few moments, Logan grinned in a way that made her blush even harder.

Then he laid a hand on her shoulder. "It's good to see you, Kristy," he said quietly. "Briana's frying up a couple of chickens for supper, after the Great Debate, and we're both hoping you and Dylan will join us. Jim Huntinghorse will be there, too."

It sounded nice. An ordinary, sane, country thing to do.

Sure, Kristy imagined herself saying. *As soon as Dylan finishes what he's started, and gets me off, we'll be right over.*

"I'd like that," she said.

Dylan, busy checking out cattle until then, spotted Logan and started in their direction.

"Have you ever heard of a company called Tri-Star?" Kristy asked Logan, as an afterthought.

She saw something in his face, so subtle and quickly gone that she immediately concluded she'd imagined it. Without replying, he turned to greet Dylan with a handshake, and the moment passed.

Attending a cattle auction brought back a lot of memories for Kristy—as a child, she'd been to dozens of them with her dad. They'd sat in the bleacherlike seats, Kristy sipping a soda, Tim drinking coffee, with the hard Montana sun beating down on their heads, even through straw cowboy hats. In the early years, Tim Madison mainly bought calves. Later on, when things started going sour, he'd begun selling off his small herd—the heifers, the yearlings, and finally the bulls.

The bidding was brisk, once it got under way, but Logan and Dylan, sitting on either side of Kristy, held their own. By the time the auction was over, they'd bought some fifty head of cattle, between them.

Checks were written. Arrangements were made to transport the animals to Stillwater Springs Ranch.

"Want to stop someplace and have lunch?" Logan asked, when the three of them stood in the gravel parking lot, preparing to leave.

"We'll hold out for Briana's fried chicken," Dylan answered easily.

Amusement glinted in Logan's eyes. "See you at the debate," he said. "Jim needs all the support he can get."

Dylan nodded. "See you there."

Kristy waited until Logan had walked away, headed toward his truck, before giving Dylan an elbow in the ribs. "You might as well have told him straight out that we're going somewhere to screw our brains out!" she whispered.

Dylan laughed, but his eyes were solemn as he looked down at her. "Aren't we?"

"Aren't we what?"

"Going somewhere to screw our brains out?"

Kristy gave a strangled scream of frustration.

Dylan laughed again. "My place or yours?" He folded his arms to await her answer, eyes dancing. "Your place is closer, but mine is more private," he finally added.

"You are *impossible!*" Kristy stormed over to the truck and got in, after Dylan opened the locks with the fob on his key ring. It was mostly bluster, though, and he surely knew that.

Dylan nodded to a passing acquaintance, then climbed in to start the engine.

"Your place," Kristy relented, stubborn to the end.

Dylan leaned toward her, widened his eyes and exuded innocence. "I'm sorry, I don't think I heard you. What did you say?"

"Your place," Kristy repeated, through her teeth.

Dylan chuckled and put the truck in gear. "That's what I *thought* you said. My place it is."

CHAPTER ELEVEN

THERE WAS SOMETHING Kristy wanted to tell him, Dylan decided, watching her moving fitfully around his bedroom dressed only in one of his western shirts, her hair moist from the shower they'd taken together, after making love until they were both too spent to do it even one more time.

Dylan, wearing misbuttoned jeans and nothing else, lay on his side on the rumpled bed, head propped in one hand, just drinking her in through his eyes, through the pores of his skin. Even in the fading sunshine slipping dust-sparkled between the slats of the window-blinds, Kristy seemed to glow as if she were translucent, formed of ever-shifting light in soft, iridescent shades.

The dog, Sam, who had jumped onto the bed at a critical moment and made them both laugh even as they were sharing a noisy climax, had been trying to keep up with her. Now, the poor mutt sank to the floor with a low whine of dismay.

"Talk to me, Kristy," Dylan said, at long last.

She stopped, gazed at him in pained reluctance. Then she gave an oh-well-what-the-hell kind of shrug and came to sit gingerly on the edge of the mattress. Realizing she'd bolt if he touched her, Dylan withdrew his hand just before it would have spanned the small of her back.

Kristy bit her lower lip and stared down at the floor, which was still littered with all of her clothes and a few of his.

"Somebody knows," she finally said, her voice so soft that he barely heard her.

"Knows what?" he asked.

"About us," she answered miserably.

He chuckled. "Kristy, this is Stillwater Springs, not New York or L.A. Small-town people pick up on things like this pretty quickly."

She swallowed visibly, nodded, as though begrudging him the point. "But this is somebody mean," she said.

"What happened?"

Suddenly, Kristy was on her feet again, pacing again.

Sam gave a halfhearted whimper of protest, worn-out.

"I keep running to you with this stuff, like some frightened child!"

"Tell me."

She spilled a story then, the words practically tumbling over each other, about visiting Web sites the night before, ones relating to the lost girl found in Sugar-foot's grave, and then receiving an instant message from somebody with the screen name Gravesitter. Even telling him the tale, she shuddered, and hugged herself with both arms, as though chilled by a harsh wind.

"Whoever this bozo was," she said, winding it up, "he—or she—said they were 'glad I was sleeping with you again,' because up till then, they thought I was *frigid!*"

Hiding a smile, because it was fine with him if everybody thought Kristy was frigid, Dylan leaned to grab his travel alarm clock and check the time. They were due at the high school gym for the debate between Jim Huntinghorse and Mike Danvers in half an hour.

With a sigh, he sat up, took the liberty of massaging Kristy's shoulders through the thinning fabric of that old rodeo shirt. Kissed her left ear. "What do you care what people think?" he asked.

She pulled away from him, leaped to her feet, nearly fell over Sam. "It isn't that, Dylan," she said, agitated. "I get it that half the town—if not all of it—probably knows we're—" she paused, reddened "—*involved*. But don't you think this particular person's information was pretty specific? Whoever this 'Gravesitter' goon is, they knew we made love *last night*. How could they be so certain unless—"

That was it. She was still freaked out because of Freida Turlow's uninvited visit. He stood, slipped his arms around her waist, pulled her close against him. "Nobody was watching us through some secret peephole, Kristy. My truck was parked in your driveway. I came down your front walk tucking in my shirttails and semi-pissed-off. Any passerby could have figured out what we'd been up to. Hell, *Logan* knew the moment he got a look at you at the cattle sale today."

Kristy tensed, let out a long breath, rested her forehead against his shoulder. "It was probably some kid who hangs out at the library—"

"One with a crush on you, no doubt," Dylan said, resting his chin on the top of her head. "Just the same, when we're done hearing both sides of the political issues and chowing down on Briana's fried chicken over at the main ranch house, you'd better come back here with Bonnie and me and spend the night. Tomorrow morning, we'll hit the hardware store, and then I'll change the locks at your place. How does that sound?"

She looked up at him, eager at first, then doubtful. "Are you sure that's good for Bonnie? My staying the night, I mean?"

He caught Kristy's chin in his hand. "Hello?" he joked. "She's *two*. This will not scar her psyche, okay?"

"It will if we make as much noise as we did this afternoon," Kristy answered, her hands moving on his bare chest in a lapel-straightening kind of motion.

He gave her a smacking kiss on the mouth and a light swat on the backside. "We'll just have to be quiet," he said. "Now, let's roll. We're going to be late." And being late, when everyone else was already seated, would draw attention, with them coming in together, both walking an inch off the floor.

Dylan saw no need to point that out to Kristy—she was already as jumpy as the famed cat on a hot tin roof.

She got dressed again, after brushing auction dust off her jeans and long-sleeved T-shirt. He put on a fresh shirt, rebuttoned his pants, combed his hair. Pulled on socks and his best boots.

He'd made light of the whole "glad you're sleeping with Dylan again" thing, mostly for Kristy's sake, but the more he thought about it, the more it worried him. He'd planned to lease a double-wide the next day, have it hauled out to the ranch and set up as soon as possible, and get started on the barn and the new house.

All well and good, but even if he changed the locks at Kristy's, there were still all those reporters to worry about, and suppose this Gravesitter freak-job wasn't just annoying, but flat-out dangerous?

Having Kristy spend the night with him was one thing. But could he expect her to move out of that big Victorian in town and share his life on a long-term basis?

He was crazy about her; he'd come to terms with that much.

In fact, he'd marry her, if she'd have him.

But did he love her? Damned if he knew. He sure as hell felt *something* for Kristy Madison, and it was powerful. But was it love?

Or was he just caught up in the sex, and the driving need to provide Bonnie with a mother?

Kristy, and any other woman worth her salt, would want more than he had to offer, right at the moment.

Still, the thoughts saddened Dylan as he filled Sam's dish in the ranch house kitchen, with its sagging floors, outdated appliances and decades of Creed history saturating its very walls. Kristy was still in the bathroom, touching up her makeup with tubes and bottles from her purse.

Probably trying to tone down the orgasm-pink still pulsing in her cheeks.

Dylan smiled at that, went outside to feed Sundance and make sure he had water to last until they got home from Logan's—it would be late, most likely, when the party broke up. Bonnie would be asleep, and he'd carry her into the house, put her to bed.

And all the while, he'd know Kristy was around. That he could see her just by rounding a corner into another room, that if he called out her name, she'd answer.

That made him feel better.

THE HIGH SCHOOL GYM was packed, the bleachers full, folding chairs set up on the tarp-covered basketball court. A podium and two folding chairs stood on the stage, and Jim Huntinghorse sat in one, Mike Danvers in the other.

Logan and Briana had arrived first, with Briana's boys, and Bonnie fairly leaped off Briana's lap when she spotted Dylan coming toward her. The toddler bounded into her father's embrace, small arms outstretched, face shining.

Kristy's breath caught at the sight.

"Daddy!" Bonnie shrieked, overjoyed. "Daddy!"

Dylan laughed, nuzzled the little girl's neck until she squealed with delight. People on both sides of the aisle smiled warmly, though a few whispered behind their hands.

Kristy knew what they were saying, of course. Or, at least, the gist of it. *Where do you suppose that child's mother is?...They're at it again, Dylan and Kristy. That's what I heard...Some people never learn....*

Dylan had turned, Bonnie riding on one hip with both arms clenched around his neck, to beckon to Kristy. She realized she'd been standing alone in the aisle, like some thunderstruck fool, and went to him. Took one of the seats Logan and Briana had saved for them. Tried to ignore the stares she felt coming at her from every direction.

She sold *poor Tim Madison right down the river. Her own father! They'll splash his story all over kingdom come, you wait and see. Movies. Books! Where will it end?*

Where, indeed? Kristy wondered.

The mayor of Stillwater Springs, a UPS driver by day, was Julie Danvers's younger brother, George. He stepped up to the podium, tapped experimentally at the microphone, frowned and cleared his throat.

A genial type, married with three preschool children, George bore a slight physical resemblance to his sister, sharing her fair coloring and blue eyes, but he was chubby and balding. He brought his kids to the library a lot, and was always cordial to Kristy.

"It is my great pleasure," George began, sounding as if he meant it, "to introduce our two candidates for sheriff."

Feedback screeched through the aging sound system.

George pulled a face and put his hands over his ears, a gesture Bonnie, seated in Dylan's lap, immediately mimicked, while the audience chuckled encouragingly.

"We need some new equipment, George!" a man called good-naturedly from the bleachers. "The school board bought those speakers in 1957!"

Everyone laughed, including the youthful mayor. It was said that George was taking college courses online, and hoped to rise to the level of state politics, or even beyond, in due time.

"Well, Fred," George retorted immediately, "I can get a special levy on the ballot if that'll make you happy. Jack your property taxes up a few hundred dollars a year."

Cheerful boos and hoots rolled toward him in a great wave in response to that, although actually, Stillwater Springs was pretty good about voting for school levies and bonds. It was just that they were still paying for two new buses and a dozen computers.

Once the din settled down, George cleared his throat again and made another attempt at the microphone. "We flipped a coin backstage," he explained, "and Jim Huntinghorse goes first."

Mike mugged a little, bringing more laughs, and Jim grinned.

He looked nervous, though—to Kristy, anyway. Leaving his suit jacket draped over the back of his chair, he stood, straightened his tie and stepped up to the mic. Jim had been a rascal as a boy, running with the Creed brothers and getting into just as much trouble as they did. Now, he had a good job managing the local casino for the tribal council.

Logan and Dylan, along with a few others, clapped and called out encouragement.

Jim quirked a grin, glanced at his ex-wife, Katherine, seated prominently in the front row of folding chairs. "Thanks," he said.

Kristy prided herself on being an informed citizen, clear on the issues before every election, local, state or national, but that night, she couldn't think of anything but the way Dylan's strong upper arm felt, pressed against hers. When Bonnie scrambled into her lap, she was moved out of all proportion to good sense.

The little girl planted a wet smooch on Kristy's cheek before settling down.

Tears sprang to Kristy's eyes.

She redoubled her efforts to concentrate, but when Jim and Mike had both finished their speeches, she couldn't recall a thing they'd said.

It was only when Dylan took Bonnie, and they all got up to leave with everyone else, that Kristy spotted the TV cameras clustered at the back of the gym.

"It's business as usual in Stillwater Springs," White-teeth was saying into a portable microphone and a lens as they passed. "Even with two separate murder investigations officially under way, folks are interested in local politics." He smiled broadly, radiating condescension and insincerity. "Small-town America, at its best."

"Jerk," Dylan remarked, close to Kristy's ear, cupping her elbow in his free hand and shuffling her past the newspeople before any of the cameras could turn on her.

"Ms. Madison!" one of the reporters called, as she and Dylan worked their way through the slow-moving crowd. Like a wreck on the freeway, the media presence made folks rubber-neck, thereby causing a clog. "If we could just ask a few questions—"

"Keep going," Dylan murmured.

Logan, Briana and the boys were somewhere behind them.

Finally, *finally,* they were outside. Kristy, feeling as though she might smother, gasped for breath.

Bonnie tried to shift from Dylan's arms to Kristy's. He restrained her.

The child shrieked in protest. "Mommeeeeeee!"

Kristy closed her eyes for a fraction of a second, and when she opened them again, Dylan was looking right at her, his expression troubled. Thoughtful.

"Hand her over," she said, reaching for Bonnie.

Dylan hesitated—that hurt, in a way Kristy wouldn't have expected—then gave the little girl to her.

Bonnie immediately settled down, deflating against Kristy's shoulder like a little balloon. "Mommy," she whispered. "Mommy."

"Shhh," Kristy said gently, patting Bonnie's small back.

They reached Dylan's truck; he unlocked the doors,

secured Bonnie in her car seat, waited politely while Kristy settled herself in front.

In the backseat, Bonnie fussed a little, then fell asleep.

"She's worn-out," Kristy said, when Dylan was behind the wheel. "Probably from trying to keep up with Josh and Alec."

"I suppose," Dylan agreed, sounding subdued as he checked the rearview mirror and waited for a break in the traffic leaving the gym parking lot.

Kristy realized he'd been looking to see if any reporters were going to follow them, and turned quickly in her seat.

There were lots of cars and pickups, so it was hard to tell. Logan's rig pulled in directly behind them, almost as if he were running interference.

Nervously, Kristy turned to face forward again, her hands knotted on her blue-jeaned lap.

"Relax," Dylan said. "The ranch is private property. If the media turns up, Logan and I will run them off with a shotgun."

It was an unfortunate choice of words, given what had happened between her dad and the still-nameless drifter that long-ago night.

Kristy automatically flinched.

Dylan heaved a sigh. "I'm sorry," he said.

Kristy drummed up a smile, leaned a little to touch his arm.

Fifteen minutes later, they pulled through the gate at Stillwater Springs Ranch, with a whole trail of cars and trucks behind them. Jim Huntinghorse was right behind Logan and Briana, with Katherine and their young son. Anxiously, Kristy stood on the running board of Dylan's truck, one hand shading her eyes from the last dazzle of summer sunlight, but she recognized all the other vehicles as those of locals. Not a reporter in sight.

Relieved, Kristy took Dylan's hand and let him help her down off the running board. Stood by while he got Bonnie out of her car seat.

There were several horses in the corral beside Logan and Briana's new barn, and Kristy found herself drawn to them. Briana fell into step beside her, as they crossed the yard, linking her arm with Kristy's.

"Aren't they beautiful?" Briana asked quietly, when they reached the fence.

Suddenly, Kristy yearned to ride again. "Oh, yes," she breathed in response. *"Yes."*

"Dylan told me about your horse, Sugarfoot," Briana said, after a few moments had passed. "It must have been a terrible loss, Kristy."

Kristy swallowed, nodded. She'd vowed, when Sugarfoot was buried, that she'd never ride another horse. At the time, it would have seemed like a betrayal. Now, she understood that she'd lost a lot more than an excellent and faithful friend. She'd lost an important part of herself.

Dylan joined them, a wide-awake Bonnie riding happily on his shoulders. With a grin, he handed the little girl off to Briana and headed inside the barn without a word.

When he came out again, he had a bridle slung over one shoulder, and he was carrying a battered saddle and sheep's-wool pad. Without once glancing Kristy's way, even though Bonnie was crowing, "Daddy! Horsie!

Ride!" at the top of her tiny lungs, he selected a paint and began fitting it with the riding gear.

Kristy watched, mesmerized by the dusty, familiar grace of the ritual—man-saddling-horse—expecting Dylan to mount up when he was finished.

Instead, he led the horse to the fence.

"Logan says this is a good one," he told Kristy.

Bonnie tried to squirm out of Briana's arms, right over the fence.

Briana held her firmly.

"You mean, I—" Kristy stammered.

"Yes," Dylan said simply.

Kristy hesitated, glanced at Briana. Looked back at Dylan.

Then she climbed up the fence rails, perched herself on top while Dylan eased the horse into position alongside. Kristy shifted to the saddle; something inside her surged and then soared as she took the reins Dylan held up to her.

She hadn't noticed Logan saddling a second horse, a buckskin gelding, in a corner of the corral. But when Dylan had opened the pasture gate, Logan led the gelding to him. Dylan shoved a foot into the stirrup and hauled himself up with the expert ease of a man all but raised on horseback.

The feeling of freedom made Kristy laugh out loud as she prodded the paint to a trot, then a gallop, then a run. The wind tossed her hair, and the good scents of grass and dirt and horse filled her like light.

Dylan was soon beside her, keeping pace easily. With a grin, he straightened his hat.

There was no need to speak—they might have been joined, one creature, soul-meeting-soul, riding those horses. It was as if they were making love, on some high and intangible plane of the spirit. The exhilaration was like nothing Kristy had ever felt before—it was exultation, it was triumph.

It was being whole again.

The ride ended too soon—there were guests waiting at the main ranch house, after all. Having crossed the wide pasture at a full run, they returned at a walk, for the sake of the horses.

Logan, Briana and Bonnie stood in the same place at the corral gate, along with Jim and the rest of the crew.

Kristy saw them all as a blur of smiles and color.

Friends.

Family.

Kristy dismounted, grinning foolishly, and stood wobbly legged holding the reins. Dylan held out his arms for Bonnie, and Logan handed her up. Then he took the paint from Kristy and led it slowly into the barn.

Kristy watched, her heart full, as Dylan took Bonnie for a brief ride. Perched in front of her dad in the saddle, the child looked transported—almost transfigured.

It's in her blood, Kristy thought. *Just as it's in mine.*

She'd ridden like that, with her own father, from the time she was six months old. In her mind, she felt her dad's strong arms around her again, heard him laughing with delight. Heard her mother calling in fitful joy, "Tim Madison, you be careful now—Kristy's just a baby!"

Coming back to the present with a jolt, Kristy sniffled once, aware that Briana was watching her.

Remarkably, Briana said, "I used to ride like that with my dad."

Kristy sniffled again, smiled. "Me, too," she said hoarsely. "Me, too."

Briana sighed happily. "It's nice to see the good things passed down to a new generation," she added, looking around at the milling friends and acquaintances. "I'd better get the fried chicken and potato salad out, before there's a riot."

"I'll help," Kristy said.

Hal Ryder, Stillwater Springs' longtime veterinarian, nodded a greeting as they approached the front porch. He'd treated Sugarfoot, and all the other animals on the Madison place, while Kristy was growing up, and before the divorce, he and Mrs. Ryder had often played cards with her parents.

"Good to see you on a horse again," he said.

Kristy choked up for a moment, nodded. Lingered when Briana went on inside. "How's Lily?" she asked. As kids, she and Doc's daughter had been summer playmates.

Doc grinned, albeit sadly. "Stubborn as ever," he said.

A sudden pang struck Kristy as she realized how Hal Ryder had aged. He seemed thinner than usual, and profoundly tired.

Before Kristy could think of a reply, he spotted someone, over her shoulder, called out a hello and excused himself.

Kristy went on inside the house, washed up in a powder room under renovation and tracked Briana to the kitchen. There, she and Briana and Katherine Hunting-horse, Jim's ex, busied themselves putting out the sizable spread Briana had prepared earlier in the day.

In the way of country people, folks filled paper plates

and plastic cups and divided themselves by gender to visit. The men went outside, to sit on the porch steps, in the grass, under trees. The women somehow found chairs inside, though a few ventured as far as the picnic table on the patio.

All the talk was convivial—the men would be discussing politics, beef prices, taxes and the rising cost of hay and gasoline. The women praised Briana's fried chicken and the renovations she and Logan were doing on the house, and let their gazes stray surreptitiously to the new Mrs. Creed's still-flat abdomen.

Amused, Kristy wondered if she might be garnering a few such glances herself, though she hadn't caught anyone at it. Briana was clearly the main focus of observation, with Katherine Huntinghorse running a close second.

Kristy was happy to be left in the dust, although between the recently discovered bodies, her budding relationship with Dylan and the option agreement she'd signed allowing Zachary Spencer first dibs on the story, she knew it couldn't last.

Katherine nudged her as the two of them stood side by side in Briana's kitchen, leaning against a counter and chowing down, as Dylan put it, on fried chicken, potato salad and various other tasty things. "Do you think Jim can win?" she asked.

Kristy didn't know Katherine very well, since she was "from away," meaning she hadn't grown up in or around Stillwater Springs, as most of the people gathered at Logan and Briana's place had. She was a mixed-media artist of some type, and looked the part, in her colorful, flowing skirt and sleeveless peasant blouse of cream eyelet. Her hair was long and dark, held back from her face by a silver barrette, and her eyes were silver-gray, fringed by thick lashes.

"I *know* Jim can win," Kristy answered. Everybody knew Jim's marriage hadn't lasted; was there a reconciliation in the offing? "He'll make an excellent sheriff."

Jim came into the kitchen from outside just then, ducking so his small son, riding on his shoulders, wouldn't bump his head. The boy—Kristy couldn't recall his name, if she'd ever known it in the first place—was about four, she guessed, and looked just like his father, except that he had Katherine's remarkable silver eyes.

A patter of neighborly applause—*here's our handsome candidate now*—rose from the women in the kitchen, but Jim's gaze, like the boy's, went straight to Katherine and stuck.

Hmm, Kristy thought.

"Dad wants to take me for a ride on a horse!" the little boy called. "Can I go, Mom? Can I go? Please?"

"Jim," Katherine said, "you'll spoil your new campaign suit."

Jim flushed; he still seemed completely unaware of everyone else in the room, save Katherine and their son. Kristy rather enjoyed feeling invisible—it would be a nifty trick next time she ran into the reporters, if she *could* disappear—and she was engrossed in the exchange between these two people who used to be married and weren't anymore.

"Sam really wants that ride," Jim said, very quietly. "And I can have the suit cleaned."

"With all the money he's making off those slot machines out at the casino," one of the women noted in a kindly jab, "he ought to be able to afford *ten* suits like that one."

More laughter followed this comment; Kristy joined in, though she rarely visited the local casino. It wasn't that she had anything against gambling; she just got bored quickly at the slot machines.

Jim seemed to snap out of his reverie, at least partly. Before their very eyes, he turned into a politician, his smile engaging, his manner easy and confident. He scanned the room, found the woman who'd commented on the slot machines. "Stella Baker," he said, making the middle-aged farmer's wife blush a little with all that noble-savage charm of his. "I thought your game was bingo."

"I played the slots last Tuesday night, between bingo games," Stella said, "and I lost my shirt."

Jim took exaggerated notice of her blue-and-white gingham blouse. The other women laughed again and Stella, pleased as a schoolgirl flirting with a new beau, blushed even harder.

"Not *this* one," she said. "I *will* say, Jim Hunting-horse, that those machines are rigged."

"Are you going to quit running that casino when you get elected?" another woman asked. This was Jolie Calhoun, Stella's best friend.

Jim set Sam on his feet, then bowed graciously to Jolie and Stella. "Yes," he said. "Being sheriff is a full-time job."

Kristy just happened to see Katherine cross two fingers on her right hand, though whether the former Mrs. Huntinghorse wanted Jim to win and leave the casino or lose and stay there, she had no way of knowing.

Little Sam raced across the crowded kitchen and

clutched at Katherine's skirt, looking up at her, his silver eyes imploring. "Mom, I *have* to ride that horse, and Dad won't let me get on alone."

Katherine looked down at her son, visibly relented, met Jim's gaze again and nodded. "Just be careful," she said.

"Always," Jim answered gruffly.

Well that *wasn't about riding a horse,* Kristy thought. Then, with a little jerk, she brought herself up short. She was turning into a snoop; pretty soon, she'd be cackling away with the rest of the hens, speculating about who was pregnant, who was having an affair, who paid too much for their new car and was putting on airs.

Jim and Sam left, headed out for the promised horseback ride, and Kristy resisted an urge to go outside and see what Dylan and Bonnie were doing.

She was helping Briana and some of the others clean up when Logan burst into the kitchen through the patio door. The look on his face froze everyone in place, and Briana was the first to break the spell.

"Logan, what is it?"

He strode past her, into a bedroom off the kitchen, came out with a couple of blankets and a pillow. His face was gray.

"It's Doc," he said, on his way out again. "I think he's having a heart attack."

Kristy had no more absorbed that when she heard the first wail of an approaching siren.

She dashed outside, only a step or two ahead of Briana.

Sure enough, Hal Ryder lay on the patio stones next to the picnic table, unconscious. Dylan pumped the man's chest while Jim Huntinghorse performed mouth-to-mouth resuscitation.

"Everybody stay back," Logan ordered, as he slipped the pillow under Doc's head and covered him as best he could with the blanket.

"We're losing him," Jim gasped, between breaths, turning his head toward Dylan.

"No way that's going to happen," Dylan retorted, still working Doc's failing heart through the thin wall of his chest. "Doc! You hear me? Hold on in there—for Lily."

Ambulance light splashed them all with red.

"Hold on, Doc," Kristy whispered, echoing what Dylan had just said. "Hold on, for Lily."

CHAPTER TWELVE

Doc's HEART WAS STILL BEATING when the EMTs rushed him away from Stillwater Springs Ranch in back of the ambulance. Kristy, holding a fitful Bonnie while Logan and Dylan and Jim Huntinghorse conferred on the patio, distractedly dazzled by the purple-gold of a spectacular Montana sunset, felt hollowed out, numb with shock.

Her own father had died in a Missoula hospital, while she was holding his hand and trying, through tears, to tell him how much she loved him, and that it was okay to go on. She'd be all right.

Though she'd meant what she said at the time, the painful truth was, she *hadn't* been "all right," not totally, anyway. Oh, sure, she'd kept right on going, like that drum-beating bunny on TV, putting on a brave front, helping people choose library books, conducting story hour, renovating her house, paying her bills—in general, coping. But she'd also flipped some internal switch, effectively shutting down yet another part of herself.

It was dangerous to love people or animals.

She'd loved Sugarfoot.

She'd loved her mom and dad.

And she'd loved Dylan Creed, although not in the way she did now.

Bonnie, squirming in her arms, gave her hair a tug, most likely to get her attention.

Oh, yes, love was a perilous thing.

Kristy's eyes burned with tears as she looked into the little face, full of trust and worry. Adult things were happening, and Bonnie didn't understand. She seemed to be debating in that lively child-mind of hers—should she be scared? She'd take her cue from the grown-ups, of course.

So Kristy straightened her spine and summoned up a smile. "It's okay, baby," she said. "Everything's okay. See? There's your daddy."

At that moment, Dylan looked their way. The strain in his face slackened a little; he said something to Jim and Logan, and came toward her. Took Bonnie easily, gave her a reassuring squeeze.

"Do you think Doc will make it?" Kristy asked, her tone deliberately light, for Bonnie's sake. Children might not understand the words that passed between their protectors, but they were masters at picking up on nuances, however subtle.

Dylan turned his head toward the road, where the dust the ambulance had raised still billowed in the air. "I hope so," he said.

"You were pretty wonderful," Kristy ventured softly, reaching out to touch his arm. "So was Jim. Obviously, your CPR skills are up to date."

Dylan made an attempt at a grin, but fell short. "Comes in handy on the rodeo circuit," he said.

They were quiet for a while. Then Kristy said, "Someone should call Lily. I know the hospital will notify her, as next of kin, but—"

Dylan nodded. People were saying goodbye, starting

to get into their cars and leave. "Looks like the party's over," he said.

"I'll let Logan and Briana know we're going," Kristy volunteered, since Dylan seemed to be rooted to the patio, now that the immediate crisis had passed.

"Thanks," he said. Burying his face in Bonnie's fluffy, flyaway hair, he closed his eyes and breathed deep.

A few minutes later, the three of them were in Dylan's truck, Bonnie sleeping, Dylan staring over the steering wheel at the road, Kristy wondering if she shouldn't have insisted on driving. Instead of heading for Dylan's place, they went to Kristy's. She needed to pack a few things, and Dylan wanted to look at the locks on all her doors, since he intended to replace them.

Winston greeted them anxiously as they entered the kitchen, and for a shaky moment, Kristy thought someone was prowling around the house again.

As it turned out, though, he just wanted his dinner, and his water bowl was nearly empty.

Dylan laid Bonnie on the living room couch, covered her with a crocheted afghan and started checking locks.

Kristy fed Winston, troubled about leaving him alone in the house while she spent the night—and maybe longer—at Dylan's. Putting the thought aside temporarily, she went into her study and found her address book.

She and Lily Ryder Kenyon, Doc's daughter, didn't correspond, except to exchange Christmas cards. It was possible—even likely—that the contact information she had was outdated, but the need to call her childhood friend was a compelling one.

After finding the number, Kristy picked up the phone on her desk and dialed. What would she say, if Lily hadn't heard about her father's heart attack? She didn't know, but she had to say *something*—woman to woman, daughter to daughter.

One ring, two, three.

Kristy was waiting for voice mail to pick up, so she could leave her name and number and ask for a return call, when a woman answered, her voice choked with tears.

"H-hello?" Lily Kenyon said.

"It's Kristy Madison," Kristy answered.

"I just got a call from someone at Missoula General," Lily told her. "My dad's on his way there with a heart attack—?"

"Yes," Kristy said, as Dylan appeared in the study doorway, hands resting on the framework at shoulder level. "I don't know how bad it is, Lily. But I wanted you to know that—well—if there's anything I can do—"

Lily thrust out a deep, tremulous sigh. "It's pretty bad, from what the woman at the hospital said. I'll be there as soon as I can. And th-thanks, Kristy. For thinking to call. It really means a lot." She paused. "Were—were you there when it happened? Dad's heart attack, I mean?"

Kristy swallowed as the image of Doc lying on the patio stones, helpless and gray, filled her mind. "Yes. It happened at Stillwater Springs Ranch—at a party. Dylan and Jim Huntinghorse gave your dad CPR until the ambulance arrived."

"Thank God," Lily murmured. A long, groping sort of pause followed. "I can't seem to think straight." After this came a heartbreaking little attempt at a laugh. "I need to book flights for Tess and me—arrange for some-place to stay near the hospital in Missoula—"

"One step at a time," Kristy said gently, as Dylan approached.

Without prompting, Kristy handed him the phone.

"Lily? Dylan Creed—"

Kristy waited while Dylan offered to send a plane for Lily and her little girl. He had a friend, he told her, who flew a jet.

Lily must have demurred, because Dylan said gently, "Okay. Yeah, I understand—your dad told Logan and me what happened. Sure—I'll tell her." He reached for a pen on Kristy's tidy desk and scrawled what was probably Lily's cell-phone number. "See you then. Hang tough, Lil."

He replaced the receiver. "Lily said to tell you thanks again. She'll call as soon as she's settled in Missoula and knows anything more about Doc's condition."

Kristy's mind skipped a track. "It wouldn't be right to leave Winston alone in the house," she said, surprising herself, since she'd planned to say something about Lily's arrival instead.

"What?" Dylan asked, understandably puzzled.

Kristy sighed, shook her head in frustration directed wholly at herself. Normally, she was the most orderly person on earth—just look at her desk, or her car—but these days, what with all that was going on, and Dylan in close proximity, her brain seemed hopelessly mud-dled. "My cat," she said. "Winston. I can't go out to your place and just leave him here."

"Fine," Dylan said, watching her closely, his eyes solemn and earnest. "We'll take him with us."

"You have a dog," Kristy pointed out.

"Sam? He's the chummy type. He'll take to Winston right away."

"Probably," Kristy agreed, fondly recalling Dylan's just-rescued dog. "But will Winston take to him?"

"One way to find out," Dylan said, with a weary grin. "Unless, of course, you're trying to backpedal here. If you want to stay with Bonnie and me, great. If you don't, that's cool, too."

Kristy bit her lower lip. *Was* she looking for an escape hatch? Winston would be happy as long as she was around, since she was his person, dog or no dog, in whichever house.

"Okay," she said.

"Okay, what?" Dylan prodded, grinning again.

Kristy took a deep breath, let it out in a rush. "Okay, we'll take Winston out to your place and see if he and Sam get along. Just let me find his crate and get a few of my clothes—"

Dylan looked relieved. "Bring something see-through, with garters," he teased, lightening an other-wise heavy moment.

Kristy gave him a poke with her fingertip and went off to find Winston's crate, used only when he visited the vet.

And his vet was, of course, Doc Ryder.

Don't die, Kristy pleaded silently, as she made for the basement stairs, off the kitchen, where she stored things like cat crates. *Lily's on her way.*

OUT AT THE RANCH, after putting Bonnie to bed and feeding Sundance, Dylan crouched in the center of the kitchen floor. Winston was making a fuss inside the crate, while Sam pressed a wet, curious nose up against the wire door, ears cocked, tail switching in uncertain little jerks from side to side.

"This isn't going to work," Kristy said in despair.

Winston took a swipe at Sam's nose.

Sam didn't move, and his tail wagged faster, with more confidence.

"It will work fine," Dylan disagreed calmly.

"Don't open that door!"

Dylan opened the door.

Sam backed up a few steps, still wagging and sniffing like mad.

Winston waltzed out of the crate, his white tail big as the brush Kristy used to clean ceiling fans at home. He stood toe-to-toe, nose-to-nose, with Sam for a few breathtaking seconds, then strolled haughtily past the dog to explore his new surroundings.

"See?" Dylan said, rising to stash the crate in the nearby laundry room.

"It *worked*," Kristy said, amazed.

"For now," Dylan agreed. "I'm going out to get your stuff and then ride Sundance over to Logan's. See if he'll stay put in the barn—I've been thinking about those bears that feed in the orchard. You mind staying with Bonnie for an hour or so?"

"We'll be fine," she told him quietly. "But how will you get back here?"

"I'll hitch a ride with Logan, or walk. It's not that far."

Kristy nodded.

Dylan brought in her suitcase, and then Winston's litter box, bag of litter and food supply. She stood watching at the back door as Dylan untied Sundance, speaking quietly to the horse all the while, and slipped a halter over the animal's head.

Sundance was skittish, but he didn't balk.

Kristy held her breath, though, when Dylan grabbed hold of the horse's glowing mane and swung himself up onto its back, Indian-style.

Sundance gathered his haunches, as if preparing to buck.

Dylan leaned to stroke the long neck and reassure the animal with quiet words Kristy couldn't make out.

Kristy laid a hand to her chest, her heart pounding. She knew horses, and Dylan did, too. But they were powerful animals, unpredictable at times, especially when they'd been abused. She'd been prepared, she realized, to see Dylan thrown. And she'd been terrified.

He waved to her, maybe knowing what she was thinking and maybe not, and rode off at an easy walk. Kristy watched until both of them disappeared into the trees.

She should go in.

Make sure Sam and Winston were still getting along.

Look in on Bonnie.

Brush her teeth and unpack.

Instead, she listened from the porch until she was sure Dylan and Sundance had had time to get through the orchard without running into a bear.

THIS TIME, SUNDANCE STAYED in his stall, as though he understood that the arrangement was only temporary.

"He's a fine-looking animal," Logan observed, leaning on the stall gate to watch as Sundance munched down on hay and a little grain.

Dylan nodded, eyeing Logan's poor collection of saddles. He'd left his own in storage after quitting the rodeo, and now he wondered whether to send for it, along with the rest of his stuff, or simply buy new.

"Heard anything about Doc?" he asked.

"He's stable, according to the people in the admitting office," Logan said, without looking away from Sundance. "We probably won't know much for a while."

Dylan wondered if his brother knew what a lucky man he was, with a pretty wife and a ready-made family. Three dogs, too, and all these horses. Cattle on the range, though some of them would be Dylan's, once the auction company delivered the fifty head they'd bought that morning. Riding up earlier, he'd taken in the old place, all alight in the gathering dusk, and felt a peculiar combination of yearning and hope.

"It was something, seeing Kristy on a horse again," Dylan said, remembering their ride across the field, just after they all got back from the political shindig in town.

Logan turned, at last, and grinned. "It was," he agreed quietly.

"What?" Dylan said, irritated by the cocksure expression on his brother's face.

"You've got it bad," Logan answered. "You remind me of a deer frozen in the headlights—or myself, when I first laid eyes on Briana."

Dylan sighed, standing there in the center aisle of Logan's fine new barn. "Truth is, I don't know *what* I've got. It's a lot different than when Kristy and I were together before—whole new ball game, as the saying goes, and a new playing field, too. And I haven't got a clue about the rules—or what the score is, either."

Logan chuckled. "Show up and suit up, little brother. That's about all you can do."

Dylan needed to shift the subject away from Kristy, at least until he could get his breath. "Lily's on her way to Missoula, to be with Doc," he said.

"That's good," Logan said, thoughtful again.

This time, Dylan didn't need to ask what was going through Logan's mind. He knew.

With another sigh, and another swipe at his hair, Dylan took the plunge. "I was real mad at you when Dad died before I could get to the hospital, Logan, and so was Tyler. It really pissed me off that you were there and I wasn't—same with Ty, I guess. Anyhow—I'm sorry. I know it wasn't your doing, my not getting to say goodbye to the old man before he went."

Logan came to face Dylan, there in that well-lit barn, and laid a hand on his shoulder. The black eye Tyler had given him at Jake's graveside was almost gone. Wounds on the outside healed fast; not so with the ones on the *inside*.

"Thanks," Logan said, his voice gruffer than usual.

"You were right about something else," Dylan went on, since he seemed to be on some kind of psychological roll. "Jake Creed was a son of a bitch."

Logan's mouth quirked up at one side—closest he could come to a grin, most likely. Instead of answering, he just nodded.

"The thing is," Dylan finished, "he was my dad and I loved him anyhow."

"Me, too," Logan said sadly. Then he roused himself from what looked to be some pretty dark thoughts, and chuckled. "Back then, I'd have swapped him out for somebody better—*anybody* better—but now, I'd just like to see him again, for five minutes, and tell the old bastard I love him, whether he likes it or not."

"Maybe he knows," Dylan mused.

"Maybe he does," Logan said.

After that, Logan went into the house for the box of old letters, pictures and journals he'd mentioned to Dylan earlier, and probably to tell Briana he'd be back in a little while. Dylan waited on the porch the whole time, envying his older brother fiercely and, at one and the same time, happy for him, too.

Doc's heart attack had been one hell of a way to end the party, and it had taken something out of Dylan, to see a good friend come so close to dying.

But he had Bonnie to go home to.

And, for tonight at least, Kristy was there, too.

It sure beat being on the rodeo circuit, crashing in this motel room or that one, sometimes by himself, but more often with a woman he'd never see again. Either way, he'd been just as lonely, because as warm and willing and even beautiful as most of those women had been, none of them were Kristy Madison.

Logan came out the front door, lugging a big plastic container jammed with stuff. "Ready?" he asked, as though it were an ordinary, everyday thing for two brothers who'd beaten the hell out of each other and then steered clear for five long years to be swapping family pictures.

Not that Dylan had anything to swap. The main house was Logan's inheritance, and so was the history of the Creeds, evidently.

On the way across the field—like Dylan, Logan never took a road if he could jostle over open ground instead—Dylan held that box in his lap and wondered if he really wanted to open it.

What he knew of the Creed legacy wasn't exactly greeting-card material.

Happy Father's Day, Dad.

Yeah, right.

Or him and Logan and Tyler mugging for a Christmas picture—the kind that usually goes out with a brag-letter run up at the copy store. He even went so far as to imagine a line from it, written in Jake's own hand. *The current wife and I are so proud...*

He made a snorting sound.

"What?" Logan asked, swerving to avoid a log or a pothole in the field.

"You remember that old aluminum Christmas tree you bought that year?" Dylan asked. "The one with the colored light thingy that turned, so the branches changed from red to blue to green?"

"I remember," Logan said. His voice sounded odd.

"Best Christmas I can recall," Dylan remarked.

Logan swallowed visibly. "Yeah. The thing was made of metal, so Dad couldn't cut it in two with a chain saw."

"It was more than that, Logan. You mowed lawns and shoveled snow to buy the thing. *That's* what made it a good Christmas."

"There weren't many presents to speak of," Logan said. "Except for those toy tractors Dad got just before the hardware store closed on Christmas Eve."

Dylan laughed. "Mine had a dent," he remembered.

"I guess he tried," Logan said. The house was in sight, and he stopped on that side of the fence. "Can you make it the rest of the way with that box?"

Dylan merely rolled his eyes. Then he said, "He tried, Logan. Maybe it was the best he could do."

Logan didn't look at him. He merely nodded once, a sharp motion of his head.

Dylan got out of the truck, lugging the box. "Night," he said. "Thanks for the ride, the stall and that tacky Christmas tree."

With that, he walked away, toward the lights, toward his child, toward Kristy. He pushed the box between the strands of rusted barbed wire comprising the fence and shinnied after it.

And when he turned around, Logan was still sitting there.

He was about to go back when his brother shifted into gear and drove off, taillights of his truck blinking cheerfully in the night.

It made Dylan think of the aluminum tree again.

He smiled.

KRISTY SAT at Dylan's kitchen table, bare feet hooked in the rung of her chair, wearing her favorite over-washed, oversize T-shirt and reading a library book. Incredibly, Winston and Sam were curled up together in a corner of the room, sharing the pile of old blankets that served as a dog-bed.

She hadn't heard a car, so when Dylan came through the back door, a big plastic box under one arm, she started slightly.

"Sundance didn't follow you home?" she asked. She'd had a shower, and her hair was still damp against her cheeks and the back of her neck.

Dylan smiled, shook his head, his eyes lingering on

her hair, her face and then the T-shirt. He shifted the box onto the counter, stepped inside and shut the door.

"You should have locked up," he said. "Stillwater Springs isn't what it used to be."

Kristy sighed. "No place is," she answered. "I didn't hear Logan's truck."

"That's because he only brought me as far as the fence," Dylan replied. His gaze seemed to be glued to her. Did she have toothpaste on her cheek or something?

"What's in the box?" she asked, taking a precautionary swipe at one side of her face, then the other.

"A hundred and fifty years of Creed memorabilia," Dylan said, crossing the room to drag back a chair and sit down. "Bonnie's all right?"

"Sleeping like a baby," Kristy said. If things had been more certain between her and Dylan, she'd have gotten up, stood behind him, massaged some of the tension out of his shoulders, the way her mother had done with her dad.

"This has been one hell of a day." Dylan sighed, tilting his head back in a tantalizing stretch. "Logan called the hospital just before I went over there with Sundance. Doc is 'stable.'"

Kristy wanted to do something for Dylan, but it was too late for coffee. "Are you hungry?" she asked.

Dylan straightened, looked at her. A grin flickered on his mouth. "Hungry?" he asked, teasing, acting as though the word was one he'd never heard before.

"For food," Kristy clarified, then felt stupid.

Dylan chuckled at her blush. "No," he said. "Not for food."

"Oh," Kristy said.

"I wouldn't turn down some good old-fashioned sex, though."

"*Dylan.* Bonnie is in the *next room.*"

His eyes twinkled, but there was a weary look in them, too. "You think people don't have sex with a kid in the next room?" he countered. "Hell, if that were so, the human race would have died out before the wheel was invented."

Kristy blushed harder. That afternoon, before they'd gone to hear Jim and Mike make their why-I-should-be-sheriff speeches, she and Dylan had practically raised the roof right off the bedroom. It had been easy then, to imagine having sex with a child in the house, but Bonnie hadn't actually *been* in the house then. She'd been with Logan and Briana.

Now, she was twelve feet away, in her pretty princess bed, a pink-cheeked, sleeping angel with little blond curls haloing her face like a gossamer aura.

"We'll just have to be quiet," Dylan said, reiterating an earlier statement.

Kristy bit her lower lip, squirmed in her chair.

"Kristy?" Dylan prompted.

"I'm not sure I can," she confessed.

"Have sex?" He pretended to ponder some deep dilemma. "You seemed to have a handle on it before."

"*Be quiet,*" she whispered. "I'm not sure I can *be quiet.*"

That made him chuckle, a throaty, ultramasculine sound that bent her nerves like grass rippling under a strong wind.

"So you think Bonnie's going to wake up because she hears the bedsprings creaking in our room and say to herself, 'For shame, I think those two are doing the nasty'? Get real, Kristy. She's two years old."

Our room. Kristy's mind caught on that phrase, even though it had nothing to do with the price of rice in China, as her mother used to say.

When she didn't answer—because she couldn't think of a single sensible thing to say—Dylan made a big drama out of stretching his delectable body and making the accompanying yawnlike sounds.

"You sit up as long as you want," he said. "I'm going to bed."

With that, he locked the kitchen door, ambled past Kristy's chair and headed into the hallway. She heard him stop to look in on Bonnie, then go on to the bathroom.

His belt buckle clinked when he dropped his jeans to the floor, then the shower came on.

Kristy hesitated a few moments, then stood up, switched off the lights and went to Dylan's room. When he came out of the bathroom, wearing only a towel around his waist, chest dotted with sparkling droplets of water, Kristy was in bed, with the blankets pulled up to her chin.

"If I get into that bed," he told her, "I'm going to make love to you. So I guess you can either sleep on the couch or take your chances."

Kristy tugged the blankets up farther, so only her eyes and the top of her head were uncovered. "Don't you dare make me yell like I did this afternoon," she blustered, her voice muffled.

"No promises," Dylan said. "Except one."

"What's that?" Kristy asked nervously.

"You are definitely going to come. Hard and often."

Heat surged through Kristy's mostly hidden body. "You are *deliberately* making this more difficult," she accused.

Dylan stood at the foot of the bed. Dropped the towel.

Kristy scrambled to switch off the bedside lamp, but it was too late. She'd seen his erection, and she was *already* on the verge of climax #1, before he'd even touched her.

Dylan immediately switched the lamp back on.

Then, slowly, he pulled back the covers, took hold of the hem of Kristy's T-shirt and hauled it off over her head as easily as if he'd done it a thousand times before. Which he probably had.

"Dylan," Kristy whimpered.

He sat down on the mattress beside her, gloriously naked and all man, and parted her thighs with one hand. "Let's test the theory," he said.

"Wh-what theory?" Kristy gasped.

"Whether you can be quiet or not," Dylan replied. And then he began to caress her, making her wet, making her writhe.

"Oh God," she said.

He continued to stroke her, easing her legs farther apart, bending once or twice to tongue and then suck on one of her nipples.

A honey-thick haze filled the small room.

Dylan increased the pace.

Kristy put a hand over her mouth, groaning aloud, her hips rising and falling with every motion of his fingers.

The bedsprings began to creak.

Kristy made a strangled, soblike sound, of need, of surrender, of woman-fury at being so easily tamed.

"So far, so good," Dylan murmured, watching her with soft, fierce eyes.

And then his fingers were inside her, while the pad of his thumb plied her clitoris.

Kristy erupted, flinging both hands upward to catch hold of the rails in the headboard, giving a long, low cry of pure, primitive satisfaction.

When the waves subsided, she lay still, breathing hard. Listening.

Dylan listened, too.

No sound came from Bonnie's room.

"Guess we're good to go," Dylan said.

"Didn't we just—er—'go'?" Kristy gasped out.

In answer, he stretched out on top of her, the light still burning on the bedside table, catching in his hair, playing over his features and his strong shoulders.

"Dylan, are you wearing—"

"No," he said. Gently, he took her right hand, still moist with perspiration, and placed it on the same rail she'd gripped during the orgasm of the century. He did the same with the other.

She knew she ought to tell him to stop, put on a condom, but the words wouldn't come out. It was as though they were huddled in the back of her throat, holding on tight, refusing to budge.

"How do you feel about trailers?" he asked.

Kristy blinked. He was about to move inside her. "How do I feel about what?"

"Trailers?" Dylan asked, bending his head to nibble idly at the length of her neck, the sensitive hollows under her ears. "It would only be temporary—until the new house is finished—"

"The n-new house?" Kristy groped to understand. All her senses were hyped up, but her brain felt swaddled, soaked in honey, drowsy and sweet.

He was inside her then. Deep, deep inside her.

She whimpered, turning her head from side to side, carried away by the rising friction, the approach of pleasure so intense she wasn't sure she could endure it. But, oh, there was no going back now.

"Stay—with me—Kristy—" Dylan ground out, driving into her hard now.

The climax seized her then, tore her apart, put her back together again. She was just beginning to catch hold of the world around her when Dylan stiffened and spilled himself inside her.

Stay with me, Kristy.

Had he really said that or, tossed about in the fiery throes of her release, off the planet, past the stars, had she only imagined the words?

At least fifteen minutes went by before either of them spoke.

"Will you live with me, Kristy?" Dylan asked then. Their arms and legs were still tangled, and his face was pressed deep into the curve of her neck.

So he *had* asked her to stay with him.

Not to marry him.

To *live* with him.

Just then, Kristy heard her mother's voice in the back of her mind, clear and crisp. *Why should a man buy the cow when he can get the milk for free?*

She laughed out loud, but at the same time, tears wet her face.

"This is funny?" Dylan asked, sounding put out, but

then he raised his head and saw the tears, and his tone shifted to one of concern. "Kristy?"

"It's—nothing," she said, trying to turn her head away.

But he turned it back, wiped away her tears with the side of one thumb. "What is it?" he pressed.

"I was just remembering something my mother used to say."

He frowned. "What?"

"'Why should a man buy the cow when he can get the milk for free?'" The cliché was so ridiculous—and so true—that she laughed again.

Cried again.

Dylan kissed her forehead, splayed his fingers and buried them in her hair. Rested *his* forehead against hers. "I'm sorry," he said.

She stroked his back. "We'd better live at my place," she said.

He lifted his head, searched her eyes. "Huh?"

"It's closer to the library," Kristy said reasonably. "It's bigger, too. And the gossips will find it a lot more entertaining, if we're right in town."

He wanted to smile, she could see that, but it fizzled. "You mean—"

"I mean," Kristy said, smiling and smoothing his hair back from his forehead, "if we're going to live together, it's going to be on my terms. I have a perfectly good house, and I intend to stay there—for the time being."

"What if it works?" Dylan countered. "Us, that is."

"What if it doesn't?" Kristy asked softly.

"Then you won't have to be the one who packs up and leaves."

Kristy merely arched an eyebrow. It went without

saying that leaving was Dylan's specialty, not hers. If things fell apart, she wanted to be *home* when it happened. That way, she could lick her wounds in familiar surroundings.

"I'm still planning to build a house and a barn, Kristy, and to raise Bonnie right here on Creed land."

"Fine," Kristy said, with a lot more confidence than she felt. "If we're still together when your new place is finished, we'll talk about it again."

He smiled, tasted her mouth. "You drive a hard bargain," he said.

"You drive a hard—bargain, too," Kristy quipped. The tears had stopped, but she was still afraid, still hopeful, all a-tangle inside.

She wasn't sure if she was ready to live with Dylan, and risk her heart. But she *was* sure of what she wanted, right then, in that bed, in that moment.

And he gave it to her, holding nothing back.

CHAPTER THIRTEEN

THE NEXT MORNING, Dylan dropped Kristy off at the library—she was hell-bent on putting in her shift, reporters or no reporters. Since there were no news-hawks in sight when they arrived, he decided he and Bonnie would go on to the hardware store for new locks. In the bright light of day, he wasn't sure it was a good idea, he and Bonnie and Sam moving in with Kristy and Winston, instead of vice versa, but Kristy was adamant. So he'd give it a try.

At a dusty little shop on Main Street, where locks and hammers and a variety of other things were sold, Dylan unbuckled Bonnie from her car seat and took her inside with him, leaving Winston and Sam there in the rig, with a window cracked. Choosing tools and supplies and wrestling a rambunctious two-year-old was a challenge, but he managed. Recalling that there were several sets of stairs at Kristy's, he bought baby gates, too. And a playpen in a time-battered box.

Bonnie would hate being tossed into a portable hoosegow, he knew, but he needed *some* way to corral the little bugger while he swapped out the locks.

Later on, when Kristy got home from work, he planned to go back to the ranch, disassemble Bonnie's fancy bed and commandeer Logan into helping him load it for the trip to town. Then the two of them could put the thing together in the small room next to Kristy's.

Of course, the plan meant revealing to Logan that he was moving in with Kristy, and he was bound to take some ribbing over that. Might as well get in practice— by nightfall, word of the arrangement would be all over Stillwater Springs anyhow, with no help from Logan. Folks would have plenty to say, right to his face and behind his back.

At Kristy's, Dylan used the key she'd given him at breakfast to get inside. He spent the next several minutes herding Sam over the threshold, along with Bonnie, and letting Winston out of his crate.

Disgruntled, the cat gave a snippy meow and disappeared into some other part of the house, no doubt bound for a private hiding place.

Sam invited himself along, much to Winston's annoyance.

Setting up the playpen took half an hour—the instructions were in Sanskrit, as near as Dylan could guess, and there must have been a hundred different washers and bolts and screws—and Bonnie raised hell when he put her in the thing, immediately tried to scramble over the side.

He filled her sippy cup from the jug of milk in Kristy's fridge, and the kid settled down. With luck, she'd go to sleep.

Without luck, she'd scream until his eardrums imploded or the neighbors called the cops.

The latter possibility didn't bother him; he wouldn't mind a word with Floyd Book, anyway. To his mind, the old man turning out to be a murderer would be about as likely as lasting peace in the Middle East, but it wouldn't hurt to get a feel for the guy's energy. Dylan had long since learned to trust the vibes he picked up from people and situations—he'd ignored them with Sharlene, but he'd come out of the deal with a daughter, too.

By noon, he'd set up all the baby gates and replaced all the locks. Mercifully, Bonnie slept through the whole thing.

He'd left his .45 locked up in the glove compartment of the truck, and he was just fetching it when Kristy showed up, carrying a bag from the Marigold Café.

"Lunch," she said, smiling.

But her face changed when she saw the gun.

"Do you intend to bring that thing into my house?" she bristled, opening the side gate in her tidy picket fence with a force that made the metal latch clink when it swung shut again behind her.

"In a word," he said, "yes."

"Must I remind you that there is a *two-year-old* living under this roof?"

Dylan grinned. "No," he said. "I'm up to speed on that one. She yelled like a banshee walking over hot coals for the first hour we were here." He let his gaze fall to the sack in Kristy's right hand. "Let's eat. I'm starved."

"Dylan, the *gun...*?"

"Could come in handy," he finished for her. "You've already had one intruder, remember?"

"Yes," Kristy retorted, "and if that *thing* had been in the house, I might have *shot* a woman I've known *all* my life."

"You're way too smart to do a dumb thing like that," Dylan reasoned. Where he went, the .45 went. He'd never had to use it, hoped he never would, but if the need arose, he meant to be ready. "I'd forgotten how you talk in italics so much of the time. It must be practically aerobic, not to mention exhausting."

Kristy stood at the base of the porch steps, still uncertain, looking downright delicious in her well-fitting black jeans and pink long-sleeved top. Letting his comment pass, she kept her attention on the .45. "Are there bullets in it?"

"No," Dylan said.

"Would you really shoot a human being?"

"If necessary, yes." Oh, yes, he'd pull the trigger under the right circumstances, with no compunction whatsoever and in a heartbeat.

For a long moment, he and Kristy just stared at each other.

Then Kristy asked quietly, "Define 'necessary,' if you don't mind."

"Don't mind at all. Any threat to you or Bonnie—or my brothers." He looked down at Sam, panting at his side. "Anybody or anything in need of looking out for."

A visible shudder went through Kristy's fine, responsive body. She was almost certainly remembering the night her father had shot that drifter and then hidden the body. "You'll put it up somewhere?"

"I wasn't planning to store it in the playpen," Dylan pointed out, "or on the coffee table."

Kristy stiffened, bit her lower lip and finally relented. "Okay," she said. "But I don't like it."

"I don't like it, either," Dylan agreed moderately, "but the reality is, it's a mean world out there, and shit happens. I'll show you how to handle the gun, how to load and unload it, all of that." At the look of rising resistance on her face, he added, "It wouldn't be safe otherwise."

Slowly, Kristy nodded, and they went inside. Dylan put the .45 on the highest shelf in the pantry, with the safety on, then went to wash up while Kristy unpacked the takeout grub she'd picked up on the way home. Bonnie woke up and gave a squall from the playpen in the living room, and Kristy hurried to fetch her. The kid was all smiles when they got back to the kitchen, cheeks flushed and eyes bright. Dylan, who had to hold Bonnie on his lap the whole time they were eating, made a mental note to bring her high chair to town, along with the little bed.

Once lunch was over, Dylan showed Kristy the shining new door handles, with their corresponding dead bolts, and gave her copies of the keys. She seemed pleased, and when she got in the Blazer and went back to the library to finish out her workday, she left a hole in the fabric of the day that Dylan had no idea how to weave back together.

He tried to interest Bonnie in cartoons, having positioned her playpen a safe distance from the TV in Kristy's study, but she was having none of that. So he loaded her and Sam up, leaving Winston to his own devices, and headed out to the main ranch.

Briana met him and Bonnie at the front door, immediately reaching out for the child, who went to her readily.

"Logan's out riding the range," Briana told Dylan with a smile, after planting a resounding kiss on Bonnie's cheek. "The auction people brought the new cattle this morning. Why don't you saddle up and find him?"

Dylan looked at his daughter, who was gazing at

Briana with the kind of adoration she usually reserved for Kristy. Felt a momentary pang. A child needed a mother, and in the long run, shacking up wouldn't pack it.

"Bonnie will be fine, here with me," Briana said.

Dylan pondered, then nodded and grinned. "Thanks," he told Briana. Then he chucked Bonnie under the chin. "Behave yourself, monkey," he said.

She barely noticed when he left, half sprinting for the barn.

There, he threw the spare saddle and a bridle on Sundance, who was fussing inside his stall, and mounted up.

Except for making love to Kristy, there was no feeling like being on the back of a horse. Together, Sundance and Dylan made for the bawling and churning dust-cloud indicating the approximate location of the herd.

The gelding was a little skittish, but eager to run, so Dylan let him.

The rush of wind felt as sweet as if somebody had left a window open between earth and heaven. Dylan bent low over the horse's neck, grinning wide and dust be damned.

The crack of the rifle shot came as a stunning affront, as such things always do. Instantly, the world went into slow-mo—the gelding stumbled and pitched forward, nearly landing on its knees, and Dylan rolled end over end above the animal's head. It seemed those somersaults went on forever, and when he finally hit the ground, he waited for the horse to land right on top of him, just as those logs had rolled down onto Jake and crushed the life out of his tough lumberjack's body.

It didn't happen.

Dylan passed out briefly, woke blinking. Stars sparked and whizzed around his head.

Sundance came slowly into focus, standing next to him, nuzzling the side of his face with a cold, wet nose. Dylan, with the wind knocked clean out of him, couldn't figure out if he'd actually taken a bullet or not. Nothing ached or burned. On the other hand, he might as well have been a puddle of consciousness, disembodied there on the hard Montana ground, for all the sensation he felt.

At least the horse was probably all right, he thought, still dazed, though the stars receded. Sundance wouldn't be on his feet if he'd been shot, or fallen hard enough to get hurt.

Dylan gulped in a breath, tried to make contact with his physical self, but it seemed as if all lines of communication had been cut. Nothing to do but wait, and hope to God the feeling came back to his arms and legs, though he'd hurt like hell when it did.

Logan rode up, seemed to slide to Dylan's side on his knees, like a baseball player trying to steal home plate without messing up the front of his shirt.

"Are you hit?" he gasped.

"I—don't know—" Dylan managed.

Logan looked him over hastily, shook his head. "You're not bleeding. Can you move?"

Dylan tried again, felt tentative messages beginning to pass between his brain and his body. He was relieved, but he braced himself for the inevitable pain, too. He knew from experience that a spill like that one, even if he hadn't broken or ruptured anything, would call for a lot of aspirin. "Somebody— There was a shot—"

"I know," Logan said. "I heard it."

"Sundance—?"

"He's okay." Saying this, Logan looked around, scanning, no doubt, for the shooter, who might try again, seeing as he—or she—had missed the first time.

"Who the hell would want to shoot me?" Dylan asked. Actually, there was a long list, but most of those guys were far away and probably wouldn't carry a grudge this far anyhow. By now, they'd have gotten themselves new girlfriends.

"I don't know," Logan replied. "Tyler?"

"He's pissed off," Dylan said, mildly disgusted, as Logan helped him sit up. "But trying to kill me? I think that's a little over-the-top, don't you?"

Logan's jaw tightened. "The shot must have come from the orchard," he said, after a few moments spent grinding away his back molars. Dylan knew his brother wanted more than anything to go racing off into those gnarled old apple trees, looking for the assailant—so did he.

And it would be a damn good way to get themselves shot for real.

Dylan assessed his arms and legs and back. Nothing was broken, but the all-over ache, so familiar from his rodeo days, was settling in for sure. Forget aspirin; he'd need to fill a horse trough with liniment and submerge himself to the eyeballs.

"Let's get you back to the house," Logan said. "Can you ride?"

"Hell, yes, I can ride," Dylan snapped, his pride stung.

Gaining his feet, with more help than he liked taking from Logan, he limped over to Sundance, soothed the horse and hauled himself back up into the saddle. For the first second or two, his head swam, and he half expected that second bullet.

Fortunately, it didn't come.

Back at the main house, a panicked Briana wanted to call an ambulance—after the sheriff.

Logan silenced her with a look.

Alec, Briana's youngest, stood beside the chair Dylan sank into in the living room.

"Did you get thrown off a horse?" the boy asked, wide-eyed.

Dylan bit back a testy *Hell, no, I didn't get* thrown. Alec was a kid, after all, and the question was an innocent one. No call to take his head off. "Not exactly," he said, measuring out the words.

Logan was already on the line to Sheriff Book.

"I'm going out there," he said, as soon as he'd snapped his cell phone shut.

"No, you're not!" Briana and Dylan chorused.

Bonnie, eyes wide with worry, clambered up onto Dylan's lap.

He mussed her hair, gave her a squeeze. It made his ribs hurt.

Some of them were probably cracked.

"Let Floyd handle this," Briana argued, frowning at her husband. "*You* need to take your stubborn brother to the emergency room."

"I'm not leaving you and the kids here alone," Logan said, but he was wavering. Dylan saw worry in his brother's dark eyes when he turned them on him. "There's some nut out there with a gun."

"Wow," Josh said, impressed. Briana's firstborn, he'd been at the computer when Logan and Dylan came in, and he still hadn't moved.

Dylan flashed briefly, in his distraction, on the IM

from Gravesitter that had unnerved Kristy so much. Of course the boy hadn't sent it, but he might know how to find out who had.

In the next instant, the thought spun off his mind.

"Let me look into your eyes," Briana demanded, stepping up to him, cupping her hands around his face and cranking upward. "Just as I thought—" She turned back to her husband. "Logan, there's a good chance your brother has a concussion."

Dylan set his jaw. "I'm all right," he insisted.

"I'm calling Kristy," Briana decided. "And what's taking Sheriff Book so long?"

"*Don't* call Kristy," Dylan said.

"It hasn't been five minutes since I called Floyd," Logan added.

"Maybe you'll have to have a cast, like I did," young Alec put in solemnly. "My stepmother hit me with a car."

"It was a van," Josh corrected.

"Enough, both of you," Briana interjected. Her gaze shifted from Logan to Dylan and back again. Then she sighed and hoisted Bonnie off Dylan's lap.

Bonnie's lower lip wobbled, then she jammed in the thumb.

"Kristy will be furious if I don't call her," Briana said. Then, with Bonnie riding on her hip, she disappeared into the kitchen.

"Do something," Dylan said to Logan. "About your wife."

Logan spread his hands. "Like what?"

If every bone and muscle in his body hadn't been throbbing, Dylan would have laughed at the bewildered look on his brother's face.

"Talk Briana out of calling Kristy," he replied, practically through his teeth. "This is going to freak her out."

"Yeah," Logan agreed. "But not like it will if she hears it through the grapevine."

Dylan sighed. Briana came out of the kitchen again, holding out a cordless phone and looking intractable.

"What happened?" Kristy demanded, before he got all the way through "hello."

He explained, though not in any great detail. First of all, he wasn't that much of a talker any time, let alone when his head was pounding, and second, he didn't remember much beyond hearing the shot and tumbling above Sundance's head like a lone shirt in a clothes dryer.

"And you think you're not going to the emergency room?" Kristy challenged tersely, when he'd finished. "Think again, buckaroo. I'll be on my way as soon as I make sure Susan or Peggy can stay until closing time—"

Dylan thought of the shooter, possibly still out there in the orchard or the cemetery or someplace even closer, with a bad attitude and plenty of ammunition. Or careening along the country roads, primed to open fire on the first car he met.

"Stay put, Kristy," he said, closing his eyes. "Sheriff Book is on his way out here right now. As soon as we know for sure what the situation is—"

She hung up on him.

He held the receiver out a little way and stared at it, confounded.

Kristy arrived at the ranch house at the same time Sheriff Book did, pale as milk and stiff-jawed.

Floyd took charge right away. Asked a lot of questions. Called in the state police for backup, since neither of his two deputies was available.

Once they arrived, bent on swarming over the whole ranch looking for either the shooter or some evidence of his identity, Kristy insisted on driving Dylan to the clinic in town. Bonnie stayed with Briana and Logan and the boys.

He didn't have a concussion, as it turned out; just a few sprains. The doctor gave him a prescription for pain pills, which he crumpled up and tossed into the waste can outside the clinic's front door.

Kristy was still so pale that Dylan thought *she* should have been the one to see a medic. "Who would *do* a thing like this?" she fretted, steering Dylan toward the front passenger door of her Blazer and all but wrestling him inside.

He tolerated the fussing. In fact, he kind of liked it.

"Damned if I know," he answered, when Kristy had rounded the rig and climbed behind the wheel. She stabbed at the ignition three times before she got the key in. "Gunnar Wilkenson probably wouldn't mind taking a potshot at me, but he isn't agile enough to come all the way down from that shack of his and hide out in the trees. Anyway, all he's got for firepower, as far as I know, is that old shotgun of his. It wouldn't have the range a rifle does."

"As far as you know," Kristy pointed out. "How about Zachary's son? What's his name—Caleb? You had a run-in with him over Sundance, didn't you?"

"He was pissed off for sure," Dylan admitted. "But trying to shoot me out of the saddle seems a little drastic."

"Isn't shooting at someone *always* drastic?" Having said that, Kristy began to tremble. Then tears swelled in her eyes.

Since they were still sitting in the clinic parking lot, Dylan leaned across the console and pulled her into his arms.

"Hey," he murmured. "You heard the doctor. I'm *all right.*"

She gave a great, snuffling sob, and he felt her tears soaking through his shirt.

He held her for a long time, his chin resting on top of her head, then said, "Swap seats with me, babe. You are in no condition to drive."

She drew back, looked up into his face, her eyes still swimming. "Neither are you."

Dylan chuckled. "We can spend all day going back and forth about this, or we can trade places, go back out to the ranch to get Bonnie and find out if Floyd and the staters found anything."

She sighed heavily. Opened her door, got out and came to his side of the Blazer, resigned.

Dylan kissed her lightly on the mouth and a minute or so later, they were cruising past the city limits.

There were Smokies all over the place when they arrived at the ranch, radios crackling, the transmissions being picked up on every scanner in the county, most likely. And there were a *lot* of scanners—the locals loved them, listened to police and fire and ambulance calls like it was their civic duty.

What was keeping that pack of reporters that had been bothering Kristy since the bodies were found?

Logan was pacing the front porch, restless as a tiger just snatched from the jungle and tossed into a cage. Clearly, he'd have preferred to be on the scene, with Floyd and the investigators he'd called in, but he had a family now. A wife, a couple of stepsons—loved ones to protect.

It made Dylan smile as he strolled up the walk, Kristy double-stepping alongside him, like she thought he might topple over any minute now.

"Any news?" Dylan asked his brother.

Logan folded his arms, leaned one shoulder against one of the posts supporting the porch roof. The pose was probably meant to look casual, but instead, Logan came off as what he was—frustrated and annoyed.

"They found a shell casing and some footprints," Logan said, sparing a reassuring grin for Kristy. "Whoever did the deed is long gone."

"Good," Kristy said, passing Dylan to mount the steps and pass Logan, too. "I need to see Bonnie."

With that, she was inside the house, the screen door banging shut behind her.

"I take it you're going to live," Logan said calmly, watching Dylan.

Dylan nodded, not bothering to climb the porch steps. "Let's go out there and see what's going on," he murmured. "With all these cops around, the women and kids aren't in any danger."

Logan grinned. "We'd better be quick," he said, with a glance over one shoulder. "If Briana spots us, we're busted."

That made Dylan laugh, despite the aches and pains, which were bound to get worse before they got better. He tossed Kristy's Blazer keys into the air, caught them again. They both headed for the rig, Dylan hobbling a little, Logan at a sprint.

It wasn't hard to find Floyd and the scene-investigation crew from Missoula; there were half a dozen cars and official vans nosed up to the edge of the orchard. The police seemed oblivious to the seventy head of cattle milling around, bawling and flinging up dust.

By Dylan's reckoning, it was a miracle old Cimarron, the white bull, hadn't moseyed over to conduct an investigation of his own. He scanned the field with a sudden turn of his head—one he immediately regretted—and sure enough, there was his rodeo nemesis, looking on from within charging distance, one forefoot pawing at the ground.

"Uh-oh," Dylan said.

The bull lowered his massive head.

"Should somebody yell 'olé'?" Logan quipped. He'd always been a bold bastard, even in his prerodeo days. Now, the damn fool seemed to *like* the idea of being skull-butted over the top of the tallest tree in the orchard.

"Somebody," Dylan answered evenly, "should yell 'look out.'" He squared his shoulders, took a slow step in Cimarron's direction. "It's me he's after," he added, shaking off his brother's hand when he reached out to grab his arm. "Tell Floyd and the boys to get into their cars. Now."

He took another step.

Cimarron pondered his options, tossed his head.

"Damn it, Dylan—" Logan protested.

"It's all right," Dylan said, without stopping or turning around. He made himself bigger in his mind, a trick a veteran rodeo clown had taught him, and took care not to look the bull directly in the eye. "This has been coming on for a while, hasn't it, old buddy?" he said to Cimarron, though afterward he couldn't recall whether he just thought the words, or spoke them out loud. "I was the last man to lower himself onto your back in a chute. You threw me. I reckon now you're curious to know why I left you here on this ranch all this time."

Behind him, Dylan heard a few raspy curses and the slamming of car doors. He didn't look back.

Maybe it was shock from the sniper incident earlier in the day, but he'd have sworn he and that animal were communicating with each other, on some intangible level. He knew what the bull was thinking and, further-more, he was convinced the reverse was true, as well.

Had he hit his head on a rock when Sundance sent him flying?

Another sound stopped him, made him look back. The lever on a rifle.

Dylan whirled, saw Sheriff Book standing about ten feet behind him, aiming a high-powered Winchester.

A little thrill went through Dylan, an adrenaline rush, in the split second he spent analyzing the situation. Kristy's suspicions about Floyd did a kaleidoscope turn in his brain; he even wondered if the sheriff had been the one to fire that shot a few hours before.

He discarded the possibility almost as soon as it came to him—if Floyd Book had taken aim at him, even on a running horse, he, Dylan, would be cooling on a slab at the county morgue by now. Despite his age, the man was a marksman.

"Don't shoot him, Floyd," he said quietly. "He's got legitimate business with me."

"He charges," Floyd argued flatly, and it was only then that Dylan realized Logan was standing right beside the sheriff, "I shoot."

"Dylan—" Logan ground out.

Dylan silenced his older brother with a shake of his head, turned back to face Cimarron. In some ways, he was facing a lot of other things, too—his own past, mostly. His dad's life—and death. His mother's accident, and Tyler's mom's unconditional surrender, alone in a tacky motel room. Losing Kristy that last time. And all the time he'd missed with Bonnie.

This wasn't high noon with a retired rodeo bull.

It was a showdown with himself.

Stand, or run.

He'd done enough running, and that left just one choice: claim his patch of ground and hold it.

"Dylan, you damn fool!" Floyd shouted. "What the *hell* are you trying to do? Prove to everybody that Jake Creed wasn't the only one in this family without the God-given good sense to be scared?"

It was a mouthful, Dylan reflected, with a slight smile, more a crook at the corner of his mouth than anything. Most likely, Floyd would have had to lower the rifle to say all that.

"You shoot this animal," Dylan replied cordially, without turning away from Cimarron, "and I'll have your badge."

"You want my f-ing badge," Floyd retorted furiously—he was old-school and didn't use the f-word lightly—"you can *have* the gawdamn thing!"

"You're scaring the sheriff," Dylan told Cimarron calmly.

Cimarron, for his part, snorted a couple of times and flung up some more dust with that right front hoof. His long tail switched at the flies trying to come in for a landing on his haunches. He seemed to be pondering everything Dylan thought or said, deciding whether to send him flying skyward or hear him out.

"I'm gonna stay right here on this ranch," Dylan went on, keeping his voice down low, so Logan and Floyd and the others wouldn't hear. "Keep you in hay and heifers for the rest of your days. You and me, we've got a bond. Because you know, don't you, that you didn't throw me that night at the National Finals. I could have made the eight seconds, but you'd never been ridden, and when it came right down to it, I didn't have the heart to spoil your record."

Cimarron cocked his head to the left, then the right. Snorted again.

"It's our secret," Dylan finished. "I'll never tell anybody that I jumped off you and made it look like a spill."

With that, he folded his arms and waited.

Maybe Floyd was right, and he *was* crazier than Jake had ever been.

Cimarron huffed and tossed his head and raised up some more dust.

Then, as if the two of them had come to an agreement, the bull turned and ambled off toward the other side of the field, most of the heifers following.

Dylan was still standing in the same place when the dust settled and Logan turned up at his elbow.

"What the hell was *that* all about?" Logan asked, his voice gruff with irritation and, if Dylan's guess was right, a certain wonder over the ways of proud bulls and former rodeo cowboys.

"I promised I wouldn't say," Dylan answered, after a long time, turning a grin on Logan.

"Floyd's right," Logan muttered. "You're certifiable."

But when they started back toward Floyd and the cluster of cops, Logan slapped Dylan's back, and Dylan managed not to wince.

He looked at the shell casing the state police had found, and at the tracks in the soft floor of the orchard. Not much to go on, for all the public money they were burning through, poking around taking pictures and samples of tree bark and even making plaster casts.

It was *Law & Order* gone country.

And whatever the hell was going on, Dylan knew, it was a long way from over.

"They think it was just some kid playing with a rifle," Logan said, as the two of them stood watching the crew pack up to leave.

"They *always* think it's just some kid," Dylan agreed. He hurt everywhere; almost wished he hadn't pitched that prescription into the trash, back at the clinic.

"You got any ideas?" Logan asked, as they started toward the Blazer.

She'd be spitting nails when they got back to the ranch house, Kristy would. There'd be a backlash that would bend the trees parallel with the ground and strip off every leaf.

Dylan smiled at the prospect as he eased himself behind the wheel, while Logan took the shotgun side.

"Yeah," Dylan said, at his leisure. "I've got some ideas—about a shot or two of whiskey, a hot bath and a certain woman anxious to soothe my troubled brow."

Logan laughed. "That isn't what I meant and you know it," he replied. "I don't know about the whiskey, but the hot bath and a sympathetic woman sound real good. If I limp when we get back to the house, will you tell Briana I got trampled by that old bull of yours?"

CHAPTER FOURTEEN

DYLAN SANK into Kristy's big claw-foot bathtub to his chin, while she sat on the edge, trying not to look at his equipment—about the only part of him that wasn't bruised or scratched from the pitch off Sundance's back.

If this were the old West, he fancied, soothed by the hot water and the beer Kristy had brought him, the brew would be rotgut whiskey, he'd have a skinny cigar clamped between his teeth and she'd be dressed up— or down—like a dance-hall girl.

The fantasy took him to full mast.

Kristy happened to be sneaking a peek right about then, and bright pink suffused her cheekbones. She looked away hastily, but not quite hastily enough.

Dylan chuckled. "Come on in," he drawled lazily. "The water's fine."

Kristy gave a little huff, stood up, sat down on the side of the tub again. "Bonnie—"

"Is asleep," Dylan said, when her voice fell away. "And haven't we already had this discussion once?"

"I'm *not* getting into that tub, Dylan. You're *hurt,* remember?"

He sighed, and hoped it sounded noble and long-suffering. "It rings a bell," he admitted. "Which is why I could use some…feminine consolation right about now."

Kristy folded her arms, teetered a little but, regrettably, caught her balance before toppling in on top of him. "I made your dinner. I ran this bath for you. I brought the beer upstairs. That *is* 'feminine consolation,' Dylan Creed, and don't you dare get the idea that I'm going to wait on you just because you're living here."

"No sex?" he asked, making sure he looked hounddog dejected.

She blushed again. "I didn't say that—exactly."

He laughed.

And his cell phone rang from his shirt pocket, said shirt being across the bathroom, on top of the hamper, and therefore out of reach.

Kristy arched an eyebrow.

"Don't answer," Dylan said.

"It might be important," Kristy objected, heading for the hamper, extracting the phone and snapping it open. "Hello?"

Dylan waited. There were calls, and there were calls, and somehow, he knew this wasn't one he particularly wanted to take.

"Never mind who I am," Kristy said into the phone, straightening her spine and lowering her eyebrows until they almost met. "Who are *you?*"

Shit, Dylan thought. *Sharlene.*

Kristy crossed the bathroom, shoved the phone at him, frowning. At least she wasn't glaring.

Yet.

"I should have known you'd be with a woman," Sharlene shrilled into his ear, before he got a word out.

"That's been my pattern so far," Dylan said mildly. "How's the boyfriend?"

Sharlene wasn't exactly a quick study, and the gibe went over her head. "He took that money you wired and *left,* that's how he is, the chickenshit—"

"Is there a point to this call, Sharlene?"

Sure there was. She wanted more money. And she'd have to say so.

"I'm in big trouble, Dylan," Sharlene said, crying now. She could turn on the waterworks faster than any woman he'd ever known, and turn them off again just as quickly, once her purpose was served. Since she couldn't have gotten word of his custody petition so soon after Logan filed it, she was going to hit him up for another infusion to her bank account. "I can't pay for the motel room we've been staying in."

"How do I know this isn't a con, Sharlene?" Dylan asked reasonably. "The boyfriend could be right there, putting you up to this."

"He's *gone!*" Sharlene wailed. "I swear it, Dylan."

Kristy started for the door, sort of slinking along, but Dylan gestured for her to stay, and there was an unspoken "please" in the motion of his hand. She walked slowly back and sat on the lid of the john.

"Any—anyway," Sharlene fumbled on, when he didn't speak right away, "I've got a proposition for you. Just listen, okay?"

Here it comes, Dylan thought, half jubilant, half resigned. She was about to offer him full custody of Bonnie—for a price. And while he wanted to raise his daughter to adulthood, it still disgusted him that Bonnie's own mother would even dream of making such a bargain.

"I'm listening," he ground out, no longer reclining in the tub, but sitting bolt upright.

Sure as hell, she surprised him.

"Well—" Sharlene's voice took on a sunny, little-girl quality that chafed Dylan's last nerve, "I was thinking we could go ahead and get married, you and me, and bring Bonnie up together. Be a real family."

Dylan closed his eyes.

Opened them again.

"Dylan?" Sharlene prompted sweetly.

"There's somebody else, Sharlene," Dylan finally managed, his gaze locked with Kristy's. It wasn't an ideal choice of words, but it certainly beat his gut response, *I wouldn't marry you if you were the last woman on earth.*

"There's *always* somebody else," Sharlene wheedled. "I don't mind if you have another woman on the side, as long as I can see other men, too."

"And that's your idea of a 'real family'?"

"Come on, Dylan! Don't be such a pain in the ass."

"This woman isn't the kind I'd have 'on the side,'" Dylan replied coldly. "She's the kind I'd *marry.*"

Kristy had turned her face away, most likely embarrassed to be overhearing Dylan's half of the soap opera, but at this last, she swung around to look straight at him. He could usually read her pretty well, but this time, one conflicting emotion after another chased across her eyes.

Sharlene was silent for a long time, except for the choking sobs—a fair indication that the boyfriend really *had* swiped the loot on hand and hit the road, leaving her behind with an unpaid motel bill and no car.

"Then I'm coming to get Bonnie," she said. "Somehow, I'll get there—I'll hitchhike or whatever. I want my daughter back—without her, I'm totally alone."

The bath was getting cold. In fact, it was giving Dylan the chills, but he didn't move to turn on the hot-water spigot. He didn't think he *could* move, even if he tried. "Look, Sharlene," he said, his voice still gruff, but gentled down a little, "don't hitchhike, okay? It's dangerous. There are a lot of creeps out there."

"I don't care what happens to me!" *Like hell, she didn't. Sharlene was all* about *Sharlene.* "I just want to get back to my baby—I never should have let you have her—"

She'd home in on Stillwater Springs like a missile, he knew she would. If Sharlene had to thumb rides with drunks and rapists and drug addicts all the way from Texas to Montana, she'd get there. And whatever his reservations, he couldn't let her travel like that, expose herself to guys who carried duct tape and box-cutters in their bag of tricks, because she was a human being and, beyond that, Bonnie's mother.

"Look, I'll get you a plane ticket," he said.

Kristy's eyes widened at that, then narrowed again.

"But there's something you need to know before you make the trip," Dylan went on grimly. "I've already filed for custody."

Another silence, leaden as a rock.

Dylan hadn't wanted to spring the custody petition on Sharlene over the phone, at least not in her current emotional state, but not telling her would have been wrong, too. This was the lesser of two evils.

"You're going to take her away from me?" Sharlene asked. This time, her voice was small, and the cracks in it were real.

Fury boiled up inside Dylan, along with pity. He hadn't had the best childhood, but Sharlene's had been even worse. She probably loved Bonnie, in her own bruised and broken way, but responsible parenting was beyond her skill set. She knew how to hustle. She certainly knew how to lie. But the next time looking after Bonnie was inconvenient—and it was, 24/7, even for him—Sharlene would dump her again.

"I want custody, Sharlene," Dylan said, very quietly, his and Kristy's gazes locked together again. "But I won't stop you from seeing Bonnie if you want to."

A few sniffles. "But I'm her *mother.* And she's all I have."

"This isn't about what you have or don't have," Dylan replied carefully. "Bonnie needs a home, a family, some stability. I can give her those things."

Sharlene gave a derisive little laugh, and it saddened Dylan to hear it. Her back was to the wall, and she was trying to brazen it through. That was a way of life for her—perennial damage control. "Sure. Until you get tired of that woman I just talked to—or until you want to rodeo again—"

Dylan stood up, reached for a towel, wrapped it around his middle. It was time to play the card he hadn't wanted to play. "Of course," he went on, as though she hadn't said anything, "there would be a settlement."

Now, he would know for sure how Sharlene really felt about Bonnie. If she told him to shove the settlement, he'd still fight for custody, but he'd be a lot more liberal when they hammered out a visitation agreement. On the other hand—

"How much of a settlement?" she asked. No tears now. Her tone was level and hyperalert.

Something inside Dylan deflated, not for his own sake, but for Bonnie's. "It's negotiable," he said. The fine supper Kristy had cooked for him earlier, after they got back from Logan's place, churned in his stomach and then went sour.

"It would have to be a lot."

Dylan's jaws felt as though they'd rusted at the hinges. He had to force his reply out. "The higher the stakes, Sharlene," he managed, in a near growl, "the more you have to give up in return."

"You want me to sign off, don't you? Agree to stay out of—Bonnie's life."

"Until she's eighteen," Dylan said. "Then it will be up to her whether or not she wants to have a relationship with you. And if you run through the money, I won't give you more."

"I have to think about this," Sharlene said.

What sort of woman had to *think* about selling her own child? He couldn't imagine Kristy, or Briana, or any other female he knew agreeing to such terms, however generous.

But at least Sharlene hadn't jumped at the hook and agreed immediately.

That was something. Not much, but something.

"In the meantime, though," Sharlene went on, cool and matter-of-fact now that she'd caught the scent of money, "I still have to eat and pay for my motel room."

"I'll wire you enough to get by on. *In the meantime,* get a job."

"Bastard," Sharlene said, and slammed down the phone on her end.

Dylan considered flinging his phone against the wall, but decided against it, since he was trying to turn over a new leaf, to be a different and better man than before. A different and better man than Jake, who, in the same position, probably would have packed Bonnie's bags for her and put her on a bus headed for Texas.

And *then* smashed the phone against the nearest wall, just for good measure.

Kristy simply watched him, standing now, wringing her hands a little. The old Dylan *would* have put a fist through a wall, and that was the Dylan she knew best.

"Y-you'd *marry* me?" she croaked.

"All you've gotta do is say yes," Dylan said. It wasn't the kind of proposal he would have envisioned—if he'd gotten as far as envisioning one, which he hadn't—him standing in a prissy-assed Victorian bathroom wearing nothing but a towel, fresh from a row with the mother of his child. And Kristy a captive audience the whole time, forced to listen to his end of the conversation and try to make sense of it.

No, he would have pictured another setting entirely. Someplace under a starry, moon-crowded sky, probably. He'd have had flowers and a diamond ring to offer, and polished his boots and ironed a shirt for the occasion.

"Why?" Kristy asked, almost in a whisper. "Because of Bonnie?"

"Partly," Dylan admitted. Except by omission, when he'd turned his back on Kristy, in front of the jail the morning after his dad's funeral, deliberately letting her believe he didn't care if the whole thing ended right there, he'd never lied to her.

"Only partly?" Kristy pressed, looking fragile.

Again, he couldn't read her. She looked alarmed, and semi-intrigued, as though she might actually consider doing something as crazy as marrying a Creed.

He couldn't answer. He was too afraid of saying the wrong thing, shifting the delicate balance.

"Do you love me, Dylan?"

He swallowed hard. "I don't know," he said.

"I see," she replied, after a few moments of mulling things over.

He went to her, cupped her chin in his hand. And she didn't pull away, though her eyes—her beautiful corn-flower-blue eyes—were full of confusion and proud sorrow. "I honestly don't know, Kristy. With Sharlene threatening to take Bonnie back—and the bodies in Sugarfoot's grave and somebody taking a shot at me with a rifle—I'm not real sure about anything right now."

"And yet you'd marry me."

"Yes."

"So Bonnie would have a mother."

"I can't deny that's a factor."

Kristy flung out her hands. "Then just about *anybody* would do, right?"

"You know that's not true. If it was, I'd have put a ring on Sharlene's finger by now."

She turned away, walked out of the bathroom, into the master bedroom. It was a frilly, beribboned place, with lace at the windows and flowers the size of dinner plates rioting on the spread, but Dylan didn't mind any of that.

The room smelled like Kristy.

It was permeated with her presence.

She stood at one of those lacy windows now, staring out into the gathering darkness. He'd have given a lot to know what she was thinking then, what she was feeling, deep down.

Was she crying?

God, he hoped not. She'd had enough reasons to cry in her life, without his adding to them.

"If I loved anybody," Dylan said, "I'd want it to be you."

She stiffened, but didn't turn around. "I want children, Dylan. And if—when—you decide to move on—well—I'm not Sharlene." She rounded slowly then, looked him straight in the eye. "I won't ever, *ever* let you take any baby of mine."

He supposed his puzzlement showed. "What are you saying?"

"That if I loved anybody, I'd want it to be you."

It felt like a slap in the face, having his own words thrown back at him like that, but fair was fair. If he and Kristy had a baby together, and then things fell apart, it would all but kill him to walk away from the child, let alone Kristy, but he'd do it. He'd do it because, as she'd said, Kristy wasn't Sharlene.

Alone or with him, she was perfectly capable of raising a child, and doing one hell of a good job at it. "I'm not going anywhere, Kristy," he said, knowing she wouldn't believe him—and why should she? "If you want Bonnie and me to leave right now, tonight, go back out to the ranch, we will. But I meant it when I said I was going to bring my little girl up on home-ground."

"What about the rodeo?" It was a reasonable question. He'd loved the game too much—like a mistress with her claws in his heart, it had always wooed him, despite his best intentions. For all practical intents and purposes, he'd chosen it over Kristy, when the chips were down.

And what a damn fool he'd been.

"I'm getting too old for that crap," Dylan said, with a rueful smile. Sure, he was young, but rodeo—especially bull-riding—was a kid's sport. "I'm tired of being on the road. Tired of eating in cafés and truck stops and sleeping in motels where the sheets haven't been changed in a week."

She pondered all that—he guessed she was doing her level best to trust his word—and it gave him hope that she was even willing to make the attempt.

"I want a baby, Dylan," she said finally. "I love Bonnie—it would be privilege to help raise her, but *I want a baby*. Of my own."

"And where do I fit into this equation, besides the obvious?"

The sadness in her eyes was almost more than he could bear. "If you stayed, and we got old together, that would be—good. If you go, I'd have our child. And I wouldn't try to keep you from seeing him or her whenever you wanted."

He supposed, under present circumstances, it was the best deal either of them could hope for. Kristy was only thirty, but she could probably hear her biological clock ticking.

"Then maybe we should give it a try," he said, his voice sounding like he had sandpaper in his throat.

Kristy's spine straightened again. Her shoulders straightened and her chin came up, though she didn't move from her post by the window. He'd instinctively stepped back by then, wanting to give her space to think, to breathe.

"We'll have to do a lot better than just *trying*," she

said. "I want this to be a real marriage, Dylan. I want a family, pictures on the mantelpiece, soccer games and Sunday school—the whole works. Even if we don't— don't love each other."

He nodded. It was a wordless promise. He *would* do better than try. He'd make it work, somehow, insofar as that was possible for one person in a relationship to do.

"We'll get a ring tomorrow," he said, when he found his voice again. "And a license."

"No rings," Kristy said quickly, with a little shake of her head.

He waited, in silence, for her to tell him why.

She took her time doing it. "My mother had a simple gold band," she said, her tone dreamy and her eyes distant. "Dad probably bought it on credit, at Sears or some- where, and by the time I was in my teens, it was scratched and dented. She treasured it, though. Because Dad put it on her finger. Because she loved him, and she knew he loved her. They lost hay crops to freak hail storms, and cattle to the bloat and a lot of other things. Once, we went a whole year with a big blue tarp tacked across our roof because we couldn't afford to repair the leaks—"

Dylan remembered seeing that tarp, as a kid, from the school bus. Some of the others had teased Kristy about it—until he pitched the ringleader head-first into a snowbank. That was the end of the digs at Kristy Madison, at least in his presence.

"But they always, *always* loved each other, no matter what," Kristy went on. "I don't want a ring until you can tell me you love me, Dylan, and mean it. And I won't give you one—not if we're married fifty years—until I can do the same."

"Fair enough," Dylan said gruffly.

In the little room next door, Bonnie let out a fitful cry, as though she knew her future was being decided by two well-meaning but very mixed-up people.

"I'll go," Kristy said, when Dylan made a move in Bonnie's direction.

He let her, since she was dressed and he was wearing a towel, and he felt rooted to her bedroom floor anyway.

All the aches welled up inside him, some of them physical, most of them not, suddenly and overwhelmingly. He pulled back the covers on Kristy's bed and crawled in, listening with stinging eyes while she spoke soothingly to his little girl, just on the other side of the wall.

Did he love Kristy?

He'd never felt what she made him feel with any other woman, but did that mean he loved her? When— and if—he ever said, "I love you" to Kristy Madison, soon-to-be Creed, he wanted it to be gospel-true. Something he'd never go back on, no matter what.

Kristy began to sing a little tune, a soft and silly lullaby, and Bonnie giggled sleepily.

The sounds snagged at Dylan's heart.

A long, long time ago, Tyler's mother, Angela, used to sing like that. She'd always sit on the side of her little boy's bed, and stroke his hair, and Logan and Dylan would lie in their rooms down or across the hall and soak it in.

Dylan had closed his eyes, and pretended he still had a mother.

Maybe Logan had, too.

Life could be—*would* be—so different for Bonnie, and for any other children that came along. All he had to do was marry Kristy, and it would happen. He imagined his new house on the ranch—he'd spent years designing it in his head—full of noisy kids, dogs and cats, aunts and uncles.

And the wanting fairly crushed him.

He was lying there, rigid, with the sheets pulled up to his waist, when Kristy came back. She sat down on the edge of the mattress and, just as if she'd seen right inside his brain, she smoothed his hair.

"Go to sleep," she said. "Bonnie's fine."

He stared up at the ceiling, where the night shadows danced, unable to look into Kristy's eyes. "It'll be a big responsibility, being Bonnie's stepmother," he said. "Think it through. Because it will break her heart if you ever decide you want out."

Kristy leaned down, kissed his forehead. "Sleep," she repeated. "You were shot at and thrown from a horse today. You need your rest."

"I wasn't thrown—" he started to protest.

Kristy chuckled and pressed one finger to his lips. "Okay, cowboy," she said. "You weren't *thrown*. But you're something the worse for wear, just the same, and you need some rest."

"I need some—"

"*Rest,*" Kristy insisted.

And she got up off the bed.

"Where will you be?" he asked. "While I'm *resting*, like some old fart in a nursing home?"

She laughed again, but it was a sad, scrapey sound. "Oh, I thought I'd go down to Skivvie's and dance topless on the bar," she teased.

"Kristy."

"I'm in a mood to peel wallpaper," she said, from the threshold.

She closed the door between them with a gentle click.

Dylan was positive he wouldn't sleep without her there.

He was wrong.

HE SLEPT LIKE A DEAD MAN, and when he woke up, the room was full of sunlight, Kristy's side of the bed was still made up and he could smell bacon cooking.

He jumped out of bed, scrambled into jeans and a shirt and hustled it downstairs to the kitchen.

Bonnie was bouncing happily in an old-fashioned high chair, the kind made of shiny wood, with a decal of a pink duck on the back, while Kristy stood at the stove, building an omelet and looking for all the world like a ranch wife cooking for a man she loved.

The scene stopped Dylan on the dining room threshold, practically took his breath away.

Kristy smiled. "There you are," she said. Following his second glance at the high chair, she added, "That was mine, when I was little. I found it in the basement last night and washed it down—looks good as new, doesn't it?"

Dylan managed a nod, crossed to kiss the top of Bonnie's head, offering a silent, desperate prayer as he did so. *Let it last.* Given that he wasn't exactly a praying man, he was a little taken aback by the power of his longing to live a thousand, a million, mornings like this one.

He looked at the retro wall clock, a green plastic teapot-shaped gizmo. Eight-thirty.

"Shouldn't you be on your way to the library?" he asked.

Kristy smiled. "I took a vacation day," she said. "Or

half of one, anyway. Susan will open for me. I'll go in after lunch. It's story day."

"Oh," he said. Given the profoundly inexplicable way he felt, it was a wonder that mundane things kept rolling off his tongue.

"Sit down, Dylan," she coaxed, a patient smile curving one side of her mouth, though her eyes still looked as though she couldn't decide between sadness or hope.

He drew back a chair at the table, next to Bonnie, and sank into it. Sam clickety-clicked it across the kitchen to lay his muzzle on Dylan's thigh, as if in sympathy for his plight. If this could be *called* a plight.

"How do you feel about stopping by the courthouse to pick up a marriage license?" he asked, and then held his breath while she poured him a cup of coffee, brought it to the table, set it down and leaned to kiss the top of his head.

The gesture both stirred his groin and gave him that little-boy-listening-for-a-song sensation he'd had the night before, when she was singing to Bonnie.

"Ready," she answered. "I feel ready."

The relief was so overwhelming that Dylan closed his eyes for a long moment. Kristy had had all night to think, after all. There was a lot going on in her life. She could have changed her mind about the wedding, wanted to forget the whole thing.

"Where did you sleep last night?" he asked, when she went to dish up the omelet. It sure as hell hadn't been with him.

"With Bonnie," Kristy answered lightly. "I was up late, though."

He risked a grin. "And here I thought you were down at Skivvie's, dancing topless on the bar."

She laughed. Inclined her head toward Bonnie. "Little pitchers," she chimed.

"Right," he said, with a sigh. Reality was already nipping at the edges of the bright morning, tarnishing them a little. Sharlene was expecting a wire, probably already hovering in some Western Union office, cursing his name. She might just blow the money and save the whole mother-daughter reunion for another time—but she might hop on a plane, too.

"Dylan?" Kristy stopped when she spoke, rimmed in sunshine from the window behind her.

He waited.

"I understand about Sharlene, if that matters. I know you have to deal with her. Just be honest with me where she's concerned, that's all."

Dylan's eyes stung. Maybe it was that golden aura shimmering around Kristy like a full-body halo. Maybe it was that she really *did* understand.

"Come here," he said gruffly, easing Sam aside with one hand.

Kristy approached, her features gradually becoming visible as she left the halo behind. He took her hand, pulled her down onto his lap.

Bonnie seemed to find that hysterically funny, and chortled with baby laughter.

"What?" Kristy asked, sort of fidgety and nervous.

"Thanks," he said, kissing the tip of her nose.

"Thanks?"

"For being Kristy."

She still seemed a little rattled. "That's the easy part," she said.

"Yeah, well, not everybody has a handle on being

who they are," Dylan answered. He'd have loved to take her upstairs, right then, peel off those sexy jeans, strip away the light blue pullover shirt and pleasure her until she melted, but it was morning, and Bonnie was awake, and the world was already in gear for the day, humming along beyond the walls of that cheerful house.

"Is it so confusing, being Dylan Creed?" Kristy asked softly, the expression in her eyes tender and concerned.

"I suppose I'm making it harder than it has to be," he admitted.

The omelet was probably getting cold, and so was his coffee. Bonnie was beating out a drum-song on the metal tray of the high chair with the base of her sippy cup. And Dylan didn't want anything to change. He wanted to be right where he was, with Bonnie and Kristy and the dog and that snooty Persian cat, forever.

Kristy smiled, kissed his cheek with a smack and got back to her feet. "Breakfast is ready," she said.

So much for forever.

CHAPTER FIFTEEN

THINGS SEEMED UTTERLY SURREAL to Kristy that morning—getting the required blood tests, applying for the marriage license at Stillwater Springs' courthouse and giving the jewelry store a wide berth because of the no-rings pact. In three short days, she kept thinking, she and Dylan would be husband and wife. *Married.*

This had been her dream, on some level, since childhood, when she was a knobby-kneed little ranch kid in homemade clothes and he was the town drunk's middle son, never actually *looking* for a brawl, but ready to tie in if one got started.

Even as a teenager, Dylan had been a formidably good lover. Now, as a full-grown man, comfortable in his skin and operating on a full complement of testosterone, he was lethal. Marriage to him meant soul-rending sex, on a regular basis. Bonnie was the proverbial icing on the cake—custody issues with Sharlene notwithstanding, Kristy was about to become a stepmother, and she knew she would excel at it. Knew she would love Dylan's child as dearly as any they might conceive together.

So why wasn't she happier?

The question was rhetorical, of course; Dylan wouldn't

say he loved her until he was sure it was bone-true, and she *couldn't* tell him how she felt because, damn it, she still had some pride.

Okay, she had a *lot* of pride. Maybe too much.

Bonnie was nodding off on Dylan's shoulder by the time the three of them arrived at the Marigold Café for an early lunch.

"Let me have her," Kristy said, from her side of the booth.

Dylan complied, and Bonnie came willingly to Kristy, stretched out on the vinyl seat, her head resting on Kristy's lap, and immediately fell asleep.

They ordered food—Kristy her customary salad, Dylan a club sandwich—and shared a chocolate milk shake because it was a celebration.

Sort of.

"If you don't want a ring," Dylan ventured mildly, once the waitress had scribbled down the info and retreated behind the counter to slap down the little bell on the pass-through to the kitchen in the time-honored "order up" tradition of greasy spoons everywhere, "I guess it follows that you won't go for a gown and veil and a cake, either."

Kristy looked wistfully down at Bonnie, entwining a gentle finger in one of the child's sweat-moistened curls. "Tell you what," she answered softly. "If we make it to our first anniversary, we can throw a church wedding with all the trimmings, renew our vows, the whole bit."

"You," Dylan said thoughtfully, "are a remarkable woman."

Kristy sighed, met Dylan's gaze across the table. "Is that a compliment?"

He grinned. "Mostly."

"'Mostly'?" Kristy echoed archly. "In what ways am I 'remarkable,' Dylan Creed?"

"You're remarkably sexy, remarkably beautiful and remarkably *stubborn.*" He paused, drew a breath, huffed it out. "I can take or leave the church wedding and all of that," he went on, his voice low and gruff. He reached across the tabletop, took her hand and played idly with her fingers, sending little thrill-flames up her arm, from nerve-ending to nerve-ending. "I even get the part about not wearing rings. But there *is* one thing that's really important to me."

Kristy simply raised one eyebrow and waited.

"I know it's getting to be old-fashioned—that a lot of women don't change their names—but I'd like you to be Kristy Creed after we're married."

He looked so hopeful, so quietly worried, that Kristy's heart teetered behind her ribs, like a circus performer on a frayed high wire. Maybe Dylan *didn't* love her, in the romantic, white-lace-and-promises sense of the word, but he cared deeply. He cared what she thought, what she felt, what she wanted.

"Kristy Madison Creed," she recited, her own voice a little husky. "I like it."

Dylan's smile was as dazzling as a sudden burst of sunshine on a murky day. "Good," he said.

The food arrived.

They ate, making plans for the remains of the day. Kristy would go to the library, and Dylan intended to draw up sketches of the house he intended to build. They'd look the drawings over that night, together, and incorporate Kristy's suggestions, then have the actual blueprints drawn up. Dylan had already spoken to Dan Phillips by cell phone that morning, and he'd scheduled a bulldozer to raze the old place to the ground.

They'd just about finished their meal when Sheriff Book walked into the café, moving directly toward their table like a man with a purpose.

Kristy felt a little frisson of fear and chagrin. This was *Floyd*, for heaven's sake. Her late father's best friend.

It was just plain crazy to be afraid of him.

But she was.

She worked up a smile.

Sheriff Book pulled off his mirrored sunglasses, nodded to her, without smiling in return, and turned to Dylan. "It was Caleb Spencer," he said immediately. "The movie star's kid? He's the one who took a potshot at you out there in the field yesterday. His father brought him into my office by the shirt collar this morning and we just got through writing him up."

Kristy's stomach clenched. She opened her mouth, found herself incapable of uttering a single word and pressed her lips together.

"Pull up a chair if you've got time," Dylan said, as casually as if officers of the law came by his table in restaurants to share such news as a regular thing.

Floyd found a chair, dragged it over and sat down.

The waitress brought him "the usual"—diet cola.

"The kid swears he fired the shot by accident," Floyd said wearily. He took a long sip of his cola and closed his eyes as it went down, like a man drinking ambrosia from a chalice. "The father is beside himself, but at least he made young Caleb turn himself in. Gotta hand it to him for that."

"Maybe it *was* an accident," Dylan speculated, surprising Kristy as much as Sheriff Book. "How old is he, anyway? Sixteen? Seventeen?"

"Sixteen, but we can try him as an adult."

"Whoa," Dylan said. "Don't I have to press charges first?"

Floyd developed a unibrow, he was frowning so hard. "He *shot* at you, Dylan. With a *rifle*."

"He's a city kid," Dylan reminded the sheriff, still acting as though people tried to blast him out of the saddle all the time. "He probably couldn't hit the broad side of a barn, even if he tried."

"All right," Floyd said testily, pausing to chafe the back of his neck with one hand, "let's assume, for the sake of argument, that the rifle went off accidentally, just the way he said it did. That still begs the question—*two* questions, actually—what the hell was a sixteen-year-old kid doing with a deadly weapon in the first place, and why was he prowling around on private property?"

Dylan grinned, raised his eyebrows. "You must have asked him that and a lot more."

Floyd sighed so deeply that Kristy half expected him to unpin that badge of his, then and there, and set it right down on the table. Just walk away from being sheriff, and let either Jim Huntinghorse or Mike Danvers have the job and the headaches and frustrations that went with it.

"Of course I did," the older man ground out. "The rifle belongs to Spencer, Sr.—we were able to verify that—and the kid claims he thought it was a dummy, the kind extras carry in movies."

"And Caleb was on the ranch because…?" Kristy finally managed to ask.

"Said he was thinking of making a movie himself, with a few of his friends from L.A. He was interested in the cemetery—didn't actually realize it was on Creed property. That's what he says, anyway."

"And you don't believe it?" Dylan asked moderately.

"Kids make movies these days. Especially rich ones, with access to all kinds of fancy camera equipment. They're fascinated with cemeteries, God knows why, so I can even buy that Junior didn't realize he was trespassing. But there's still one mighty big hole in his story, obviously."

"Why the gun?" Dylan mused. Kristy, the sheriff and the whole Marigold Café might have disappeared— he'd tuned out of his immediate surroundings, Dylan had, to ponder the problem.

"Hell, yes, 'why the gun,'" Floyd grumbled.

Bonnie stirred, sat up and crawled into Kristy's lap.

"You've got to press charges, Dylan," the sheriff insisted, while Dylan went right on drifting amid his own thoughts. "You let a kid get away with something like this, and the next thing you know, he's taking out a dozen people in a high school cafeteria because one of them beat him to the last piece of pizza."

Kristy soothed Bonnie by giving her some of Dylan's French fries and what was left of the chocolate shake.

"Maybe," Dylan agreed, slowly coming back to himself. His gaze lit on Bonnie, and another grin twitched at the corner of his mouth. "I'll want a word with young Caleb Spencer before I decide one way or the other, though."

"You're just going to let him walk," Floyd accused,

disgusted. "Why, Dylan? Because you were a wild kid once and you turned out okay?"

"I didn't say I wouldn't press charges, Floyd," Dylan answered patiently. "I said I wanted to talk to the boy first."

"You're a damn fool even to go that far, in my opinion."

"Hell, Floyd, you can come up with a more imaginative insult than that," Dylan remarked. "I trust you've got Billy the Kid locked up in the local hoosegow?"

Floyd snorted at that, scraped back his chair with a noise that made Bonnie's eyes widen, and Kristy's, too.

"I wish," the sheriff growled, looming over all of them like a bear risen onto its haunches to bat at bees with both paws. "Bail's already been set and paid, thanks to Mr. Hollywood and you'll-never-guess-who."

Dylan chuckled, shook his head. "Logan?"

"Logan," Floyd confirmed grimly. "Lawyers! The kid shoots at his own brother, on his own ranch, and Logan Creed signs up to defend the little bastard without a qualm!"

Kristy was a little thrown by this news, but Dylan took it in stride.

"Everybody deserves defense counsel," he said.

"You Creeds," Floyd said, in parting. "You're all crazy."

"So I'm told," Dylan agreed, apparently amused.

Kristy, on the other hand, felt a hot flush of indignation suffuse her face. After all, *Bonnie* was a Creed, and in three days, she would be one, too. She started to protest Floyd's remark, albeit belatedly and with no particular retaliatory phrase in mind, but stopped at a slight shake of Dylan's head.

He'd shoved aside what was left of his food, as Kristy

had, and was turning a ballpoint pen he'd found by the napkin holder end over end, pressing the clicker down on the tabletop with each rotation, then snapping it up again with a rhythmic motion of his thumb. Judging by his expression, one, Dylan was unconcerned that there was indeed a hole in Caleb's story, and two, he didn't see Logan's willingness to defend the boy as any sort of brotherly betrayal.

Kristy, quite the contrary, wanted to stand toe-to-toe with her future brother-in-law and demand to know what he could possibly be thinking, accepting Caleb's case.

Sheriff Book cleared his throat, signaling a change in subject and an imminent departure. "Kristy," he said. "You doing okay? Seems like the majority of those reporters have moved on, but there are a few still lurking around."

"I'm doing fine," Kristy replied, a little stiffly.

"I spoke to Doc last night," Floyd went on, replacing his bad-ass country sheriff sunglasses. "He's off the critical list, but he won't be coming home for a week or two. Asked me to keep an eye on his place while he's in the hospital."

At the mention of Doc, Kristy softened a little. "Is Lily with him?"

Floyd nodded. "She and the granddaughter," he answered. "Once Doc gets his walking papers, Lily and the little girl will be moving here to look after him until he's a hundred percent." A spare grin rested on Floyd's mouth for a fraction of a second, then vanished. "If I didn't know better, I'd swear that old coot had himself a heart attack just to get Lily back home."

"Can Doc have visitors yet?" Dylan wanted to know.

The waitress appeared with a check, and he handed it back with money to cover both the meal and the tip.

"Just immediate family," Floyd said. "Since the granddaughter is underage, Lily's the only one who can get in."

Dylan nodded.

Kristy made a mental note to contact Doc's part-time secretary, Donna, and ask if there was anything she could do to help get the Ryder house ready for Lily, her child and a certain gossipy but loveable old veterinarian.

The sheriff offered a few quiet words and left.

Dylan dropped Kristy off at the library, along with Bonnie, her diaper bag and the ever-present sippy cup. He'd protested the idea at first, but Kristy maintained that Bonnie would enjoy story hour and, anyway, she'd be taking the child to work with her a lot, in the near future.

Once Dylan had gone, and Kristy had dropped Bonnie's gear off in her office and herded the toddler into the play area, within easy sight of the main desk, Kristy listened to an update on the morning's events from Susan with half an ear. Later, she broke up a minor scuffle between two very young brothers over a toy, and she kept an eye on the line of public computers along the wall, too.

The users were a real cross-section of the town's population.

Ranchers scanned agricultural publications online.

Teenagers surfed and chatted.

Housewives printed out grocery coupons.

Kristy, mainly focused on watching over Bonnie and doing her job at the same time, thought distractedly of

Gravesitter, and wondered once more if she'd seen the mystery person time and time again, right there in the Stillwater Springs Public Library.

Briana brought Alec and Josh in for story hour, and they immediately gravitated toward Bonnie. Both boys were solicitous of her, like big brothers, and the scene made Kristy smile.

Briana, meanwhile, approached the desk. "Is it true?" she asked, with a friendly grin.

Kristy returned the grin—she was peeved at Logan, not Briana—and pretended to be confused. "Is *what* true?"

"The town's buzzing," Briana said, with mock impatience. "You and Dylan had blood tests at the clinic, and *then* you were seen going into the courthouse together. The supposition is wedding bells."

Kristy laughed, shook her head. "I've lived in this community most of my life," she said. "And it never fails to surprise me, the way word gets around so fast. It's almost spooky."

"It's true?" Briana asked eagerly. "You and Dylan are getting married?"

"It's true," Kristy said, after looking both ways.

Briana made a fist and pumped the air with it once, exuberantly. *"Yes!"*

"It'll be a very simple ceremony," Kristy went on, reassured that no one else had overheard, though she couldn't think why she should be, since the news had obviously traveled the whole loop already. "Probably in my living room. Of course we want you and…Logan and the kids to be there, but we're keeping the fuss to an absolute minimum." She lowered her voice. "And,

Briana? *Definitely* no bridal shower, just in case that idea should cross your mind."

Some of Briana's earlier enthusiasm dissolved, and a small frown creased the space between her perfect eyebrows. "Okay," she said, and sighed. A long pause followed. "What was that little hitch about—the one just before you mentioned Logan's name?"

"According to Sheriff Book, Logan is defending Caleb Spencer," Kristy said carefully. She didn't want her feelings about that coming between her and Briana. They'd been friends from the first, and soon they would be in-laws, after all. Almost sisters. "I just—well— Since Dylan could have been killed—"

Briana sighed. "They're all out at the main ranch house hashing it out at this very minute," she said. "Logan, Dylan, Mr. Spencer and Caleb. That's why I brought the boys to town for ice cream and story hour. So we wouldn't be underfoot. Logan hasn't said much about the case, except that it really *isn't* a case and he believes Caleb's version."

"Why?" Kristy asked. "Why does he believe Caleb?"

"I'm not sure," Briana admitted. Her gaze swung to her two boys, both of whom were doing their best to entertain a delighted Bonnie, her green eyes full of gentle pride. Her voice went soft. "If I had to guess, though, I'd say he doesn't want Caleb to wind up in prison if there's a chance he's just a kid who made a stupid mistake."

Kristy recalled Dylan's reluctance to press charges until he'd spoken to Caleb personally. She'd do her best, she decided, to reserve judgment and let Dylan deal with the situation as he saw fit.

So she simply nodded, and when a good crowd had

gathered, she settled herself in the play area and read three more chapters of last time's Nancy Drew mystery.

THE KID LOOKED SORRY, Dylan thought, seated next to his famous father on Logan's living room couch and fidgeting a lot. Of course, it remained to be seen whether Caleb Spencer was sorry he'd nearly injured or killed a man and a horse, or sorry he'd been caught.

Zachary Spencer, for his part, had faded to gray, and there was a grim set to his mouth. He'd done the right thing, making Caleb face the consequences of his actions, but he clearly intended to do whatever he had to do to look out for his boy, too.

Which made him a father, Dylan concluded.

He wondered what Jake Creed would have done, if he or Logan or Tyler had gotten themselves into a fix like this, and only part of the answer came to him. First order of business: tan their hide, but good.

After that, who knew?

Logan occupied the big armchair, so Dylan, the most recent arrival, pulled the computer chair over to join the circle.

"Tell us your version of what happened yesterday, Caleb," Logan said, taking the lead.

Perry Mason in jeans, shit-kickers and a T-shirt, Dylan thought, smiling to himself. This was an entirely new aspect of Logan's persona.

Caleb started to cry. "I've already told you," he sniffled. "I told my dad. I told the sheriff. How many times do I have to go over the same stuff?"

"Tell us again," Zachary ordered quietly.

Caleb's gaze moved to Dylan's face, and the boy

made a visible effort to suck it up and carry on. "I was real mad at you when you took that horse away from me," he admitted. "But I wouldn't have *shot* you for it."

"Why bring the gun to the cemetery, Caleb," Dylan began evenly, "if you were just scouting for a movie location?"

The boy's sigh seemed to come from the soles of his expensive sneakers. A tremor went through him, and he sniffled again. Wiped his eyes with one forearm. "My friend Toby Phillips was supposed to meet me in the cemetery. I'd told him about the gun—my dad says it used to belong to John Wayne—and Toby wanted to see it for himself."

Dylan and Logan exchanged glances. Both of them knew Toby—he was Dan Phillips's kid brother. From what Logan had said on the cell phone, prior to Dylan's arrival for the powwow, Toby was an honor student, had never been in trouble and aspired to make movies someday.

Logan leaned forward in his chair, rested his forearms on his thighs and regarded the elder Spencer impassively. "As I understand it," he said, "you were thinking of buying some property around Stillwater Springs."

Dylan frowned. Waited.

"Yes," Spencer said, with a sigh. "Some outfit called Tri-Star bought the land I wanted right out from under me, though, so I'm back to square one. If it wasn't for those bodies found on the Madison place, Caleb and I would have gone back to L.A. and none of this would be happening."

Ah, yes, Dylan reflected. Spencer had taken out some kind of option on Kristy's story. Or, more properly, her *father's* story.

"Where have you and Caleb been staying?" Logan asked, in the tone of a man who already knew the answer, but wanted everyone else to hear it.

"We've got an RV," Spencer replied, playing the game. "At that park outside of town, just past the casino."

"Not the kind of digs you're used to, I suppose," Logan observed.

Spencer smiled, but it was brittle, that smile, and soon fell off his face. "It's an adventure," he said. "You know, father and son. Roughing it."

Logan nodded sagely. "And you brought a rifle with you from L.A.?" he asked, his tone moderate.

"Just the Duke's," Zachary replied. He sure looked the part he was playing—devoted dad, stunned by his otherwise perfect son's behavior—but, then, he was an actor. "I have a large collection of movie memorabilia—especially items from westerns. That one is a favorite, and since I knew we'd be away from home for the summer, I decided not to leave it behind and risk having it stolen. We've had several break-ins, for all the security measures I've taken. A couple of days ago, I saw a virtual duplicate in a gun shop in Missoula—they're unbelievably rare, so I bought it. Caleb mistook that rifle—which is real, of course—for the collector's piece."

It was a convoluted story, to Dylan's way of thinking. Just convoluted enough to be true. But there was still an important detail that hadn't been mentioned.

Dylan looked at Logan.

Logan nodded slightly.

"Why was the gun loaded?" Dylan asked, watching both Spencers the way he would opponents at a high-stakes card game. There would be "tells," poker jargon for the unconscious ways people gave away exactly what they most wanted to hide.

"I'd taken it to the range to try it out," Zachary said. "I *meant* to unload it as soon as I got home, but the phone rang—" He paused, shook his head, looked for a moment as though he might break down and cry, just the way Caleb had earlier.

It was too late for the loaded-guns-kill speech, and Zachary Spencer probably didn't need to hear it, anyway. He'd been damn lucky not to learn his lesson the hard way.

Spencer's eyes were earnest as he looked into Dylan's face. "If somebody has to be prosecuted," he said, "it ought to be me. I'm the one who left that rifle where my son could find it. I'm the one who forgot to unload it."

Now that he'd had a chance to assess the situation, Dylan agreed with Logan's take on the matter. Caleb Spencer was spoiled, but he wasn't a killer.

"I won't press charges," Dylan said.

Both Caleb and Zachary looked almost sick with relief.

"But," Dylan stipulated, "I do think I should have some kind of redress. After all, I could have broken my neck—or lost a good horse."

"You want money?" Caleb's father asked, patting the front of his golf shirt as though feeling around for a checkbook.

"Not money," Dylan said, tight-jawed.

"What, then?" Caleb asked, looking wary.

"Help training Sundance," Dylan answered, watching the boy's eyes widen. "You've got a few things to learn about working with horses. Of course, if you're not interested—"

"I'm interested," Caleb broke in, neatly confirming Dylan's suspicions. "I *like* horses."

"You have a mighty peculiar way of showing it," Dylan observed, recalling how the boy had meant to go after the gelding with a lunge-whip, out there in the road. Would have, if Dylan hadn't stopped him.

Caleb flushed. "I guess I lost my temper," he said.

"You lose your temper with that horse, or any other living thing, and I'll lose mine—with you. Not a pretty sight, I can tell you."

The boy nodded solemnly.

Logan indulged in a brief grin.

"Until my barn is finished, there won't be much horse-training going on. Sundance is boarding here at Logan's for now, but he still needs feeding and currying and regular exercise. His stall has to be shoveled out, once a day anyhow, and Logan has his own horses to take care of, not to mention his lawyering, so I'll be over regularly to see to the gelding."

"And I get to—have to help?" Caleb asked, leaning forward from his perch on the edge of the couch.

"Yep," Dylan said. "Six o'clock, every morning, for the next couple of weeks." He let his gaze drift to the boy's feet. "Get yourself some decent shit-kickers," he advised, in closing. "This is a working ranch, not a basketball court."

AT FIVE SHARP, Dylan pulled into the library parking lot, got out of his truck and sprinted up the front steps. It promised to be a slow night, but Kristy was bushed from keeping up with Bonnie all afternoon. Once story hour was over, and Briana and her boys and the other kids had left, the child had morphed into a holy terror.

She'd helped Kristy pick up all the library toys, and promptly scattered them again at the first opportunity.

She'd pulled a whole row of books off a low shelf before Kristy caught her.

And then she'd screamed "Daddy!" and "Poop!" alternately until the whole place cleared out. Even Susan, the die-hard, had pleaded a headache and made a hasty exit.

Maybe, Kristy thought, sagging with relief when she saw Dylan come up the stairs and through the front door, she'd bring Bonnie to work with her again.

Someday.

The little girl shrieked with joy when she saw Dylan, and ran to him as fast as her toddler's legs would carry her. He laughed and swung her up into his arms, then planted a smacking kiss on her cheek.

"How was it?" he asked Kristy. The grin in his eyes indicated that he already knew.

Kristy rubbed her temples with the fingertips of both hands. Sighed so hard that her shoulders rose and fell.

Dylan laughed. "I tried to warn you," he said.

Was it crazy to be so glad to see a man who wouldn't say, "I love you"? Kristy wondered. She *was* glad to see Dylan, and not just because it would mean a respite from taking care of an angelic hellion like Bonnie. Just by being there, he seemed to charge the atmosphere with something entirely new, an unseen electricity, a sense of expectancy and possibility.

She went back to her office to fetch the diaper bag,

brought it to Dylan. "I'll close up around seven," she told him, "unless there's a last-minute rush."

He grinned again, in that slow Dylan-way that curled Kristy's toes and made things dance inside her. "Nothing worse than a bunch of readers on a rampage," he teased. "Bonnie and I will have supper ready when you get home."

Someone promising to have supper ready when she got home.

When had *that* happened before? Not since she lived on the ranch with her parents, certainly. She'd been coming home to an empty house for a long, long time.

"Okay," she said, standing on tiptoe to kiss Bonnie's cheek.

The little girl giggled and dodged, then craned to kiss her back.

"Did you speak to Caleb?" Kristy asked, following Dylan as far as the front door.

"Yes," Dylan answered. "I'll tell you about it over supper."

With that, he leaned to place a light, brief and very tantalizing kiss on her mouth, then turned, with Bonnie in the curve of his left arm, and the diaper bag slung over his right shoulder.

Somehow, he managed to look drop-dead gorgeous, even walking away with the child and her gear.

Once he'd gone, the library seemed as silent as an undiscovered tomb, somewhere deep beneath the Egyptian sands.

Kristy busied herself neatening shelves, restocking returned books, washing out the employee coffee pot and setting it up for morning. All that time, she had one eye on the clock—*she,* Kristy Madison, who had *never* in her whole life been a clock-watcher. In the Madison household, the habit had been on par with Communism.

Just as she was about to close up, a young boy came into the library, dressed in a long black coat. Kristy had seen him before, and though she didn't know the boy, it didn't take a rocket scientist to conclude that he was an outsider. While there were always a few rebels in any group, most of the high schoolers in Stillwater Springs were ranch or farm kids. They wore jeans and boots and although some of them probably smoked marijuana, beer was still the most popular drug of choice.

She was tired.

She was hungry.

She wanted to get home to Dylan and Bonnie. Yes, Bonnie, even after the hair-raising adventures of the afternoon.

Maybe that was what drew her to the boy—all her usual defenses were down. "We're closing soon," she said sunnily, not wanting to discourage further library patronage, or make this obviously different kid feel unwelcome.

"I just want to check my e-mail," he said.

He had a spider tattooed to his neck, and piercings in his ears, eyebrows and—Kristy winced inwardly— even his lower lip.

"Okay," Kristy said.

He logged on to the first computer in a row of several. It was the newest one, but still antiquated.

"Do I know you?" Kristy asked.

He turned, looked up at her curiously. Solemnly. Such old eyes, in such a young, if desecrated, face. "I come around sometimes," he said. Translation: Go away, lady. I'm busy here.

Still, Kristy hovered. She couldn't help it.

The boy turned back to the computer, his fingers flying deftly over the keyboard.

Presently, he swung around again. "You want something?"

Kristy shook her head. But she didn't move away. "What's your name?" she asked.

"Davie McCullough," he answered, his blue eyes dipping to her name tag. At least, she *hoped* it was her name tag. The bit of plastic was pinned directly above her right breast, and she resisted an urge to unpin it and move it higher up. "What's yours?"

Kristy didn't reply.

Davie rounded to face the computer again, sending off go-away vibes in the way only teenagers can do.

At last, he gave up. "Okay," he said. "You win. I'll leave."

"Be sure to come back tomorrow," Kristy replied. "We'll be open until nine."

"Right," Davie mocked, homing in on the front door.

Kristy took a deep breath. Gathered her courage. "Gravesitter?" she asked.

CHAPTER SIXTEEN

"I BEG YOUR PARDON?" Davie said. If he'd recognized the screen name, if he was indeed Gravesitter, he gave no outward indication at all.

"Never mind," Kristy said, her smile wobbling a little. *Color me with one foot in my mouth,* she thought.

As soon as Davic had gone, she locked the door and turned the Open sign to Closed. Normally, she would have hurried back to her office for her purse and any books she'd decided to borrow over the course of the day, and leave by the back way. The longer she lingered, after all, the greater the risk of someone showing up and staring at her plaintively through the glass in the door until she let them in for "just one book." Of course, that one book always evolved into *several,* all painstakingly chosen.

That night, she stayed where she was, watched Davie McCullough slink away down the sidewalk, head down, his hands stuffed into the pockets of his black opera coat. He seemed to be shrinking inside the huge garment as he moved farther and farther away, almost as if it were swallowing him fold by fold.

It wasn't dark yet when Kristy reached home—it would be several hours before the sun set—but lights burned in the kitchen, and the glow warmed her heart.

Dylan was inside. Bonnie and Sam, and Winston, too.

A complete world, contained within the walls of a single house in an obscure Montana town.

Kristy quickened her step.

Home wasn't a house, she thought, or a piece of land.

For her, it was one man, one little girl, a cat and a dog. Wherever they were, *that* was home.

She paused just inside the gate in her white picket fence, soaking in the present moment—*this* time, *this* place. The infinitely precious *right now.*

The back door was open a little way, and she could hear the washing machine chugging away on the utility porch, dishes clattering in the kitchen beyond, Bonnie's small voice piping her favorite litany, "Daddy! Daddy! Daddy! Poop!"

Kristy smiled and simultaneously wiped away a tear with the back of one hand. Year after year, she'd soldiered bravely on, always smiling and maintaining that her life was *fine, wonderful, perfect in every way.*

Then Dylan had come back to Stillwater Springs, and brought Bonnie along for good measure. And suddenly, without them, her life *wouldn't* be fine, wonderful or perfect. It was a kind of vulnerability she hadn't counted on, hadn't even considered. Wasn't sure she could endure.

How could she have forgotten what a dangerous risk it was to love so fully that she thought her heart might burst? Hadn't she learned anything from losing her parents, and Sugarfoot, and that younger, wilder Dylan?

While she was thinking these thoughts, the screen door creaked and Dylan stepped out onto the porch.

"Hey," he said.

Embarrassed to be caught standing there staring at her own house as though she'd never seen it before, Kristy marshaled all her forces and got moving again.

"Supper ready?" she asked, hoping she sounded—well—*normal.*

"My world-famous beans and wieners." Dylan grinned, coming down the steps to meet her, gathering her close for a moment, kissing the top of her head. "You open a can and a package of hot dogs, mix them together and throw the whole works in the microwave. I'm expecting the Food Channel to offer me my own show any time now."

Kristy laughed, because if she hadn't, she'd have cried. Her emotions were so very close to the surface these days, such a tangle of sweet hopes and wild fears, and she had zero hope that that would change anytime soon. "Sounds fabulous," she said, but the words came out sounding broken, and Dylan gripped her shoulders and held her back a little way to look directly into her face.

Inside the house, Sam began to bark in cheerful, semifrantic yips, Winston hissed, and something crashed to the floor. Something heavy, that shattered.

Dylan immediately turned and bolted back into the house, and Kristy was right behind him. At the threshold, Winston shot by them like a furry little comet, darting outdoors, and Sam ratcheted up the barking until Kristy wanted to put her hands over her ears.

Bonnie, strapped into her high chair, had nonetheless managed to upend a bowl of salad on the supper table, and lettuce leaves, tomatoes, shredded cheese and ceramic fragments covered the floor.

"Bonnie *bad,*" the little girl said solemnly.

Kristy laughed with relief, because the child wasn't hurt, and Dylan, surely feeling the same way, immediately began cleaning up.

"Bonnie's *not* bad," Kristy said, unfastening the toddler from the confines of her high chair and hoisting her into her arms for a resounding cheek-kiss.

"Jury's still out on that one," Dylan remarked, carefully gathering up the pieces of the broken bowl. "Was this special?"

Kristy swallowed. The bowl had been her mother's and her grandmother's—possibly even her *great*-grandmother's. She said what any of those women would probably have said, in a similar situation. "Bonnie's okay. That's all that matters."

Remember, Kristy, she heard her mom telling her once, as a child, when she'd accidentally dropped a special ornament while decorating the family Christmas tree one December, people *are important. Things are just things.*

Dylan, crouching there on the kitchen floor, looked up at her. "I'm sorry," he said. "I should have seen that the dish was old, and left it on the shelf."

"*People* are important, Dylan," Kristy said. "Things are just things."

Bonnie struggled to get down, but there were still bits of broken pottery on the floor, so while Dylan went to the utility porch for a broom and dustbin, Kristy carried the child to the playpen in the corner of the kitchen and set her inside.

Bonnie immediately pitched a fit.

Dylan came back, gave a shrill whistle through his front teeth.

Bonnie went silent, her eyes enormous, not with fear, Kristy knew, but with awe.

"Can you teach me how to do that?" Kristy asked. Such a skill would come in handy at the library, and not just when Bonnie was around, either.

Dylan chuckled. "You're born with the ability to whistle like that, Kristy," he told her. "It can't be taught."

Kristy supposed, regretfully, that he was right. If she'd possessed the whistling gene, the gift would have manifested itself before now. Since yelling and spanking were both out, too, she'd have to find another way to divert Bonnie from her temper tantrums.

She washed her hands at the kitchen sink, went to the fridge, got out the makings of another salad and started chopping.

Bonnie curled up on the floor of the playpen, stuck one thumb in her mouth and drifted off. Sam tried to stick his muzzle between the bars and lick the top of her head, probably thinking she'd been imprisoned and wondering how to stage a jail break without opposable thumbs.

"Peace." Dylan sighed, dumping the remains of the previous salad and the last of the broken bowl into the trash, then putting the broom away.

"Did Bonnie eat?" Kristy asked, as they sat down to greens served up in a plastic storage bowl and that old Montana standby, beans and wieners.

"I shoveled some of that toddler-goop into her mouth earlier," Dylan answered, after tossing a fond glance in his daughter's direction. "She spit most of it back at me, but I figure enough went down to hold off starvation."

Kristy smiled, relaxing. It had been a long, emotional day, but she was home now, with a man who cooked—sort of. There were plans for the new house and possibly the barn on the counter, neatly rolled and secured with a rubber band.

"You went ahead and had the blueprints drawn up?" she asked.

Dylan shook his head, watching her with a forkful of salad greens poised halfway between his plate and his mouth. "No," he said. "Those are just the sketches we talked about."

A soft warmth spread through Kristy. She didn't expect to make a lot of changes to the designs, but she did want to have some part in the process, however small. "Oh," she said.

"You look exhausted," Dylan commented. "Good thing I've got a surprise planned for after supper."

"A surprise?" Kristy asked, pausing. "What?"

Chandelier-swinging sex? An engagement ring and an "I love you" to go with it?

The sex was distinctly possible. When it came to the ring and the declaration, though, she knew she was getting carried away.

"It wouldn't be a surprise if I told you, would it?" Dylan asked.

They finished supper. Dylan gathered Bonnie up and took her upstairs to get her ready for bed. Kristy re-trieved a disgruntled Winston from the backyard, let Sam out for a few minutes and cleared the table. Overhead, the plumbing rattled, and water swooshed through the pipes.

Dylan was a brave man, Kristy thought with a smile. He was giving Bonnie a bath.

Remarkable. She'd never dreamed one of Stillwater Springs' bad boys would turn out to be such a first-class father.

Let alone run the washing machine, which went into the spin cycle at that moment, and put supper on the table.

Her dad would have fought a whole pride of lions, bare-handed, to protect her and her mother. But she'd never known Tim Madison to wash a dish, prepare a meal or do laundry.

Dylan returned presently—by that time, Kristy had brewed coffee and wiped the table clean in preparation for viewing the sketches—his shirt soaked. He grinned and hauled it off as he crossed the kitchen, heading for the utility porch, and came back tugging a T-shirt over his head, fresh from the dryer.

He grabbed the rolled-up sketches and brought them to the table.

Kristy sat down in the chair closest to his, after pouring them each a cup of coffee, and enjoyed the scent of Dylan's still-damp skin and hair, and the newly laundered T-shirt.

He bumped his shoulder to hers, then popped off the rubber band and unrolled the large pieces of drawing paper.

And there was the house, drawn with colorful strokes, front view, back view and interior floor plan.

Kristy drew in her breath. She'd never guessed Dylan could draw so well, and the detail was amazing—even the light switches were there. Clearly, he'd been designing the structure in his mind for years, just as he'd said.

"I'm impressed," Kristy said.

"Good," Dylan replied, watching her again. "Here's the kitchen. State-of-the-art everything. I originally planned on slate floors, but with the munchkin around, cushioned vinyl would be a better bet."

"Definitely cushioned vinyl," Kristy responded. The house was just a sketch, done on cheap paper with colored markers, but she could see it in her mind, even imagine herself living in it. The cupboards, the appliances, the combination breakfast-alcove with the overarching windows—the thing had come to life.

It took her breath away.

"Here's our room," Dylan went on, almost shyly, indicating a spacious area with its own fireplace, a gigantic master bath and a private patio. "The nursery's here, and I'm guessing we need three other bedrooms besides, not counting the guest quarters on the other side of the living room—"

"Dylan," Kristy breathed.

"What?"

"It's—incredible." She frowned as her gaze caught on a smaller room with a strange object drawn in the center. "What's this?"

Dylan chuckled. "Mechanical bull," he said.

"Mechanical—?"

"Nothing adds zip to a party," Dylan informed her seriously—or, at least, she *thought* he was serious "—like a mechanical bull."

"What?" Kristy asked, with a twinkle. "No indoor bowling alley?"

Dylan grinned, leaned over to kiss her lightly. "I thought about a room totally dedicated to sex, but the kids would find it for sure, so that's out."

The kids. Plural, as in more than one. Kristy gave a sudden, pealing laugh, more from delight than amusement. "*That* I would have objected to," she said.

"But you're okay with the mechanical bull?"

"Sure, as long as you don't expect me to ride it."

"You'll ride it," Dylan said, with such confidence that Kristy suspected he might be right. "The floor will be sawdust, with rubber pads underneath. The rest of the room will look like an old West saloon—"

"How long, exactly, have you been thinking about this?"

"Quite a while," Dylan replied. "I used to lie alone on motel room beds, while I was still rodeoing, and move possibilities around in my head. After a while, it all fell into place."

There was something touching about the thought of Dylan lying in some lonely room, planning a house. Not, she supposed, that he'd been alone as often as he probably wanted her to believe.

"See anything you'd like to change?" he asked, and his face was as open as Kristy had ever seen it. Was his heart, by any chance, open, too?

She shook her head. "It's perfect."

And it *was* perfect, except maybe for the mechanical bull, and even that might turn out to be fun.

It almost made up for seeing her folks' old place go to some outfit called Tri-Star.

"Here's the barn," Dylan said, switching to another sketch, just as carefully planned as the one of the house had been.

There were twenty stalls, plus a special, larger one for foaling mares, as well as ample space for storing grain and hay. A tack room, a small office and a studio apartment completed the ideal stable.

"We'll probably need some help around the place," Dylan explained, tapping the center of the apartment with the tip of one finger. "This would suit most ranch hands, I guess."

Kristy almost laughed. Her parents' whole house probably wasn't as big as that apartment attached to Dylan's barn.

"The mortgage will be horrific, Dylan," she heard herself say. Shades of the old days, when fear of fore-closure ran through the farms and ranches like another creek, invisible but swift of current, often reaching flood-level.

"What mortgage?" Dylan asked.

Kristy blinked. "Surely—this will cost a fortune—"

"Yeah," he agreed. "It will. This room over here? That's a sort of family-study—the kids can do their homework there, and things like that."

"Dylan," Kristy said, determined to pull him back from the brink of financial ruin. *"Millions."*

"Millions?"

"That's what a place like this would cost."

"Yeah, I know."

"But—"

"It's a relief to know you didn't agree to marry me just to get your hands on my money," Dylan joked.

"I know you've done stunt work, and won a lot of championships, but this—"

"I got a lucky break in the stock market once. Well, more than once, actually, but the first time clinched it."

"What *are* you talking about?"

"Logan started a company several years ago," Dylan answered. "Do-it-yourself legal services kind of thing. I'd just picked up a sizable paycheck at the National Finals in Vegas when it went public, and for once I was a couple of jumps ahead of the bill collectors, so I paid my taxes and plowed the rest into Logan's outfit. We weren't speaking back then, Logan and me, but I knew he had a good head for business so I decided to take a chance. Third best thing I ever did."

"Third best thing?" Kristy echoed, still reeling a little.

Dylan wound a finger in a tendril of her hair, close to her ear, and hot shivers of response rushed through her. "First best thing would have to be a tie between fathering Bonnie and coming back here to marry you. Second, well, that's whichever one isn't first."

Kristy smiled, even as tears filled her eyes. "Some logic, Creed."

"Works for me," Dylan said, rolling up the sketches again, snapping the rubber band back on. "If you're good with all this, I'll get the plans drawn up right away."

She nodded, still in something of a daze.

The interlude was so sweet, so delicate, that Kristy was sure something terrible would happen to end it. This wasn't paranoia; it was based on bitter experience.

"About that surprise," Dylan said.

He stood and pulled Kristy to her feet. Left her standing to lock the back door and shut off the coffee-maker. It was wasteful, Kristy reflected distractedly, since the pot was mostly full, but on the other hand, they could always nuke it the next morning.

They left the darkened kitchen, Winston and Sam following them up the rear stairway, and Dylan stopped to look in on Bonnie as they passed her door.

"Go on," he urged, when Kristy hesitated in the hallway. "I'll be along in a minute or two."

Kristy nodded, stood a moment longer and then walked into her room.

The covers were turned back, and the sheets were scattered with yellow rose petals so fresh that Kristy caught their marvelous scent even from the doorway.

Things shifted and tumbled inside Kristy, wants and needs and, conversely, a sense that with Dylan, she had no physical boundaries, no secrets. He could lay her soul bare as easily as her body. In the throes of their love-making, she lost herself, as a separate human being, and became part, not just of Dylan, but of something cosmic.

She heard him come in behind her, close the door softly.

She, the librarian, who read three books in a slow week, couldn't come up with a single word.

Dylan stood behind her, wrapped his arms around her waist, bent his head to kiss her neck. Outside the door, Sam whimpered softly for admission, and Winston scratched officiously at the wood.

Dylan sighed, stepped back from Kristy, went to the door.

"Later," she heard him say to the animals.

Miraculously, the scratching and whimpering stopped.

Dylan shut the door again, and gave her backside a squeeze as he passed, headed for the bathroom. She heard the water go on in the tub.

And still she didn't move.

She just stood there, drinking in the sight and scent of those rose petals.

"Kristy."

She turned just her head, saw Dylan in the bathroom doorway, arms folded, leaning one shoulder against the frame.

"That isn't the whole surprise," he said.

"Oh," Kristy murmured. She wasn't sure she could *handle* another surprise; she was still absorbing rose petals, and the incomprehensible idea that Dylan, one of Jake Creed's rowdy sons, could spend millions building a house without needing a mortgage.

Dylan held out a beckoning hand.

Kristy went to him, switched off the light when she entered the bathroom and saw the candles—at least a dozen of them—flickering romantically on every surface. Dylan had run a bath for her, and there were more rose petals, pink this time—a trail of them leading to the tub like some magical path through an enchanted wood. White petals floated luxuriously on top of the water, which was redolent of the petals and lavender and just the merest touch of gardenia.

Kristy was speechless.

Dylan began undressing her, very slowly and very gently.

When she was naked, he handed her over the side of that plain claw-foot tub like a courtier helping a queen step onto a barge. She sank into bliss and water.

Kneeling beside the tub, Dylan bathed Kristy, and while the motions of his hands were more reverential than sexual, rhythmic, almost hypnotic, so lightly did he caress her, all five of her senses and several she'd never known she had were aroused to a fever pitch.

The candlelight, dancing across Dylan's face, awakened her eyes.

Soft music, seeming to come from somewhere better than earth, floated around her ears.

The water, the air, and Dylan's hands touching her, everywhere and nowhere at all.

The mingling of roses and gardenias and man tempted her nose.

And taste? Well, that was the most prevalent sense of all. The want of Dylan, the need of him, tingled on her tongue.

This is a man who does not love you, a voice deep inside her warned, but the wanting drowned it out, forced it to the floor of Kristy's psyche like a bit of flotsam caught in a riptide.

Kristy gave herself up to Dylan, surrendered completely, allowed her senses to riot, unchecked.

At some point, he stripped off his clothes, and while the water drained slowly around them, he took her, brought her to the fiery heart of creation itself with a series of hard, deep thrusts.

Kristy clung to him as she came, and then came again.

And when he reached his own release, she somehow knew.

They'd conceived a child, she and Dylan.

They'd conceived a child.

MUCH MORE SEX like last night's, Dylan reflected, trying to will some starch into his knees while he made a predawn breakfast for Bonnie, and he'd die of sheer ecstasy, long before his time.

Oh, but as the old saying went, what a way to go.

The sun was barely edging the eastern horizon, and Kristy was still sleeping, curled up in a warm, naked little ball in the bed they'd shared. Leaving her was one of the hardest things Dylan had done in a long time, but if he was going to be at Logan's barn by six, he had to hustle.

Would Caleb show up, the way they'd agreed?

He had no idea. He hoped so, though.

He'd wrestled Bonnie into a set of clothes before bringing her downstairs. She'd be in the way out at the barn, he supposed, but she was a Creed kid, so she had to learn to be around horses. And he'd meant what he'd said to Caleb the day before, about Logan having enough to do looking after his own responsibilities. If she got the chance, Kristy would probably volunteer to take Bonnie to the library with her again, but two days in a row of riding herd on a hellcat-in-training was more than anybody could expect.

So Dylan scribbled a note on the blackboard, under Kristy's perpetual grocery list, explaining that he and Bonnie and Sam had gone out to the ranch to tend to Sundance. Dan Phillips was going to look the sketches over, then turn them into blueprints, but he didn't add that information, since there wasn't room.

Did the woman *always* need broccoli, baking soda, yogurt, cereal and cat food, or was she just haphazard about erasing things off the board as she bought them?

Dylan pondered the mystery, with a slight smile curving his mouth, as he locked the back door carefully behind him and carried Bonnie to the truck, Sam gamboling happily alongside.

The drive out to Stillwater Springs Ranch was uneventful, except for Bonnie yelling "poop" at regular intervals. Dylan knew she'd already done the deed back at the house in town—she just liked saying the word.

With any luck, she'd get tired of it before she started college.

Caleb was waiting by the corral fence when Dylan arrived at Logan's, dressed in jeans, a T-shirt and brand-spanking-new boots. His father must have dropped him off, because there weren't any extra vehicles in sight, just Logan's truck and Briana's navy-blue Beamer, a gift from her loving bridegroom.

Dylan smiled to himself.

Once upon a time, Logan had been a heartbreaker, running through women—including two wives—like a drunken sailor spending his paycheck. But that was before Briana Grant and, by extension, her sons. Logan loved those boys as if they were his own; that was obvious by the way he joked and wrestled with them, and allowed them to follow him all over the ranch.

Dylan understood—if Kristy had come as a package deal, like Briana had, he'd have loved her kids simply because he loved her.

Loved her?

Wait a second. He wasn't prepared to go that far.

Caleb waited shyly while Dylan parked the truck and got out. After hoisting Sam to the ground, so the dog could run around in happy circles and then lift his leg against the old pump handle over by the fence, Dylan began turning Bonnie loose from the car seat.

She was impatient, which made the whole job that much harder, and when Briana came out of the house, smiling, her intentions clear by the purposeful, take-charge way she walked straight toward him, Dylan was secretly relieved.

Briana greeted Caleb with a cool nod as she passed him.

"You're up early," Briana remarked, taking Bonnie from Dylan as she looked up into his face.

"Caleb and I are going to see to old Sundance," Dylan answered. He braced himself, expecting Bonnie to pitch a snit, but she didn't. She cooed and tugged at Briana's braid, perfectly willing to be spirited away into the house.

"Have you had breakfast?" Briana asked, and this time, she took Caleb in, too, though somewhat grudgingly. "Logan's still putting away pancakes."

"I'm good," Dylan said, and out of the corner o eye, he saw a flash of disappointment in Caleb's f "I'm not sure about my horse-wrangling buc though," he added smoothly. "He might hav a hotcake or two."

Briana, deftly bouncing Bonnie on he finally turned a full-fledged smile on the n kid. "Are you hungry, Caleb?" she asked. "Y come to all the pancakes you want, if you are.

He blushed so hard it looked painful, then nodded. "Dad bought me a couple of breakfast sandwiches at the drive-through in town, before we came out here, but things like that wear off quick."

"I suppose they do," Briana agreed, tossing Dylan a grin after the kid went by them, all but sprinting for the house.

Dylan followed, with Briana. He'd downed a couple of bowls of cereal back in town, and reheated a cup of coffee before setting up a fresh pot for Kristy, but he could definitely use a jolt of caffeine.

And maybe a pancake or ten.

AT FIRST, Kristy thought it was Dylan, stretched out on the bed beside her, but there was something wrong about the slight slope of the mattress and the odd, jerky meter of the breathing.

Kristy peered through her lashes, and instantly bolted to her feet with a raspy shriek of terror. A person—somehow familiar but definitely *not* Dylan—reclined on his side of the bed, clad in jeans, a heavy turtleneck sweater—and a ski mask.

"Dylan!" Kristy shrieked, though she knew he wasn't in the house.

"He's gone." The figure rose off the bed. "Left at least an hour ago, and took the baby with him."

Kristy's sleep-sodden, fright-spiked mind struggled with that niggling sense of recognition. She'd have given anything for Dylan to walk through the bedroom doorway right about then, but she was wildly grateful to know Bonnie was safely away.

"Who are you?" The question sawed at Kristy's throat. Made her raise one hand to her neck. In the next instant, she realized she was naked and snatched up the bedspread to cover herself.

The intruder reached under the sweater and brought out a small pistol. Kristy had no idea what kind it was, or what caliber; it was enough to know it could kill her—along with the child she and Dylan had started the night before.

"Put on some clothes," the prowler said. The voice. Familiar, like the form, but disguised somehow. Just out of Kristy's mental reach.

Shivering, Kristy moved slowly to her bureau, took out jeans and a short-sleeved pullover, scrambled into them while keeping the bedspread in place as much as she could.

Would a rapist order her to get dressed?

"What do you want?" Kristy demanded, more confident once she had clothes on. She wished she'd let Dylan show her how to use that pistol of his. Was it still on the pantry shelf downstairs in the kitchen, or had he taken it with him, wherever he'd gone? "How did you get in here?"

"Questions, questions." The ski mask came off with a tug of the intruder's gun-free hand, and there was Freida Turlow. "Did you think changing the locks would keep me out? There are a dozen ways into this house—I found them all while I was growing up, but evidently, you haven't, for all the things you've torn up and replaced."

Kristy's mouth had fallen open. She had to will her jaws to work before she could reply.

"Freida! Are you insane? Coming in here with a gun—lying down on *my bed*—"

Freida's face hardened instantly. Her eyes had a queer, glazed look, as though they were focused on some scene only she could see. "Where is it?" she demanded.

"Where is *what?*" Kristy countered, honestly puzzled and already easing, a fraction of an inch at a time, toward the door. If she could just get out of that room, then down the hallway and the stairs—

"My diary!" Freida spouted furiously.

Kristy, on the verge of bolting, froze instead. She might be able to outrun Freida, but not the bullet.

"Is that why you tore out the closet wall in your old room? You were looking for a *diary?*"

"I know you have it!"

"Freida, I *don't* have it. You must have taken it with you, when you moved out, and simply forgotten—"

"I didn't forget! I meant to come back for it—I thought I had plenty of time before we closed escrow—but you were always here, with some wood-flooring salesman, or that guy who was going to replace the furnace, or that handyman measuring for bookshelves—"

"Why now?" Kristy asked, strangely calm, considering that she was looking straight down the barrel of a pistol, one Freida Turlow apparently knew how to use, from the easy way she handled it. "I've lived here for a long time. You clearly had copies of my old keys. Why wait?"

"Because Brett said he had it. For a while, I believed him. I gave him money, let him use my car, sleep on my couch. But when he went into treatment after that last run-in with the law, I went through everything my dear brother owns. And he *didn't* have the diary."

"He could have hidden it someplace," Kristy suggested reasonably. She was stalling for time now, waiting for a chance to make a break for it—and pretty certain that chance was never going to come.

"He's not smart enough to do that!"

Kristy took a risk. "Brett was obviously smart enough to blackmail you," she pointed out diplomatically.

Freida raised the gun. "You watch how you talk to me, Kristy Madison," she said. "You're nothing! The daughter of a stone-cold killer—" Something changed in the other woman's face then, something elementally frightening.

"What was in the diary, Freida?" Kristy pressed quietly.

"You already know. You *have* it."

"Okay, I have it," Kristy said, on to Plan B—God,

please let Plan B work. She had to get the gun away from Freida and run.

"Then you know what's in it," Freida murmured, looking confused now, even a little disoriented, as though she might be losing track of her whereabouts, if she'd ever had a handle on reality in the first place. "You know I saw your dad drag that drifter out of the bed of his pickup and dig a hole under those trees, and throw him inside. *You know* I killed that Clarkston girl and buried her in the same place, on top of Sugarfoot. And *since* you know all that, I'm going to have to kill you."

CHAPTER SEVENTEEN

KRISTY BARELY HEARD the sound on the stairs, over the thud-thud-thud of her heart, but it didn't raise her hopes of being rescued before Freida Turlow shot her to death. She was sure it was only Winston, and what could he do?

"Why?" Kristy asked. "Why did you kill Ellie?"

Freida's face contorted with some horrible emotion. Or was it a horrible memory? Both, most likely.

"You'd think she was a saint, the way everybody carried on when she went missing," Freida sputtered, checked-out again. Or still. "Well, let me tell you, she *wasn't*. She took my boyfriend—got him to sleep with her and made sure I knew about it. Rubbed my face in it. He liked her better, she said—"

Kristy swallowed. "Sheriff Book?" she asked stupidly. Rather than being a one-man-woman, Freida was generally considered the *any*-man type. It was just that Floyd was the only one of Freida's lovers Kristy could recall, stressed as she was.

Freida gave an ugly, contemptuous snort. "That fat old man? He didn't even have the guts to stand up to his wife and get a divorce!"

The sound came again, nearer now, a slight creak in the hallway.

Freida frowned, listening hard.

Run away, Winston, Kristy thought desperately. *Run away.*

She wouldn't have put it past Freida to shoot the cat, if he startled her or simply because he'd decided to live with Kristy instead of moving on with his original mistress.

"Who's there?" Freida demanded, turning aside from Kristy and raising the gun, gripping it in two hands, like someone on TV. Someone *used* to guns, and proficient with them.

Kristy lunged at her, but even in her madness, or perhaps because of it, Freida had the instincts of a wild creature, cornered and prepared to kill to escape.

She swung her clasped hands, still holding the pistol and striking Kristy in the face, sending her hurtling backward onto the floor. She landed hard on her backside, blood streaming from her nose; she was dazed and coldly, calmly certain that this was it.

She was going to die.

But suddenly Floyd Book loomed in the doorway to the hall, a blurry shape. A blurry shape with a service revolver in one hand. "Put the gun down, Freida," he said evenly. "This is all over."

Freida *didn't* put the gun down. She didn't even lower it. "You know who my boyfriend was, Floyd?" she taunted. "Don't pretend you didn't hear, because I know you did. It was Mike Danvers. The man who wants your job."

"Put the gun down," Floyd repeated wearily. "I don't want to have to shoot you, Freida, but I will."

"Oh God, Freida," Kristy pleaded, unable—and

afraid—to get up from her sitting position on the floor, "do what he says. *Please—*"

And that was when Freida whirled on Kristy, gun raised. "You took Mike. You took my house. You even took my damn *cat—*"

She pulled the trigger.

Simultaneously, Floyd fired from the doorway, a flame flashing briefly from the end of his gun barrel.

Kristy screamed as Freida whirled to one side, like someone performing a ludicrous and graceful dance in slow motion, and then fell to the floor, still gripping the little pistol in her right hand. The pistol that had clicked, but not actually gone off.

There was blood—her own and Freida's. And with it came the memories, vivid, crimson ones. Her dad, loading the body of that drifter into a wheelbarrow, in the sultry darkness of a summer night.

With the help of Floyd Book.

Floyd was staring down at Freida, as though he couldn't believe he'd actually shot her, but he was still holding the service revolver.

Kristy couldn't have spoken if it would have saved her life.

Floyd had been there, on the ranch, the night of the killing.

Slowly, as if unaware that Kristy was in the room at all, Floyd crossed to Freida, knelt beside her. She stirred, groaning, on the floor. The sheriff set his revolver down, activated the radio on his belt.

"We need an ambulance at Kristy Madison's place," he said to the dispatcher in his office. "Someone's been shot, and it looks pretty bad."

Kristy simply stared at her father's old friend, waiting for him to realize that she'd remembered. That she'd seen him clearly, a part of that traumatic scene so long ago. She tried to gather her scattered wits, make a plan, get out of there before he shot her dead to keep her from telling what she knew, what she'd been suppressing all this time, but she couldn't think.

She didn't want to die.

She wanted to marry Dylan, and love him with all her heart, even if he didn't love her in return. She wanted to see Bonnie grow up. She wanted to train and ride Sundance—

Dear God, there were *so many* things she wanted to do.

"You'll be okay, Freida," Floyd said, in a strange, gentle voice. "You'll be okay. Just try to lie still."

Until then, it hadn't registered with Kristy that Freida was alive, though very badly injured.

Floyd reached for the bedspread, still lying where Kristy had dropped it when Freida ordered her to get dressed, and tucked it around the woman, careful not to cause her pain.

A moment later, his gaze swung to Kristy. "I wondered when it would come back to you," he said quietly. "That I helped your dad bury that damn worthless piece of—"

Kristy swallowed hard, struggled to get to her feet, still unsure whether Sheriff Floyd Book would gun her down if she made any sudden moves. Now that some of the shock-fog was clearing, she thought she might actually survive this confrontation—would the man have called for an ambulance for Freida if he meant to kill her?

He might, Kristy decided. Because he could use

Freida's gun, wipe it clean of his fingerprints, and then put it back in Freida's grip, so only hers would be on the handle and trigger. All he'd have to do was say *Freida* had fired the fatal shot—he'd tried to stop her, but just hadn't been quick enough.

If that was his intention, though, he was taking his time about it.

Was it because Freida was conscious, and therefore conceivably a witness? Or because he'd already summoned an ambulance, and some neighbor might hear the second shot and check the clock?

Kristy felt the blood drain from her brain, causing a dangerous dip toward unconsciousness. She gripped the edge of her bureau, somehow managed to stay on her feet. The front of her shirt was soaked red, but the bleeding had stopped. She was pretty sure it had, anyway.

"What really happened that night, Floyd?" she asked. Her voice seemed to come from somewhere far away, instead of inside her, where there was only numbness and the bleak hope that she would walk out of that room on her own two feet.

Floyd sighed heavily, smoothing Freida's hair back from her forehead, murmuring to her to hold on, the ambulance was coming. "Tim called me, after the shooting, and he was in a real panic. Afraid he'd go to prison, or even be executed, and you and your mother would be on your own. In those days, Kristy, it was even harder for a single woman to support a child than it is now, and they were in debt up to their ears, as you know. I came right out to the ranch, and I tried to calm Tim down, tried to reason with him, but he wouldn't listen. He begged me to help him bury the body, so I did. You have to understand, Kristy—we were in the army together, your dad and me. Saved each other's lives half a dozen times, over in Vietnam. I couldn't turn my back on him and besides, I'd have killed that drifter, too, if I'd found him in my little girl's bedroom."

Kristy heard a siren in the distance. Eased herself onto the edge of her bed, too shaky to stand. "He wouldn't have been convicted—would he?"

Floyd sighed. "Probably not," he said. "But don't you see, Kristy? He and Louise were barely holding on as it was. A long court case, and all the legal fees—how was he supposed to pull the family through something like that?"

Kristy bit her lower lip, absorbing that. "You're not going to kill me?"

Floyd gave a raw chuckle. "Now, why would I do that?"

"To shut me up?"

He shook his head. "You read too many thrillers, kiddo. Branch out a little."

"Then I guess you—saved my life."

"Not much gets by you," Floyd said. This was the Floyd she knew and trusted, the one who'd sat at her parents' kitchen table all those times, drinking coffee and eating apple pie and talking about Vietnam until Kristy's mother insisted that he and Tim change the subject.

"How did you know? That I needed help, I mean?"

"Like I told you before, I make a habit of cruising by here every so often. Hell, this town is so small, I cruise by every house in it, half a dozen times a day. I was about a block away, and old Mrs. Beckings, across the street, popped out of one of those lilac bushes of hers and flagged me down—said she'd just seen a burglar pry open your cellar door and slip inside. Sure enough, that old padlock had nearly rusted through—Freida probably sprung it with a stick or something. I came in the same way, figuring you were probably at work, and would have locked all the doors, and I was about to call out when I heard a scream from up here, so—"

"That was me," Kristy said. A shudder went through her as she recalled opening her eyes and seeing a ski-masked figure lying on the bed beside her. She looked at Freida, lying there on the floor. "Did you hear what she said, Floyd?"

"About me being a fat old fool who wouldn't leave his wife?" He seemed grimly amused. "Hell, it's the truth."

"Not that," Kristy said. "She told me she killed Ellie Clarkston. Over Mike Danvers."

"Yes, I heard her say that."

The siren gave another shrill bleep and, moments later, someone hammered at the front door.

The paramedics, of course.

"I'd better let them in," Kristy said, forcing herself to stand.

"I'll do it," Floyd offered. "You stay here with Freida."

Kristy shook her head. Being alone in a room with Freida Turlow, incapacitated or not, was more than she could manage.

Dylan tore into the driveway, wheels flinging gravel every which way, just as Kristy opened the front door for the paramedics and both of Floyd's deputies. He left the engine running and jumped out of the truck, vaulting over the fence and darting across the lawn.

Kristy met him at the bottom of the porch steps.

One of the paramedics asked if she was all right.

Kristy looked down at her bloody shirt and nodded that she was.

Dylan had taken note of the blood, too, of course. Gripping her shoulders, he closed his eyes tightly for a moment, breathing hard. When he looked at her again, he said, "I saw the ambulance— I thought—"

Kristy dropped to sit on one of the steps.

Dylan sat beside her, wrapped an arm around her as she began to tremble.

The story poured out of her: waking up to find she wasn't alone in the bed, Freida raving and brandishing the gun after she'd pulled off the ski mask, confessing to the Clarkston girl's murder, Floyd appearing in the literal nick of time.

If it hadn't been for footsteps clattering on the stairs just inside, they might have sat there, the two them, for hours, Dylan holding Kristy tightly, Kristy glad to be held. But the paramedics had already loaded Freida onto a gurney, and they were in a hurry to get her into the ambulance and race away.

Dylan got up first, pulled Kristy off the steps so the EMTs could pass. Floyd walked slowly in their wake, like a man in a stupor.

Kristy remembered the tender way he'd spoken to Freida, after shooting her, and how he'd covered her with the bedspread in an effort to keep her warm until she could be moved.

Maybe he *had* loved Freida Turlow.

And maybe he was simply the good man Kristy had known for so long.

"You going to be all right, Floyd?" Dylan asked him huskily.

"God damn this job," Floyd muttered, as though no one had spoken to him at all. "God *damn* it."

Kristy touched the sheriff's arm. She wanted to promise that she'd never tell anyone—besides Dylan—that he'd helped her father bury a body, then cover up the truth about what had happened. She owed him that much, she figured, because if not for Floyd Book, she'd be dead by now. The trouble was, she couldn't get the words out—they were all snarled up in her throat.

"It's all right, Kristy," Floyd said, turning to look down into her face. "Soon as I get back to my office, I'll call the state police and turn myself in."

Dylan's jaw dropped. For once, *he* was the speechless one.

"Freida's been blackmailing me all these years—though I didn't figure out who was behind it until today. It'll be worth whatever comes now just to be free of that."

Kristy nodded.

One of the deputies had gone with Freida in the ambulance. The other circumspectly took his boss by the arm and ushered him toward a waiting squad car.

Kristy hurried to catch up. "Freida said there was a diary," she told Floyd quickly. "She was sure I had it, sure I knew what she'd done."

Floyd stopped again, there on the sidewalk, while the deputy stood holding the front passenger door of the squad car open for him. "I have the diary," he said. "Brett Turlow gave it to me, before he went into treatment. Said he'd been holding it over Freida's head for years, and now he'd get back at her for signing off on him the way she did."

"Then you *did* know?" Kristy marveled.

"Hell, no," Floyd said gruffly, and she believed him.

"I figured it was stuff about Freida and me, when we were together. Came close to burning the thing a couple of different times. Now, I'm real glad I didn't."

"Do you think you'll be arrested?" Kristy asked, as the sheriff stooped to get into the squad car.

"Maybe," Floyd said. "Maybe not. I'll have to resign right away, that's for sure, and I guess I could lose my pension. Once word gets around that Freida killed a girl over him, Mike Danvers won't have a chance in hell of getting elected, even though I'll eat my hat if he had anything to do with the murder. And that means Jim Huntinghorse will be the new sheriff." The lawman sighed heavily, plunked himself down on the car seat. "I don't imagine he's got the first idea what he's getting into."

Kristy reached into the car to lay one hand on Floyd's shoulder. "Thank you," she said. "Thank you for saving my life."

Floyd leaned forward a little way, to look around Kristy at Dylan, who was standing close by, watching and listening in silence. "You take care of this lady, young Mr. Creed," he said. "She's a keeper."

"I'll do it," Dylan vowed, putting an arm around Kristy and pulling her close against his side.

As soon as the squad car pulled away from the curb, Dylan hustled Kristy into his truck, and they headed for the clinic, even though she swore up and down she wasn't hurt.

X-rays and a thorough examination confirmed what Kristy had known all along—she was going to have some bruises and maybe even a black eye, but she'd suffered no serious injuries.

By the middle of that afternoon, the reporters were

back in town, some posted in front of the sheriff's office, others practically at Kristy's front door. A team of evidence technicians, accompanied by high-ranking members of the Montana State Police, had cordoned off her bedroom, in order to take photographs and pluck up fibers with tweezers, she supposed.

Kristy sat with Dylan at her kitchen table, Winston curled on her lap. Now that the immediate danger had passed, she was calm enough to be scared out of her mind. Dylan had put a call through to Logan, while she was being poked and prodded at the clinic, and Logan was already geared up to defend Floyd, if things came to that.

At that point, no one knew exactly what would happen.

"I don't think I can sleep in that room again," Kristy confessed.

"I'll be with you when you do," Dylan said.

She gave a completely humorless little laugh. "This is like getting back on a horse right after you're thrown, isn't it?"

"Same principle," Dylan agreed, with a ghost of a grin. "It won't be that long until the new place is done. In the meantime, we'll deal. Get on with our lives."

Kristy sucked in a sudden, gasping breath. "I completely *forgot* about the library!"

Dylan smiled. "Folks will cope," he told her. "As soon as the police are done upstairs, we'll go out to the ranch and get Bonnie. Or I could call Briana and ask her to bring her by."

Kristy merely nodded, still distracted. She'd failed to open the library before, once when she had the flu, and couldn't get out of bed or even grab the phone on her nightstand to call Susan or Peggy for backup, and another time when she'd had a bad case of cramps in the night and thought her appendix was rupturing. But she'd never *forgotten.*

Then again, she'd never been held at gunpoint, in her own home, by a woman who had once been her baby-sitter, either.

Babysitter.

Gravesitter.

Kristy's shock-addled mind made the leap. Was *Freida* Gravesitter? Had she been the one to send that scary IM?

She might never know. And that was a hard thing to accept.

"What?" Dylan asked, evidently reading her expression.

Kristy told him her theory.

He didn't offer an opinion, one way or another.

When his cell phone rang, Kristy jumped. He frowned, checked the caller ID panel and then answered.

"Hello, Logan."

Kristy let out the breath she hadn't realized she'd been holding. It wasn't Sharlene, then, calling to make some threat about taking Bonnie back. The relief was almost as great as when she'd known for sure that Floyd Book wasn't going to shoot her.

"Okay," Dylan said. "Yeah—right. Thanks."

Kristy leaned forward in her chair, waiting for him to click the phone shut and say something.

When he did, the room seemed to tilt crazily to one side, then the other.

"Freida Turlow died in the ambulance," he said.

Tears sprang to Kristy's eyes. Even with all that had gone on, she hadn't wanted *this* to happen.

"Oh my God," she whispered, then gulped back a rush of bile. "And Floyd?"

"There's an investigation pending," Dylan answered. "According to Logan, that's routine, whenever a police officer has to shoot someone."

Kristy doubled over, arms wrapped around her middle, and let her forehead rest on the tabletop. Dylan rubbed her back.

"It's pretty obvious that Floyd shot Freida in the line of duty," he told her quietly. "He isn't under arrest or anything like that. But he's got a lot of questions to answer."

Kristy straightened. Looked him in the eye. "He's told them that he helped my dad bury that body, and then kept the secret. Won't he be in trouble for that?"

Dylan considered. "Probably. But I don't think he'll go to jail, Kristy. Neither does Logan."

"What will happen to him, then?"

"I don't know," Dylan answered. "Logan should be able to shed a little more light on that, once he gets here. He'll stick close to Floyd until the state police are through questioning him, though."

Floyd Book, being questioned by the state police.

It was incomprehensible.

Floyd was an Eagle Scout leader. He was a member of the Rotary and Lions clubs. He taught Sunday-school classes, and he'd been a good husband to Dorothy, at least since her accident.

What would become of Dorothy, if the state decided to prosecute Floyd for the cover-up? She and Floyd had no children, no immediate family, as far as Kristy knew.

"This is awful," Kristy said, starting to get out of her chair. "Floyd's wife—she's in a wheelchair and—"

Dylan eased her back down. "Word's out by now," he said gravely. "The neighbors will look after Dorothy. This is Stillwater Springs, remember?"

Kristy nodded. For all the town's faults, collective and individual, people rallied around whenever trouble came. When she'd come home from college for her parents' funerals—first her mother's, then her dad's— she'd barely been able to navigate the house for all the concerned friends who'd come to sit with her, and the casseroles and bakery goods they'd brought had crammed the freezer to capacity.

Dylan left his chair to make her a cup of tea.

Briana arrived, bringing Bonnie and Sam, and Logan got there soon after that.

Kristy, glad to have something to do, filled Bonnie's sippy cup and put her into the playpen where, miracle of miracles, she sat quietly, drinking her milk and finally toppling over on one side to sleep.

Watching, Kristy wondered if she'd ever be able to sleep again, especially in that room upstairs, where she'd almost died.

Logan joined Briana and Dylan at the table, all of them drinking coffee and talking quietly.

"I know you're probably pretty upset right now," Logan said solemnly, as Kristy sat down at the table. "But I need you to tell me what happened here today, Kristy. Floyd's answers were pretty jumbled—he was having chest pain, from the stress, so the police decided to hospitalize him overnight."

This brief speech earned him a glare from Dylan, which he ignored.

Slowly, carefully, Kristy repeated the awful story,

aware that it was one she'd have to tell again, and yet again, possibly under oath in a court of law or before some investigating committee.

Logan listened without interruption, his face revealing none of what he was thinking.

When Kristy finished, he nodded, as though she'd confirmed something he'd already deduced.

"He saved my life," Kristy said. "Won't that carry some weight with the judge or the grand jury or whoever decides things like this?"

"Most likely," Logan replied.

"Why can't they just let him go?"

Logan sighed. "He's a cop, Kristy. Sworn to uphold the law. He helped dispose of a body and then covered up what happened. He did give me Freida's diary—I haven't had time to do more than scan a few pages, but there's enough in there to convince anybody that he's known, at least since that journal came into his possession, what happened to Ellie Clarkston. And it's possible, if the prosecutor gets involved, that the state will claim he was covering up for Freida, the way he did for your dad, because they were involved."

"He told me he hadn't read the diary, Logan, and I believed him."

"He also said," Dylan put in, "that she'd been blackmailing him for years, anonymously, because she'd seen him helping Tim bury that drifter. What do you suppose she was doing out there in the dark, anyhow?"

"Kids used to roam all over the countryside at night," Logan reminded his brother. "We did." He reached over, took Briana's hand, squeezed it lightly. "If she had a reason, it'll be in the diary."

Kristy nodded. "What about the statute of limitations?" she asked, clutching at straws. "Hasn't it run out?"

"There is no statute of limitations on murder," Logan told her.

"But Floyd didn't—"

Just then, one of the evidence techs came down the rear stairway and announced that they were finished, and they'd be leaving now. The detectives stayed, however, and battered Kristy with quiet, pointed questions, and she was glad Logan and Dylan were there, and Briana, too.

Dylan and Briana offered silent moral support, and Logan made sure Kristy's rights were respected.

Logan didn't mention the diary to the police, Kristy noticed. Clearly, he wanted to read and perhaps photocopy it before turning it over to the authorities.

The detectives thanked Kristy politely and left.

Once they were gone, the house seemed to let out its breath.

Briana glanced at her watch. "Alec and Josh are at the pool," she said. "I'd better pick them up." She leaned over to kiss Logan, then stood. "See you at home."

He nodded, his eyes shining as he looked at her.

At the door, Briana paused, swept Kristy, Dylan and Bonnie up in a glance. "You're welcome to come and stay at our place, if you've got the heebie-jeebies or anything."

"Thanks," Dylan said, when Kristy didn't speak. "But we'll be okay."

Briana hesitated, as though she'd like to argue, then went out.

"You're sure you don't want to come out to the ranch for a while?" Logan asked. "It's still your home, too, you know."

Dylan smiled, shook his head.

Logan stood to go.

"If you hear anything about—about Floyd, will you call?" Kristy asked.

"I'll call," Logan confirmed.

He'd barely stepped out the door before Kristy was on the kitchen phone, dialing the sheriff's home number. She wouldn't stop obsessing about Dorothy Book until she knew the woman wasn't alone, stunned by the news that her husband was under investigation *and* in the hospital for chest pain. If indeed she'd *heard* the news at all. Poor Dorothy might be sitting there, waiting for Floyd to get off work, like any other day, with no idea what had happened.

Carla Adams, a neighbor of the Books', answered on the second ring. "If you're a reporter—" she began tersely.

"It's Kristy Madison," Kristy said.

"Kristy," Carla said. "Good heavens. Are you all right?"

"I'm fine. The question is, how's Dorothy?"

"Baffled," Carla replied sadly. "I've tried to explain, but she doesn't understand. She keeps asking if one of us will call Floyd and ask him to bring home hamburgers for supper, because she doesn't feel like cooking."

Kristy closed her eyes against the image of that poor, bewildered woman, but it stayed with her. "Someone will be staying with her?"

"One or another of us will be here for the duration."

Kristy sighed with relief. "That's good," she said.

"It's the only option, right about now."

"Is there anything I can do?"

"I'll let you know if we need help," Carla promised gently.

"Thanks, Carla."

"You take care of yourself, Kristy. It's no secret, what you've been going through, over what happened. I just want you to know that we're on your side—the town, I mean. We all remember Tim and Louise, and they were good people."

That time, Kristy couldn't answer at all. She nodded and hung up.

And because she desperately needed something to do, she found an apron, tied it around her waist and began making supper.

THE NEXT DAY, Floyd Book was released, though the investigation would continue for months. He promptly returned to Stillwater Springs, announced his resignation and went home to look after his wife.

Logan had already handed the diary over to the state police, and he brought a copy by the library for Kristy to read. She immediately put Susan in charge and slipped into her office, alone, to devour every word.

She was desperate to understand what had happened, even though it was all in the past—so far in the past.

She read through a blur of tears how a teenage girl had seen two men she'd known all her life burying a body under a copse of trees on Madison Ranch. The handwriting was jerky and strange, the spelling that of someone much younger than a high school junior.

Freida had been spending the night by the creek, on a dare from some girls at school, by her account. And once she'd realized what it was Tim Madison and Floyd Book were actually doing, she'd been so terrified that she'd hidden in some bushes until the sun came up.

If she had ever blackmailed Kristy's parents, she'd made no record of it in the diary, but she'd hit Floyd up for money, never revealing her identity of course, and he'd paid promptly. He'd probably never suspected a teenage girl to be behind the demands, but Kristy still wondered why he hadn't used his resources as sheriff to run her down.

Guilt, she supposed. On some level, Floyd Book had believed he deserved to be blackmailed, maybe even that he was getting off easy.

Freida spent the initial loot on a prom dress. She didn't say how the money was transferred.

Oddly, even as she continued to collect on what she'd seen, Freida had begun to develop a schoolgirl crush on Floyd. She wrote about how good he looked in his uniform, and how she'd like to have his children, and began to map out a plan of seduction long before he'd actually succumbed to her charms.

The most chilling entries, of course, concerned Ellie Clarkston. How she'd spoiled things by waltzing into town and stealing Mike Danvers right out from under Freida's nose.

Freida's description of the actual murder made the small hairs stand up on Kristy's arms.

> I shouldn't be writing this down. But I can't tell anybody, and I can't hold it in, either. I killed Ellie Clarkston.

She'd underlined that last sentence, in bold strokes of her pen.

I told her Mike wanted to see her about something important, in that copse of trees between the Creed place and Madison Ranch. I was the go-between, that's what I said. She was so smug, and spiteful. She called me "Message Girl." Well, when she went to meet Mike, she found out she wasn't so smart after all. I got there first, and I was waiting. I hit her in the back of the head with a rock, and when she was down, I hit her again and again, until she died. I had to take off all my clothes afterward, and wash them in the creek, and myself, too, and wait for everything to dry. She sat propped against a tree, all that time, looking at me with her dead, staring eyes. It took me three days to dig that hole, and I was scared to death the whole time that somebody would catch me, or the coyotes would drag her stupid slut carcass into plain sight and someone would find her and put it all together. I'm not sorry for what I did. I'm NOT SORRY. She brought it all on herself. Nobody—NOBODY—takes what's mine.

"Nobody takes what's mine," Kristy repeated, cold to the marrow of her bones. *You took Mike—you took my house—you even took my damn cat—*

Sickened, Kristy stopped turning pages, pushed the stack of copy pages away, unable to read any more.

Somehow, she got through the rest of that day.

Dylan got her through the night. They didn't make love—her emotions were too raw for that—but he held her, in the safe circle of his arms, and when she cried because terrible memories crowded around the bed like shadows, he stroked her hair and murmured that everything would be all right. They'd get through this, together.

But he still didn't say the words that would have made all the difference in the world.

He didn't say, "I love you."

CHAPTER EIGHTEEN

THE WEDDING, as Dylan and Kristy had planned, was a civil ceremony, held in her living room. Bonnie attended, of course, wearing a lacy pink dress and little patent leather Mary Janes Kristy had hastily chosen for the occasion, and Logan, Briana, Josh and Alec were there, too.

There were no rings in evidence, though Kristy had secretly bought a broad gold band for Dylan, and tucked it away for safekeeping, just in case.

Briana had insisted on bringing flowers—bright splashes of zinnias in varying shades, charmingly arranged in a Mason jar. *It's a wedding,* she'd insisted, when Kristy protested, looking askance at the bride's simple blue polka-dot sundress and sandals.

Dylan wore jeans, his best boots and a crisp white shirt, with the cuffs rolled partway up his forearms.

Logan, the best man, brought a digital camera.

Judge John Etterling performed the ceremony, and the whole thing was over in what seemed like five minutes.

The judge accepted payment and made a hasty departure, and after he'd gone, Logan explained that Etterling would be the one to preside over Bonnie's custody hearing.

"You heard from Sharlene?" Dylan demanded of his brother, the lawyer. It was the first thing he'd said since "I do."

"I wasn't going to tell you until later," Logan admitted, with a sigh. "She wants to tell her side of things."

"Great," Dylan muttered. Kristy knew he wasn't surprised, but he'd hoped for more time. So had Kristy.

"Where are you going on your honeymoon?" young Josh, Briana's elder son, asked. "Mom and Logan went to *Las Vegas*."

"What happens in Vegas," Alec, his very precocious little brother, quipped, "*stays* in Vegas."

A tender yet smoldering look passed between Briana and Logan.

"You've got that right, kid," Logan said, rubbing a hand over his stepson's bristly haircut.

Briana smiled dreamily, but the expression was quickly gone, replaced by worry. On her, even that looked good. "It's just one thing after another in this family," she remarked. "In this *town*."

"Is there a cake?" Josh asked, cutting to the chase. The honeymoon question had gone unanswered, and not by accident.

Dylan and Kristy hadn't even *discussed* a honeymoon.

"No," Kristy said.

"Yes," Dylan contradicted, at the very same moment. She glanced at him, puzzled.

"Relax," her husband—*her husband*—said, obviously, by the muscle twitching in his cheek, not taking his own advice. Was he already having doubts? Wishing he hadn't married her? Wanting to give rodeoing one more try? "It's the kind you buy in a box, in the freezer section."

So much for champagne, little silver bells, doves made of sugar, and tossing the bouquet, Kristy thought, a little sadly. She'd married into the Creed clan, of her own free will and with her eyes wide open, and the only guarantee was good sex and lots of it.

The rest, she'd have to figure out on her own, probably by trial and error, though Briana, with a little more experience under her belt, might have a few pointers to offer.

They ate the cake.

Kristy put a sugar-frenzied Bonnie down with her sippy cup in the playpen, for a badly needed nap, and Briana, Logan and the boys offered congratulations, and left. On his way out the door, Logan leaned to kiss Kristy's cheek and whisper, "Hang in there, babe. He's so crazy about you, it's a wonder he's got his boots on the right feet."

Bemused, Kristy went upstairs—being alone in the bedroom still jangled her nerves, but it was getting easier—and swapped out the sundress for her usual jeans and a tank top. When she got back to the kitchen, Dylan was putting crumb-gooey cake plates into the dishwasher.

"Dylan," Kristy said, pausing on the bottom step of the rear stairway, one hand on the newel post. "What have we done?"

AS SCREWED UP AS the wedding had been, from Dylan's viewpoint, the wedding *night* had been a spectacular success. But with the morning, it was business as usual—Kristy ate a quick breakfast, refusing to look at him unless he stood toe-to-toe with her, which he did a couple of times, out of pure obstinacy, and dashed off to the library in her Blazer.

"Some honeymoon, huh, kid?" he asked Bonnie, after Kristy had gone.

Even Winston and Sam looked a little long in the face.

"Poop," Bonnie said gravely.

Too late, Dylan realized the word had been a warning, not a comment on the state of her father's love life.

After he got the kid cleaned up, the three of them, him and Bonnie and good old Sam, headed out to the ranch. Caleb had probably been and gone by then—it was nearly nine-thirty—but since he wanted to give his sketches to Dan Phillips to turn into building plans, Dylan hit the road.

It was a hell of a lot better than sitting around waiting for Sharlene to call and announce that—surprise!—she was right there in Stillwater Springs and ready, willing and able to be a mother to her child.

Caleb, as it turned out, had already fed and groomed Sundance; when Dylan arrived, he was leading the horse patiently around by a lead-rope in Logan's front yard. For all his distractions—the custody suit, the marriage that *wasn't* a marriage, the revelations about Floyd Book—Dylan was pleased to see the kid. Might be there was some hope for him after all.

"You're late," Caleb said.

"I got married yesterday," Dylan answered. That was more information than he would have given most people, but he figured he owed Caleb some kind of explanation, after ordering him to be at the barn every morning at six o'clock. He took Bonnie out of her car seat, hoisted Sam down, too, and headed toward Caleb and the horse.

Bonnie toddled at Dylan's side, holding on to one of his pant legs.

"Horsie!" she said.

It was an improvement on "poop," anyhow.

Logan came out of the barn just then, looking way more like a rancher than the slick lawyer Dylan knew him to be.

"Why don't you fetch that beat-up old saddle on the peg just inside the tack room door?" Logan said to Caleb, sweeping a giggling Bonnie up into his arms at the same time.

Once Caleb had gone off on the errand, Logan turned to Dylan. "For a man who just married a beautiful woman, half again too good for you, you don't look all that happy."

Dylan swept off his hat, slapped one thigh with it, put it back on again. "S-h-a-r-l-e-n-e," he spelled out, for Bonnie's sake.

Logan arched an eyebrow. "We can handle her, Dylan," he said.

"I wish I had your confidence," Dylan replied, as Caleb reappeared with the saddle. "But, then, it's *my* k-i-d who might be taken away, not yours."

Logan slapped his shoulder. "B-o-n-n-i-e," he replied, with a grin, "is my n-i-e-c-e. You think I don't have a stake in this?"

Dylan sighed. "I guess you do," he admitted. "But s-h-i-t, I'm s-c-a-r-e-d."

Josh and Alec burst out of the house at that moment, whooping greetings at Bonnie. Logan smiled and set her down—she was already kicking to get free—and she and the boys went back inside, each of them holding one of her hands.

Briana met them at the door, smiling.

"Can we stop s-p-e-l-l-i-n-g now?" Logan asked.

"Judge Etterling," Dylan sputtered, resisting an urge to slap his hat against his leg again. "What if he decides in Sharlene's favor? The man doesn't have a sense of humor."

"He must," Logan joked, probably trying to lighten the mood. "He married you to Kristy Madison, didn't he?"

Dylan spared a grin. "That's Kristy *Creed* now," he said.

"Etterling is a fair man, Dylan," Logan went on, watching with some amusement as Caleb gamely tried to saddle Sundance, who kept sidestepping him. "I'd have requested another judge if he wasn't."

"If you say so, I believe you."

"Hot damn." Logan chuckled. "You believe me. Make a mark on the calendar—we'll pick up a freezer cake on this day every year from now on, to celebrate."

"Hugely funny," Dylan said. Unable to watch the greenhorn-and-pony show any longer, he moved to take the saddle out of Caleb's hands and show him how to put it on right.

"Can I ride him?" Caleb asked eagerly.

Dylan made sure the cinch was tight, held Sundance's reins and spoke soothingly to him, which was an answer in itself.

Caleb mounted up—it took a couple of tries, but he finally made it—and beamed down from the saddle.

Dylan felt a surge of liking for the kid—his initial impression of Caleb had been wrong, and that was a relief to know.

"Let go of the reins," Caleb said.

Dylan complied. "Go easy," he warned. "And stay where I can see you."

Caleb gave a long-suffering sigh. "All *right,*" he said.

"He'll be fine, Dylan," Logan said quietly. "I've been watching him since he got here. He's serious about doing this right." He shoved a hand through his dark hair. "Come inside for a minute. There's something I want to show you."

Dylan frowned. More family memorabilia? He hadn't even had a chance to go through the stuff Logan had already given him.

But he followed his brother into the house, glancing back at Caleb and Sundance a couple of times as he went.

In the cool, shadowy living room—Briana and the kids were laughing in the kitchen, and it was a good sound, a *family* kind of sound—Logan went straight to his desk and pulled open a drawer. Brought out a legal-size sheaf of documents.

"What's this?" Dylan asked, scanning the cover page. The heading read, Tri-Star Cattle Company, Inc., and there was some legalese jargoning around underneath it, in the requisite small print. The name was faintly familiar to him, but he didn't remember why.

"I bought the Madison place," Logan said. "The bank formally accepted my offer yesterday afternoon."

Dylan didn't know what to say. He was too stunned.

"You want in?" Logan asked.

"Huh?"

"Do you want to be part of Tri-Star?" Logan prompted. "It's set up for the three of us to be equal partners, if you agree to the terms. You, me and Tyler."

"Good luck roping Ty in," Dylan said ruefully, wishing things were different. "He'd sooner go into business with the devil."

Logan's mouth quirked up at one side, meaning he was trying to smile, but he couldn't quite manage it. "What about you, Dylan? You want to be a cattleman? Help me make something of this ranch and this family?"

Something spiky knotted itself up in Dylan's throat, making speech impossible. So he just nodded.

Logan slapped him on the shoulder.

"Good," he said, sounding relieved. "Good." His eyes were suspiciously bright.

"Kristy's folks' house," Dylan began. "I don't want it torn down unless she agrees."

"Fair enough," Logan said, his voice husky. "You'll have as much say in what happens with that land as I do."

"Then there's one more thing," Dylan answered. His eyes itched, so he ran the sleeve of his shirt across them once. The sniffle was probably allergies, he told himself. "Sugarfoot's grave. We have a concrete vault poured and bury that horse right, and for good."

"Agreed," Logan replied, recovering a little.

"Are you always going to be this easy to deal with?" Dylan grinned.

Logan laughed. "Hell no," he said. "*Hell* no."

Sharlene Creed—she could call herself whatever she wanted, couldn't she, and the name suited her plans—got off the bus in Stillwater Springs, Montana, stretched her legs, and let the dumbo farm boy collect her suitcase for her. He'd been in the seat next to hers since Reno, and the damn fool thought she was going to sleep with him.

Sharlene smiled slightly. She'd as much as promised him that, of course, played the damsel in distress so he'd pay for her food when the bus stopped, carry things for her and keep the creepier passengers at bay.

Now, Jimmy what's-his-name had served his purpose. So long, Jimmy.

Stretching, Sharlene admired her slender figure in the front window of the gas station/convenience store where the bus had stopped. Her hair was dark that month—a drugstore dye job, but it looked good—and pulled up into a ponytail that brushed her nape and made her look at least ten years younger than she was. Her black jeans and sleeveless white eyelet top were some the worse for wear, after the long bus ride from Texas, but a shower, a change of clothes and fresh makeup, and she'd be ready for anything.

"I can't wait to introduce you to my folks," Jimmy Hayseed said. He wouldn't be a bad-looking guy, if he lost forty pounds and had his teeth fixed. And ordered the magic acne cure off TV.

"Look, Jimmy," Sharlene began, in a regretful purr, "I've got some things to do, so—"

"They own the Sundowner Motel," Jimmy announced, grinning. He hadn't heard a word she'd said, but that was a man for you. Men didn't *listen,* unless you were saying exactly what they wanted to hear. "I'm sure they'd be glad to put you up for free, just like you was company. Things have been slow at the Sundowner since that new Holiday Inn went in out by the casino."

Sharlene was intrigued. Dylan sure as hell wasn't going to offer her a place to stay—not right away, anyhow—and renting a room would put a serious nick in her already-pitiful funds. "I wouldn't feel comfortable," she said shyly, and as sweetly as she could, given that she was dead sick of Jimmy-twig-dick. For one thing, his deodorant had failed him—at least three bus stops back. "You know, sharing a room, under your folks' own roof—"

"Me, neither," Jimmy said, still grinning. "My mom would throw a hissy fit. She's a good cook, though, and she runs a clean place. She's been after me to get a girl-friend for years, so she'll make you right welcome." His meaty shoulders moved in a shrug beneath his dirty T-shirt. "I'll just go out and stay at the farm."

I'll just bet she's been after you to get a girlfriend, Sharlene thought, behind her Girl Scout smile. *Good luck with that, bozo.*

"I *am* a little short on funds," Sharlene confessed, almost simpering. She hated simpering, but so far it had worked on every man she encountered except Dylan Creed, so she pulled it out of the old toolbox.

"I know," Jimmy replied cheerfully, beginning to sweat under the afternoon sun. "That's why I think you ought to stay with Mom and Dad, at the Sun-downer, until we're ready to—well, you know—*tell* people about us."

Tell people about us. Sharlene deserved an Oscar, by her own reckoning, for not throwing up on his shoes.

"Okay," she said, batting her false eyelashes. "If you're *sure.*"

That technique hadn't worked on Dylan, either, but Jimmy Cricket here was a whole other species from her baby girl's lovin' daddy.

A little over an hour and a half later, Sharlene was settled in a seedy room at the seedy Sundowner Motel on the other end of Main Street, and practically a member of the family.

She showered.

She put on fresh clothes and a touch of lip gloss.

And then she scarfed down the chicken-fried steak, mashed potatoes and creamed peas Jimmy's delighted mother whipped up just for her, right there in the kitchen behind the motel's check-in desk.

Time enough to tackle the Dylan problem later.

In the meantime, she'd play it cool, gather her strength. She'd landed on her feet—just like she always did.

KRISTY WAS MYSTIFIED when Dylan showed up at the library, right at quitting time, without Bonnie or Sam in his truck. He hardly gave her a chance to lock up before he had her by the hand, pulling her down the sidewalk.

"Where—"

"You'll see," Dylan said.

She let him hoist her into his truck, like the storied sack of potatoes, and sat there wondering what this was all about.

He volunteered nothing at all. Just turned on the radio, tuned it to a country station and hummed along with the music as they traveled the length of Main Street and then on toward the ranch.

Maybe, she speculated, he'd decided to lease that double-wide trailer after all, and move her and Bonnie and the pets out there until the new house was finished.

But he turned in at the tilting mailbox—with *Madison* still stenciled on the side—and they bumped and jostled over the rutted road until they were parked in front of the old house she'd grown up in.

Tears filled her eyes at the sight of it.

So many memories, some good, some terrible.

When had she let go of it? All she knew was, she *had* let go.

"What?" she whispered. "Why are we here?"

Dylan unfastened his seat belt, turned to unfasten hers and place a soft kiss on her mouth. "Because it's yours," he said. "This place, I mean. You can tear it down or you can restore it, or whatever."

"I don't understand. The Tri-Star people—"

"*Logan* is Tri-Star, Kristy," Dylan said, his lips still very close to hers. His breath was warm and mint-scented and it made her mouth tingle in anticipation of more kisses—so much so that it was a moment before she realized exactly what he was telling her. "And as of today, so am I."

Kristy's eyes widened. Her mouth moved, but no sound came out.

Dylan chuckled, his rein-roughened hand resting lightly against her cheek. "What'll it be, Mrs. Creed?"

"I'm—" She paused, swallowed. "What about Sugarfoot's grave?"

"It'll look like Grant's Tomb by the time I get done with it," Dylan said, resting his forehead against hers now. "Sugarfoot's not going anywhere, babe."

"You and Logan bought Madison Ranch?"

Dylan pulled back a little ways, looking worried. "Is that a bad thing?"

She considered the question, then shook her head. "I guess not. But I know I mentioned Tri-Star to you, and you just let me think—"

"I didn't know, Kristy," Dylan said. "Logan just told

me today. He offered me a third of the company, and I bought in."

"Will you still be able to afford that fancy house, with the mechanical-bull room?"

Dylan laughed, quietly at first, and then with a gusty whoop of delight. "Yeah," he said. "I can still afford the house."

"I don't know what to say."

He leaned past her, his upper arm brushing her breast, and opened the glove compartment. Took out a small black velvet box.

Kristy's heart did a reverse bungee jump, practically coming through the top of her head.

"Well, I know what to say," Dylan told her, flipping open the box with his thumb. A knuckle-to-knuckle wedding-and-engagement-ring combo nestled inside, glittering like trapped stars. "I love you, Kristy. I have since we rode the school bus together. I was just such a damn—*Creed* that I didn't know what I was feeling."

Tears slipped down Kristy's cheeks. "Y-your ring," she half sobbed, half laughed, "is at home, in my nightstand."

Dylan's eyes twinkled. "You bought me a ring?"

She nodded, not even bothering to dab at her face with the back of her hand. "I was hoping—"

Dylan waited.

"I love you, too. And it goes way back. I was such a geeky kid, and you teased me and pulled my pigtails, but when the chips were down, you defended me." She closed her eyes for a moment, savoring everything, then opened them again, so she could look at Dylan. "Do you remember when we started junior high, and your dad made you get those school pictures taken?"

"Yeah," Dylan said slowly. "I guess."

"You guess. Well, I still have mine. You didn't give it to me—I traded Tyler a whole week of lunchroom desserts for it."

Dylan laughed again. Kissed her again. "Ty was always a businessman," he said, somewhat wistfully. In fact, it was almost as if he was talking about someone who'd died a long time ago.

"He drove a hard bargain," Kristy said, smiling moistly.

Dylan took her hand, slid the wedding ring onto her finger first, then the engagement ring. Door-knockers, both of them.

"I think satellites can pick the sparkle up from space," Kristy commented, enjoying the look of those rings—*Dylan's* rings—twinkling on her left hand.

See, Mom? she asked silently. *He bought the cow, even though the milk was free.*

"Nothing but the best for my missus." Dylan grinned, kissing her knuckles. And that felt even better than the rings.

They were quiet for a long time, then Dylan turned and looked toward the house. "If you need a while to decide, it's okay," he said.

Kristy wasn't tracking all that well. "Decide?"

"The house?" Dylan reminded her. His eyes were soft, but blazing with blue fire. She couldn't wait to get him home and—well, *that,* but she was eager to get that gold band on his finger, too.

She studied the sad old house, with its sagging floors and broken windows, and sunken roof. A shred of the blue tarp still clung to one of the warped shingles, after all these years, fluttering softly in the breeze.

"Let's take it down," she said.

"You're sure?"

She nodded. She'd had a lot of happy times in that house, with her mom and dad, but it would always be the place where something horrible had happened. "I guess it's my way of letting go of the past and moving on," she said.

Dylan kissed her forehead. "Understood. I'm doing some letting go and moving on myself."

"If you hadn't just given me these rings," Kristy informed him, "I'd be pretty worried about that statement."

"I'm here for the duration," Dylan said. "Till death do us part."

"Till death do us part," Kristy repeated.

And she would always remember that as the moment she truly married Dylan Creed, with her whole heart, her whole body, her whole mind and spirit.

CHAPTER NINETEEN

SHARLENE WATCHED Dylan working with the yellow horse for a long time, the way she'd watched him from the alley the night she'd left the baby in his truck behind that crumby card-joint in Vegas. He'd stripped off his shirt, and the sun glinted in his golden hair, and his muscles moved like graceful cords under his skin.

She'd tracked him here, to Stillwater Springs Ranch after borrowing Jimmy's mother's old Buick. It had been three days since she'd rolled into town on that bus, days she'd spent sizing things up. Exploring her options.

Now that she was expected to clean up after the few tourists who chose the decrepit Sundowner over the shiny new Holiday Inn, in return for board and room, her mood had dipped considerably.

She studied the woman, slim and blond, with one of those scrubbed-looking faces, holding *her* little girl and practically eating Dylan up with her eyes.

According to Jimmy's mom, Florie, the two of them were married now.

The flash of the rings on the woman's left hand was proof enough.

Sharlene bit her lower lip. So much for the big plan

of becoming Mrs. Dylan Creed and reaping all the accompanying benefits. She was totally screwed.

It was just as this thought passed through her head that Dylan seemed to sense her presence. He stopped what he was doing, handed the long lead-rope off to a teenage boy standing nearby and started toward her.

The woman—Kristy, Sharlene thought her name was—stood back for a few moments, then came on ahead, bringing the child Dylan called Bonnie along with her.

Sharlene waited for the kid to shriek with delight at seeing her again, and strain to be taken into her arms, but she didn't do either of those things. She screamed and tried to crawl right down the neck-hole of the Kristy-woman's blouse.

Dylan put a hand out, and Kristy stopped, a little way behind him, soothing the baby. Murmuring to her.

Dylan's expression was so cold as he approached Sharlene that she actually felt a physical chill, right there in that sun-washed pasture across from the big ranch house.

One by one, the last of Sharlene's hopes crumbled.

Dylan wasn't going to give in and marry her so he could help raise the kid. He wasn't going to move her into a big fancy house, buy her a new car and give her a handful of credit cards.

And he wasn't going to give Bonnie up without a fight.

Dylan Creed, Sharlene knew, could put up one *hell* of a fight.

"I'd like to see her," Sharlene heard herself say, in a stranger's voice, soft and sad, "when she's older."

Dylan absorbed that. Said nothing.

He didn't even nod.

"Like you said on the phone," Sharlene struggled on. "When—Bonnie's eighteen, if she wants to see me, well, I'll want to see her."

Still, Dylan didn't speak.

"I—I need money, Dylan."

He finally spared her a nod, but nothing more.

"A *lot* of money."

"As soon as the proper papers are signed," Dylan said, glaring at her, his fists knotted at his sides, "you'll have your settlement."

She glanced at Bonnie. The little girl—*her* little girl—was glaring at her now, in the same way Dylan was. Both her arms were wrapped tightly around Kristy's neck, and her whole body seemed to scream, *Don't let go.*

"Okay," Sharlene said, trying to squeeze out a few motherly tears. Inside, she was thinking of where she'd go next, and what she'd buy. Who she'd be able to attract, with a chunk of money drawing interest some-place, and no kid always yammering for attention.

"That's it?" Dylan echoed. "Just 'okay'? It's that easy to walk away from your own daughter?"

Sharlene felt a flash of shame, but she didn't take the bait. Arguing with this man would get her nowhere—just like always.

"But, then, you've had some practice at that, haven't you, Sharlene? Walking away, I mean?"

"Don't be mean," Sharlene cooed.

"Spare me," Dylan said. "Wherever you're staying, Logan—that's my lawyer—will bring the papers by tomorrow. Have somebody read them over, if you want. Once they're signed and notarized, you'll have your money."

Sharlene nodded, trying not to look too pleased at the prospect. She wouldn't have been happy in this shit-hole town anyway, she figured. There wasn't even a movie house, for pity's sake, or an outlet mall. What did people around here *do* on a Saturday night, anyhow? Sit around and spit-shine their shoes for church?

She'd have gone stark crazy within a week.

"Okay," she repeated.

"The terms are pretty stiff, Sharlene," Dylan went on, slowly and carefully. Did he think she was stupid?

Well, yeah, he probably did.

And she didn't give a rat's ass what he thought, as long as his check cleared the bank.

"No more money, Sharlene. *Ever.* And you don't come within three states of Bonnie without my say-so. Are we clear on that?"

Sharlene glanced toward Kristy again, unable to hide her contempt. "I'll go you one better, Dylan," she said. "Double the settlement, and your pretty bride there can *adopt* Bonnie."

For once in her short acquaintance with Dylan Creed, she'd actually managed to surprise him.

"You're serious?"

"I'm serious."

Dylan turned, looked at Kristy.

Kristy nodded, holding Bonnie a little tighter.

Dylan put out his hand to Sharlene. "It's a deal."

AT TEN O'CLOCK THE NEXT morning, in one of the public rooms at the library, the agreed meeting place, Sharlene signed away all rights where Bonnie was concerned, snatched up the check Dylan had written and kicked the dust of Stillwater Springs, Montana, off her feet so fast that Kristy was amazed. Apparently, she'd persuaded poor Jimmy, the latest in what was probably a long line of suckers, to drive her to the airport in Missoula.

"It's over?" Dylan asked Logan, sounding shell-shocked.

Logan, looking spiffy in his suit, grinned. "It's over," he confirmed. He turned to Kristy. "When do you want to start adoption proceedings?"

She and Dylan had talked about that most of the night. Dylan wanted her to be sure—it was a big step, adopting a child, after all. A major commitment.

"How about yesterday?" Kristy asked, beaming.

Logan laughed, took another folder out of his briefcase and slid it down the table toward her. "We aim to please, here at Creed, Creed and Creed—sign and I'll file the petition."

Kristy's eyes widened. She looked at Dylan.

He looked at her.

"Got a pen?" she asked Logan.

And she wrote her name, Kristine Madison Creed, on every line Logan pointed out.

"When will Bonnie be my daughter, too?"

"I think Bonnie's *already* your daughter," Logan replied. "Legally, there's a six-month waiting period, then a hearing. Sharlene won't come out of the woodwork wanting to put on the brakes, Kristy. She'll forfeit a serious chunk of her settlement if she does, and we spread it out over a period of fifteen years to make sure she couldn't stash it somewhere outside the country and then try to take Bonnie back."

Dylan took a tight hold on Kristy's hand, pulled her

close. "About that honeymoon," he said. "Where would you like to go, Mrs. Creed?"

Logan cleared his throat, gathered his papers and left.

Kristy simply stared at him.

"I'm serious," Dylan insisted, but his blue eyes were full of twinkling mischief. "We need a honeymoon. Where to?"

Kristy grinned. "Well," she said, straightening his collar, "I know this place where I used to lie in tall grass with my lover and look at the stars—"

She felt him go hard against her. "What about Hawaii? Or Mexico? Or Las Vegas?"

"All I want to do, Dylan Creed, is lie down in the tall grass again, with my husband, and love him with everything I've got."

He laughed, and she barely had time to pick up her purse, he pulled her toward the door so fast.

As they crossed the library, Susan called out from behind the main desk. "Zachary Spencer has called five times about that movie deal. What am I supposed to tell him?"

"Tell him to forget it," Kristy called back. "In the kindest possible way."

Susan seemed determined to keep them right there, in the library. "Did you vote? The special election is today, you know. Mike Danvers dropped out over the Freida scandal and Julie's threatening to have an affair just to get back at him. So that means Jim Huntinghorse is running unopposed."

They were almost at the door.

This time, Dylan answered. "Then I guess he won't need our votes," he said. "*Goodbye,* Susan."

"If anyone else calls," Kristy added, "tell them Mr. and Mrs. Dylan Creed are away on their honeymoon."

Dylan opened the door and all but pushed Kristy through it.

She looked back once, and saw Susan blush, and then smile and waggle her fingers in farewell.

HIGH ON THE PRIVATE HILL, in the sweet, tall grass of the meadow, Dylan and Kristy made love. When it was over, they lay still for a long time, recovering and gazing up at the broad Montana sky, their clothes still askew.

"I can't believe it," Kristy said. "I'm a wife, a mother."

"Bonnie's going to be a handful," Dylan reminded her quietly.

Kristy laughed. "Bonnie's *already* a handful. Pure Creed, through and through."

"We're a wild bunch," Dylan agreed. Then he shifted onto his side, propping himself up on one elbow and looking down into her face. "That's a good thing, from your point of view? Bonnie being a Creed?"

She stroked his cheek. "It's better than good. Besides, I'm a Creed now, too, remember?"

"We have a long and dishonorable tradition of raising hell," Dylan said. "There's a lot to live down."

An overwhelming tenderness swept over Kristy. "The past is over, Dylan," she said gently. "And the future starts right now." She paused, bit her lower lip.

"What?" Dylan prompted, with a slight grin.

"It's too soon to pee on a stick or anything," Kristy said, "but I think I'm pregnant."

Dylan's face lit up. "How can you know a thing like that?"

"I just do," Kristy said.

Dylan kissed her lightly. "I like the idea," he said. "You have any names in mind?"

"If it's a boy," Kristy replied, remembering another time, when they'd had conversations like this one, "I think we should call him Timothy Jacob, for our dads." When Dylan's face changed slightly, she hastened to add, "*Or* Jacob Timothy."

Dylan plucked a piece of grass and used it to tickle her chin, but the expression in his eyes was solemn. "I think that's more forgiving than I can manage," he said. "I don't have any problem with calling our son Tim, but naming him for Jake—"

"I won't insist, Dylan. But don't you think it's *time* you forgave your father?"

"I've got some getting ready to do first," Dylan replied honestly. "Besides, I'm hoping we'll have a girl. A little sister for Bonnie." He grinned, tossed aside the blade of grass when she slapped at his hand to make him stop tickling her. "Maggie Louise?"

"Maggie Louise," Kristy repeated, smiling, even though her eyes burned. Her mom would have been so proud to have a granddaughter, and one named for her at that.

Dylan kissed her again, more thoroughly this time. "I do love you, Mrs. Creed," he said, leaning to kiss the length of her bare collarbone. "That much, I'm sure of."

Kristy crooned and arched her back as Dylan's mouth traveled toward her right breast, leaving a tracing of fire dancing on her skin.

Mrs. Creed.

It sounded so good, and so right. And she loved her husband, now and forever.

That much, she was sure of.

* * * * *

Can't get enough of the Creed men?
New York Times *bestselling author*
Linda Lael Miller brings you a brand-new tale
starring Tyler Creed and the woman
who always loved him.

Look for MONTANA CREEDS: TYLER
by Linda Lael Miller,
available April 2009 from HQN Books
at your favorite retail outlet.

THEY WERE TWENTY MINUTES outside Stillwater Springs when they spotted the man and the dog walking alongside the highway.

Something about him jarred Lily, a combination of familiarity and alarm.

"Stop," Hal commanded urgently. "That's Tyler Creed."

And I thought this day couldn't get any worse.

Lily pulled over and put on the brakes, while her father buzzed the passenger-side window down.

"Tyler? Is that you?" he called.

The man turned, flashed that trademark grin, dazzling enough to put a heat mirage to shame. Damn it, it *was* Tyler.

All grown-up, and better-looking than ever.

And here she was, with her back and thighs glued to the car seat and her hair tugged up into a spiky mess.

He approached the car, the dog plodding patiently at his heels. Bent to look in at Hal. When his gaze caught on Lily, then Tess, the grin faded a little.

"Hey, Doc," he said. In high school he'd been cute. Now he was drop-dead gorgeous. His eyes were the same clear blue, though, and his dark hair still glistened, sleek as a raven's wings. "Lily," he added in grave greeting.

"Get in," Hal said. "We'll give you a lift to Stillwater Springs."

"Don't you have a car?" Tess ventured, fascinated, straining in the hated "baby seat" to get a look at the dog.

Tyler grinned again, and Lily's stomach dipped like a roller coaster plunging down steep tracks. "It broke down on a side road," he explained. "No tow trucks available, so Kit Carson and I started hoofing it for home."

"Hoofing it?" Tess echoed, confused.

"Walking," Lily translated.

Tyler chuckled.

"Well, get in," Hal said. "That sun's hot enough to bake a man's brain."

Tyler opened the back door of the Taurus, and he and Kit Carson took their places alongside Tess, the dog in the middle. Delighted, Tess shared the last of her crackers with Kit.

"Obliged," Tyler said.

"My daddy died when I was four," Tess said. "In a plane crash."

Lily tensed. Oddly, Tess often confided the great tragedy of her short life to strangers. With counselors and well-meaning friends, she tended to clam up.

"I'm sorry to hear that, shortstop," Tyler told her.

"Is hoofing it the same as hitchhiking?" Tess asked. "Because hitchhiking is *very* dangerous. That's what Mom says."

Lily felt Tyler's gaze on the back of her neck, practically branding her sweaty flesh.

"Your mom's right," Tyler answered. "But Kit and I didn't have much choice, as it turned out."

Lily sat ramrod straight on the sticky vinyl seat. Concentrated on her driving. She'd thought a lot about Tyler Creed since she'd hurried out to Montana to keep a vigil at her father's bedside, but she hadn't expected to actually run into him. He was a famous rodeo cowboy, after all—a sometime stuntman and actor.

"Where shall we drop you off?" she asked sunnily when they finally, *finally* hit the outskirts of Stillwater Springs.

"The car repair place," Tyler replied.

Lily had forgotten how sparely he used words, never saying two when one would do. She'd also forgotten that he smelled like laundry dried in the fresh air, even after he'd been loading or unloading hay bales all day. Or walking along a highway under a blazing summer sun. That his mouth tilted up at one corner when he was amused, and his hair was always a shade too long. The way his clothes fit him, and how he seemed so comfortable in his own skin…

Do not think about skin, Lily told herself.